LAST CHANCE

My Last Chance

Copyright © 2021 by Domenico Simone. All rights reserved.

This is a work of fiction. Names, characters, places and incidents are products of the author's imagination or are used fictitiously and should not be construed as real. Any resemblance to actual events, locales, organizations or persons, living or dead, is entirely coincidental.

No part of this book may be used or reproduced in any manner whatsoever without written permission, except in the case of brief quotations embodied in critical articles and reviews. For more information, e-mail all inquiries to info@mindstirmedia.com.

Published by Mindstir Media, LLC

45 Lafayette Rd | Suite 181| North Hampton, NH 03862 | USA

1.800.767.0531 | www.mindstirmedia.com

Printed in the United States of America

ISBN-13: 978-1-7365224-0-0

MY LAST CHANCE

Written by
DOMENICO SIMONE

Should one's entire life journey be determined solely by a major innocent screwup?

Mid-morning, the roads shimmered and the motionless haze melded houses and trees into a steamy purgatory. Not a typical New England late-spring day. Hoping that Rocky would be home, Kelly sped furtively through the streets. Ahead, a youngster labored over his bike's pedals on and off the sidewalk, seeking the shade from adjacent houses. Not far behind him, a derelict dog was hauling its legs toward the same, sniffing the scorching earth on its way. *What a pitiful thing*, Kelly thought. Then dashed inside the house and pleaded with him once more.

He turned, his owllike eyes bulging. "Unplug those goddamn ears. I said, I don't have it!"

"Rocky, for a whole week we've been promising her."

Rushing out the door, he pointed his index finger at her. "No, *you* did that!"

The roar of his 96 black Corvette was like bullets piercing her temples. She snatched her keys and stormed into a cloud of smoke and spattering dust as she gazed at his skidding tires darting around the corner of their street. How did he get to be so heartless? She jumped in her 91 white Subaru, floored the gas pedal, and screeched away. The disk-jockey's fuzzy vocals announced Gregg Roile's birthday, born on that same day June 17, 1947. Then he went on about Roile's stay with the band Journey and how much he loved their song "Don't Stop Believing."

"My friends, from New Haven's number one station, please relish this beautiful tune."

"Follow the way till you reach your dreams, you keep on movin'… don't stop believing. "

Kelly braked to a sudden halt inches from the walkway leading to the school's main entrance. Hope leaned against one of the door's glass panels, shaded by the overhang above. She could be smiling and laughing with her schoolmates instead. Behind her, on the inside, a dowdy woman dragged a mop over the lobby floor. Kelly jumped out of the car and rushed over. Placed her hand on Hope's shoulder and crouched down. "Honey, I'm sorry. I still can't believe they wouldn't let you go."

Hope, face stained with tears, looked straight in her mom's eyes. "I told you. I told you they wouldn't let me go without the money!"

Kelly reached for a tissue in her back pocket, pushing her little angel's long deep brown hair away from her face and gently wiping the tears away. "Your dad had already left the house, I'm really sorry."

Hope cupped her mom's face. "My friends laughed at me; you understand?"

"I do. Believe me I do." Kelly looked away. She remembered that day when, about Hope's age, she waited in the lobby, hoping her mom would bring her lunch money. She waited and waited, stomach growling, only to watch some of her schoolmates smiling and blabbering, and others laughing. It's got to be a curse. She turned to her little angel and held her tiny hands in hers. "Trust me, I feel your pain."

"Mom, even as they stepped on the bus, they laughed at me. They laughed and laughed."

The tears streaming down her little angel's face were like blood whooshing out of her heart. She stood up, lips pursed. *For twenty fricking dollars*, she thought, face changing colors faster than a chameleon's skin. *For eight years, we've been doing things his way. Eight darn years and look where it got us.*

She grabbed Hope's hand. "Come on!"

***

Minutes later, Kelly parked her car across from the diner and stared at the steps leading to the front door. She had never filled out a job application, but watching her daughter subjected to one form of humiliation or another because her husband refused to let her to work was no longer acceptable.

"Mommy, are we going for lunch?" Hope asked.

"No, we can't afford it."

"Mom, why is it that my friends' parents always have money, and you and Dad don't?"

"That's why we're here." Kelly jumped out of the car and headed for the door. She had met the owner on one of those rare occasions when Rocky brought them there for a Sunday treat. The first step, her stomach started coiling, her chest tightened, and she hesitated. Then took a deep breath, tightened her fists, and slowly conquered the remaining steps. Kelly watched the hostess leading a couple to their seats. Her insides were now hard as a rock, and her face red hot, droplets of sweat surfacing over her forehead. Invaded by a moment of doubt, she twisted and headed toward the exit.

"Ma'am, I'll be right with you!" The hostess's voice caused her to stop, one leg out into the foyer.

"I was just going to make a phone call," she replied, pointing to the public phone. Then stepped back inside. *I need to do this*, she thought, *and I must do it.* Took a deep breath, walked back to the spot where the couple that was now being seated had been standing, and waited for the hostess to return.

"Is it just you?" the hostess asked her.

Kelly moved closer to her and whispered, "I'd like to see the owner."

"Can I ask you why?" the hostess said.

"Tell him that…" Her body switched postures. "Just tell him a customer would like to see him." Waiting for the hostess to say something, her body switched posture again. "Just tell him that Kelly would like to see him." Then she stepped to the side and rested her back against the wall next to a picture window. She peeked at Hope, whose anxious eyes quickly found hers.

The hostess approached her with a snobbish look. "He'll be with you shortly."

"Thank you." Besides the owner, who was now making his way down the aisle, thank God none of the customers' faces looked familiar.

"Hey, I remember you." The owner's black mustache widened over his chubby face. "Pretty women always leave a stamp in my heart."

She turned red as customers swung their heads to look at her. "Thank you."

He extended his hand. "Kelly, what can I do for you?"

"Sorry, it's been a while. George, right?"

"Don't worry, sweetie, I scramble for names all the time."

"The last time I was here with my husband," she whispered, "you mentioned that if I ever wanted to be a waitress to come and see you."

"I remember that. I remember that big guy of yours staring at me with his owl-like eyes when I said that to you."

"I know, sometimes he can be rude and not realize it."

"Well, right now, I don't have an opening for a waitress." He scanned her up and down again. "But if you don't mind starting as a busboy, I could use you for the afternoon shift."

"Since this would be my first job ever, I guess starting at the bottom would be the right thing to do."

George fingered his double chin. "I like that, smart and honest."

"Does that mean you're hiring me?"

He motioned the snobbish hostess for a blank application. "Fill this out and bring it with you Monday at one."

That meant she only had the rest of the day and the next to get ready. Rosita had promised to watch Hope if she ever needed her to. Wrestling to hold the surge of ecstasy, she extended her hand. "I promise you won't regret it."

"I'm sure I won't," he replied with a smirk. He headed back to his office, muttering, "She's one of the hottest women I've ever…"

I can't believe I'm finally going to be working, Kelly thought, smiling. She was going to be able to buy Hope new clothes and things when she needed them without having to beg anymore, and maybe even bring her there for lunch occasionally. *Thank you, God, thank you.*

"Mommy, what happened?"

"I got a job; can you believe it?"

"Oh Mommy." Hope cuddled against her. "I'm so happy for you, but Daddy doesn't want you to work, what if he says no again?"

"When things change, people have to change too."

"You know how crazy he gets when we don't listen to him."

"I know, but this time he has to understand and accept that I too go to work."

Hope's face sagged. "Where will I stay while you work?"

"Honey, that's why we're going over to Rosita's. She always said she would love to babysit you, and you like her too, right?"

"Yes, but she's not my mom."

"Honey, we need to do this, and remember what I just said. When things change, people must change too, and that goes for children as well." But Kelly was worried. She hadn't talked to Rosita in a while; what if she couldn't do it anymore?

***

Rosita stood on the threshold; mouth stretched wide in her signature smile. "Amores, what a pleasant surprise. Come in!" A hug and two kisses to Hope, and a hug and a kiss for Kelly.

"Rosita, I'm sorry to barge in on you."

"You're always welcome." Rosita closed the door and led them to her kitchen table. "Please sit?"

"Thank you."

"Refreshment?" Rosita asked, holding the fridge door open.

Hope didn't hesitate. "Yes, I'm crazy thirsty."

"Thank you, Rosita, we're not staying long," Kelly said.

"OK, I pour three glasses. One for Hope, one for me, and if you get thirsty later, here is one for you too." She moved the colorful vase full of seasonal flowers to the side, placed the glasses in front of them, and sat across from Kelly. "I'm so happy to see you guys."

Kelly's chair screeched under her. "Rosita, I got a job."

"That's great, but why you're just smirking when you should be excited?"

"I still have to deal with Rocky later, and I only have the rest of today and tomorrow to get ready for it, and…"

"And what?"

Hope glanced back and forth from her mom to Rosita.

"Is your offer to babysit my angel here still open?"

Rosita turned to Hope. "Amore, you be happy to spend lots of time with me?"

"Will you take me to the playgrounds again?"

Kelly had stopped taking Hope to the park because it always sparked an argument with Rocky, at times leading to fights that left them not speaking for days or even weeks, worse than the fights they often had about her wanting to go to work.

"Yes, mi amor, and everywhere else I go. You like to go watch TV now?"

Hope got on her feet, ready to sprint to the living room. "Mommy, can I?"

Kelly sensed that Rosita wanted to talk to her alone. "Just for a little while but be careful with the clicker."

Rosita waited for Hope to leave the room. "Kelly, what time you go to work?"

"The only shift he has open is in the afternoon. He asked me to be there Monday at one."

Rosita leaned forward. "You know how much I love to babysit her," she whispered, "but last week, my boss changed me to the day shift."

Kelly's earlier fear transpired, and her chair became a sinkhole. If she were to tell George that she couldn't start on Monday, he would think she was an unreliable jerk.

"I'm sorry, Kelly, but why now all of a sudden?"

Kelly grabbed a tissue from the table and wiped the corners of her eyes. "Maybe I did overreact this time and should just forget about it."

"What happened?"

"I don't know if I—"

"If you should tell me? I thought we could talk about anything."

Rosita and her husband Carlos, both in their early forties now, had emigrated from Peru a decade earlier. He was a department manager in a factory, and she took care of the house and continued her education toward a law degree, while at the same time eagerly trying to have children. After all the alternatives available in their country were exhausted, they gave up. Sometime later, their relatives who lived in New York City persuaded them to move to the States by telling them that there were doctors here who could help them. Once the paperwork for their green cards came through, they didn't hesitate and left their native country. After several attempts here too, reality sunk in, and they finally gave up trying.

New York City was too expensive for them, and through a friend, they got jobs in the Naugatuck Valley area, he in construction and she in an all-night coffee shop. Ten years or so later, they still worked at the same places, lived on the second floor of their two-family house, and rented the first floor for extra income.

Kelly and Rosita had met at a local grocery store when Rosita's wallet fell out of her pocketbook and Kelly sent Hope to take it to her. Rosita was so happy and appreciative, she invited them to her house for lunch that same day, which sparked the beginning of their special friendship.

"Rosita, I know. I'm sorry." Kelly glanced at Hope who was fully absorbed in her cartoons. "Hope was supposed to go on a school trip today, the last of the school year. Throughout the week, I have been asking Rocky to give me the twenty dollars she needed, but he kept saying tomorrow, tomorrow. This morning, while he was half asleep, I asked him again, but he totally ignored me. I rushed her to the school, hoping to convince the trip organizer to let me pay for it later, but she wouldn't budge. I thought I still had enough time to run back home and steal it from him if I had to. He yelled at me and stormed out of the house. I rushed back to the school and found Hope outside, crying her heart out." She wiped the corners of her eyes again. "That's when I decided that I had enough."

"That's terrible. Why you did not come to me? You know I help you."

"I know, Rosita. I know, but I can't continue this life of static poverty. It breaks my heart, especially during the holidays and her birthdays."

"That's terrible, but you shouldn't let it get to you. I'm sure there are other people out there worse off than you."

"But in our case, it doesn't have to be that way. I'm young, healthy, and willing to work."

"When you first hinted that he did not want you to work, I thought it was because you didn't need to."

"You know what's ironic, Rosita? My father started pushing me to earn my own way with babysitting jobs the day I turned fourteen, and now I have a husband who refuses to let me work and we're broke."

"Then it must be jealousy."

"I think he's got a nineteenth century brain in a twenty-first century body."

"Kelly, most men are insecure, but let's face it, you're eight years younger than he is and getting prettier, while he has already begun his downhill journey."

Kelly's body shifted on the chair. *I remember that big guy of yours staring at me with his owl-like eyes when I said that to you. Was George hinting the same?*

"OK, even if I find a way to help you, what if Rocky says no again?"

Kelly took a slow sip of juice. "I was planning on telling him tonight at dinner, but maybe I should just forget about the whole thing and go on with the miserable life I'm destined to live."

"You're talking crazy now. You finally found the strength to go this far and now you want to give up?"

"He's going to flip out."

"Maybe you should leave Hope with me for the rest of the day," Rosita said.

Kelly stared at a flower wilting over the edge of the colorful vase. "You know, my dreams growing up were to go to college, get an excellent job, travel for a while, get married, buy a big colonial house like my friend Angela's parents, and then build a family, in that order. Instead, on my sixteenth birthday, I got pregnant."

"I know that. What I don't know is what were you thinking."

"I was naïve and madly in love. "

"Kelly, in my old country, my papa would've killed me."

"My father threw me out of the house and disowned me. If that wasn't enough, he made my family turn against me too. But I still felt that having my baby was the right thing to do. Yes, I wasn't happy that my dreams came to a sudden stop, but I never regretted my decision to give birth to that beautiful angel there."

"And what did you do when he threw you out of the house and all?"

"Rocky's father, Sicilian like my grandfather, made sure we got married to save his family honor and took us in to live with them."

"That was nice of him."

"Yes and no."

"Why do you say that?"

"His father was like an army general, and Rocky didn't get along with him either. So, a few months after we were married, Rocky found a three-bedroom ranch for lease with an option to buy. It was a nice house. It had a circular driveway, a sunken living room, and a fireplace too. We leased all the furniture and moved in. At first, I felt strange going from high school student to wife, but we became a happy family. Then he had an excellent job and worked steadily every day while I took care of the house, our little angel, washed and ironed all the clothes, and cooked all the meals. Maybe because I was just a child myself, but in some strange ways I felt that my dreams, even if not in the order I had planned them, were becoming reality."

"And you couldn't see that side of him because there was no need for you to work then."

"That's true, we had pretty much everything. He was different then. Then, five years or so after we got married, his company moved to China and he lost his job of eleven years. That's when all the craziness began. Within a year, we lost the house and most of the furniture in it."

"You know, they say that God works in mysterious ways. And I think what happened to you this morning was to let you gather the strength to do exactly what you did. Go home and stand up to him."

Kelly looked straight in Rosita's eyes. "You're right."

"That's the Kelly I like to see."

"I'll pick Hope up as soon as I can." She stood up, ready to go.

"Wait," Rosita said. "After you leave, I will take Hope with me and go see my boss. I don't know what excuse I use, but I tell him I want to go back to the night shift, or I quit."

"No, Rosita, don't do that. I'll find some other way."

"But I wanna help you."

"I know." Kelly hugged her. "But I don't want you to lose your job over this."

"Remember, you're like the daughter I could never have, and Hope is like my granddaughter."

"Thank you, Rosita." Kelly guided her chair under the table.

Rosita followed her to the door. "You be strong, and don't forget that mi casa es tu casa."

***

Kelly's house was less than a half mile away. Realizing that she was entering her driveway a bit faster than usual, she slammed her foot on the brakes, but the car still bounced off one of the deeper potholes before coming to a full stop inches from the house door. She backed the car a couple of feet, turned the ignition off, and gazed at the peels of green paint about to fall off the siding. Going from a beautiful ranch to a crumbling six-hundred square foot converted garage, and he still didn't want her to work. She turned to the passenger seat, pulled the application out of her pocketbook, and stared at it. *Fill this out and bring it with you on Monday at one.* Yes George, whatever it takes, I'll be there.

As she was having the little conversation with herself, an unfamiliar car pulled in the driveway and parked to her left. A man in his early sixties with stringy salt and pepper hair and a belly choking the steering wheel waved at her with a half-smile. He stepped out of the car and started walking toward her. Not recognizing him, she rolled the windows up, pressed the door locks down, and followed each of his moves.

"Come out, got talk to you."

"Who are you?"

Her voice, muffled by the glass, wasn't loud enough. "Whar you say?"

"Who are you?" she yelled.

"Mr. Casale, you landlord!"

Mr. Casale had emigrated from Italy in his mid-thirties, and although his English was somewhat broken, his shrewdness was never affected by it. Over the years, he was able to accumulate a small real estate empire.

She unlocked the door and stepped out. "I'm sorry, I didn't recognize you at first."

"Is OK. Two years ago, my head had more hair."

"What can I do for you?"

He looked away from her. "I have no good news for you."

"What happened?"

"See, the bank wanna me to pay my mortgages on time. They no wanna hear me that my tenants pay late."

"Why you're telling me that?"

"Today is the seventeen, and I don't have your money, capisce?"

"That's got to be a mistake. Rocky always pays you on time."

"That's what that sceccu tells you?"

"Why would he lie about that?"

"Kelly, I know you two from when you was babies. Your grandfather was honest and religious, no his grandfather. You took after yours and he took after his. This is no the first time he pays me late, but this is the first time he is late like this."

"I can't believe this!"

"Before I rent him the house, I call the owner of the house you was living. You wanna know what he tell me?"

"Yes," she nodded.

"He tell me that he was feeling bad to push you and you daughter out, but no him."

"Mr. Casale, please? I'll make sure that he gets the money to you as soon as possible. And from next month on, I'll be on top of it myself."

He brushed his salt and pepper strings back with his hand, cupped his large-double-chin, and stared at her for a while. "If he bring me the money by Sunday night, OK. If no, Monday morning, I call the lawyer."

"I'll make sure that he does." She shook his hand. "Thank you, Mr. Casale, thank you." She watched him leave, stepped inside the house, and slammed the door behind her. Knickknacks from the top of the kitchen cabinet splattered all over the brown vinyl floor.

The house was like a furnace with a mildew odor. If outside was like being in purgatory, inside was like being in hell. She stormed inside and pushed the kitchen window wide open. Threw her pocketbook and the blank application on the kitchen table and headed straight for their tiny bathroom across from the front door. There, she wrestled with the rusting shower knobs until the water flowed lukewarm. Took off her sneakers and her sticky white-cotton T-shirt and threw them on the living room floor. Did the same with her jeans-shorts and pink panties. Naked, she stepped inside the shower stall. Threaded her hair over her shoulders and let the water flow across her face. *We could be heading for a homeless shelter and he still doesn't want me to work.* She grabbed the shriveled bar of soap and soaped herself all over. *This time I'm not backing down. Even if he beats me up, I'm not.* Her eyes shut tight, she remembered a more serene time: laying on a patch of plushy green moss alongside a placid brook, surrounded by ancient boulders, the sun peeking through the dense trees and Rocky gently pulling her shorts and panties down around her ankles.

With her legs bent halfway, her head stretched upward, her hair covering her face, his hands everywhere, her hands everywhere, moving faster…"Yes," she sighed, landing on her knees. "Yes, don't stop. Yes!"

***

The phone woke her from her ecstasy. She stared at the splashing water, then at her surroundings, and then down at her hands resting between her thighs. Stood up at once and shut the shower off. Wrapped a bath towel around her chest and hips. As she hurried to the phone, she stepped on a small ceramic shard.

"Is there anything else you want to throw at me today?" she asked the universe. Snatched the receiver off the hook. "Hello?" Only shrieks echoed from the other end. She slammed the receiver back onto the hook. "Go to hell!"

It was 4:42. She stepped in front of the small mirror above the sink. As her left hand searched for a spot with less back-wear, her right hand was whooshing her brush through her hair. Annoyed at playing peekaboo with the mirror, she threw the hairbrush into the sink. "This stupid mirror must be as old as my great-grandmother. And this dinky sink too."

She dumped her clothes in the washer. Gazed out the window. *I should just tell him straight out the moment he steps through that door.*

She went to the master bedroom and slid her feet into her pair of over-used brown-slippers, then hurried to Hope's bedroom, where the only decent size closet in the entire house was located, grabbed his favorite short black dress, and put it on. Grabbed her pair of embroidered black panties from the bottom drawer, also his favorite, put them on and hurried back to the stove. Filled a pot with hot water and turned the knob to low for some Angel hair pasta she had bought on sale. Perused through the small freezer and shuffled packages around until she found one with two chicken breasts and one with broccoli. Dropped them inside the pot, placed the big frying pan on the stove, poured a half cup of olive oil in it, and got that started on low. Skinned two garlic cloves, chopped them, and added them to the searing pan. Then, while gathering the knickknacks from the floor and the fragments of those that had broken, she heard Rocky's roaring Vet approaching. Her eyes shifted to the clock. 5:20. Hid all the pieces in the cabinet below the sink and started working on the chicken breasts.

He stood on the threshold, staring at her. "Fuck, that smells good."

"You're home early."

"You have a problem with that?" He shut the door behind him and headed straight for the fridge, grabbed a can of beer, snapped it open, and gulped, heading straight for their three-seater grey suede sofa. "That's what I mean."

She shook her head.

"Is Hope back from the trip yet?"

"Really?"

"Yeah, really."

"She never stepped on that bus."

"Why not?"

"Didn't you see it was snowing?" She sneered at him, her voice packed with irony.

"Fuck you."

"'No money, no trip.' Those were the organizer's exact words."

"Fuck her too. There will be another one."

"She was crying hysterically when I picked her up. Her heart has been scarred forever."

He headed for the fridge for another beer. "She'll get over it."

"And what makes you so sure that she will."

"You know how many things I wanted at her age and never got?"

"That was different, especially for an immigrant like your father who was struggling to build a new life in a new world."

"Don't matter, I got over it, and she will too."

"Is that so?" She glared at him. "You must be lucky because I never got over things that were supposed to happen and never did."

He flopped back on the couch and took a long gulp. "So, where is she then?"

"She's at Rosita's house."

He was about to swallow another gulp and nearly choked instead. "That fucking Rosita? Why don't you tell her to adopt one of her own!"

"So that I can lose the last friend I have?" She snapped the bag of broccoli open and dumped it in the searing pan.

He leaped up and held his index finger near her face, shouting, "You wanna know who your real friends are?" Pulled a small stack of mixed dollar bills from his pocket and flashed it before her eyes. "These are your real friends!" Flashed it again. "These, you get it?"

"And you couldn't spare twenty dollars for her this morning?" Eyes flooding, she turned away from him.

"This morning I didn't have it," he muttered.

"Where did you get it then?"

"None of your business."

"Is that the rent money?"

"What're you talking about?"

"Mr. Casale came by this afternoon. He told me that if we don't pay the rent before Monday, he'll have us evicted."

"That old man." He shook his head. "With all his money, what's his problem?"

"The rent is due by not later than the tenth of the month, and today is the seventeenth, which means that it's our problem, not his."

"Few days, what's the big fucking deal?"

"If your boss pays you a week later than he is supposed to, wouldn't that be a big deal for you?"

"That's different."

"No, it's not."

"Is dinner ready?"

"If that's not the rent money, then where did you get it?"

"Is dinner ready?"

"Forget it, the damage is done anyway. Hope begged me to leave her with Rosita for a while longer." She grabbed the box of angel hair from the counter-top and dumped it in the boiling pot.

"And you decided it was OK without asking me first?"

"I'm sorry, I forgot to bring my cell phone with me. Did you have yours with you?"

"Fuck you."

"After what happened this morning, I thought it would be good for her to get her mind off it." The chicken breasts were fully defrosted. Kelly brought the pot to the sink and let chilly water run over them. Squeezed them until no more water dripped, grabbed the butcher knife, and started slashing them into small bits. Sprinkled them with salt, pepper, and garlic powder and dumped them into the sautéing broccoli.

"Aren't you hot with that dress on?" He looked puzzled.

"I thought you love this dress on me."

"Yeah, so what?"

She rolled a couple of Angel hair strings around a fork and placed them in her mouth. "Couple more minutes and dinner will be ready."

"It's about time."

Black underwear and nothing else under her dress drove him insane. His eyes were glued to her back every time she bent down or stretched up to get something. He crushed the empty beer can in his huge hand and threw it on the coffee table. "Bring me another beer." He took his soaked T-shirt off, dried his long light-brown hair and face with it, and threw it on the coffee table. His body was as tan and ripped as that of a lifeguard, a byproduct of mowing other people's grass, racking soils, and spreading seeds over new lawns. At six-plus feet tall and around two-hundred pounds, his size was quite intimidating.

"At your service, sir." She shut the burner under the pasta, drained the water, and slowly eased it into the searing chicken and broccoli pan. Stirred it and turned the knob to low. Took a beer from the fridge and brought it to him.

He grabbed the beer with one hand, and with his other, he pulled her over until her chest pressed against his. Set the can down and slid his giant hands under her dress. "Since Hope is not here, let's get laid."

"Later," she replied with a smirk, trying to pull away.

"Why not now?" He gripped her tighter and started fondling her.

She sealed her legs and rested her arms over his shoulders. "I thought you were starving."

"I was." He locked her butt in his left hand, pulled her dress up above her hips. "But now I want to get laid first."

"Please, let's eat first."

"No, I want you now!" He forced her down and dragged her hand over his penis.

"This isn't the right time, please?" she pleaded.

"It is for me!" He pushed her on her back, snatched her panties off, and began to fondle her even faster.

"The food will burn, please stop!"

"Fuck the food."

After a stubborn struggle, she succeeded in snatching her hand away and pushed him back far enough to lock her legs tight. "I said no! Not now!"

"Bullshit!" He planted his legs on her knees and spread her legs open. "I'm your husband and I'll take you whenever I want!"

"Get off me," she yelled, pushing on his chest with both hands. "I said no!"

"Goddammit, keep these legs open!" He pulled them apart again and held them there with both his hands, pushing his penis against her to penetrate her.

She pounded his chest with every ounce of strength left in her. "No," she screamed, "you're raping me!"

"Shut up."

After pushing him few more times, she was able to wiggle her way out from under him. She stormed back to the kitchen.

Half-naked, his shorts hanging below his buttocks, his face a rectangle of rage, he lay down speechless, staring at her. "Next time that window will be shut."

Looking like she had just been wrestled by an angry dog, she was walking around the kitchen, hands shaking, right eye twitching relentlessly. "Monday I'm going to work," she said out loud.

He grabbed the beer from the coffee table, took a long gulp. "What did you say?"

"Monday, I'm going to work!"

"You're not going any fucking where!"

There was a time when his imperial attitude made her feel protected and secure, but now she was beginning to hate it. She clutched the edge of the countertop and gave him a long sneer. "I am too! Our daughter shall never again be embarrassed like that. Never. We live in the richest country in the world, in the year 2000, and for twenty lousy dollars, we scarred Hope's heart forever," she yelled. "For twenty fricking dollars, don't you get it?"

He sprung up. "I will not let you embarrass me."

"Embarrass you?" She shook her head.

"My mother was the wife of an immigrant and she never worked. None of my aunts did, and neither are you." He pointed his index finger at her. "You stay home where you belong, cooking and cleaning for me like you have been, and like my mother did for my father, and her mother before her."

She stared at him, face ghost-like, right eye twitching.

"Maybe you need another fucking child to keep your mind off that bullshit."

"Are you crazy, bringing another child into this destitute life of ours?"

"I thought you loved children!"

Her face changed as many colors as a rainbow as she yelled, "Home is where I belong?" She turned around and shut the burners off. "And you even have the guts to call this a home."

He rushed toward their bedroom. "What's wrong with it?"

"Look around you. In case you've forgotten, we live in a converted garage with prehistoric fixtures and decaying furniture from the seventies."

"Fuck you." He slammed the bedroom door.

"We live in the country of opportunities for all and look at us!" she yelled through the door.

Man, what the fuck got into her? He grabbed something from her nightstand drawer and put it in his pocket. Must be that Rosita spoiling the hell out of her. He opened the door and leaned against the doorjamb. "The richest country in the world, my ass," he said, shaking his head. "Did you take a ride through the Valley's main streets lately? Where thousands of people once used to feed their families, now are like war-zones full of ghost-hosting buildings. The land of opportunities was when you could go from one good-paying job to a better one at wish."

"I'm not stupid, I drive by there too. But the people who you used to work with all moved on with their lives. Many re-trained themselves and got jobs in new trades. Instead of wasting your time and money at the bar with your friends when your boss has no work, why don't you do the same?"

He grabbed her by her arms. "Fuck you!" Shook her. "First, my buddies are my business. And second, don't you think I'm mad as hell that most of the companies that could have a job for me moved overseas? 'You're a toolmaker?' they say, laughing. 'Man, you're outdated.'"

Kelly sobbed. "That's not what you said when you dragged us here. 'Honey, don't worry, this is only temporary. I'll do whatever I need to, even work two jobs if I have to, and we'll move out of here in no time.' Isn't that what you said?" She freed her arms from his stranglehold and rushed to the kitchen sink for a sip of water. "It's almost two years now, and here we are still in the same dump with you still working at a seasonal job, and you expect me to care about you being embarrassed if I go to work?"

"I put food on the table and keep us warm in the winters, don't I?"

"Don't you get it? I want a better life for us, and with both of us working, we can do it."

"I won't have people laugh at me." He pointed his index finger at her again. "That's it. I'm the boss of this house, and you're not going anywhere!" He grabbed another beer. "Like you lived in a fucking castle when I first met you, right?"

"I wasn't even sixteen."

"You're the one who got fucking pregnant!" He slammed the door and was gone.

She pushed dinner to the side and dragged herself to the table. Her head dropped on her folded arms, and as her eyes drifted to a close, Saturday June 6, 1992 flashed before her brain's eye. "I was so young. So young and so naïve…"

***

Even though it was her sixteenth birthday, that Saturday of 1992 had started just like any other Saturday. She went home to grab a bite to eat and found her drunken father with an angry look on his face sitting at the kitchen table, a shot of whiskey in one hand and his other hugging the whiskey bottle. He told her that she should quit school and get a full-time job, and when she yelled back that she wanted more from life than just a factory job, he lost it.

She evaded his closed fist and ran out of the house as fast as she could. Got to the public phone and called Rocky, who picked her up with his 89 Z28 Blue Camaro. They drove to his favorite area of the upper-level section of Derby's Osborndale State Park. There, he handed her a cassette with "November Rain," her then favorite song by Guns and Roses, and wished her happy birthday. At first, she refused to smoke a joint with him because she had never smoked marijuana before, but after Rocky kept insisting, she joined him. While they were joking and laughing, and making out in between, Rocky's friend Jay showed up in his Red Corvette with a cooler full of beers. They chatted for a while and before Jay left, Rocky took four beers, shook Kelly awake, and persuaded her to drink two beers. Then, with a blanket in one hand, and the other hand helping her stand straight, they walked to a hidden spot under an oak tree. Dusk had descended. He helped her lay down and they started making out. When she realized that they were totally nude and he was ready to penetrate her, she tried to stop, moaning that she was still a virgin and was afraid to get pregnant. He assured her that would never happen because he knew what he was doing.

***

Suddenly, the door burst open and her head sprang up, her face whiter than snow.

"I'm the fucking king of this castle!"

She tried to snatch the pint of whiskey from his hand. "Give it to me, you've had enough already!"

"I'm the king here and I do whatever I want with my slaves." He jerked her hand away and pinned her to the wall, his gorilla-like body pressing against hers, sticking his tongue in her mouth.

She swung her face to the side. "I'll never let you kiss me, stinking like that."

"Oh yeah? I'll show you who the boss is!" He held her arms tight against the wall. Gulped the rest of the whiskey and threw the empty bottle to the floor, then started dragging her toward the couch.

She wrestled to free herself from his stronghold. "You're drunk, let me go!"

"You go nowhere until I say so." He dragged her by the hair to the window, shut it, and then closed the door. Pulled her face closer to his. "Just like you not going to work!"

"Please let me go!"

"Not until we finish what you started."

"What I started?"

"Who the fuck told you to wear that dress, those sexy panties?"

"You're right, we should finish what I started. Let go of me first."

He wobbled his index finger near her eyes. "Don't fuck with me. I'll beat the shit out of you."

She lifted her body up, and barely sticking her tongue in his mouth, kissed him with her eyes closed.

He pushed her down on the couch and pulled her dress up above her breasts. "That's what I mean."

You disgust me, she thought, watching him wobble and drool. As he unraveled his feet from his shorts and underwear, she kicked her legs, and like a lightning strike, hit his groin with all the strength she could exert. She jumped off the couch and ran straight for the door.

"You fucking bitch," he screamed, falling on his back with both hands glued to his groin. "I'm gon' kill you!"

***

"*Dios mio*, what happened to you?"

Kelly's long black curly hair was tangled like a wheat field after a nasty tornado. Her dress was wrinkled like she'd tussled with a mad dog, her eyes blood shot like she hadn't slept for days, her body shaking with her hand over her heart, and her lips gasping for air. "I had to do it."

"You had to do what?" Rosita rushed her inside.

Kelly paced around the kitchen table, nipping at her nails. "I kicked him bad, really bad. He's going to kill me."

"Honey, please?" Rosita pulled a chair out for her. "Sit, he's not going to kill nobody."

Hope rushed out of the living room and coiled herself around her waist. "Mommy, why you're crying?"

"Don't worry, honey, I'm fine."

"Did Daddy hit you?"

"No, we just had one of those stupid fights. Please, go back and watch TV."

"It's because of the job, isn't it?" Hope asked as she walked back to the living room.

Rosita filled a glass of ice water and placed it before her. "Drink, you'll feel better." Sat beside her, winked at her with a smirk. "What happened, he didn't like the dinner?"

Kelly took a long sip, labored a smirk of her own. "We never got that far."

"I just don't understand. He can't provide for the family the way he should and doesn't want any help from you either. He must be crazy or very jealous. Either way, you better watch yourself."

"This time was my fault too. I shouldn't have dressed up the way I did. But I figured that preparing one of his favorite dinners, and wearing his favorite dress and all, would put him in a better mood to hear me out."

"If I had to change Carlos' mind about something, I would have done the same. We're women, and that's what we do."

"Poor Hope, she looks worried. Kelly, go on."

"One word led to another, and another led us to a big fight. He swore at me and stormed out the door."

"There has to be more to it for him to mess you up like this."

"I had planned to tell him after dinner." She peeked into the living room, to make sure that Hope was focused on her cartoons, and went on to tell Rosita what happened step by step

"Hijo de puta (son of a bitch)," Rosita said, shaking her head. "You did the right thing. He has no right to force himself on you."

"But I disobeyed him, Rosita, and that was wrong."

"No, not in today's world, and especially in this country. Listen to me." Rosita placed a hand on Kelly's shoulder. "He has no right to run your life as if you were a slave of his."

"But the man always has the last word. In my grandparents' house, it was that way. With my own parents, it was that way, and in Rocky's parents' house, it was that way too."

"And your house has been the same way, right?"

"Yes, it has."

"And where has it gotten you?"

Kelly took another sip of water. "I don't know what to do. A few hours ago, it all seemed so simple, but now I am totally lost."

"Kelly, I see it this way. All along, your desire of wanting to work and your wish to get the strength to persuade him was like a chick at the end of its incubation period, pounding its soft beak against the inside of the eggshell, hoping to break through. This morning, by you going to look for a job and finding one, it was like the same chick opening a little hole on the tip of the shell and looking at the light for the first time. Now your destiny calls for you to break through the rest of that eggshell. Go to work on Monday, and let life take its own course from there."

"Rosita, he was furious. If I go home pretending like nothing happened, he's going to put me in a hospital for sure and forget about the job. If I go and beg for forgiveness, life will go back to normal, and forget about everything. I don't know what to do."

"Kelly, we have our guest bedroom there. Tonight, and as many nights as you need, you and Hope will be our guests. And listen, it's his selfish and devious mind that has created this pointless issue, and the sooner you let go of this male superiority thing, and stand up for yourself like you did tonight, the better off you'll be."

"I made a bigger mess of everything, didn't I?"

"No, you didn't. But if you surrender now, for sure you'll be his slave for the rest of your life."

"Rosita, even if I were to take your advice, I still have to figure out what to do with Hope while I work."

"Well, I went to my boss and told him that if he didn't change my shift back, I would quit. He was shocked but didn't hesitate." Rosita's grin exposed her perfectly symmetrical white teeth. "I couldn't let this chance of spending lots of time with your little angel slide."

Kelly's face brightened. *Only my mother would do something like this for me.* She gave Rosita a long hug. "Rosita, God bless you."

"Like I told you earlier, you're like the daughter I could never have, and that little angel there is like my granddaughter. You're staying with us."

Kelly had never told Rosita how much Rocky hated her. "Rosita, this will enrage him even more, and I don't want to involve you and Carlos in this mess."

"That's why we have the police, isn't it?"

"I know, but—"

"Listen, if he hasn't allowed you to work till now, he's not going to change his mind anytime soon, because that will give you the taste of freedom, and make him feel less of a man. And if you really want to better your life, and that of your angel, Monday you go to work as you had wished."

Kelly placed her elbows on the table and thought for a while. "Rosita, you're right. This is the time."

Rosita's face shone. "Carlos should be home soon; I'll ask him to bring you to your house tomorrow when Rocky is not around and help you pack as many clothes and things as you can."

"What if he shows up when we're there?"

"Don't worry, Carlos will have his cell phone with him."

CHAPTER TWO

The next day Carlos drove Kelly to her house, parked at a safe distance, and waited for Rocky to leave. After his Vet sped away, they waited to make sure that he wouldn't come back to get something that he might have forgotten, drove to the house, and quickly got busy gathering clothes and things for her and Hope. They were almost done when the roaring of a loud engine outside the house froze them in their paths. Carlos looked through the blind and saw a big pick-up truck idling in the neighbor's yard. They drew sighs of relief, loaded all the boxes in the car, and took off like a couple of thieves.

***

Kelly was putting Hope to bed when Rosita's phone rang.
Rosita recognized Rocky's voice but played dumb. "Who's this?"
"You know who I am, just put her on the goddamn phone."
"She is sleeping right now."
"I don't care if she's dying, you put her on the goddamn phone, or I will come over and…"
"And what?" Rosita yelled. "You take one step up my stairs, I'll have your butt behind bars in no time."
Kelly, who was now standing next to her, said, "Rosita, please let me handle it."

"Who does he think he is?" Rosita handed her the receiver and stood next to her like an angry bear protecting its cubs.

"What do you want?"

"You bitch. Get your clothes and get your ass back home!"

"Haven't you done enough harm to us already?"

"After what you did to me, I haven't even gotten started."

Pacing around, eyes watering, Kelly said, "You keep that up, and for sure we'll never come home again."

"You forgot the vows you agreed to when we got married? To be faithful and honor me for the rest of your life?"

"No, I haven't, but you must have forgotten yours."

"Getting a job without my permission, is that how you honor me?"

"Trying to rape me, and keep me a penniless slave, is that how you honor me?"

"Where the fuck is this job anyway?"

"I'll tell you when I feel like. Just like you're going to tell me where you got that money."

"There you go, girl." Rosita patted her. "Let him put his feet in someone else's shoes for once."

"After we got married, you didn't work for years and were OK with that."

"Then you were a good provider, but now we're broke."

"I have plans to make a lot of money soon."

"I've heard that crap too many times over the last couple of years."

"Come home and we talk about it."

"So that you can beat me up?"

"You come home right now; I'll pretend this never happened."

Hope, in her pajamas, ran to the kitchen, wrapped her arms around her mom, and cried. "Please, tell Daddy to stop fighting."

"Rocky, did you hear that?"

"I did, but it's you who should stop being a bitch."

Rosita held Hope's hand. "Come on, honey, let's get you back to sleep."

"Since I'm nothing but a bitch, why do you still want me around?"

The receiver went silent.

"I can't stand being a penniless housewife anymore. Why can't you understand that we need me to go to work?"

"You've been a housewife since we got married."

"That's true, but I can't keep begging you for money when Hope needs things and when I need a new pair of panties or anything else. I am tired of that; don't you get it? I'm tired."

Rosita came back and stood right next to her, an arm around her shoulders.

"Then go fuck yourself, and don't count on me for anything. No rent money when you move out of your friend's house, and no child support."

She dropped the receiver and started crying.

"Honey, don't panic, we're here for you."

"No, Rosita, I better just go home and pray to God to look after us."

"Don't do it, Kelly. This is your last chance. You went this far, don't back down now. Remember, God helps those who help themselves."

Kelly wiped her eyes with the back of her hands and hugged her. "I'm so darn confused."

"Kelly, once I heard this saying, 'It's better to live one day as a lion than one hundred as a sheep.' You're smart and strong, you've got to fight."

***

The next day, they had just finished lunch, Rosita was washing, and Kelly was drying. "I just hope he doesn't come around and do something crazy at the diner."

"Don't run ahead of yourself. It will take him at least a couple of days to figure that out. By then you'll have already shown George what kind of person you are."

"I hope so."

"Hey." Rosita shouldered her. "If he does something crazy, you go to the police and put a restraining order on him."

"Rosita, you should have been an attorney."

"You know, I make mistakes too. We were madly in love and rushed to get married. After we moved to this great country, I did think about continuing my education, but because I was too scared that my English wasn't good enough, I never took that step. You're young and smart, and the step you're taking is the right one. And once things settle down for you, who's to stop you from going back to school too?"

"Rosita, I think my destiny is leading me to being a single mom and working full time. I doubt if I'll ever be able to do that."

"Don't ever say never." Rosita looked at her watch. "Go, go get ready, you have to be at work in less than an hour."

"Hope, where are you?"

"Here, Mommy." She was sitting on the living room floor, quietly shuffling her few toys in the pink Barbie backpack that her godmother Angela had brought her from California couple of years earlier.

Kelly stood at the door for a moment and stared at her.

Hope turned around with her green eyes glittering. "Now you can buy me new toys, right, Mommy?"

"Soon, honey, soon."

MY LAST CHANCE

"But what if Daddy stops you from working?"
"Honey, we can't afford to let him do that anymore."

CHAPTER THREE

Kelly roamed around looking for a parking spot that couldn't easily be seen from the road. She parked behind the diner next to a cluster of overgrown bushes. She took a long deep breath. "I can do this."

Butterflies whirled in her gut, and prickles of joy coursed up her back. The snobbish hostess was walking a couple to their table, and George was next to the double swinging kitchen doors chatting with a couple of customers sitting at the counter.

"Why are you so early?" the snobby hostess asked, staring.

"Since it is my first day, I figured it would take me at least fifteen minutes to get my uniform and get ready."

"I see." She chewed gum as she spoke.

"Hi Kelly," George hollered making his way toward her as if he had just seen an old friend.

Kelly blushed. "Hi George."

He looked at his watch. "You're pretty early?"

"I don't like to be late."

"So, you're ready to get going then?"

"As ready as I could ever be."

"Then follow me."

The friendly way with which George welcomed her caused the butterflies in her gut to diminish. He turned around and headed toward his office. Picked up two black, short sleeve dresses, and handed them to her. "These are our standard uniforms. The lady's room is over there, try them on, and let me know which one fits you best."

Other than being an inch or so further above her knees, the smaller size fit her perfectly. She wasn't too happy about the low cleavage line, which exposed more of her breasts than she was comfortable with. She thought about telling him, but as she approached his office, she decided to leave it for another time. "I think this is the one. What you think?"

George scanned her from head-to-toe. "Hell yes. That fits you like a glove."

Shy, she looked down. "I think so too."

"Come on, I'll have you train with Sandy. She is my best waitress and has been working for me the longest. But remember, you work as a busboy for now. If what I see is good, as soon as a spot is available, I'll give you a chance at waitressing."

"Thank you, I wouldn't expect any more."

Sandy was a slim woman in her fifties, sprouting wrinkles around her eyes and lips. For the first couple of hours, step-by-step she showed Kelly where all the tableware was kept. She explained how to clean the tables quickly and efficiently, and how to properly set them. Fully focused, Kelly absorbed her instructions like a sponge, and when she felt a bit overwhelmed, she took notes. In no time, with a smile and an eager look on her face, she was handling pretty much everything she had just been taught. Except for the snobbish hostess, whom she caught sneering at her couple of times, the other waitresses and the kitchen crew were all smiling and encouraging her throughout. While clearing a four-seater table, she noticed customers backing up at the register. Quickly, she rushed to the waitress station and gathered all that she needed to set the table back up.

George, sitting in a booth, chatted with a female customer while watching Kelly's every move. He looked at his watch. 6:45. She was supposed to leave at 6:30. The place was getting packed again. He walked over to her with a smile, "Kelly, you know what time it is?"

"No, I don't have a watch," she replied, hurrying to get the table fully set.

"The clock is right there, look." George pointed above the coffee station.

"Oh my God. I'm so sorry, I didn't—"

"That's OK. Finish what you're doing and then go."

"It was so busy; I didn't realize it was that time already."

As he walked away from her, he said, "Don't worry about it. I wish some of the other ones would do the same."

***

"That's the face I love to see." Rosita greeted her. "Your shorts look like a checkerboard. Go change."

"It's OK, Rosita, they'll dry in no time."

Hope, who was glued to the TV as usual, heard her voice. "Mommy, you're back!" She ran over, jumped in her arms, and gave her a kiss on the cheek. "I missed you."

"I missed you more." Kelly held her tight and kissed her forehead. "Go back to the TV for a while longer, I need to unwind a bit."

"And then we go home?"

"No, honey, we're not going home."

"But I thought yesterday you said—"

"The other night, you heard us arguing. Daddy is terribly angry that I'm working. If we go home now, we're going to fight even harder, and I don't think you want to see that again, do you?"

"No," she shook her head, "but I told you he didn't want you to work."

"But if I don't work, how're we going to get your new toys and pay for your school trips next year?"

"I see."

"Let's give him some time to cool off, and then we will see."

"OK…" Hope smirked at her mother and strolled back to the living room.

"I feel so bad, but you were right, Rosita. I can't be a sheep anymore."

"Don't worry, she'll come around. Tomorrow I'll take her to the playground," Rosita said. "Carlos will be late for dinner. Here, sit next to me and tell me about your very first working day."

Kelly extended her legs under the table, leaned her head over the chair's top rail. "I can do this. I can."

"I never had any doubts, and I know you can do everything you put your mind to."

"You know, Rosita, even though it's only a busboy job, as time went by and I was doing more and more on my own, I felt so proud of myself. I have never experienced that before."

"To feel that worthiness is great, isn't it?"

"As I walked to my car, I felt as if I had grown inches taller." Kelly shook her head. "All these years, what a waste."

"I'm so proud of you. But remember, he'll come around, they always do. And when he does, you need to stay strong, no matter what."

"It's just a matter of time, I know."

CHAPTER FOUR

Two days after summer had officially started, it was Kelly's fifth day on the job. It was a sweltering day and unusually slow for 1:30 in the afternoon. On her way back from punching in, she waved at George who was on the phone with a sad look on his face.

"Kelly, wait, I need to talk to you."

She turned back and leaned against the office door jamb with a puzzled look on her face. After a few seconds, George hung up and motioned her to sit across from him.

"Did I do something wrong?"

"No, Kelly, but I do have a problem."

She exhaled a sigh of relief. "Is it something I can help you with?"

"Yes and no." He leaned forward. "Sandy was in a car accident this morning and is banged up pretty bad."

"Oh my God." She cupped her face in her hands. "I'm so sorry."

"I'd love to get my hands on that young jerk who hit her."

"George, I can't believe it. How bad is she?"

"She suffered a few fractured ribs and a fractured knee. The doctors said it could be at least couple of months before she can resume her normal life."

"That's terrible."

"You think you're ready to give it a shot at being a waitress?"

Of course, working as a waitress was her current goal, but she never expected to achieve it that way, and that soon. "I think I can, but It won't be easy to fill Sandy's shoes."

"Here." He handed her an order pad and a pen. "Go ahead, give it a try, and if you get stuck, just ask the other waitress for help."

Even though she had only known Sandy for a brief time, she liked her very much. She strolled out of the office, eyes watering.

Sometime later, a young couple walked to her side and sat in one of the four-seater booths. Kelly stiffened. She took a deep breath and approached them with the menus. A couple of minutes later, armed with a bit more courage, she went back, took their orders, served them, and later handed them the check with a wide smile. Then she snuck to the lady's room, and after making sure no one was in there, she took a deep breath and looked in the mirror. "I did it! I did it!"

Not long after, she served four guests, also from beginning to end, and by the time she was through with them, all the fears of failing had vanished. The rest of the afternoon she moved around as if she had been at that job forever, while George, unknown to her, was discreetly observing her performance, smirking. At the end of her shift, he came out of the office and called her to join him in one of the booths where he normally sat to observe his operation.

"Kelly, are you sure you didn't lie when you applied for this job?"

"Why? What's wrong?"

"You work like you have been at this forever."

"Really?" Her eyes glittered. "Honestly, besides babysitting in high school, this is my first job ever. I just like to learn things as fast as possible and do them the best way I can."

"You're a rare breed these days." George shook his head. "What am I going do with Sandy when she comes back?"

"Does that mean you're going to keep me on as a waitress?"

"Use that booklet well. And If sometimes you make mistake, don't tear up the page and throw it away, just write voided across it, and go on to the next one." He got up. "I'll see you Monday."

**

She had parked her car in the same secluded spot she had been using since her first day at the job. Excited to tell Rosita of her unexpected promotion, she rushed to her car, and as she was about to turn the engine on, she heard a loud roar, turned around, and saw Rocky's Vet speeding in her direction. "He's going to hit me!" Shaking like a leaf, she crouched her head between her knees. His tires swirled and screeched to a sudden stop lengthwise behind hers. As she was rushing to lock all the doors, he jumped out of the car and headed straight to the driver's side.

"I got talk to you, open the window!"

"If you don't get away from me, I'll start screaming. Get away!"

"I just wanna talk to you. I won't touch you; I swear."

She stared at him. "OK, but only if you stand in front of that blue car there, and if you take one step toward me, I'll scream so loud, your ear drums will burst."

"All right." He looked like a homeless person with his dirty shorts, wrinkled T-shirt, droopy face and hunched back. He dragged his feet to the spot she had pointed to, twenty feet or so away.

Slowly, she opened her door halfway, got out, and stared at him over the roof top. "What do you want?"

He leaned against the passenger door of the blue car. "The house is dark and empty. I miss you guys."

"Let me understand. You miss having your slaves around?" Only days earlier, she wouldn't have had the courage to talk to him like that, unless they were in the middle of a fight.

"I shouldn't have said those things, or act like I did." He shook his head. "I just had too much booze that night, that's all."

"And what about the other times when you didn't have that much booze."

"OK, you're right, maybe I do have a problem that I need to work on."

"Who told you I worked here?"

"Nobody. I came home for lunch today with one of my boss's pick-up trucks. I parked a few houses down from Rosita's and waited for you to get out. When you did, I followed you here." He took a couple of steps forward.

"Stop right there or I'll scream!"

"Listen, I am not angry anymore. Yes, my fucking balls still hurt, but I am not looking for revenge. This is crazy, I just want us to get back together."

"It's too late."

"You're gon' throw eight years away and have Hope grow up without a father just like that?"

"Let's say we were to come home, then what?"

"I'll do what I need to do to make good on my promises." He paused. "I'll work two jobs and whatever else I need to do to get us a house like we had before."

"I've heard that story so many times that it's beginning to sound like the vanishing lyrics at the end of a song."

"Talking this far apart is weird. I have no intention of touching you, please?"

He had been the only man she had ever intimately known. And being alone night after night for the first time in eight years, she was beginning to feel sexually starved. "I tell you what. Move your car away from mine and stand on the passenger side of my car. The doors there are locked, and mine will stay halfway open with the engine running."

"OK."

He drove his car to an empty spot and walked back. Maybe he was beginning to see how important they were to him.

"Stand right over there."

"Isn't this better?" He lit a cigarette and leaned his arms over her car roof. "OK, here is the deal. You will…" He looked away from her, took a few more puffs, threw his cigarette on the ground, and squashed it a few times.

"Hope is waiting for me."

He pulled the pack of cigarettes from his shirt pocket again and lit another one, while Kelly's fingers were playing with the car roof as a keyboard. "And soon it will be Christmas too, she said."

"All-right. OK." He rested his arms back on the car roof and stared away from her. "I'll go along with you working if…"

"If what?" She frowned with her eyes squinted.

"I am still your husband, right?"

"Yes, you still are."

"You still gon' have the supper ready for me when I come home from work, and wash, and iron my clothes as usual?"

"I get out of work by 6:30, so I could have supper ready by 7:30."

"I'm OK with that. What about when I want sex, are you gon' always be ready for me?"

"You know I love to have sex with you as long as you're not drunk or trying to rape me like last time."

"That was the booze, it's not gon' happen anymore."

"What if we argue and you get drunk again?"

"I promise you." He held his right hand up. "I swear, I'll never do that again."

If he was serious about her working, which he seemed to be, that was a ninety-degree turn from where he had been over the last few years. Of course, he could be lying, but how could she know that unless she gave it a chance? "So, that's it?"

"There is one more thing. When I'll be making the same money I was making before my fucking company moved to China, and I get the house of your dreams, we go back to the way we were."

"No." She shook her head. "That's a no-no. For the first time in my life, I've experienced a sense of pride that I never knew existed, and I am not letting it go even if you build me a castle with servants."

He turned away from her, lit another cigarette, and stared at the pavement wordlessly. With his eyes flooded, he shook his head couple of times. "Will you consider working only a few hours a week?"

The last time she had seen him like that was at his parents' funerals. If she said no, they couldn't stay at Rosita's forever, which meant she must rent her own place, furnish it, and that would require money that she didn't have. If she said yes, he might come around and they would all be happy. After all, she still cared a lot about that big baby. And if it didn't work out, she would have a chance to save some money so that she and Hope could then move into a place of their own. "We'll cross that bridge when we get to it."

With tears dripping from the corner of his eyes, he pled, "Please, I feel lost without you guys?"

Whether those tears were genuine or crocodile tears after swallowing its prey, only the future could answer. "If you're serious, I'll think about giving it a try."

"Can I come closer?"

She hesitated at first. "I guess so."

His face brightened. He rushed around the car, held her by her arms, pulled her close to him and latched his lips on to hers. Grabbed her butt and pressed his groin against her.

His erection caused her to implode in his arms like a deflating doll. His hand slowly made its way under her uniform and up her thighs.

Their tongues whirling in each other's mouths, an oncoming car's headlight flashed directly into her eyes. She pulled back at once. "Please, stop."

"Let's go home, I am ready to explode."

"No." She pulled her hair back. "Not that fast.

"Why not?"

"Even if I decide to return, I'll have to let Rosita know first." She gave him a quick kiss on his lips, got in the car, and drove away.

His eyes stared at her car merging onto the road. *That fucking Rosita.*

***

"You had to work late?"

"No, Rosita, I was detained for a while. I'll tell you after dinner." She nodded in Hope's direction.

"I see."

After they had gorged on spaghetti and meatballs, Hope headed for the living room to put her cartoons on. Kelly cleared the table, took the three half-full glasses of wine, and placed them back in front of their respective chairs.

Kelly wiped the dishes as Rosita handed them to her, her mind pondering. In such a brief time, they had grown to be more like family than just friends, the kind of family that Kelly always longed for growing up. If she went back to Rocky, Rosita and Carlos were going to be heartbroken.

"So, what held you up?"

"You were right, Rosita."

"I was right about what?"

"'He'll come around,' you said to me last week, 'they always do.'"

"I knew it."

Kelly dried the last dish, wiped her hands on her apron, and sat down across from Carlos. Rosita followed. Kelly sipped her wine. "I had just started my car when he showed up."

"Who told him where you worked?"

"This afternoon, he was watching my car from down the street and followed me to work."

"He tried to do anything bad?"

"No. Actually, he was like a totally different person. Maybe he's finally coming to his senses."

"Kelly, remember that when the devil charms you, he's after your soul."

"That's true," Carlos added.

"After all these years, he finally agreed for me to work."

As each word came out of her mouth, Rosita and Carlos sensed that they might not have the girls around for much longer, and their faces sagged.

"Kelly, once you told me that your grandfather used to say, 'Wolves change their furs, but never their habits.' Make sure you keep that in mind."

"Rosita, his eyes were flooded with tears when he begged me to move back. The last time I saw him like that was at his parents' funerals. I really feel that he might be ready to come around."

"Sounds like you made up your mind already."

"Rosita, no, but if he were as serious as I thought he was when he told me that he would stick by his promises, I will consider it. Those fights about me going to work would stop, and our relationship could go back to our happier days, or even better."

"I understand." Rosita picked up a napkin and wiped the corner of her eyes. "It's just that I got so used of having your guys around all the time that—"

"Rosita, if I decide to go back with him, you're still going to watch Hope when I am at work, aren't you?"

"You bet I am."

"Then you're still going to see us almost every day. The only difference will be that we'll not be sleeping over, but that would have had to change because eventually we would have had to move into our own place somewhere."

"I know." Rosita nodded. "I thought about that a lot, but it would have been down the road somewhere."

"I will miss you guys a lot too," Carlos said. "It's been great to come home from work and cheered by your little angel there, and then have dinner with a bigger family."

The corners of Kelly's eyes began to drip. "Guys, I'm behind grateful to you, thank you."

"Kelly, let me say it again. Since we first met, I always thought of you as the daughter I could never have, and Hope as my granddaughter. And this week you've allowed us to live that dream." Rosita wiped her eyes again. "As long as God will keep us around, we'll always be here for you. Just be watchful of that charming devil."

"I will. Trust me, I will."

CHAPTER FIVE

Kelly was rushing around to get dinner ready while Hope quietly played with her toys and watched her cartoons.

Rocky's ego had been fractured, and his mind was tortured thinking of all the men that would flirt with her. However, the house was full again and the stove was on, the same as it was, and the same as it will be because the plans to end her journey of defiance had earnestly been brewing since she had left. He took a few steps, looked at her. "Man, that smells really good."

Apologizing that the dinner would take a little longer, Kelly greeted him with a smile of her own.

Before their week apart, he would have made a big deal about it, but knowing that fucking Rosita was always ready to host them with her open arms, he had to be extra careful if he wanted his plans to come to fruition. He kissed her cheek. "I'm sure it'll be worth the wait." Peeked inside the sizzling pan. "What're you making?"

Hope ran over, jumped in his arms, and gave him a hug and a kiss.

"I'm making shrimp over angel hair pasta."

After she had dropped their clothes and stuff off, and before she brought Hope back to Rosita's house and embarked on her second week of work, they had gone shopping with the hundred dollars' worth of tips she had been able to accumulate. For the first time since they had been married, she proudly did the shopping with money that she herself had earned.

"Can't wait to devour it."

Kelly slid her hands up his chest and gave him a teasing kiss. "By the time you take your shower, I promise it'll be ready."

While he was in the bedroom, he opened her nightstand drawer and shuffled things around for a while.

"Dinner is ready!" Kelly called. "Hope, come on, put your toys away, shut the TV, and go wash your hands."

Rocky sat in his usual chair. "You know, nothing feels better after an exhausting day at work than a freshly scrubbed body and a set of clean clothes."

Smirking, Kelly filled his dish to the rim with pasta, topped it with a generous quantity of shrimp and sauce, and placed it in front of him. Then she made a smaller dish for Hope, the same for herself, and placed them in their spots. Handed him the bottle of Chianti with a corkscrew and asked him to do the honors.

He filled two glasses, placed one in front of her, and held his up for a toast. "To our lives, back to normal."

She took her glass, held it up. "And to your working wife."

"That too," he replied looking down at his dish.

Kelly placed the first forkful in her mouth. *To our lives, back to normal.* Maybe the new reality hadn't sunk in yet.

Minutes later, Rocky was finished eating. He grabbed his glass of wine and gulped the rest. Took the bottle, gave Kelly a lascivious stare, filled his glass again, and refilled hers. While Kelly cleared the table and started washing the dishes, he lit a cigarette. "Was that your uniform you had on Friday night?" he asked, puffing and sipping.

"Yes, why?"

"It fits you well, and black looks great on you, but the cleavage line is too low, and the length is a bit too short."

Kelly secretly agreed but she wasn't about to jeopardize her job. "You're right. I told George that, and he said when he orders the new batch, he'll take care of it."

Rocky frowned. *He and those fucking pervert customers of his looking at my woman's gorgeous legs and down her tits.* "When is that gon' happen?"

"I guess when these get damaged or begin to look old."

He plopped on the couch. That meant he would have to put up with that shit for three to four months. Hope looked like she was about to fall asleep. He caught Kelly's attention. "I think she's ready for bed."

Kelly lifted Hope in her arms and whispered, "I need to shower first."

"I've been drooling for a week, make it quick."

After a while, he heard the squeaky bedroom door open. He turned the TV off and zoomed in there. A comfortable breeze swished through the crevice at the bottom of the window, a tiny night light from an outlet on the bottom of the wall outlined her flawless naked body, her long curly black hair framing it down to her hips, a sight that would lead even an angel to penance recitals. He locked the door, snatched his clothes off and fused his body to hers. *That's what I mean*, he thought as she guided him inside her, before their coiled bodies wrestled relentlessly from one side of the bed to the other, breathing each other's breath, bathing in each other's sweat, incessantly moaning until their fireworks discharged the final blasts. His body ambled to her side, and hers deflated with fading jolts.

She stared at the ceiling in disbelief. It had taken only a couple of days apart before she had missed sex with him. If it is true that for a marriage to work, sex should account for at least fifty percent, in theirs, it must account for a hell of lot more.

She got up and walked to the kitchen for a quick glass of water. Then laid next to him again, wrapped her leg around his butt, and her arm around his back. "You ready?"

He peered at her, eyes half-shut. "You serious?"

"I told you to watch what you were wishing for."

"Did you take your pill?"

She pushed him flat on his back and sat on top of him. "Of course, I have no intentions of getting pregnant."

***

The rain wasn't about to slow down anytime soon. She placed her pocketbook over her head, ran for the door, and went straight to the lady's room. On her way back, one of the waitresses with eyes ready to pop out of their sockets froze in front of her. "Kelly?"

Perplexed, Kelly stared back at the chubby face. The girl looked awfully familiar, but she couldn't place where she knew her from.

"Kelly Nolan. I can't believe it's you?"

The girl rushed to hug her like an old friend. It had been a long time since someone had addressed her by her maiden name. Mutely, Kelly played along with the greeting as her mind continued to churn.

Finally, the girl let go of her, stepped back, and scanned her up and down couple of times. Then she looked around and whispered, "I still remember a number of boys skipping school for days when they found out you were dating an older guy."

Kelly could now see a picture of a thinner her. "Gilda from Derby High?"

"No foolin', do I look that different?"

"I'm sorry, it's been so long since I last saw you."

"Yeah, now I'm not only stupid, but fat too."

Gilda's boyish style haircut was gone. Now she wore her hair long and parted in the middle. She was a lot chubbier than she used to be. To her credit though, her extra weight was voluptuously dispersed throughout her body, including her breasts. Relieved to have avoided the embarrassment of not remembering her in front of her coworkers and newly made friends, Kelly placed her hand on Gilda's shoulders. "Gilda, you look great."

Gilda primped her hair and smiled. "I can't believe you work here too. You know, everyone has been talking about this new waitress Kelly, but I never thought it was you. You were so smart, I always pictured you in a big job somewhere outside this valley."

"Gilda, I'm very flattered, but crap happens and here I am."

Throughout their early school years, they were never best friends but occasionally hung out. They lived in the same neighborhood then, and Kelly had sometimes helped her with her homework. But it had been eight years since they last saw each other.

"OK ladies." George pointed to his watch. "It's time to take over your sections."

Gilda sneered at him. "Just a minute." She turned back to Kelly. "Hey, after work let's go for coffee at the donut shop next door."

"Huh, I don't know if I can."

Kelly wasn't sure if it was a clever idea to rush back to the future that fast. Besides, having supper on time for Rocky was her main concern now, especially because it was only her second day of work after they had made up.

"Come on, please, it's been so long?"

"I'll think about it."

By the end of their shift, Gilda had persuaded her. They grabbed their pocketbooks and were on their way.

Gilda held the door open. "Come on, we got so much to catch up with."

"Gilda, I have to have dinner ready by 7:30, so I can only stay for a brief time."

"It can't be 8:00 or 8:30?"

"No, it can't."

"Tell Rocky you're with me. He used to be over my house a lot before I introduced you guys on that unforgettable Memorial Day party. I'm sure he hasn't forgotten who I am."

By then almost everyone had a cell phone, including many teens. It was the closing of the century novelty to have, but not for the Esposito family, at least not yet, and Kelly was embarrassed about it.

"Kelly, it's not a big deal, I lie to my husband all the time."

She knew Rocky when he was young and single with a decent job and plenty of money in his pocket, Kelly thought, she has no idea how erratic he can be now. "First, I don't have a cell phone, and then— "

"Here, you can use mine."

"No, it's OK." Kelly pushed her hand back and headed for her car.

"Where're you going? It's only a couple hundred feet, let's walk."

"It'll be quicker to go home from there."

There were no customers ahead of her, and only a handful of them sitting at various tables. It had been a long time since she had been in a coffee shop, or anything like it, as a customer. "I'll have a small black coffee please?" While saying that to the young boy on the other side of the counter, Gilda walked in. "Gilda, what would you like?"

Gilda shouldered her away from the register. "No, this one is on me. I invited you, and I am treating." She looked up at the menu.

"I'll have a medium coffee with cream and sugar." Winked at the boy, "Extra cream and heavy on the sugar."

"Yes ma'am. Will that be all?"

"How fresh are those round donuts filled with cream there?"

"They were brought out of the kitchen about half an hour ago."

"I'll take one." Then she turned to Kelly, pointing to a table near one of the picture windows. "Let's grab one of those."

She sat across from Kelly and took a full bite of the succulent yellowish-cream donut. "I know, I shouldn't be eating all these calories." Her muffled voice heaved through her mouthful.

"Gilda, if you enjoy it, why not? I'm not a fan of sweets, but I do make an exception during the holidays. I even drink espresso without sugar."

"I could never do that." Gilda placed the last bite in her mouth, wiped her hands, and took a long sip from her coffee. "So, how did you end up working at the diner anyway?"

Among other things, Kelly now remembered that Gilda was excessively nosy and a gossiper. She was good at digging things out of people and then blabbering with anyone willing to listen. Perhaps that was her way to get the attention she constantly longed for, not realizing that in the process she used to hurt people. When Kelly was eleven, her grandfather died, and the subsidy to pay the rent for her family's three-bedroom ranch in a middle-class neighborhood died with him. By the following month, she and her family had moved into a two-bedroom apartment in one of the Valley's lower-class areas. She was devastated by the move. Not long after, she got into a fight with two of the most snobbish girls in her school who had been mocking her for several days. By the time other girls broke them apart, Kelly's lips were swollen, and the two girls' eyes were black and blue. Gilda wasn't even present at the fight, but wasted no time learning about it and delivering the news to Kelly's parents. That evening, hoping to avoid a whipping, Kelly hid in her building's furnace room for a while. Later, she stood across the street, looking up at her apartment until all the lights went off. Waited a bit longer, and quietly snuck into the bedroom she shared with her brother and went straight to bed. But with her stomach lamenting for food, her sleeping was fitful at best. As if that wasn't enough, the next morning her father pulled her out of bed for an early beating instead of an early breakfast. It took months and multiple apologies before Kelly talked to Gilda again. Was she different now?

"Gilda, for my first job, I had to start somewhere."

"No foolin', is this your first job ever?"

"Other than babysitting, yes. And to be honest, I'm really enjoying meeting new people, and the feeling of worthiness that comes with it."

"Shit, I have been working the 10 p.m. to 6 a.m. shift since I graduated from high school. And except for when I popped my two children out, and a couple vacations here and there, and some sick time, I have never missed a day."

"So, the afternoon shift is not your normal one then?"

"No, and I wish I didn't have to work there at all."

Kelly stared at her. "Why is that?"

Gilda's thin lips tightened, her nostrils flared, and her dark gray eyes narrowed. "Trust me, they'll get to you after a while."

"What do you mean, they'll get to you. Who?"

"The customers. Many men are rude, especially at night after the bars close. And some of them are plain pigs, peering up our uniform every chance they get." She shook her head. "And some, when we bend down to place the dishes in front of them, they rub their elbows against our breasts, and sometimes even against our crotch."

Kelly's eyes rolled over. "That's disgusting, thanks for warning me."

What Gilda left out was that when a customer was young and hunky, drunk or not, she was the one to initiate the crotch rubbing, not the other way around. And while at it, she would take her sweet time taking his order, and then her sweet time placing the dish in front of him while quietly arranging an escapade in his car, or in the bush behind the diner, if there were no other customers around to be served, or right after work if the hunky decided to return.

"So, what did you do all these years?"

"I'd rather not talk about it just now."

"How many children you have with that charming hunk of yours?"

"Just one, that's all. Her name is Hope, and she is a little over eight now. You're also married, right?"

"Yeah," Gilda replied lazily as her eyes focused on a woman walking toward the counter.

"How many kids do you have?"

"Sorry. I have three of them. My five-year-old Melina, my seven-year-old Tommy, and my twenty-six-year-old husband Kevin."

"I see."

Gilda peered at the lady at the counter again. "Isn't that Angela, your best friend from high school?"

Kelly took a good look at her. "No. Angela is still living in Santa Monica anyway."

"You guys were inseparable. Are you still friends?"

"Of course we are, we just don't talk as often because it's too expensive for me. The last time I spoke to her, she was considering moving back with her parents in Woodbridge, a couple of miles down the road from here."

"Must be nice to have rich parents."

"Growing up, her parents were like any other middle-class family, and lived in a modest two-bedroom ranch in Derby, right across the street from where my family and I used to live." She sighed, eyes watering. "Then her father got involved in real estate and finally made it big. I must say though, Angela never let it go to her head."

"I can't wait until I graduate."

"Graduate from where?"

"From that community college in Waterbury. In a few more semesters, I'll be a legal secretary."

"Gilda, I'm so proud of you. I wish I could say the same about me."

"I knew you never came back to school after you had your daughter, but you never went back at all?"

"My husband believes that kids have to be brought up by their mothers. After begging him for couple of years though, I did manage to get my High School Equivalency Diploma."

"Why did you have to beg him for that?"

"He also believes that for a woman going to school is a waste of time."

"Are we talking about the same charming Rocky that girls used to stand in line for?"

"I was aware he had dated a few girls, but I didn't know he was in such a demand."

Gilda gave her a tight-lipped smile. "He looked up to my dad a lot, and almost every time he came over to visit, he had a different girl with him, but after he met you, we only saw him one more time before you guys got married."

Why was she telling her those things? "Gilda, as long as it was before he started dating me, that's fine."

"Sounds like he has fallen out of touch with reality though. My classes are full of housewives."

"How do you manage to take care of your kids, work, and go to school?"

"When it comes to that, my husband pitches in a lot. He works from 9 to 5, and in the morning, he gets the kids ready for school and takes them to the bus stop on his way to work. I pick them up when they get out, and when he gets home, he takes care of them for the evening so that I can get to school by 6:30. We do that four nights a week, and when I get out of school, I come straight to work from there."

"My Rocky would never go along with that. I am lucky that he is finally allowing me to work."

"Kelly, that's either bullshit or he must make a lot of money."

Kelly's face sagged. "Before he lost his job, he used to, but since then, we've been just about surviving."

"What's his problem then?"

"He is one of those old-fashioned Italians who got terribly spoiled by his homemaker mother and was molded by his fascist father."

"Are you saying that you guys weren't doing well, and he still demanded you stay home doing nothing?"

Kelly's body flinched. "Pretty much. I brought Hope to school and picked her up, I washed clothes, I cleaned the house, I cooked for him every night, prepared his breakfast and lunch for him every day, spread my legs whenever he wanted me to, and the rest of the time waited around the house just in case he called."

Gilda chuckled. "Please, don't take this the wrong way, but the 'spreading of my legs' sounds exciting to me."

"Don't get me wrong, on that part, I have no complaints at all."

"Being that tall and muscular, he must have a big one, does he?"

Kelly couldn't believe what she was hearing. She stared. "Gilda?"

Gilda realized that what she had asked was totally out of line, and her face turned redder than a hot pepper. "I'm sorry. That was stupid of me. It's just that I got so excited for you." Got closer to her. "See, my husband isn't into sex much, and when it does happen, he is so small, I just lay there and pretend to get excited while I wait for him to finish."

"I feel bad for you, but—"

"Kelly, I'm really, really sorry. Please forgive me?"

"OK, apology accepted."

"Anyway, you just went along with everything else?"

"Growing up, I was always told that that's what a wife is supposed to do. I watched my grandmother do that, my mother, and even Rocky's mother. So, until now, I have been doing exactly what I was taught."

"That's bullshit. I forget; how many years older than you is Rocky?"

"Eight, he's thirty-two now."

"You should have stuck with someone our own age. Someone like Cody."

"I don't think our age difference is an issue though."

"You know, Cody was really crazy about you. When you didn't return to school the following year, and he found out you were pregnant, he got really depressed. Did you have something going with him before you started dating Rocky?"

Here she goes with the digging, but Kelly didn't care because she had nothing to hide. "Every now and then we hung around the bowling alley in Derby." Her eyes switched to the coffee cup in her hand. "We made out a couple of times, but just kids' stuff, that's all."

"Must not have been kids' stuff for him, because it took him a long time before he started to act normal again."

"I'm so sorry to hear that."

"But he turned out OK after all, he's a cop in Ansonia now, and as far as I'm concerned, the handsomest one there."

"Cody is a cop where I live?"

"Is that where you guys live now?"

"Yes."

"Then I'm sure you'll run into him. If not around the city, you will at the diner because sometimes on his way to Derby after work, he stops to get something to eat."

"It would be nice to see him."

"You know, since you started working here, men keep talking about how pretty and sexy the new waitress is."

"Gilda, come on, please? I'm just a regular woman trying to help my family to a better future."

"Maybe that's why Rocky never wanted you to work, he must be jealous, but that shouldn't give him the right to stop you from living your life."

Kelly's temples began twitching. When she first applied for the job, George had insinuated that too. Days earlier, Rosita told her the same. And a couple of years before, during her short coffee visit while home for the winter holidays, Angela said it too. *If true, then he has been using his beliefs and traditions only as an excuse to stop me from working and going back to school.*

"Hey, cheer up. I can still see that spunk in your eyes."

"Gilda, thank you."

"Listen, some Sundays I go up to my school's library to study. Would you like to ride up with me and do more catching up?"

"That would be exciting, but Rocky doesn't always work on Sundays." The clock above the sales area marked seven. "I've got to go now."

"Standing up for yourself should start right now."

Kelly picked up her pocketbook from the chair next to hers. "It's been great to see you again, but I need to go get supper ready."

"Whatever. How about Fourth of July, are you guys doing anything?"

"No, why?"

"We're having a pool party and it would be nice if you guys come. There will be a few couples with kids around the same ages as ours."

"Hope would love that, but I have to—"

"I know, ask Rocky first." Gilda wrote her house address and her cell number on a napkin. "Here, you don't have to call first, but it would be nice so that I can brag about you coming."

"We'll see."

She was proud of Gilda's change in attitude toward school, but also a bit jealous because universities had sought her out years before she even graduated, and here she was now, twenty-four-years-old with only an equivalency diploma. *You were so smart, I always pictured you in a big job somewhere outside this valley.*

With tears dripping from the corners of her eyes, Kelly accosted the sidewalk in front of Rosita's house and stared at the thick rain hitting her windshield as she remembered the moment when she told her mother she was pregnant. It was a hot and humid day with a thunderstorm brewing, and she was in her bed in a fetus-like position, crying her heart out when her mother told her, *Kelly, what do you want me to say, that I told you so a million times? Or beat you up until you're black and blue like my father would? You're a child. A child, bearing a child. I hope you realize that you have just turned your life upside down. Now you must grow up fast. All your dreams about college, a career, and traveling are shattered.*

***

"Mommy, those raindrops hurt my head."

"The hails mixed with it hurt you, not the rain. Go dry yourself. Better yet, go take a shower and put your pajamas on."

"But it's too early."

"I don't want to hear it." Kelly clutched Hope's shoulder and hauled her to the bathroom. Rushed back to the kitchen area, grabbed a thick glass tray from the refrigerator with chicken wings, thighs, onions, and potatoes that she had seasoned before going to work, covered it with an aluminum foil, turned the oven to 375 degrees, and placed it inside.

"Honey, are you done yet?"

"Yes, I am!" Hope walked out of the shower and headed straight for her bedroom.

Kelly hurried to the bathroom, snatched her clothes off, and stepped under the shower. *Hey, once the baby is a little older, there is no reason why you can't go back to school. I didn't plan to be a father this soon, but I promise to do my best, and your dreams have only been derailed not shattered.* Rocky's words from when he proposed echoed through her thoughts, the roaring of his Vet muffled through the outer walls.

He walked straight to the fridge, snapped a can of beer, opened it, and took a long gulp. "Is anybody home?" The pleasing aroma drew his attention to the stove. He opened the oven door. "The fucking dinner is not ready!"

"Hi Dad," Hope shouted but before she had a chance to jump in his arms, he held her back. "Where's your mom?"

Hope turned away, her face wilted, and strolled to the couch. "I'm sorry, I was just gon' hug you, that's all."

"You can do that later, watch TV for now!"

Kelly rushed out of the bedroom in her jean's shorts, hair still damp. "You're home already?" She approached him with her arms open, but he shook his head and turned away from her. "What's wrong?"

"Dinner isn't ready."

"By the time you clean up, it will be."

"Bullshit." He walked away, turned around. "Goddammit, I knew this was gon' happen, that's why I don't want you to work!"

"I am sorry, I was—"

"Bullshitting with the cooks and that fucking owner, right?"

"Please, Dad, stop fighting," Hope shouted from the couch.

"No, I ran into Gilda, and—"

"And forgot that I need my dinner ready when I walk through that door!" He thought for a couple of seconds. "Who, that Gilda?"

"Yes, that Gilda that first introduced us. She works at the diner too. We hadn't seen each other since I left school, and after work she invited me for a coffee at the donut shop next door. Then, one word led to another—"

"We made a deal, didn't we?"

She walked over to him. "You're right, and I promise you, it won't happen again. Look at me."

He turned and fixated his owl-like eyes to hers. "It better not!"

"You're the only man I ever had, and the only man I ever wanted." Got closer to his ear. "I'll make it up to you in there," she whispered, nodding toward their bedroom.

Later, she had just finished chewing on her last bite and noticed he was wiping his dish with a piece of bread. Got up, walked to the counter. "There are some wings and more potatoes here, would you like them?"

"Mommy, can I have some too?"

"You and Daddy can split them." She picked up the tray, scooped one wing and half of the potatoes and placed them in Hope's dish. Walked around the table, but he held her hand back.

"I'm full, give it to her."

"But you were— "

"That's not the first time I wiped my dish with the bread, is it?"

She walked to Hope's side again and put the rest in her dish.

"Thank you, Dad. I was so crazy hungry tonight."

Kelly placed the empty glass tray in the sink and went back to her seat. Her glass still had some wine left in it. She took a sip. "Gilda invited us to her Fourth of July pool party."

He reached for the ashtray. "After all these years, why now?"

"She has two children around Hope's age. Every year, she invites several couples around our age who also have kids, and Hope could have some real fun."

"Oh Mommy, that would be great." Hope clapped.

"Fuck Gilda, and her guests too."

"Watch your mouth, please?"

"Don't worry, Mommy, I hear that word at school every day."

"Nobody is going anywhere."

"And why not? You used to be friends with her too. She told me that before you and I met, you were over at her house a lot."

He kept puffing like he hadn't even heard a word she had said.

"I thought was nice of her to invite us after we didn't talk or see each other for so many years."

In his own unorthodox way, Rocky loved his wife and his daughter, but still held a silent rage with everyone who had anything to do with his premature marriage, including his father, who had told him, "You got her pregnant and now you marry her! If you embarrass our family, I'll strangle you with my bare hands." He hadn't spoken to his father until he was on his death bed years later. As for Gilda, he blamed her for having introduced them at that point in his life. "I don't care if I don't see her for another eight years."

"This would be an opportunity for Hope to make new friends, and who knows, you might even make some connections for a better job."

"I got my own plans; I don't need any help."

She sighed. "Hope, help me clean the table please?"

The only audible sounds were those of the water flowing, the sponge rubbing against the dishes, an occasional car passing by the house, and utensils dropping onto the countertop.

Rocky stared at them as they went about their chores. If he was gon' get laid later, he should do something fast. "OK, I'll think about it."

Wordless, Kelly looked at him with an elusive smile.

"Thank you, Dad." Hope gave him a long hug and a kiss on his cheeks. "Can you believe it, Mom? I get to swim for a full day!"

Kelly hugged Hope and looked straight in his eyes. "You better not disappoint her this time."

He got up and headed for the couch. "I wanna go to bed."

She knew that when he said he wanted to go to bed straightforward like that, he meant he wanted to have sex.

CHAPTER SIX

Kelly reached out to feel the bed, but Rocky was already gone. Then, at the sight of her nightgown wrinkled behind recognition, she hopped out of bed with a smile. Saturdays and Sundays were her days off. She hurried through the house and opened the windows to a sunny New England spring-like day, even though it was July first.

Sometime later, she was sitting at Rosita's kitchen table. Hope was in the living room playing with her toys and watching cartoons, and Rosita was standing near the stove waiting for the coffee pot to stop brewing. "I called you right before you came over, but there was no answer."

"I finally had a chance to go visit Sandy, she is home from the hospital."

"How's she doing?"

"It's going to be a while before she can get around without a walker. Other than that, she's doing good."

"How are things with you and Rocky?"

"They're going pretty good."

"No more fights?"

"We did have a minor argument when I didn't have supper ready for him on time, but— "

"It's always only about him, isn't it?"

"It's going to take time, but it looks like he's coming around. This morning, he got up and went to work without waking me up to prepare him breakfast and lunch. Something I never remember him doing before. Our last argument was my fault. I was thirty minutes late with the dinner."

"Thirty minutes and he argued about it? My Carlos sometime waits a couple of hours and it's never a big deal."

"Rosita, I did agree that my work shouldn't interfere with getting dinner ready by 7:30."

"He should worship you, because I don't think there are many women who would put up with his crap."

Kelly looked toward the living room with a smirky face and whispered, "In some ways, he does. Since we got back together, there hasn't been one night that we haven't had sex. And on weekends, when he is off from work, two times a day."

"Don't tell me no more." Where Rosita grew up, those were things that one didn't openly talk about.

"Please, don't judge me."

"You're still young, I understand, but what if you get pregnant again?"

"That can't happen, I take my pill every night."

"Then I better have the guest bedroom nice and ready for the Fourth of July."

"What you mean?"

"Me and Carlos are planning to have a cook-out here with you guys."

"Oh no." After all Rosita had done for her and Hope, especially over the previous couple of weeks, the last thing Kelly wanted to do was to disappoint her. "I promised Gilda we'd go to her pool party."

Rosita's face drooped. It would have been her first Fourth of July cook-out ever, and she had also planned it to celebrate Kelly's first job.

"Since Fourth of July is Tuesday, I thought that asking you today was enough time."

Kelly rested her hand over hers, "I'm sorry Rosita." Then thought for a while. "Wait, what if you and Carlos come with us at Gilda's party?"

"We never even met her."

"I am planning to bring a tray of macaroni with chicken and broccoli, and you could bring a tray of Paella. I think Gilda would love that. What do you think?"

"I don't know if Carlos—"

"Come on, Rosita, I'll call her as soon as I get home and let you know."

***

Rocky stormed into the MacDonald's parking lot with his company truck and parked in a secluded spot out of sight from the main road. He went in, used the bathroom, freshened up, and stood next to the entrance door, scouting the cars coming in. *The fucker should have been here already.*

At that moment, Jay drove his red Vet slowly into the parking lot.

"Man, I got to get back to the shop before my boss flips out," Rocky said.

"Hey," Jay said, "I am not screwing my car up for anybody. And remember, beggars can't be choosers."

Fuck you, Rocky thought.

After graduating from high school, Jay had decided to grow his drug dealing business. Being the smart weasel that he was, and determined to make a lot of money, within a few years, he had managed to stay out of jail and do extremely well for himself and several guys working for him. His face was still boyish, his general attitude still friendly, but in business he had become heartless and vindictive. If double crossed, he would turn on you like a cornered rattlesnake.

"You wanna coffee?" Rocky asked.

"Yes," he replied, adjusting his designer jeans and his fitted black-T-shirt. "How the hell are you anyway?"

"I'm stuck in a tiny boat full of cracks, far from shore, and I can't swim."

"You turned into a philosopher now? What're you saying?"

"Man, my life is sinking. Find a quiet table and I'll tell you."

In their high school days, Rocky's charm had secured plenty of girls for himself and for his friends. Jay was one of the beneficiaries, and to make up for it, he used to supply him with marijuana at a cheaper price and would make up the difference by overcharging others.

Jay took a sip of coffee. "So, tell me about this sinking boat."

"You said that if I wanna work with you to just ask.'"

"That was a while ago."

"Fuck, what difference does it make?"

"Times have changed a lot since then. Now cops are a pain in the ass."

"They always were." If Jay would not work with him, the second part of his plan was out the window.

"Not really. Now they watch everything you do. How you live, where and how much money you spend, and whether your job or business can provide you with that lifestyle."

"Look who's talking. You don't seem to hide much yourself with your new Vet and your designer clothes."

"Have you forgotten that I bought that liquor store a couple of years ago?"

"What the fuck does that have to do with it?"

"Come on, man, get smart."

"Jay, I need to make a lot of money and fast."

"What kind of mess did you get into now?"

"It's that wife of mine."

Jay had loved and admired Kelly from the very first time he met her on that summer afternoon at Osborndale Park when he brought Rocky the beers and more marijuana. He would have killed for a woman like her. "Your sweet caring Kelly, what could she have possibly done?"

"She just got a job at the diner and I got to get her out of there."

"Why?"

"I just can't stand her working there."

"Rocky, I don't get it. Didn't you just tell me that you need money?"

"Yeah, but not at that cost. That owner makes them wear a short uniform with one of the lowest cleavage lines I have ever seen, displaying their tits as if ready to bounce out of their chest."

Jay laughed. "What happened to you? Remember that time at the park when I said that you were falling in love with her and you answered, 'Sure, just like all the other ones.'"

"You were right, so what?"

Jay laughed again. "Listen, being obsessed about men getting a peek at her legs and boobs is not real love, it's jealousy."

"I'm not jealous."

"Rocky, I'm sorry. It's just that I never expected you to turn out like this. You were the macho man, remember?"

He smirked. "And I still am, but that doesn't mean I have to approve of my wife dressing like that."

"I don't know if you really love her, but I do know that she does love you. Men can drool as much as they want over her boobs and legs, she would never cheat on you."

"I don't give a fuck, I hate her working there, or anywhere."

"I can't believe you've turned out to be this crazy."

"Man, that's not funny."

"Sure, Rocky." He smirked, placed his arms on the table and leaned forward. "So, you're gon' show her a pile of hundred-dollar bills and she's going to quit her job?"

"Not right away, but when I get her a house like we used to live in, I'm sure she will. She hates the house we're in now, and that's how she conned me to allow her to work."

"I don't blame her. No offense, but you guys went from a gorgeous ranch to a…"

"To a what?"

"Forget it. Are you gon' tell her that you'll be selling drugs?"

"No way, she would flip out."

"Then, where you gon' tell her the money come from?"

"I have a plan."

"I'm listening."

"Can't tell you yet."

"Then I can't do business with you, sorry." Jay got up at once, ready to leave.

Rocky grabbed his arm. "Where you are going?"

Jay noticed two families nearby, staring at them. "Let go," he said with a cool tone and sat back down.

Rocky leaned forward, grabbed his arm again, and whispered, "I need to do this, and you need to trust me."

"I know you still drink. What if you get stopped for DWI when you happen to be carrying a stack of hundred-dollar bills on you. How're you going to explain your way out of that?"

"How would you do it?"

"That's my liquor store money, remember?"

"I don't have an answer now, but I'll come up with one, I promise."

Jay studied him for a while.

"Man, you need to trust me."

"You fuck up once, it's all over." Jay got up. "I'll call on you soon."

Rocky followed him to his car. "Do we have a deal?"

Jay lowered the window a bit. "I said, I'll call on you soon."

***

Rocky stood at the bathroom door. "Screw the party, it's not gon' be hot enough for the pool."

Kelly was leaning forward and to the side, looking through the largest clear spot on the mirror, touching up her mascara. "I've already checked the weather report, and it's going to be 78 degrees at midday. That's good enough for swimming."

"You women are unbelievable. Put those huge tweezers away so I can shave."

"And you men are a pain in the butt. I'm almost done."

He closed the door behind him and squeezed between her butt and the wall to get to the toilet. "Why are you so thrilled about this fucking party anyway?"

"Why shouldn't I be? The last social gathering we attended was at your boss's house right before your company shut down."

"Why not drive down to the beach and hang around, just the three of us?"

She put her tweezers back in her pocketbook and sneered at him. "First, I will not let you disappoint Hope this time. And second, I already had Rosita change her plans for us." She moved away from the mirror. "You don't have to go if you don't want to, but we are going."

Never in a million years would he allow her to go to a social gathering by herself, even knowing that he would have the worst time. *Soon*, he thought with his macho smirk on. *Soon, her head will be back in the sack where it belongs.*

The day was shaping up to be a perfect Fourth of July. By 11:30, it was already 75 degrees, sunny with a perfect blue sky, only a few scattered clouds slowly moving westward.

"Hope, look," Kelly said, pointing to her left as she was turning the corner onto Gilda's street. "Remember when we used to live there?"

"I do, Mommy. I used to love it, why did we move?"

She turned to Rocky, who looked like he was going to a funeral. "Daddy and I are planning to get another house just like that one, right, Dad?"

He grinned at Hope. "Yes, we are."

Kelly parked behind a line of cars. "I think we're here."

Hope clapped. "Yes, I can't wait to jump in the pool."

"Rocky, can you please take this?" Kelly asked.

"Did you have to wear those shorts?" he whispered as he bent next to her.

"Do I have many choices?" she whispered back, handing him the tray. "And what's wrong with them anyway?"

"I just saw part of your ass when you bent down."

"Look, Mommy," Hope said. "Rosita and Carlos are here!"

Their green Toyota was slowly entering a space alongside Gilda's neighbor. Kelly waved at them.

Rocky, his top lip vanishing below his bottom one, clenched the macaroni tray. "You said they had changed their plans because of us, but you never told me they were coming here too."

"Since the party isn't at our house, I didn't think it was a big deal." She shut the trunk and greeted them. "I am so happy that you decided to come."

"We didn't want to lose this chance to spend a full day with you and Hope." Rosita waved hesitantly at Rocky, and he mutely jerked the tray up and down in response.

Carlos opened the trunk and pulled the still warm Paella tray tightly covered with aluminum foils.

Holding her hair to the side, Kelly lowered her face over the tray. "Wow, it smells great."

Rosita and Carlos followed her towards Gilda's house, and Rocky, shaking his head, followed a few feet further behind them.

The backyard was full already, guests flattening the well-manicured lawn by hitting shuttlecocks, or wrapping horseshoes around a dowel, or playing bocce. A dozen kids were jumping in the pool, laughing, shrilling, and splashing water everywhere. Kelly gripped Hope's shoulder and held her back.

A deck was setup with two large coolers alongside the wall; two long picnic tables were draped in red, white, and blue; and a few picnic tables were already occupied by guests sipping on drinks.

Gilda was busy going in and out of the kitchen, prepping and carrying trays of various meats to her husband, a thin short man busy firing up the grill. She saw Kelly and company approaching the steps. "There you are!" She placed the two trays she was carrying on a table next to the grill and rushed down the steps. "Hey guys," she hollered, waving her hand above her head to get everyone's attention. "I'd like you to meet my other friends. This is Kelly," she said, pointing at her with a proud smile. "The tall man in the back is her husband Rocky, this gorgeous young lady here is their daughter Hope, and …"

"And these wonderful people here," Kelly said, "are my good friends Rosita and Carlos."

Gilda shook Rosita and Carlos's hand. "I'm very happy to meet you, welcome to our party."

Gilda's husband glared at his wife.

"Oh, sorry." Gilda pointed to her husband with a smirk. "And that guy there, ready to cook for us all, is my husband Kevin."

Kelly, Rocky, Rosita and Carlos introduced themselves to Kevin. Then Rosita turned to Gilda. "Here, I made paella for you."

"Oh, it smells out of this world! I'm drooling already."

"Gilda, you look great," Kelly said. "I love your hair like that, and I like this dress."

Gilda's hair was braided and wrapped around in a bun. She wore a knee-length white dress that showed off her cleavage. "If my hair were as curly as yours, I would wear it down just below my shoulders. As for my dress," she smirked touching her hips, "this extra weight doesn't allow me to wear jeans shorts like you."

"Goddammit, when you gon' take this off my hands?" Rocky muttered.

She gave him a scornful look. "OK?"

Gilda waited for Rocky to walk away and moved closer to Kelly's ear. "He's still a hunk though."

"And a pain in the you-know-what."

"Most men are. Let's leave everything here for a minute, I wanna introduce Hope to my kids and all the other children."

Meanwhile, Rocky grabbed a beer and approached a couple of guys who were leaning against the railing talking about football.

Gilda returned and told Kelly, Rosita, and Carlos. "Come on, let's go inside."

"My God, I can't believe your house looks exactly like the one we used to live in around the corner from here."

"You guys used to live in one of these houses?"

"Yes, I think you can see part of the backyard from your deck."

"How long ago was that?"

"Little over two years."

"It's a little less than two years that we moved here. Wow, we could have been neighbors. Why did you guys move?"

Kelly hesitated a bit. "We had a five-year option to buy it, then Rocky lost his job and…"

"That's a shame."

"The sunken living room and that fireplace there bring back many good memories. And except for the cabinets and the furniture, even the dining and kitchen area are the same."

"We replaced the cabinets when we bought the house."

"How many bedrooms and baths you have?"

Gilda had a proud look on her face. "Let me show you the rest of the house." They went through the two and half baths, the three bedrooms, the two-car garage, the laundry room, and lastly the finished basement with a sizable pantry to one side. "The builder who built this whole block only used three different sets of plans. The house you lived in must have been built with the same set of plans as ours."

"It had to be." On their way back to the kitchen, Kelly's throat knotted, and her eyes watered.

Rosita noticed Kelly's resentful expressions and patted her back. Then she turned to Gilda. "I want to help you, what do you need to do next?"

"Don't worry, Rosita, I'll be fine."

"You have a lot of people to feed out there. Carlos, you go outside and mingle with the other guests. Kelly, you do the same, and I'll stay to help."

"Rosita, I can handle it, I do this every year."

Rosita held Gilda by her arms. "Can I have an apron please?"

Kelly strolled through the deck and headed straight for the pool. In a revolving caravan, kids lined up behind the steps, ready to dive right back in and splash water in all directions, while laughing and shrilling at each other. She walked to the end. From there, if it weren't for a few pine trees separating Gilda's property line, she could have seen the house that she used to love. She propped her chin in the palms of her hands and watched the kids. Hope was having the time of her life, and that put a smile over the sorrow that had descended over her face.

"Mommy, Mommy! Look how fast I can swim."

"That's good, honey, but be careful."

She leaned her head to one side and peered at her old circular driveway. The black mailbox was still there. That early spring morning a couple of years earlier, the last time she opened it, tiny rivulets of melting dew rushing down its side, mimicking the tears flowing through her high cheekbones. *For whatever its worth, I'd like you to know that I really tried to work with your husband, but twelve months of empty promises…I'm sorry.* "That landlord did go out of his way to help us," she muttered under her breath. "If I had only stood my ground then."

"Kelly!" Gilda shouted from the top of the deck. "The food is ready."

Kelly wiped her eyes with the back of her hand.

"Come on!" Gilda waved her over. "And please get the kids out of the pool."

"We're coming." On the deck, a spread of food covered the two tables, and coolers with sodas, and beers, and wine, and water, and tea for a hundred people. In no time, after Gilda made the announcement, the tables swarmed with children ahead and grownups behind.

Gilda took a spot at the end of the line and Kelly and Rosita stood right next to her.

"Kelly, did you see Cody?"

"Cody from high school?"

"Yes. I can't believe you didn't see him when you were leaning on the edge of the pool. He was only yards away, and from time to time he looked your way."

"Who's Cody?" Rosita asked.

"Look," Gilda nodded toward the middle of the line. "A few people down from Rocky. The tall guy with dirty blond hair there."

"No way, he was short," Kelly said.

"Kelly, that was eight years ago, we were only sixteen then."

Rosita looked at Gilda. "He's a policeman in Ansonia, right?"

"How do you know that?" Kelly asked her.

"I've seen him driving around in the police car couple of times."

"He turned out great. Tall, handsome, and a nice career ahead of him." As Gilda was saying that, a chubby blonde girl approached from behind and whispered, "Hey, is she the Kelly you told me about?"

"Yes. Kelly, I'd like you to meet my good friend Crystal here. She is also studying to become a legal secretary. And this is my newly made friend Rosita."

"Hi Rosita," Crystal shook Rosita's hand and turned to Kelly. "It's really nice to meet you. Gilda has told me how great of a student you were."

"I just tried the best I could, that's all."

"I hope we get to chat when you come up the school to visit," Crystal said before walking away.

"Gilda? I only said I'll see, I never said I was going to."

"That little slut," Gilda whispered, "she changes men like we change clothes."

Rosita and Kelly looked at each other with vigilant eyes.

Kelly, Hope, Rosita, and Carlos, sat around a small table close to the pool. Gilda moved from a group of guests to another, playing the host. Rocky sat at a table not far from the coolers, still with the same two guys that he had started talking to when they first got there.

"This is a very nice party," Rosita said. "Thank you for insisting on us coming."

"Yes, thank you, Kelly," Carlos added. "Nice people and delicious food, what else can one wish for?"

"Gilda's parents there," Kelly pointed them out, "used to have great parties every holiday too. I guess it runs in the family."

"You have been friends for a long time?" Rosita asked.

"We were never really that close, but when we were in high school, we'd sometimes go to her parents' parties. By the way, that's where I met Rocky, Memorial Day of 1992. It seems like yesterday."

"So," Carlos said, "Rocky knew Gilda then too?"

"He used to work with her father."

"I can't wait to meet Angela too," Rosita said.

"Next time she comes home, I'll make sure we come over for coffee. Growing up, she and I were like one."

"Mommy, I wish you become like one with Gilda too," Hope said. "I love this pool."

"I know you do; you've been in it since we got here." She got up, gathered their empty dishes, "I'll be right back." She headed for the garbage pail next to the bushes that defined Gilda's property line, some twenty feet or so to the left of the deck. As she crossed the lawn, men's eyes were glued to her model-like body.

Cody, armed with couple of empty dishes, walked over and stood right behind her. "Hi Kelly."

She turned around and stared at him, wordless.

"You don't remember me, do you?"

"I do now. Gilda pointed you out earlier when you were in line for the food. But you're right, I wouldn't have recognized you if she hadn't."

A smirk erupted on his handsome face. He extended his hand. "You're prettier than ever."

She hesitated for couple of seconds, made sure that Rocky was not looking at them. "Thank you." With the corner of her eye, she spotted Rocky staring at them, fuming. She pulled her hand back at once. "Enjoy the party."

"We should meet for a coffee."

"I would, but I don't think my husband there would like that."

"I know, I heard about him."

"What you mean?"

"You know that I am a policeman in your town, right?"

"Gilda did mention that."

"Well, cops do talk to each other."

"Why, what has he done now?"

"They say he has a very hot temper."

"That's true. That's why I better go before he flies the coop."

Peering at her back, as she walked up to the deck to the cooler with sodas, he said, "If you ever decide to…"

Rocky didn't waste any time. "Who's that fucking guy drooling all over you?"

"Just a guy I went to school with."

"He wasn't acting like a guy you just went to school with. Did you ever go out with him?"

"No." She stood up with four soda cans in her hands. "He was just shocked to see me after such a long time."

"You better not be fucking lying to me."

CHAPTER SEVEN

Rocky dialed Jay's number, lit a cigarette, and started pacing around the foyer, oblivious to the people staring at him. *Fuck!* He snapped the receiver on the hook. Grabbed another quarter, jabbed it into the slot, and dialed his house number. Still no answer. Walked back to his seat and took a long gulp of beer. Sam, the owner, and bartender, was leaning on his elbows, cozily whispering to a sexy blonde.

"Hey, Sam," Rocky shouted. "Watch my stuff."

"Go ahead." Sam gestured but glanced at Rocky with loathing.

Jay hurried inside and glanced around the bar. He didn't like doing business with people around, but Rocky had the money from his first week of dealing and he wasn't confident enough to leave it with him any longer than he needed. Walked over to Sam. "Hey, man, how're you doing?"

"Not bad." Sam winked toward the blonde. "Not bad at all, what about you?"

"I guess not as good as you," Jay said, winking toward the blonde too. He subtly pulled a tiny bag from his shorts pocket and shook Sam's hand with it. "Has Rocky been around?"

"That psycho?" Sam pointed down the counter. "Those are his keys and his beer." He filled a tall glass with an icy cold draft and handed it to Jay. "A salute, this one is on me."

"A salute." Jay raised the glass to his mouth.

Rocky was approaching his seat and saw him. "Jay, come on, I got to get going."

Jay sat next to him. "Keep it low. In this business, we operate like moles, not like traveling salesmen."

"Sorry, man. I had a long fucking day and can't wait to get off these dirty clothes and take a long cold shower." Raised his glass and took a gulp. "Fuck, it tastes like piss. Sam," he shouted, "bring me another one."

"Here you go again." Jay grabbed Rocky's arm. "We don't need no goddamn spectators." He walked to the end of the bar. "Sam, please bring us another round."

"That fucker cares more about getting in that blonde's panties than his customers," Rocky said as Jay approached his seat again.

"Wouldn't you?"

"She doesn't waste time with married men."

"She is smart. Besides, your wife is prettier and sexier than her."

"Would you eat spaghetti and meatballs night after night after night?"

"If they tasted as good as my grandmother used to make them, sure. Anyway, let's get down to business," Jay whispered. "You have my money?"

"Yes," Rocky replied with a proud look on his face. "Do you have more stuff for me?"

"If you work with a cool head, I'll always have it for you. Give me couple of minutes to get to my car and then follow me." He caught Sam's attention, placed twenty dollars on the counter. "I'll see you soon."

Rocky followed him to his red Corvette and sat in the passenger seat. Counted his share of the stack of bills he had staunchly guarded and handed him the rest. "Not bad for the first week, right?"

Jay flipped through the stack. "Not at all." He handed Rocky a brown paper shopping bag. "There is plenty of powder in there. Like I told you inside, work with a cool head, and you're gon' make a lot of money."

"That's the idea." Rocky stepped out of the car.

Jay lowered the passenger side window and motioned him to stick his head inside. "Next week, we'll meet somewhere else." He turned the ignition on. "I'll let you know where, but remember, we work like moles."

"I get it, man, I get it." On the way to his car, he mumbled to himself, "I'll show her what I'm capable of."

***

Kelly's shift was over, and she was about to leave when Rosita called to tell her that they were still shopping and would drop Hope off late. The day before, on Sunday, Kelly had made and cooked a pot of meatballs with tomato sauce, and now the only thing she had to do was cook a pound of spaghetti, warm up the meatballs and sauce, and dinner would be ready. She took her shower, turned the simmering meatballs and sauce to low, and dropped the spaghetti in the boiling pot.

Rocky walked in with a wide smile. "Hi."

She'd take that entrance from him anytime. With a smile of her own. "Did we win the lotto?"

"Some like that." He grabbed his usual beer.

She grabbed his arm. "Dinner is almost ready, and I got us a bottle of Chianti to go with it."

"OK, I get a glass of wine then." He opened the bottle, filled two glasses, handed her one, and raised his to hers. "A salute, to a great future."

"A salute." Bewildered, she took a quick sip. "So, what's this fuss all about?"

He winked at her. "I'm gon' take a shower first."

"I'll be waiting." Her skeptical look followed him through the bathroom door.

By the time she was through half of her dish, he had devoured his, and was already sipping on his wine and puffing on his cigarette. She started to clear the table for washing up.

"Babe, don't do that now, have a seat."

Babe? It must have been years since he had called her that. She wiped her hands on her apron and sat back down. "OK, I'm all ears."

With the cigarette in his left hand and the wine in his right, he gulped the wine like a shot of whiskey and followed it with a long puff. "Soon, we'll have our own house like the old days."

She didn't know whether to laugh or weep. They had zero savings, didn't have a checking account, and she had just started working. How was he planning to buy a house? He must be losing it.

"You just gon' stand there and say nothing?"

"That would be great, but where would we get the money?"

"I had a long talk with my boss today. I told him I needed more money, and if he couldn't help me, I was gon' look for another job. He didn't like the idea of losing me, thought about it for a while, and then offered me a forty percent partnership starting with September first. Babe, only six fucking weeks from now."

She hadn't seen his face shining like that in a long time. "That's great news."

"Isn't it?" He reached for her hand. "We can once again be a real family. You'll be home taking care of the house and us, and I'll be the breadwinner as it's supposed to be."

Be home taking care of the house and us as it's supposed to be? That statement angered her, but why ruin that peaceful moment? "My grandfather used to say, you don't know if it's a fish until the hook is out of the water."

"What're you saying?"

"When I see the results and we have moved into our own house with you making enough money to at least support the lifestyle we used to have, then we'll talk about the rest."

With his temples twitching, he thought for a while. "OK, that's a deal."

CHAPTER EIGHT

The restaurant was unusually slow for that time of the day.

Jody and Francis were the other waitresses on duty.

Kelly sat on the last stool next to the kitchen door. "Jody, it's so dead in here. If I didn't need every penny I can get, I'd go right back home."

"I was thinking the same," Francis said. "Jody, what about you?"

Jody laughed. "Sure, why don't we do that, and early morning tomorrow we'll all meet at the unemployment office?"

"You can see the asphalt flickering; I could be at the beach instead."

"Nice wish, Francis." Kelly winked at her, then looked up at Jody. "Is George around?"

"No, he went to visit some of his relatives in New York City and will be back in the morning. Anyway, that's what he told me."

Francis heard the door open and turned to look. "Oh boy, here comes the geek. I can't believe in this heat he still dresses like that."

The guy approaching the register wore a light blue two-piece suit, a white-cotton long-sleeve shirt, a striped red and blue tie, and a pair of black dressing shoes. He must have been in his mid-forties, and wore black framed prescription glasses, his light brown hair brushed to the back of his rectangular head.

Jody took a second look. "Yes, there must be something wrong with him."

"I only served him couple of times," Kelly said, "and he never once looked up at me."

Francis moved closer. "I served him couple of times too, and I still don't know the color of his eyes, or if he has them at all. He's got to be a nerd."

"If I'm not mistaken," Jody said, "he's started to come around more often since you started working here. I only see him on your shift."

"Really? Then George should give me a raise."

"Keep wishing. You'd be more likely to get a snowstorm than get a raise from George this time of year."

The guy stood at the register, waiting mutely.

"Sir?" Francis caught his attention right from where she was standing, something that she would never do if George were around. "You can sit wherever you choose."

He walked between the tables and sat in one of the window booths a few feet from where an elderly couple was seated.

Jody smirked at Kelly. "What did I tell you? He must know that that section is normally yours."

"That's good, I can use the extra tips." She got up and went to punch-in, and on her way back she walked straight to the guy's booth. "Sir, what can I get you?"

With his eyes focused at the two-page menu, he scanned it from left to right and right to left couple of times before looking up at her.

"I think I served you before. I'm Kelly, what's your name?"

"Does it make any difference?" he mumbled, looking at the menu, his face now deep red.

"No, it doesn't. So, what can I get you?" She took his order and rushed it to the kitchen. When she came out, Jody and Francis were still chatting in the same place. She sat down and whispered, "He's definitely weird."

"What did he say to you?"

"When I tried to introduce myself, his face got blood-red, and then he muttered, 'Does it make any difference?' That didn't make any sense."

"I didn't hear him, but I did see the expression on your face. I honestly believe he has a thing for you because when you're on, he always tries to sit in your area, and when he can't get a seat there, I noticed he follows your every move. Don't worry, you'll get used to it." She laughed. "When I was younger with a nice body like yours, well, almost like yours, I used to catch guys sneaking peeks at me all the time, especially when I bent down for something. After a while, I actually enjoyed it."

"Jody, that's crazy."

By the time the weirdo's order was ready, a handful of people had come in. Francis sat most of them in Kelly section, which had been practically empty since her shift had started.

On her way to deliver his order, the old couple waved for their check. Kelly placed the plates down before him. "Sir, can I get you anything else?"

"No."

She added up the check for the old couple, smiled, and handed it to them. They placed a tip under a glass and slowly made their way to the register.

Kelly rushed to the table to clean and set it. "Thank you, and I hope to see you soon."

The old lady smiled at her. "You will."

She took the three-dollar tip, placed the dirty dishes on a tray, and took them to the kitchen. Then, armed with a white cotton rag and a bottle of cleaning agent, she sprayed the table and started meticulously wiping it. While bending over to reach the furthest end of the table, she noticed the weirdo leaning so his head was in line with his knees, a hand grabbing a knife from the floor while he looked up her dress. At once, she stood up, turned around, and shouted, "Hey, what do you think you're doing?"

The customers seated nearby jerked their heads toward him. His face turned as red as a red-hot pepper, sweating from his pores. "What? What?" he muttered, body shaking. Then before Kelly had a chance to shout again, he bolted up, grabbed a twenty-dollar bill from his pocket, threw it on the table, and stormed out of the place with his head down.

Shaking, Kelly rushed back to the counter. "Jody, did you see that? He just did what you were saying."

"So, he got a nice peek at your beautiful ass." Jody placed a hand on Kelly's shoulder. "Honey, listen to me. Don't let it get to you. Like I said, it comes with the territory." Smirking, she shook her head. "I wish it still happened to me."

"Or to me," Francis added on her way to the kitchen.

"Well, I don't like it. But if it happens again, I don't care how old or young the jerk is, I'll run over and slap the bastard."

"Honey, forget it. The way you embarrassed him, he won't come around for a long time, if ever again."

Kelly couldn't believe they got so used to that crap that they joked about it. She played the scene of the jerk looking up her dress over and over until her shift was over.

As she left, Gilda walked in. "What're you doing here? Your shift starts at eleven."

"I know, it sucks. One of the evening waitress's son is sick, and I'm gon' be stuck here until tomorrow morning."

"I'm sorry."

"Kelly, you look sad. What's the matter, you didn't make enough tips?"

"I'll tell you later."

Gilda grabbed her arm. "Come on, I'll walk you out."

They leaned against Kelly's car.

"Gilda, you were totally right; some customers are plain pigs." She looked away. "This guy was staring up my dress while pretending to get a knife from the floor. Today was so hot, I decided to wear just my bra and my underwear." She stared at the ground, eyes flooding. "I'm so darn angry, the bastard saw me practically nude."

"Every now and then, you get jerks like that. But if George made us wear long pants, then we would complain about them being too hot. Like I told you, it happens to me too. Try to shake it off for now. In the future though, try to be more aware of the people around you before you bend down to do something."

"If Rocky finds out about this, he will—"

"Don't worry, who's gon' tell him?"

"Maybe this job can't be forever for me either. Is your offer to take me up to your school still open?"

Gilda smiled. "How about this Sunday?"

"But the offices will be closed on Sunday, won't they?" She paused. "Plus, I don't think Rocky will be working. How about Monday morning before my shift?"

"Kelly, are you thinking of going back to school?"

"It's just a thought for now, that's all."

"I am so happy for you."

"Gilda, not so fast. Even if I decide to go back, I'd have to convince the king first."

"Bullshit, you stand your grounds. He has no right to dictate your life to that extent."

"So, can we go on Monday then?"

"Let me see. I could ask my neighbor to watch my kids for a couple of hours. OK, I'll see you Monday morning at my house."

"That's great. If I'm lucky, I'll see you then."

"Kelly, that's not about luck, it's about standing your ground."

"I just hope he doesn't put me in a hospital when I tell him."

***

That morning, she had prepared chicken nuggets sautéed with broccoli. Took it out of the refrigerator and placed it on the stove with the burner at low. Then filled the pasta pan with hot water and placed it on the stove with the burner set to high. Got Rosita on the phone and asked her if Hope could stay with her for a bit longer than usual.

"Kelly, going back to school is a good thing, why would he get upset?"

"When I wanted to go to night school to get ready for the G.E.D. exam, he wouldn't let me. He told me that it was a waste of time for a housewife. So, I bought the books and studied at home, but with college, I can't do that."

"Studying at home was not a waste of time but going to school for it was. Like I told you, he is sickly jealous, and that proves it even more."

"You know, thinking about all the things he stopped me from doing over the years, and all of you that know us are saying or hinting the same, I'm beginning to see it that way too."

"Kelly, when people get to be that possessive, they go loco and can be dangerous. You be careful."

"I hear his car." Kelly rushed to the cabinets, picked up a package of angel hair, and glided it into the pan.

As he was easing the door behind him, he smiled. "I know that smell from a mile away, chicken and broccoli over angel hair."

"You're right." She looked at him with an elusive smile. "Did you have a good day?"

"Not bad at all." Walking toward the refrigerator to get his usual beer, he stopped behind her and squeezed her crotch. "Is it ready for me?"

"As always, but dinner first."

He snapped the beer can open, took a long gulp, and strolled to the couch. "What's with that uniform still on?"

As usual she hated lying, but she had concluded that if she needed to lie to avoid unnecessary arguments, she was willing to do it. "Rosita called to say that Hope wanted to stay there for dinner and chatted for a while. So, if I went to take a shower first, your dinner would've been late, and we don't want that, do we?"

"You bet your ass we don't!"

He dove into his dish like a lion diving on its freshly killed pray. "Man, this is so good."

With a fork in her right hand and a spoon in her left one, she was slowly rolling the pasta around a piece of chicken, pondering if that was the right time to tell him.

He got another beer and went to lay down on the couch.

Still searching for the moment, she started washing the dishes. Gazing at her hands, she said, "Rocky, I'm thinking of going back to school."

His eyebrows quirked. "What?"

"I'm thinking of going back to school."

His face creased. "First you wanted to go to work, and even if it is against my traditions, I let you go. Fuck, now you want to go to school too, why?"

"Why not?" She finished drying the utensils and put everything away.

"If you're already tired of working, just stay home. You're not going to school!"

Kelly, that's not about luck, it's about standing your ground. "Yes, I am."

"I'm gon' make a lot of money soon, what the fuck you want to go to school for?"

She was about to tell him what happened at work, but that would have been self-destructive because for sure he would have demanded that she quit at once. "So that if whatever you're planning doesn't work, I can make enough money for both of us to better our chances of getting out of this rat-hole."

"And what school you're thinking of going?"

"The college that Gilda goes to. I'm driving up there on Monday with her to check it out."

"That fucking bitch. I had the feeling that that Fourth of July party was going to be trouble somehow."

"Watch your mouth, please, she's not a bitch."

"She is too. I know her a lot better than you, you'll see."

"Maybe you do, but since our lives crossed paths again, she has been very nice to me."

"What the fuck is going on in that head of yours?"

She fluttered her hand at him. "What the heck is going on in yours? I followed you like a puppy dog all along and look where it got us. I'm ashamed of living in this rat-hole. Ashamed!"

"I don't give a fuck!" He pointed his index finger at her face. "I married you to be my housewife and that's what you're gon' be. You lucky I'm letting you work until I get us a house and now you want to go to school too?"

"That's a lie! I remember as if it was yesterday with my mother present when you asked me to marry you, you said, 'Hey, once the baby is a little older, there is no reason why you can't go back to school. I didn't plan to be a father this soon, but I promise to do my best, and your dreams have only been derailed, not shattered.' You remember that?" She walked to the sink to get a sip of water.

Enraged, his eyes followed her to the sink.

She drank half a glass and turned around. "Later, you changed that to when Hope would start school, and I went along with that too. You remember that?"

"I don't remember shit." He walked back to the coffee table to get his beer. "Besides, aren't you too old to go to college?"

"That is my problem."

He stared at her for few seconds. *Fuck, she'll be pregnant soon anyway.* He walked to the table and sat in his place. "All right, sit down and listen."

What kind of crap was he planning on pulling now? She sat. "Go ahead."

"When I agreed for you to go to work, I said that when I made enough money to get us a house of our own, you would quit, right?"

"That's another lie. Maybe that's what you thought of saying. You asked me if I was willing to work less hours, and I said we'll cross that bridge when we get to it."

"That's the same fucking thing for me."

She was going to argue but decided to let it go and see where he was going with it.

"If I go along, the same goes for school too. Once I get the house, you quit them both, and until then, don't ask me for any help with school, your daughter, or anything else. And I want dinner on time, the clothes washed and Ironed, and the house clean. Do you agree?"

Staring at him, she thought, *If I say no, who knows where this argument will lead. If I say yes, and he succeeds in buying us a house, I'll have to be ready to face this same crap then. At that point though, I'll be so far ahead that by then he might just get used of the idea of me working and going to school.* "OK, we'll do it your way."

A devious smirk spouted over his lips. "I'll show you what I can do."

"Me too."

CHAPTER NINE

Kelly peered out the bedroom window at a clear blue sky with a piercing sun. Excited, she took a quick shower, and got dressed in her jean's shorts, her white T-shirt top, and her new light-blue sneakers, the first pair of shoes she had purchased with her own money since she had been married. She was extremely proud of them. On her way to drop Hope off at Rosita's, the fantasy of sitting in a classroom after so many years made her gut roil.

Gilda rushed out of the house, got into the passenger seat. "I'm so excited for you. Let's go."

Kelly hugged her. "Thank you for taking the time."

"What're friends for? Get on to Route 8 north, from there we get onto West 84, and not even couple of miles after that, we get off, and the school isn't far from there. You do know how to get to Route 8 from here, right?"

"Gilda, I did live like a hermit these last few years, but I still had to do things for the house and take care of the kids." She placed the car in drive and headed out.

"Wait, I thought you only had one daughter."

"And I thought you only had two children."

Gilda laughed. "You almost got me there."

"I borrowed one of your lines."

"So, what did you do to convince Rocky?"

"After a brief argument, I had to agree that when he buys a house similar to the one we used to live in, I'll quit both my job and school and go back to being just a housewife again."

"Are you kidding me?" Gilda looked at her with her mouth agape. "I would never take that shit."

"If the past few years after he lost his decent job are any indication of what he can do on his own, he is never going to be able to buy a house by himself, which is one of the reasons why I'm seriously thinking of doing this. I figured, if I get a degree and a decent job, it could be our only way out of this stagnant life we have been stuck with for so long. To be honest though, even with all his crazy ways, I still feel that same spark I felt for him the first time I met him at your parents' house."

"I remember that day very well." *If I had known that he would show up without one of his older girlfriends*, Gilda thought, *if I had only known.*

"I just have to work around his old-fashioned traditions and his stubbornness."

"Kelly, you might not know this, but I had a few relationships before I married my husband, some of which were almost as serious, and if there is one thing I learned, it is that most men are just like babies."

"Gilda, as you know, I got pregnant at the end of my sophomore year, and he was the first and last man I have ever intimately known. But you're right, he acts like a child when he doesn't get his way. He turns into a giant baby beast."

"My Kevin is much smaller than me and knows better. So, when he gets in those childish moods, instead of fighting me, he just stops doing his share of chores. You know what I do? I move to phase two.

I get migraine headaches twenty-four seven and sexually starve him until his attitude reverses back to my expectations. And even though he is not into sex that much, like I understand your husband is, at some point it does get to him. That's the power we have over men, and there is nothing wrong with using it."

"It wouldn't work with Rocky; he would get even angrier and cause even bigger arguments. Besides, when you do that, don't you get sexually starved too?"

"Come on, Kelly, they starve easy. Us women can go without sex for much longer than they ever can, that's just nature."

"Not me. When he ignores me for more than a few days, my body goes into a craving mode. That would not be a good strategy for me, but thanks for the advice."

"You don't know for sure until you try. Trust me, it works. Just like it worked for the few moms I convinced to try it. Our exit is coming up." She pointed.

Kelly slowly guided her white Subaru around the ramp and proceeded following Gilda's detailed directions.

She parked in a spot close to the main entrance doors. "I can't believe I'm about to do this."

"You're not changing your mind, are you?"

"No way. It's just that until a few days ago, this was just a dream."

"Don't get your hopes too high though, we still don't know if they're gon' take you for this semester."

Out of the elevator, they headed for the registration office. The layers of anxiety on Kelly's face could have been peeled, but that didn't stop her from sneaking a quick peek through every office and classroom that had the doors ajar, allowing herself to recall the familiar scent of her last days of school that summer of 1992.

"Kelly, come on," Gilda hollered, "we've got a lot to do."

"I'm sorry, I just can't help it."

Gilda kindly asked the clerk for the courses' booklet. Mrs. Alston, who knew Gilda well, got up from her cubicle and walked over to the window. "I thought you registered already, what you need that for?"

"For my friend here."

Kelly took a step closer to Gilda. "Hi, I'm Kelly."

"Miss, you are kind of late. What did you say your name was?"

"Kelly." Her right eye started twitching. "Kelly Esposito."

"Mrs. Alston," Gilda pleaded, "it's important that she gets in this semester, can you help us out?"

"As you know, I don't have much saying in deciding who gets admitted and who doesn't, or even when." She looked at Kelly. "If you already know what you'd like to major in, I suggest you go talk to that dean and see what he can do for you."

"Thank you, Mrs. Alston." Gilda grabbed Kelly's arm, pointed to the room around the corner. "Let's go in there and figure this all thing out."

"Gilda, why are all these computers here?"

"They're for the students to use."

"Gilda, I just learned how to use our cash register at work, the closest I have ever been to one of these." She touched the one on the side of their table. "The last time I checked out a book from the library though, I did see one there."

"I am surprised you guys don't have one at home. They're not that expensive nowadays and are helpful in many ways, even for the kids. I wouldn't worry though." Gilda gave her a smirk. "Knowing you, in no time you'll learn how to use them better than anyone here."

"I hope so."

Gilda opened the courses booklet. "So, what you think you want to major in?"

Kelly had always dreamed of getting a college degree, but she had never given what to major in much thought. "I've always been good in math. Maybe accounting, what you think?"

"That's a great field, I wish I had that inclination."

They spent some time choosing the courses that Kelly needed to start with, and that were also available Monday through Friday in line with her work schedule, which called for her to leave school no later than 1:45 p.m.—enough time to go back to Ansonia, get her daughter from school, drop her off at Rosita's and get to work by 2:30. A tight schedule by any means, but Kelly had insisted she could handle it. They wrote it down and headed for the Dean's office with their fists clenched.

A blonde lady in her late thirties greeted them with a pleasant smile. "What can I do for you?"

"We need to…" They both found themselves saying. Then looked at each other and Kelly nodded at Gilda to go on.

Gilda turned to the secretary again. "We need to talk to the dean."

"Mr. DeSantis just headed down the cafeteria for a break, isn't there something I can do for you?"

"Mrs. Alston told us that Mr. DeSantis is the only one who might be able to help us. Can we just wait for him here?"

"That's what those chairs are for." She smiled and went back to do her things.

Gilda stared at Kelly's twitching right eye. "What's up with your eye?"

"OK," Kelly said, placing her hand over it and her face turning red. "When I get nervous, it takes a life of its own."

"You don't have to cover it," Gilda whispered. "It's just that I have never seen an eye twitching so fast."

"Sometimes it goes on for minutes before it goes back to normal."

"Don't be nervous. If they don't take you now, then we'll get you ready for next semester, and Rocky better go along with it, or else." Gilda made a fist.

Kelly smiled. "Trust me, it's not that simple."

Their eyes turned to a tall handsome man in his late thirties with short salt and pepper hair, wearing a fitted dark navy-blue suit, a white shirt, and a dark-purple tie.

"Are you ladies waiting for me?" He took a second look at Gilda. "We've met before, haven't we?"

They stood up at once. "We did, in my Dean's office not too long ago," Gilda said, words stumbling. "And this is my friend Kelly. We were told that you might be able to help her, can we steal a few minutes of your time?"

"Step in my office, please."

Gilda went first, Kelly next, and he followed them. He motioned them to take a seat in the chairs facing him.

Kelly noticed that he peeked at her legs as he shuffled papers in front of him. She resettled her body, knees braced, her hands over them, and her chest straight.

"So, Kelly, what can I do for you?"

Her eye had slowed down but not quite to a full stop, and she hoped he wouldn't notice it. "I'd like to…"

Gilda noticed her hesitation. "Let me take it from here." She turned to Mr. DeSantis. "See, Kelly is new at this, and I came with her to help. She would like to enroll for this semester, but Mrs. Alston from the registrar's office told us that it might be too late and sent us here to see if you can help."

"And what makes Mrs. Alston think that I can just flip my fingers and warp time back?" He paused. "At times, I have had returning students registering late and I helped them do that, but to get a new student in with less than two weeks before classes start, I wouldn't even know how to go about it. There is the S.A.T. she would have to take, then we'll have to request her high school transcript and on and on." He looked straight into Kelly's eyes and shook his head. "I don't think I can help you."

Kelly's face sagged. On top of the world one minute and down the pits the next. "I'll take whatever test you want me to take, and as for my high school transcript, I have my G.E.D. diploma I can give you. Please, if I don't start this semester, I might not have this chance again."

The dean gazed at her. "I'm sorry, but what do you mean you might never have a chance again?"

"See, Mr. De Santis," Gilda said, "it's a complicated story, but I promise you that if you can help her in any way, you will never regret the effort. Not because she is my friend, but you are looking at one of the most intelligent people I have ever had the luck to know. Throughout our school years, from first grade to the tenth grade, Kelly was among the top ten students in our school every year, and most of the time, she was either first or second best."

Kelly sat still with her heart pounding and her eyes floating back and forth between Gilda and the Dean. She never knew that Gilda thought that much of her to put her own reputation on the line for her like that.

"That's impressive," the dean said with a dubious look, and then thought for a while. "OK, give me couple of days, and I'll see if I can pull some strings. In the meantime, just in case I get some positive responses, be available to take the S.A.T. at once."

This revived hope. "I'll do whatever I need to. Thank you, Mr. DeSantis. I promise, you won't regret it."

"Don't go celebrating yet." The dean shook Kelly's hand. "I'm only promising that I'll try my best. Leave your phone number with my secretary, and I'll have her call you as soon as I have something."

She gave the secretary both her house and her work number with a detailed schedule of where she was going to be for the next couple of days.

Once out in the hallway, Gilda shouldered her. "Isn't that great?"

"No, I think he just wanted to get rid of us."

"What makes you think that?"

"Somewhere there, I had regained hope, but he's never done anything like this before. What makes you think that he is really going out of his way to help someone who he doesn't even know?"

"Kelly, at this point, the best we can do is wait and see."

"That's true, but I'm not going to celebrate yet."

"Isn't he a hunk though?"

"Gilda? First, you're married, and second, he is much older than you."

"I don't think he sees it that way. I saw how he peeked at your legs when we first sat down, and not just once."

"He did?" Kelly pretended not to have noticed it herself.

"Uh huh!"

"Gilda?"

***

Kelly looked at the clock. Five minutes after seven, shit. She rushed to the bathroom. Hope was already out of the shower, drying off. "Honey, get your pajamas on, and watch the pots on the stove for me. I'll be out in couple of minutes."

"Why you want me to watch the pots for?"

"If they start boiling too much and spill over to the side, turn the gas knobs to the off position. You think you can do that?'

"Yes, I can."

Her heartbeat rose when the phone rang as she toweled off.

"Mommy, a lady on the phone wants to talk to you," Hope yelled through the door.

She was disappointed that it wasn't the school calling but was happy to hear from Angela telling her that she had moved back with her parents. After they chatted a bit, Kelly cut her off by scheduling a date at their favorite Italian coffee shop for a cappuccino.

Rocky stood on the threshold and watched her hurrying around the stove with her nightgown on. Slammed the door behind him. "Fucking dinner is not ready again?" Rushed to the fridge and grabbed a beer.

"Will be ready in few minutes."

He took a long gulp. "It's past 7:30, and you wanna go to school too?"

Her day had not shaped the way she had hoped at all. Mr. DeSantis's secretary never called, causing her heartbeat to rise and fall like a yo-yo throughout the day whenever the phone rang. Her replacement at work showed up late. Angela had moved back home unexpectedly, and now she was expected to justify to the imperialistic and unreasonable mind of her husband why dinner was not ready exactly by 7:30. "Should I have the dish waiting for you at the door like a dog?"

He grabbed her arm. "You better watch it."

"Hey, Dad," Hope yelled from the couch.

Kelly jerked her arm away, repulsed. "Please spend some time with our daughter."

"Now you're getting cocky too?"

"I am cocky? You better look in the mirror."

He sat in his chair. "Just give me the food."

"Why are you like this again?"

"Why is dinner late again?"

"Angela called me. We hadn't talked for a while and—"

"That Angela again?" he raged. "Tell her to marry some rich and famous queer down there, so that she can stop bothering us."

"She has moved back here with her parents. And I would appreciate it if you wouldn't talk like that about her, she has always been my best friend and always will be."

"Let's see where we're going with this. You want to work, go to school, and spend time with your friends. First was Rosita only, then you added Gilda, and now Angela again. Where the fuck does that leave me?"

Hope stopped watching TV and turned around, ready to cry. "Daddy, please stop fighting."

Kelly sneered at him. "Honey, don't worry, we're not going to fight."

He grabbed another beer.

Kelly placed dishes on the table. "Do I tell you who to hang out with?"

Fuming, he started eating.

"We agreed that my responsibilities are to have dinner on time, keep the house going, and take care of all Hope's needs, but not for you to tell me who I can talk with and who I can't. Yes, I was a little late tonight, and this has only happened two times in the two months I have been working. I'll try my best to make sure that it doesn't happen again, but I won't go back to being the hermit that you were turning me into."

His jaw dropped. *What the fuck was he gon' do with her?* In two bites, he had swallowed a full meatball.

"Hope, please shut the TV off and come to eat."

"OK, Mommy, I heard you."

"I am the man in this house, and I decide when and where you go." He pointed to her chair. "Sit down."

A wave of heat slithered through her body like flames bursting out of a fireplace. Slower than a turtle, she guided tiny clusters of spaghetti from her dish to her mouth as she stared at him devouring his. *To be honest though, even with all his faults, I still feel that same spark I felt for him the first time I met him at your parents' house.* What she had told Gilda earlier flashed through her mind, but was she really being honest with herself?

***

Kelly handed the check to a couple who was ready to leave. She felt like she was at a family wake. Three days, and no call. Perhaps being a waitress and a housewife for the rest of her life was her destiny and no longer her choice.

Francis joined Kelly at the counter. "Are you sick?"

Jody was wiping the counters. "Kelly, your face has looked like midnight all afternoon. Do you have your monthly friend?"

"No, but it's after five and I really thought that the school would have called me by now."

"Shit." Francis rushed back to the register and grabbed the phone. "I'm sorry, who're you looking for? Hold it. Kelly, there is a lady on the phone, asking for you!"

Kelly stared at her, mute.

"Hurry up!"

She rushed over. "Hello."

"Hi Kelly, this is Mr. De Santis's secretary."

She had been looking forward to this call for the last three days, and now, fearing the worst, her lips froze.

"Kelly, are you there?"

She rested her hand over her speeding heart. "Yes."

"We just heard that they're going to allow you to take the SAT."

The words reached her mind like echoes from a mountaintop.

"And if your score is good, Mr. De Santis will help you register this semester."

"Really?"

"Yes, he was able to pull few strings, like he promised he would, and now it's up to you."

Exhaustion suddenly became hope. "When do I do that?"

"Be in my office by 10 tomorrow morning and bring your G.E.D. diploma with you."

"I sure will, thank you."

She gave Francis a long hug. "I can't believe it! I was just thinking that it was never going to happen."

The handful of customers had all turned their heads toward the commotion, and a guy seated at the counter asked Jody if she had won the lotto.

"No, she didn't win the lotto, but the news she got is bigger than that for her."

This time her replacement showed up a few minutes earlier. Right at 6:30, she stormed out of the place, and in no time was at Rosita's house, rushing up the two flight of stairs. *I can't believe this is happening.*

"Kelly, what's that big smile for?"

She hugged her. "I think going back to school might happen."

"Let's go inside and sit before your heart pops out of your chest."

"Hi Mommy," Hope yelled, running toward her. "We'll be in school together."

Kelly picked her up and gave her a kiss. "You mean at the same time."

"Yes, that's what I meant."

Rosita filled a glass of ice water. "Drink it, you look like you need it."

"Thank you."

"So, when you're starting?"

"Actually, before I know for sure, I have to take the SAT test, and that's tomorrow."

What if you don't do good?"

"I must, I can't afford not to."

***

Dean De Santis's secretary smiled at her. "Come in, please."

"Thank you." Kelly approached her desk, a swarm of butterflies roaming her gut. "I'm ready."

The secretary picked up a manila folder. "Follow me. Dean De Santis asked me to supervise you."

Kelly waited for her to step out and walked alongside her. "When will I get results?"

"He hopes that by Monday we can call in for the results, but he suggested you take the test regardless, and if worst comes to worst, we'll use it for next semester."

"I really need to get started this semester."

"Based on my experience with this dean, when he gets this involved, he usually gets results. He instructed me to fax your test out immediately. After you finish, if you think you've done well, I would go ahead and start to get the tuition money and everything else ready."

"Do you know where I could go for a student loan?"

The secretary thought for a while. "This late, I would go to the bank down the street."

"I really appreciate what you're all doing for me."

The secretary opened the door to the computer room. "Even allowing you to take this test with just a few days until school starts is unheard of. I have been working here for over ten years and never experienced a case like yours. Someone up there must be looking out for you."

Kelly followed her to the table and sat down. "Maybe my mother."

"What do you mean?"

"When cancer took her away from me, she was only forty-three years old."

The secretary placed a hand on Kelly's shoulder. "I am deeply sorry to hear that."

"Thank you. It was hard losing her so soon; she was a good person."

"Then I'm sure she is the one. Here, this is the test, and these are three sharpened pencils, use them well." She looked at her watch. "You have three hours and fifteen minutes, three hours for the test and two breaks, one of five minutes, and one of ten minutes. I'll be sitting right there." She pointed to the other side of the room. "Good luck."

"Thank you." Kelly organized the test papers in front of her. This was it.

***

Less than two hours later, she had completed the test. She went straight to the bank.

A teller waved her over. "May I help you?"

"I need to get a student loan, what do I do?"

The teller smiled. "You are in the right place, but not with the right person. See that gentleman on the phone there, he is the person to talk to. Have a seat on one of the chairs to the side of his desk and when he gets off the phone, he'll call you."

"Thank you."

While Kelly waited, she took her notes from her pocketbook. What she had saved was probably just enough for the books. She determined that she would need around eight hundred dollars.

Just as she lifted her head, the man motioned her over. She approached his desk. "Hi, I'm Mrs. Kelly Esposito."

He shook her hand, "Mr. Hogan. Please have a seat."

"Thank you."

"Mrs. Esposito, I understand you need a student loan, is that right?"

"Yes, and I have no idea how to go about it. Can you help me?"

"That's why we here, but you're a little early for next semester."

MY LAST CHANCE

"No sir. I'll have to start classes next Thursday the 31st."

Mr. Hogan leaned his elbow on the desk and looked straight in her eyes. "Mrs. Esposito, if I were to take your application today, it would still take at least five working days for the approval, and tomorrow is already Friday."

Each word coming out of his mouth was like a bullet piercing through her skull. She stared at him in absolute silence for few seconds. "Are you saying to forget about the loan?"

"No, Mrs. Esposito, I am saying that we need at least a week to process your request."

Without the loan, her dream of going to college would be shattered. Her mind began to churn on overspeed for an alternative. If she could get the school to wait a few days for her tuition money, then he would have enough time to approve it. "What do you need from me?"

He handed her the loan application. "Fill this out and bring it to me with a letter from your college admission office detailing the list of the courses you'll be taking with their costs. Do that as soon as possible, and I'll take it from there." He sat up, shook her hand. "It was a pleasure meeting you."

"Thank you, it was a pleasure meeting you too." She took a couple of his business cards, looked at the clock hanging on the wall behind the tellers. 12:20. That should give her enough time to go back to school and get the letter. If she needed to be late for work, it would be her first time ever, and George should be OK with it.

At the school, she rushed to the registration's office window and stood behind two students already in line.

Peeking behind the cashier, she was looking for a desk with the manager name plate on. One desk was empty and the other ones were occupied by women. She also saw Mrs. Alston writing something. After a couple of minutes, the last student in front of her handed the cashier a check and left.

"Young lady, you're next."

"Hi, I'm not here to pay for my registration. I need to get a letter from the person in charge of this office."

"Then why are you standing here?"

The student in line behind her and the few employees from inside the office looked at her as if she was a troublemaker.

With an unwavering stare, she got closer to the window. "Ma'am, I am not here to bother you. I need to talk to your boss, so that I can ask her for a letter that the bank needs to release the money for my registration."

"My boss went to a convention and won't be back until the end of next week. Move aside, so that I can attend to the next in line."

"Ma'am, with all due respect, I have waited in line for my turn and I am not moving aside until you tell me who I can talk to in this office that could help me. I only have an hour before I must pick up my eight-year-old daughter from school in Ansonia, twenty minutes or so from here, feed her, bring her to my friend's house and be at work. I need this letter today, please?"

Anger spilled from the cashier's face. "Young lady, that's not my problem!"

Every desk had a name plate except for the empty one. The name plate on Mrs. Alston's desk read Mrs. Allison Alston, assistant office manager. Mrs. Alston got up and walked to the window. "Of course, it's our problem. Isn't helping students with their registrations part of our job?"

Kelly looked toward the ceiling. *Thank you, Mom.*

The cashier's face turned blood red. Now she probably wished to shrink and disappear. "Yes, but—"

"There is no but. Young lady, step through that door to your left and I'll see what I can do for you."

"Yeah, way to go, girl," a young man with long hair at the end of the line shouted.

"I'm sorry if I seemed to be too persistent, Mrs. Alston, but I really need this letter."

Mrs. Alston, who was holding the door open for her, said, "Don't worry, it's that time of the day when fatigue and hunger pair up."

Kelly sat across from her.

"Weren't you here with Gilda few days ago trying to register for this semester?"

"Yes ma'am, and—"

"I'm sorry, I don't remember your name."

"Kelly Nolan Esposito."

Mrs. Alston moved some documents to the side. "I heard you saying you're from Ansonia."

"Yes ma'am, but I grew up in Derby."

"Really?" Mrs. Alston's chubby cheeks glowed. "I am from Naugatuck, but my first love was this handsome Italian guy from Derby. It was a long time ago, but I still get soft when I think about him."

"Those Latin lovers are something else, aren't they?"

"They are. I overheard that the bank wouldn't release the money for your tuition. Why?"

"I just came from there," Kelly replied. "You know, the bank down the street." Took one of Mr. Hogan's business cards from her pocketbook and handed it to her. "He needs a letter from this office outlining the courses I would be taking, and the cost. And this is the list I came up with from the curriculum outline for an accounting major."

Mrs. Alston looked at the list, and then at the business card. "Are you sure that this Mr. Hogan knows what he is doing, and isn't wasting your time and ours?"

"No ma'am, it's not quite like that. As you know, I'm the one who's late. He gave me the application and said that if I get it to him soon enough, together with the letter from this office, I should be approved within a week, just in time for me to register for this semester."

As she was talking, the convivial look on Mrs. Alston's face was fading. She leaned forward. "Kelly, based on what I know, there is no way you'll get the loan approved in time to register for this semester. Why don't you take your time and get ready for next semester?"

Kelly's face sagged. "Mrs. Alston, I can't do that. I have to start now, or I might never be able to."

"I don't understand. You're still young, what difference can a semester make?"

She looked away from her. "A difference between life and death, If not of my body, of my soul."

"I don't get it."

Kelly wasn't comfortable sharing her personal problems with total strangers, but to stand a chance, it was crucial to let Mrs. Alston in. She took a deep breath.

"It's a long story, but I'll get right to the heart of it. My husband is an old-fashioned man. He believes that a woman's place is at home, barefoot and pregnant, and whose job is to look after his children, run the house, and be available to his every desire and needs at the flick of a finger. When we got married, I was sixteen, and he was twenty-four, and that suddenly halted my life-long dreams of going to college."

Mrs. Alston's blue eyes were now glued to Kelly's watery ones, absorbing every word that came out of her mouth.

"Along the way, there were many arguments about me getting a job, or going to school. Then, this past June, when I didn't even have twenty dollars to pay for our eight-year-old daughter's last school trip of the year, I stood my ground and finally persuaded him to allow me to go to work and got a job as a waitress at a diner. A few days after I started working, I ran into Gilda who also works there. We had been school mates from first grade up through high school but hadn't seen each other since I got married. We had coffee and revived our old friendship. When she told me that she was going to school, and how much she was looking forward to getting her legal secretary diploma, my dreams of going to college resurfaced. I approached my husband about it, and after another argument, he reluctantly agreed as long as I don't ask him for financial help, I take care of the house just the same, his current lifestyle doesn't get affected in any way, and when he gets the right job making good money again, I'd have to quit both work and school." She stared away from her, with tears appearing in the corners of her eyes.

Mrs. Alston cupped her face in her hands. "Go on."

"I know my husband all too well, and it's only matter of time until he changes his mind. I figured, if I'm already in school when that happens, it will be much more difficult for him to stop me because by then I'll have student debt on our shoulders. See, I always loved school and had great plans, then the summer before my junior year, I fell in love with him and on my sixteenth birthday, I got pregnant."

Mrs. Alston was enchanted by her sincerity, eagerness, and her sense of urgency. It wasn't the first case she had come across where girls got pregnant in high school, and years later came around to get their lives going again, but none of them ever seemed as eager and resolute as the girl standing in front of her. "It's none of my business, but since your husband seems to be your main problem, have you considered divorcing him?"

"No. I'm his wife of eight years, and we have a beautiful daughter together. Plus, I'm Catholic, and I was brought up with the principle that divorce is immoral, and should only be the last resort, if ever."

"And if along the way, like you said, he wants you to stop both school and work, then what?"

"I know it's a gamble believing that he can change, but that's all I have. He seems to be adjusting to me working, and I can only hope that in time, he will adjust to me going to school as well. What I do know for sure is that if I don't get a higher education and a better job, we'll never get out of the hole we're in."

"Kelly, I have never met your husband, but what you call old-fashioned, I call abusive. Nevertheless, I'd like to help you, but even if I write you the letter for the bank, you still aren't going to get the money before next Thursday, and that will be too late."

Kelly's right eye started twitching. "Could I attend classes as a guest student for those few extra days that it will take for the loan to come through?"

"I don't think so. There have been times when we have allowed students to sit as guests for a class or two, but never for an indefinite number of times, and for five classes."

"There has to be something that can be done. When I was young and confused about something, my grandfather used to tell me, 'Remember, a river is a collection of many streams and creeks.'"

After a minute of total silence, Kelly's face lit up. "Mrs. Alston, what if I sign a letter stating that I owe the school the amount needed for the tuition, like a loan, and when I get the loan from the bank, I'll pay it off."

"You just can't take no for an answer, can you?" Smirking, Mrs. Alston shook her head. "Since I have been working here, we have never done anything like it, but that might work if my boss goes along with it."

"Can you please talk to your boss then?"

"What about the SAT?"

"I took it this morning, and Dean De Santis's secretary told me that they could get the results by Monday."

"Why am I not surprised?" Mrs. Alston handed Kelly a pen and yellow pad. "Write the phone number where I can reach you this afternoon, and I'll let you know."

With a renewed sense of hope, Kelly's face glowed. "Thank you, Mrs. Alston, I'll make you proud of me, I promise."

Mrs. Alston's secretary, whose desk was on the outside of her cubical, got up, stood in front of her, and said, "can I get you a cup of tea Mrs. Alston?"

"No, thanks. I must admit though, for a while there I was about to lose it, but then something clicked that made me look at her from a different point of view. She is a highly intelligent young lady and highly creative, and I love that about people. I am going to do whatever I can to help her, of course, after I do some snooping around. Please, get me Dean De Santis on the phone?"

At that moment, her secretary's blushing face was wishing to be anywhere else on the planet but there. With her back hunched, she rushed back to her desk and dialed the Dean's number. "Mrs. Alston would like to speak with you, hold on please?" She placed her hand over the receiver, looked at Mrs. Alston over the cubical. "Your desk or the manager's office."

"Here it's fine." She thought it would be better for the rest of the office to eavesdrop on the conversation, just in case.

"Mr. De Santis, I know you must be busy, so I get right to the point."

"Thank you, Mrs. Alston."

"What's with this young lady Kelly Esposito besides being very persistent?"

"And highly intelligent, I might add. This morning, she took the SAT in almost half the time that takes our average student, and because of that, before sending it out I took the liberty to flip through it. I couldn't believe my eyes, for every question that I know the answer to, she had it right."

"I'm not surprised."

"Wait, it gets even better. I called the Derby school district, and after an hour or so, they got back to me with her entire file. Kelly was in the school's top ten students from first grade to her sophomore year, with most of those years ranking first or second. They also told me that three respectable Universities had shown interest in her with a full scholarship before she quit school the summer of nineteen-ninety-two."

"And she had to stop all that because she got knocked up when she was sixteen by a guy eight years older than her, who believes that a woman belongs at home barefoot and pregnant. What a shame."

"Is that what happened?"

"Yes. Let's try to rescue her. You'll do your share with the admission, I'll do mine with her tuition, and let's get her back to school before it's too late."

"Yes, she will be a good role-model for our school."

Immediately after she hung up with the Dean, she handed her Secretary Mr. Hogan's business card. "Put him on the phone too."

Her secretary quickly dialed the number. "Hold on please," she looked over the cubical again. "Mrs. Alston, he is on the line."

"I understand that this morning you had a meeting with a Kelly Esposito, you remember her?"

"How could I forget; she is an unusually persistent young lady."

"Yes, but she is also very intelligent, and we like to help her."

After Mr. Hogan stated that he didn't see any problem for her to qualify for a student loan, they discussed various approaches that would lead her to register on time and settled on a similar option that Kelly had suggested; to have her sign a one-page document stating that she assigned the loan proceeds to the school.

***

While Kelly was hugging all her co-workers about the great news that Mrs. Alston and the bank had agreed to work with her on the loan, Rocky had just wrapped up a sizable deal in a secluded spot behind Sam's bar and was organizing his dollar bills of fives, tens, twenties, and quite a few fifties. He stashed a small plastic bag of cocaine in his right sock and drove off.

He had just turned onto his street when a police car flashed his lights behind him. *If he frisks me, I'm fucking done.*

Rocky slowed down and pulled to the side of the road. He looked through his side mirror and realized that the cop getting out of the cruiser was his old buddy Joe, who used to hang out with him at clubs throughout the county, looking for partying girls. At times, they even shared girls for a night or two.

"Rocky, what's wrong with you?" Joe shouted. "This is the second time I've caught you going through this stop sign."

"Sorry, man, it's just that I have been having some issues with my wife and my mind hasn't been quite the same."

"You better focus on one thing at the time. When you drive, it's the only thing you ought to be focusing on."

"I know, man. It won't happen again."

"It better not, because I'm not the only cop working this area anymore. One of the other cops once told me he hates your guts."

"Who's this guy? And what have I done to him?"

"Back when he was in high school, you took the girl he was in love with away from him."

"I never stole a girl from any guy I know."

"His name is Cody, and he was in love with Kelly. You might not know him, but he knows you."

"That so? What he looks like?"

"As tall as you, with dirty blond hair. Fit." Joe handed Rocky a warning ticket. "Next time, I'll have no choice but to book you, capisce?"

"I get it, man, I get it." Rocky placed the warning ticket in his glove compartment. Looked up at him. "Don't you guys have anything more serious going on?"

"The chief has received many complaints from the surrounding neighbors that a lot of people don't respect this stop sign and decided to police the area heavily, especially from four to nine p.m."

"That's nice to know, I'll be extra cool from now on, I promise."

"Remember, our job is to make sure that people follow the rules so that no one gets hurt. Go now before I change my mind, go!"

"Thanks, man." Rocky put the car in gear and slowly drove toward his house. Looked in the rear mirror. "Fuck you all."

As tall as you, with dirty blond hair. Fit. Goddammit, that could be the same guy that was talking to her at Gilda's party.

Hope was playing with her toys on the coffee table, occasionally peeking at the TV. "Dad, why are you late? I'm starving."

"I had to work late. Where is your mom?"

"Outside in the back, getting the clothes."

To save money in the summer months, Kelly dried her laundry on a clothesline she herself had installed. At the sound of Rocky's heavy steps coming from Hope's bedroom, she spun around with her hand over her heart. "You almost gave me a heart attack."

"Not now, wait until we get laid first."

"And what makes you think I want to?" She took the last piece from the clothesline and headed for the house.

He followed her. "Who's this guy Cody?"

"Cody who?" She turned the light on and started putting clothes away.

"The guy who had a serious crush on you back in high school?"

Her hands froze. "That Cody?" She laughed. "My God, that was so long ago. Where the heck did that come from?"

He started pacing behind her. "While I was waiting for my boss at the bar in Derby to go over the partnership documents, this guy a few stools down said he remembered me picking you up from school with my blue Camaro. Then he went on to say that when I married you, it was a big deal in your school because Cody got sick over it. Did you ever go out with him?"

If she told him the truth, a big fight would start. She turned around. "I have to admit, he was cute, and so were other boys who also had a crush on me back then, but I chose you." She opened her arms to give him a hug.

He stepped back. "Did you, or not?"

She turned away from him and shut the drawers. "No."

"He's a cop here in Ansonia now, did you know that?"

With a casual air, she started for the kitchen. "No, I didn't."

He followed her. "He is from Derby, why did he choose to be a cop in Ansonia and not in Derby?"

She peered at him. "Why don't you ask him?"

"Maybe because he knows you live here?"

"Rocky, please?"

He walked to the fridge, got a beer. "I'll get to the bottom of this, and when I do…"

CHAPTER TEN

Classes were supposed to start the following day. On their way to Hope's school, Kelly decided not to drive herself insane waiting for them to call. She gave Hope a hug and a kiss. "Honey, I'll see you later."

Kelly decided to stop at Mrs. Alston's office first. The cashier, the same one she had issues with the last time she was there, acted as if nothing had happened. "Good morning, I don't see Mrs. Alston at her cubicle, is she in?"

"Good morning, Mrs. Esposito. No, she called and should be here within the next thirty minutes or so. If you like, you can wait in the computer room there."

"OK, thank you." Kelly grabbed a magazine and started flipping through it. Half-an-hour passed and still no sign of Mrs. Alston. Kelly waited for the cashier to be free again and approached the window. "Please, when Mrs. Alston comes in, tell her that I went to Dean DeSantis's office for a moment."

The dean's office door was halfway open. Kelly knocked and spoke to the secretary. "Can I please see you for a minute?"

"Kelly, come in. As matter of fact, Mr. DeSantis just asked me to get in touch with you."

"I hope it's good news."

Mr. DeSantis heard her and stepped out of his office. "Yes," he said, extending his hand. "Congratulations, Kelly, you did extremely well on your SAT. They're going to fax us the official results before the day is over."

The weight of a mountain lifted from her shoulders. "Does that mean I'm in?"

"Yes, if that glitch with the student loan can also be resolved today."

Just as quick as the mountain she had been carrying on her shoulder had lifted, another one quickly took its place. "What glitch? Mrs. Alston told me that everything was set to go on Friday."

"So, you haven't spoken since?"

"I was at her office just now, and I was told she was running late."

"Kelly, you've made a great impression with everyone here who met you, and we're all trying our best to see that you become one of our students this semester."

"Mr. De Santis?" The secretary interrupted. "Mrs. Alston would like to see Kelly in her office as soon as possible."

"Go ahead, Kelly," the Dean said, rushing her out, "and good luck."

With an anxious look on her face, Kelly sat across from Mrs. Alston.

"Kelly, as I told you Friday, the good news is that the bank agreed to go along with us and are waiting for you to sign the release of the loan before they proceed any further. The sad news is that I can't get in touch with anyone above me to sign this agreement that the school will accept in lieu of your tuition until the bank can release the check directly to us."

"But Friday you told me that it was approved."

"Yes, my boss approved it over the phone, but she is not here to sign it. In her absence, something like this needs to be signed by someone higher up than myself, and I haven't been able to track anyone down since I last spoke with you."

"We've worked so hard to get this far. Please, I can't give up now."

"You're right. Here, take this." She handed her the standard school letter with the list of the courses and its relative tuition costs. "Together with your loan application, bring them to the bank. There, you will sign their loan documents and the release of the loan to the school, and have Mr. Hogan give you a copy of both with your original signature on. In the meantime, I'll keep trying to reach one of the eternal vacationers to sign this last piece of the puzzle."

Kelly took the letter and rushed out of the office.

Minutes later, stomach growling and her mind roiling, she was seated at the bank waiting for Mr. Hogan to get off the phone. *You're a child. A child, bearing a child. I hope you realize that you have just turned your life upside down. Now you must grow up fast. All your dreams about college, a career, and traveling are now shattered.*

She looked up. *Mom, I'm trying to make everything right, please give me a hand.*

Then she noticed Mr. Hogan waving her over and rushed to his desk. "I'm sorry, I was thinking of all the things I still have to do before school starts tomorrow."

"We all have those moments."

"Here is the letter from the school and here is my loan application."

He took them, and then skimmed through the letter. "I see you want to major in business."

"Math was one of my favorite subjects in high school. I figure it's only natural to go in that direction."

"With an associate degree in accounting, you'll have no problem finding a decent job." Then he looked at her application line by line. "Everything seems in order, so let's move on."

"I really appreciate what you're doing for me."

He leaned back and looked straight in her eyes. "Mrs. Esposito, I've really enjoyed doing this for you, but I have to tell you that you must be incredibly special to someone. Since I have been in this business, I have never seen an unusual situation moving this fast, and practically flawless."

Flawless? she thought.

He got up. "I'll be right back with copies for you to sign."

***

Back at school, she approached the cashier's window for the fourth time that day. The cashier was free and walked straight to the door to let her in.

"There you are." Mrs. Alston got up. "Let's go to my boss's office."

"Here is the signed release you asked for." Kelly placed it on the desk before her. "Have you found someone?"

"No, I have been on the phone all this time trying, and it's driving me insane." She sat silent for a while then leaned forward. "Come closer."

Kelly moved her chair closer, eager to listen.

"Kelly, over the years, I have paid close attention to people who succeeded in life, not only among the students that crossed my path, but also successful people in general, and what I have found to be common among them all was their desire, their hard-working nature, their focus, and their determination to get where they wanted to go. Watching you do everything you were asked beyond anyone's expectations, you strike me as one who possesses all those qualities, and I am not allowing them to go to waste. I'm going to sign this agreement myself; I'll take care of your registration process so that you can start school tomorrow, and if I get fired over it, let it be."

Kelly couldn't allow her to put her career on the line for her. "Mrs. Alston, I don't think that's a good Idea."

"Shhh! Now I really understand how important this is to you, and perhaps to our school too. I'm going to handle all the paperwork myself and hold it in my desk until the loan comes through. Hopefully, no one will ever have to know what happened."

She was ready to jump with joy, but Mrs. Alston held her hand and motioned her to stay cool. "If you show too much excitement," she whispered, "someone here might uncover my plan. Do that in your car on the way home if you need to. Just make sure to show up for classes tomorrow."

"Thank you, Mrs. Alston. You'll never regret this, I promise you."

Driving home, she cried with joy. "Thank you, God. Thank you, Mom. This time I will not mess up."

She still had enough time to stop home, call Gilda, get ready for work, pick Hope up from school, bring her over to Rosita, and go straight to work from there.

"Gilda, tomorrow I'm starting classes, can you believe it?"

"Kelly, slow down before you have a heart attack. What did you do to make it happen?"

"With persistence and a little help from above. Thank you for introducing me to Mrs. Alston and Dean DeSantis. Without their dedication, it wouldn't have happened."

"I thought Rocky wasn't going to help you with the money?"

"And he isn't. I've got a student loan for the tuition and the rest I will handle with my job, even if I have to work extra hours."

"Did you cut him off?"

"What you mean?"

"You know, fake headaches and so on, like I told you to do when he gets stubborn?"

"Oh, you mean have I stopped having sex with him?"

"Yes, did you?"

"I can't do that; he would go crazy. Come to think of it, I was supposed to get my period few days ago."

"Shit, I hope you're not pregnant."

"I can't be, I take the pill every night."

"That would be a disaster for you. First time around, you had to quit high school because of it, and now it would be college."

"It's not happening."

***

After spending all that time between school and the bank, she didn't have a chance to get the dinner's main course prepared that afternoon. So, instead of stopping at Rosita to get Hope firsts, she decided to drive straight home to make Rocky sautéed chicken and broccoli over Angel hair.

Shit, I hope you're not pregnant. Gilda's words kept resonating in her thoughts. She decided that first thing in the morning, she was going to make an appointment with her gynecologist.

As she was about to go take her shower, the roar of his car froze her in her tracks. She turned around and walked right back to the stove.

He walked to the refrigerator for a beer, face long. "I heard you registered for school today. Where the fuck you got the money?"

"From a bank, where else?"

"How did you do that without my signature?"

"They didn't ask for it."

He turned the TV on. *Fuck, now she can borrow money on her own too.* Took a long gulp of beer. "Where is Hope?"

"Still at Rosita's. I came home first to make sure that dinner would be ready on time. I'll go get her while you start eating."

"It's OK." He smirked at her. "Then let's go for a quick one."

"Right now?"

He grabbed her butt with both hands. "Let's go."

She pulled away. "We can't, my period is late, and I'm worried."

"You've been taking the pill, haven't you?"

"Yes, and that's the one thing that gives me hope it's a false alarm."

"I wouldn't worry, but if you think we shouldn't do it because of that, that's OK."

"Tomorrow, I'm making an appointment with the gynecologist."

With a sinister smirk, he walked back to the fridge for another beer. The money he had been paying that half-ass crooked pharmacist was paying off. One done, one more to go. All her school shit and work would soon feel like just a bad fucking dream.

CHAPTER ELEVEN

On her way to class, a sudden influx of goosebumps rushed across Kelly's back. She was the first student there. She sat in the front row.

When class began, Kelly gave the room a casual scan. It seemed evenly divided between sexes. Except for one lady in her thirties, and the two older gentlemen sitting at the back of the class, she was the oldest student there.

Kelly's schedule consisted of two classes on Monday and Wednesday from 9 a.m. to 11 a.m., and three classes on Tuesdays and Thursdays from 9:45 a.m. to 12:45 p.m. She had to get to Hope's school by no later than 1:30, feed her, take her to Rosita and get to work by 2:30. Her schedule was demanding, but the sacrifices were worth every bit of it. By the time she got through her classes for the day, her anxieties were replaced by a high sense of worthiness and confidence. The first pay phone she came across, she stopped and dialed Angela's father's business number.

"Kelly, I was just thinking of calling you and letting you have it," Angela said.

"I know, but a lot of things have happened since I last talked to you. Listen, tomorrow is Friday, and I don't have classes, how about meeting me at the Italian coffee shop in Derby around twelve or so?"

"OK, you're forgiven."

"See you there." She hung up, and headed for her car with her head up, a smug smile, and her mind roiling years into the future.

MY LAST CHANCE

***

The blue sky ushered in a few clouds and hosted a sun so strong that its heat flickered over the asphalts like ghostly waves, resembling August more than September.

Kelly hadn't seen Angela since Christmas. She got to the coffee shop early and sat at one of the two tiny tables outside the shop, now shaded thanks to the midday sun that had just crossed over.

"Hey, girl?" Angela giggled.

Kelly hugged her. "Look at you, looking like Marilyn Monroe."

Growing up, Angela's hair had been long and wavy and deep brown. Now her hair was short and blonde, but her attractive round face with her high puffy cheeks was still the same. Being the only child of a wealthy real estate broker, she was able to do things that the average person could only dream of. She had gone to college in L.A., and after she graduated, had decided to live there. She was an inch or so shorter than Kelly with couple extra pounds on her and a noticeably deeper cleavage. Men of every age going in and out of the shop tried to make eye contact with both women. They weren't called queens for nothing back in high school, where girls coveted, and guys drooled over them.

"I needed a change, so I decided to become a blonde."

"Angela, you look great. But you left L.A. for this?"

"Listen, girl, when you live there for a while, you realize that it's not what it has been built up to be. You never know who you can trust and who you can't. From one day to another, someone who you thought was your friend is the latest one to backstab you."

The barista placed two cappuccinos on the counter. Angela insisted on paying, and both walked back to their table while taking short seeps from their cups. Kelly looked at the car that Angela had driven. "You know, I should envy you, but instead I'm really happy for you."

"That's my mother's Mercedes, and until I get my own car, she is letting me use it from nine to five only."

Kelly chuckled. "Your father is going to make his only daughter, his forever princess, sacrifice like that?"

"Yes, he is. They aren't so happy with me. They told me that I wasted my time and their money in L.A., and now I must earn my own way. He expects me to work with him and learn every aspect of his company."

"I feel so sorry for you," Kelly joked. "I had to fight just so that I could go to work as a waitress, and we don't leave in a 5000 square foot home in Woodbridge."

"You're right, I shouldn't complain. They always gave me everything I ever needed and wanted, and I haven't given them the grandchild that they crave. Sister, enough about me now. Yesterday, you sounded thrilled, what's going on?"

"I'm finally back in school."

"That is so fabulous, where?"

"This college in Waterbury for now, where I'm planning to get an associate in Accounting. With that, I hope to get a decent job to start with, and from there I'll see. By the way, you remember Gilda?"

"Gilda? No, should I?"

"Of course, you should. Back in high school, she used to yearn to hang out with us."

"No, I don't remember her."

"She was pretty, chubby, shorter than us, and always happy?"

"Wait, is she the girl that introduced you to Rocky at one of her parents' parties?"

"Yes, that's the one."

"What about her?"

"She has been working at the diner since she graduated from high school. And since I started working there, we have become close. She is the one who steered me back to school and helped me with the registration process. Had it not been for some of the connections she has there, I would have never been able to register for this semester."

Angela giggled. "Wow, she sounds like a game changer for you."

"What you mean?"

"I was just thinking. You met your husband because of her, and that changed your life then. Now she steered you back to school, which is going to change your life now."

Kelly cupped her chin. "That's an interesting point."

"Kelly, there are good angels and bad angels all around us. In L.A., I only seemed to attract the bad ones."

"She is a nice person. I'm sorry we didn't let her closer to us back then."

"Is Rocky OK with you going back to school and work?"

"I'm not sure how to read him anymore."

"What you mean?"

"I know he isn't happy about me going back to school, and he isn't happy about me working, but he seems to go along."

"Maybe he is finally coming to his senses and needs some time to adjust?"

"That's what I'd like to think too. But if that was the case, why did he make me agree that when he gets a better job and buys us a nice house, I'll quit both school and work and go back to being just a housewife?"

"Girl, no way. That's crazy of him to demand that. And it's even crazier of you to go along with him if that's not what you want."

"Of course, it's not what I want. You remember when I used to tell you about my dreams of going to college, getting a big job somewhere, traveling for a while, buying a big house, and then falling in love and building a family?"

"I remember it well, and your studying efforts and your grades reflected that."

"Angela, those dreams never died. The only difference now is that they are not just for me but for my daughter and him too, but I must go along with his demand because if I didn't, for sure those dreams would remain just that. Maybe that's why he pretends to be cool about it because he thinks this is only temporary."

Angela whispered, "Hey, if worse comes to worst, you can always divorce him."

"No way, I couldn't do that."

"Why not?"

"First, it might sound crazy after what he has been putting me through, but I still love him. And second, I am Catholic, and we don't normally do that."

"Sister, that's bullshit. You know how many Catholic women choose divorce over a miserable life?"

"I know, but—"

"Kelly, if you go back to being a housewife only, the Kelly I remember is going to be miserable for the rest of her life."

"That's not going to happen because…" Tears started to form in the corner of her eyes.

Angela placed her hand over Kelly's. "Because of what?"

"He is not capable of delivering on his promises. He is too limited to get another big job, and that's why I agreed. Not because I intend to quit work or school."

"What if you're wrong though and he delivers, then what?"

"I don't know." She shook her head. "Darn it, I lied to him in a big way. Even if my goal is to build a better life for all of us, it's still wrong to lie like that."

"Look, I lie to men too when it's necessary," Angela said, hoping to cheer her up. "But I am not you, and I know how honest you are. However, I do believe that if someone lies also for the benefit of the people one is lying to, like in your case, that lie is justified. And if in time he ends up accepting the new you, it was all worth it."

Kelly wiped the corner of her eyes. "Thanks."

"Our cappuccinos are getting spoiled, maybe we should go for a nice scotch on the rocks somewhere instead?"

"Angela, no way, I don't remember the last time I had whiskey."

"But I do," Angela teased. "Remember when we used to sneak into my father's bar in the finished basement of our Derby home?"

"Please, don't remind me of those days."

"You mean our masturbation days?" Angela whispered.

"Did you have to go there?"

One day, when they were around twelve, the girls had snuck into Angela's parents' finished basement's bar, drank two shots of whiskey each. Drunk, Kelly started telling Angela the story of how she had discovered masturbation as a refuge from fear. Angela asked her to show her how, and soon Kelly was in the shower stall with her back leaning against one of the sides, her legs bent a little, her jeans shorts and her panties down to her knees, rattling her vulva area, and Angela was sitting on the toilet, her back against the tank, her skirt up, her panties down, and her legs stretched wide open, imitating Kelly's actions.

"Kelly, those were fabulous days."

Kelly's face got redder than an ardent flame. "Angela, please?"

"Girl, you're the one who got me started."

"I was trying to tell you the story of when I ran away from my father who was chasing me to beat me up, but you never let me finish it." She stared at the shimmering asphalt. "I was scared as hell looking back at him chasing me with his belt in his right hand folded in two. I ran down the basement and hid in a corner behind a big furnace. It was pitch dark and I was terrified. I crouched in a corner with my trembling hands tight between my thighs, and after a while I felt a pleasing sensation running through my body that I had never experienced before."

"That's right, before you finished the story, I asked you to show me, and that was the first time I experienced an orgasm."

"My god," Kelly whispered, "I can't believe you brought that day back to my front lobe."

"So what? That's probably the most important thing I learned that early in life, and I thank you for it, because it's one of few things that gives me power over men."

"What do you mean?"

"It gives me sexual independence. OK, it's not like the real thing, but sometimes I'd rather do that than submit to all kinds of abuse from some jerk just to have sex."

"Angela, we need to find you a good husband."

"Don't tell me that you don't masturbate anymore."

"Angela, how did we get on this subject anyway."

Giggling, Angela looked Kelly straight in her eyes. "You don't?"

"Lately, I wouldn't even have the strength to. The other strange thing that has happened with Rocky is that since I started working, he wants to have sex every night."

Angela's eyes were ready to pop out of their socket and her mouth opened like a fish out of water. "Wow, I hope you're not complaining about that."

"No, but I'm puzzled about it, and also worried now."

"Worried about what?"

"That I haven't gotten my period this month and it was due about a week ago."

"You're not on the pill?"

"Of course, I am. But what if they didn't work? I've heard of that happening to other women."

"I've heard that too, but that's very rare."

"That would be a disaster for me now."

"You can always get an abortion."

"Angela, are you crazy?"

"I know women in L.A. that did it, and they said it was a simple procedure."

"It doesn't matter, that's a life we're talking about."

"Sister, some say it's a life at conception, some say after few weeks, some say after few months, it's all a mess. I say it's up to the woman if she wants to have one."

"I totally disagree. If your mother and mine had decided to have an abortion when they were pregnant with us, we wouldn't be here now. And if I had an abortion, Hope wouldn't be here either."

"That's true too."

"Before I started working, we used to do it two or three times a week. Now it's almost every night, I don't get it."

"Maybe his mistress left him, and you must fill her spot too." At the look on Kelly's face, Angela quickly added, "I'm only kidding."

"Hey, one never knows. According to Gilda, he was a ladies' man before he hooked up with me. But I'm not the kind of person to go snooping around. If he ever did that, then a divorce might be justified."

"Does Rocky have a brother?" Angela said jokingly.

"Angela, come on. To answer your question, yes, I still masturbate. I do that when I am either stressed out, afraid, or upset about something. Just like that night behind the furnace. Somehow it relieves my stress or fears, even if it's only temporary."

"Let's face it, we're a pair of libidinous creatures."

"Maybe we are."

"About my godchild, when can I see her?"

"What time is it?" Kelly reached for Angela's hand and looked at her gold watch. "She'll be out in twenty minutes; would you like to follow me to school and surprise her?"

"That would be awesome. Then I'll hang around the house with her until you get ready for work."

"No, that's not possible. I'll be rushing, preparing her lunch, and getting ready."

"I can help you with her lunch."

"No, not today."

"You know, lately I've been getting this feeling that I'm not welcome in your house anymore," Angela said. "Has Rocky revived his old line that I am a bad influence on you?"

"That might still be true with him, but that's not the reason why I have been trying to keep you away from our house." Her head wilted, and her eyes stared at the table. "I must confess, I'm ashamed of where we live now. When Rocky lost his job, we couldn't afford to keep up with our lease purchase payments and lost it. Then we moved into these six hundred square feet converted garage. It was supposed to be a temporary move until Rocky found another decent job. That was over two years ago."

Angela placed her hand on her shoulder. "Girl, look at me. You shouldn't be ashamed about that, at least not with me. You're like a sister to me, and family shouldn't keep these things from each other's. Besides, I know what you're capable of, and now that you have taken a stand, you will turn things around."

Wiping tears with the back of her hand, Kelly looked at her friend. "I hope so."

"Kelly, regardless of how small the inside is, or how crumbled it might be on the outside, I'm sure that it is so spotlessly clean and organized, even a president wouldn't mind being hosted there. When you're ready to have me over, you let me know."

The heavy clot in Kelly's head began to dissolve. "Angela, you have no idea how much this has been bothering me, and I'm sorry I didn't tell you this when you called."

"Kelly, remember when you used to tell me that people should be judged for who they are, and not what they have. So?"

Kelly got up. "Are you coming to the school then?"

"Yes, of course."

***

For the first time in all her school years, she had been restless for the duration of the class with her mind swaying between the lecture and her visit to the gynecologist at eleven-thirty that morning. The class ended at eleven, and the instant the professor dismissed class, she stormed out, something unusual for her. Throughout her twenty-minute drive, her mind roiled over the possible test results. *God, please let it be negative. I promise I'll abstain from sex forever.*

The short stocky doctor chuckled when Kelly explained why she was there. He examined her chart. "Mrs. Esposito, why do you think you're pregnant?"

"After I gave birth to my daughter and you put me on those pills, I never missed my period once except for this month."

He looked at her over his thick glasses. "And you have been taking them religiously?"

"Yes."

"What other changes have you noticed in the last few weeks?"

Kelly thought for a while. "Little over a week ago, my pelvic hurt badly for couple of days, and everything around it was redder than normal, but went away shortly after. The other thing I noticed this morning, those jeans there, they barely fit me now, but a month or so ago, they were loose."

"OK." He handed the folder to the nurse. "Please get on the table and lay down."

The nurse helped her to get in the right position, and the doctor proceeded with her physical examination. A bit later, he stood up. "Do you have the pills with you?"

She asked the nurse to get her pocketbook from the countertop. Picked up the box with only a few pills missing and handed it to him.

"Yes, these are the ones I prescribed you." He looked straight in her eyes. "Right now, I can't give you an answer, but—"

Those words pierced through her scull like a bullet and everything around her suddenly went dark as if all the lights had been turned off at once. Her school, her job, and all her dreams were once again been crushed. "This is not happening," she cried. "It can't be true, it can't!"

"Mrs. Esposito, please calm down," the nurse said, holding her by the shoulders.

"Please," the doctor echoed. "I didn't say that you are, or that you aren't. I'm only saying that— "

"You don't understand, this must be a curse."

"Mrs. Esposito, hear me out. After I delivered your daughter, I told you that for you to get pregnant again was nearly impossible, but not totally. With the pill, there is a six percent or so chance of unintended pregnancies. Your symptoms and everything I see today are positive signs, but to be totally certain, we need to do an HCG test. The nurse here will take your blood now. We'll send it to the lab and should get the definite results, I'd say by not later than Tuesday next week."

"Can you get it done any faster?

"I'll try my best, but I can't guarantee it."

"Please?"

"Mrs. Esposito, I will personally call you the moment the test results are in." He shook her hand and walked out of the room, shaking his head. There were women that would kill to get pregnant.

"Listen," the nurse whispered on her way out. "If you want to get an abortion, I'll direct you to the right place."

Kelly stared at her wordlessly.

***

She had parked her car on the opposite side of the doctor's office. It had only taken her a minute to reach the office when she arrived, but it took her more than ten minutes to get back to her car now. If she were pregnant, it meant that she would be giving birth by May, the end of the spring semester. The tears flowed freely. "God, please have mercy on me."

***

Later that day, after she left a message for Angela to call her, she plopped on the couch and put the TV on, her mind everywhere but on the screen. Six women out of a hundred, and one had to be her.

"Mom, are you deaf?" Hope yelled from her room. "The phone is ringing."

Kelly dragged herself to it. "Hello?"

"Hey, girl, Dad told me you sounded down. What's wrong?"

Kelly looked toward Hope's room to make sure that she wouldn't hear her. "I might be pregnant."

"Shut up, that's crazy."

"No, I'm serious. And I'm angry and confused. My doctor is sending my blood to the lab and I'll know for sure in few days."

"That really sucks if you are."

"I never really believed in curses before, but now I'm beginning to wonder."

"Don't be too harsh on yourself, shit happens. You've just got to deal with it more selfishly."

Kelly broke into tears. "I'm tired of taking one step forward and ten back."

"Girl, you're one of the smartest and strongest women I have ever known, don't let me cry too."

"Damnit, since I had Hope, I've always been so cautious."

"Listen, girl, I know how you feel about abortions, but you have to be realistic now."

"I can't do that. I just can't."

"Kelly, I dated this older guy back in L.A. who once told me, 'The road to the mountaintop is not always straight, but those who persist through the slopes, valleys, and spirals will ultimately get there."

"How many more of those slopes, valleys, and spirals do I still have to overcome?"

"Kelly, maybe you're just putting the cart before the horse, as they say. Wait for the final test and then you can think about what to do."

She heard Rocky's car approaching. "He's here, I must go now."

Rocky walked straight to the fridge as usual. "You've been crying, what's your problem?"

"Nothing!"

"What you mean nothing, you look like you just came from a fucking funeral?"

"Hi, Dad," Hope hollered from the threshold of her bedroom door. "Mommy punished me."

"Good, go back in there and I'll see you at the dinner table." He looked at Kelly. "Soon, I hope."

"I might be pregnant."

"No way. You told me you were taking the pill."

"Yes. The doctor will know for sure by Tuesday."

He turned around and walked to the couch. "Did you tell him you're taking the pill he gave you?"

"Of course. He even double checked the box to make sure that matched his prescription, but also told me that there is a six percent chance of unintended pregnancies. I must be one of those six percent victims."

A mild smirk surfaced on his face. *I got give that pharmacist a bonus. Even the doctor couldn't tell that the box was fucked with.* He laid down on the couch and took a long gulp. "Six percent? I wouldn't worry about it."

"And what if I am, how do you feel about it?"

"I wouldn't be happy, but we deal with it like we did with Hope."

Kelly dumped the macaroni in the boiling pan. "How are we going to move out of this house, get at least the necessary furniture for the new baby and everything else with your pay only?"

"Don't worry about that, I'll be making the money for all of it."

She stirred the macaroni one more time, and as she was turning the knob to the off-position, Angela's words from earlier resonated in her. *Don't be too harsh on yourself, shit happens. You just got to deal with it more selfishly.*

***

For the next few days, she did only what was expected and nothing more. At work, she hardly spoke, took the customers' orders, served them, and only forced a smile when unavoidable. At home, she barely prepared dinner and spent most of her time on the couch, longing for time to pass. She spoke to Hope only when necessary and acknowledged Rocky once in the morning and once in the evening before she lowered the TV volume and stared at the screen, her heart beating faster, her eye twitching, and her temples pulsating.

Tuesday morning, on her way back from dropping Hope off, she slammed the door behind her and thought, *today my life could be over.* It was only ten after eight, and she didn't have to be in school until 9:45. Stepped inside the shower, face up, and let the lukewarm water stream down for a while. Then with a towel wrapped around her body, she was drying her hair when she heard the phone ringing. Ran over, snapped the receiver off the hook. "Hello?"

"Mrs. Esposito, this is the gynecologist's receptionist. The doctor would like to talk to you."

"Yes, please?"

The doctor got on the phone. "Mrs. Esposito, you are not pregnant."

Wordless, she stared at the floor, mouth agape.

"Mrs. Esposito, are you there?"

"Yes, can you say that again, please?"

"OK, you-are-not-pregnant."

"Thank you, doctor. Thank you so much."

"You are very welcome. Like I told you years ago, it's difficult for you to get pregnant again, even if you try."

"What happened with my period then?"

"I'm not sure. It could have been a bad batch of pills. You take care, but don't wait two more years for your next appointment."

Her knees weakened and her legs slowly kneeled to the floor as she smiled, widely. "I'm not pregnant," she cried out loud. "Thank you, God. Thank you! Thank you!"

The curse had been averted and her goals remained intact, at least for the time being.

***

That afternoon, Rocky stopped by the diner to ask Kelly about the results of her pregnancy test. She was busy serving customers, so he sat at one of the stools next to the kitchen door and ordered a coffee. Once free, she approached him and gave him the exciting news that she wasn't pregnant and that the doctor had told her that even if they tried, it would be difficult for her to get pregnant again. He smirked, told her to take care of the bill, and rushed out, saying he had something important to take care of.

Later, over Rosita's house, she and Hope were almost out the door when Kelly remembered that she had promised to cover for someone on Saturday. "Rosita, I almost forgot. Can you watch her this coming Saturday from 11 to 5?"

"No, I can't. I'm sorry, but Saturday morning, we're driving to New York City to visit my cousin. We made the plans last weekend; I wish you told me before."

"George asked me on Tuesday, but I was so involved with school that I forgot all about it. Don't worry, though. Go and have a wonderful time, I'll figure something out."

CHAPTER TWELVE

Friday evening, Kelly peered at the clock. 7:45. Hope was watching her favorite cartoons, and Rocky hadn't come home yet.

"Hope, look at me for a second. Tomorrow, if my boss is OK with you being there, you'll come to work with me."

"OK, I like that."

As Kelly was walking to the couch to join her, the phone rang.

"Kelly, how're you doing?"

"Who's this?"

"I know it's been couple of years, and I'm sorry, but have we become total strangers?"

"I said, who's this!"

"My God, you really don't recognize me. This is your brother Carmine, how're you doing?"

After graduating from high school, Carmine had moved to San Francisco where he landed a job with an Internet startup that paid for his college. Intelligent and determined, he got his four-year degree in only three years, and quickly moved up the ladder.

"Good, and you?"

"Not so good." His voice heaved with sadness. "I'm back in the valley for few days, and I'm staying here at the Marriott in Shelton."

"That's a lovely place. I stay at the Marriott too whenever I travel around the world."

"Kelly, this is not the time. I came up because Dad is on his last days. I guess all that booze has finally caught up to him."

"I thought he was already dead."

"He'd like to see you guys. He cried when he asked me to tell you."

"My eyes spilled rivers of tears because of him. I was a child when he practically threw me out of the house." Her stomach was in knots. "I'll go see a strange dog dying before I go see him."

"I remember how badly he treated you, and as a father, I agree he doesn't deserve it, but he is still a human being seeking forgiveness as his candle melts down to its base."

Now she was crying. Over time, she had succeeded in resting that part of her life in the remote section of her brain, but her brother's sudden appearance had now roiled them to her front lobe again.

"I'm really, really sorry for how things turned out with you and Dad." Carmine paused for a while. "You do what your heart tells you, but I think you should go see him, if not for him, for you."

"Where is he dying?"

"At a hospice in Branford."

"I've got to go now." She wiped the corners of her eyes as she sat next to Hope.

"Mom, who was that?"

"Someone who dialed the wrong number."

She stared at the ceiling as her mind played the scene of her and her father that infamous day of her sixteenth birthday.

***

MY LAST CHANCE

Ross Dolan, sitting at the kitchen table with his left hand cuddling a full shot of whiskey and his right hand tightly cuddling a half-full bottle of the same, shouted, "Did you make any money today?"

Why was he bugging her again? "Dad, it's Saturday, remember? When people are home from work, they watch their own kids."

He gulped his shot. "Aren't you sixteen today?"

"That's what the calendar says," she replied, walking toward the fridge. "You actually remembered it."

"Every morning, as I walk through that factory door, my mind plays the day you were conceived, frame by frame, over and over." He poured another shot and gulped it at once.

"Dad, what's that supposed to mean?" She sneered. "The only thing you ever did on the birthdays that I can remember was to give me a cold shoulder."

"I don't celebrate mine, why should I celebrate yours?"

"I don't know. Maybe because I am your daughter, and that's what parents do, especially on their sixteenth birthday." Somehow, that day she did expect something. Something like a vanilla ice cream cake with sixteen burning candles, surrounded by friends and family singing to her like Angela's parents did for their daughter. She grabbed a slice of boiled ham, a slice of American cheese, stuck them between two slices of white American bread, and cut it in half.

"You all know the way to the fridge, but none of you know how it gets filled. I hope you were out looking for a real job this morning."

Her throat tightened into a knot. Anxiously gasping for air and rushing for the kitchen sink, she coughed and spat everything but her guts out. When the last bread crumb trickled down the sides of her face, she grabbed paper towels, wiped her face, and gave him a disdainful look. "You want me to pay for the little bit of food that I eat too? Isn't it enough that I have been giving you half of my money and paying for all my clothes and stuff since I turned fourteen?"

"Yes, something like that!"

"But how can I work fulltime, go to school fulltime, and keep my grades up?"

"That's simple. Quit that goddamn school and go to work." He gulped another shot and slammed the table with his fist. "I am sick and tired of supporting you all!"

"I can't quit. I love school, even my…" *Kelly, I am overly impressed with you.* Her math teacher's words from days earlier echoed through her thoughts. *I haven't had a student scoring a perfect hundred on that test in quite some time. Keep it up, honey, and the sky will be your limit.*

"Go to night school like other people do! Wasn't it enough feeding you for sixteen years?" He poured another shot and gulped it even faster than the previous ones. "There're still plenty of factory jobs out there where you can make decent money."

What had she ever done for him to be so angry at her? "I'm not quitting! I want more from my life than just a factory job."

"Is that right?" He stood up, fists firm on the table. "I am tired, you hear me! I'm sick and tired of working day in and day out for you guys!"

"You guys? We didn't choose to be born; you did that for us! If you stop spending all that money on your stupid booze, we'd all be better off."

He swung around the table, grabbed her by her arms, and pulled her face inches from his. Raised his right fist ready to strike. "Don't you ever, I mean, *ever* dream of telling me what to do!"

She held his arm back from hitting her. "If you ever try this again, I'll have you arrested!" She snatched the other arm from his stronghold and ran out the door.

***

The roaring of Rocky's Vet disrupted her thoughts. She rushed to the kitchen.

Rocky stepped inside, long hair glued to his jaws, water dripping down his face and arms, and grease marks scattered all over his shirt and jeans.

Kelly chuckled. "Did you get run over by a car and left in the pouring rain?"

"And you're fucking laughing?" he replied with a long face. "I had to go back to the shop and fix a fucking mower that I need in the morning."

"Dinner is ready. The faster you clean up, the faster we eat."

Rocky devoured his food, rushed to the fridge, grabbed another beer, and headed straight for the couch.

While puffing a cigarette, he flicked between the few channels over and over.

Kelly was washing the dishes. "What's bothering you?"

He stared at her for few seconds and turned his attention back to the flicker.

She put everything away and joined him on the couch. She looked toward Hope's bedroom to make sure that she was still in there. "I'm ready for you."

He pushed her hand off and slid a few inches away from her. "Not tonight."

She got closer to him again, leaned her head back to meet his eyes. "We can have sex without worrying now, isn't that great?"

He gave her a frigid look.

"Why are you pushing me away?"

His anger was deepening. He gulped his beer and grabbed another cigarette. "I had a fucked-up day, that's all."

Realizing that the ingredients for a fight were brewing, she got up, walked to Hope's bedroom to make sure she was asleep, and on her way to their bedroom, she teased him with a smile. "If you change your mind, I'll be more than ready for you."

CHAPTER THIRTEEN

"*Mommy, I thought we were* going to work?"

"That's at 11." Kelly crouched down and held her arms. "I took you here to meet your grandpa."

"To meet Grandpa?" Her eyes squinted. "But Mommy, once you told me that both grandmas and grandpas were up there with Jesus?"

A couple of years earlier, while Kelly and Hope drove back from school, Hope had asked why all the other kids had grandparents and she didn't. At the time, to tell her that they had all died sounded like a logical answer to get rid of the issue, but now she had to scramble her way out of the corner she had placed herself into. She noticed the nurse at the receptionist desk eavesdropping. Pretending to straighten Hope's purple blouse collar up, she whispered in her ear, "I'll explain it to you later."

There were beds with people waiting for their last breath in every room they passed. Most of them looked old and skinny and tired, while some looked much younger, but just as skinny and tired. Around midway there, her thoughts darkened like a winter night. *Is this how it all ends?* She let go of Hope's hand, pulled her sunglasses off, and wiped the corner of her eyes.

Just before they approached her father's room, she stopped, crouched in front of Hope again. "Listen, Grandpa is awfully sick," she whispered. "Don't get scared, OK?"

"I won't," Hope whispered.

The room was big and white. There were four hospital beds, all equipped with intravenous equipment from which tubes stretched to the patients' arms. Some rested sideways in a fetus-like position, and others leaned on their backs with their legs stretched to the end of the beds, their faces up toward the ceiling, their eyes shut, and their open mouths wheezing. Their jaws were sunken, their lifeless wrinkled skin whiter than milk, as if all the blood had been drained out of their bodies.

"Mommy, let's go," Hope said softly. "I don't like this place."

"I don't either, but we need to say hi to your grandpa." Her eyes searched the four beds a couple more times before she recognized him.

"Mommy, is he my grandpa?" Hope whispered, pointing at the bed in front of them.

"No." Kelly placed a hand on Hope's shoulder and pointed toward the other bed. "He's the one over there."

"Why doesn't he move?"

"They're all napping."

Kelly had just finished saying that when his head turned. He gave them a long stare, tears dripping on to the pillow. With her lips pursed, Kelly stared back. *Why don't you run me out now, you son of a bitch?* she thought. *Everything could have been so different.*

Slowly, he turned his head straight, grabbed both sides of the bed rail, and pulled his body up, so that his head sat a little higher on the pillow. He looked straight at Hope. "God, you got so big since I last saw you," his feeble voice ambled out of his dried paper like lips.

Puzzled, Hope looked at her mom and shook her head.

"What you mean since you last saw her?" Kelly said. "You never met her."

Exerting the top half of his body to his right, Kelly's father reached for the small tissue box on the nightstand. "That's true, and I'm so sorry," he muttered, wiping his tears, "but every chance I had, I watched you play at your school playgrounds."

As each word limped out of his mouth, the signs of rage on Kelly's face grew harsher. *He threw me out of the house because of her, and now he pretends to regret that they never met each other.* She grabbed Hope's hand and brought her to his side of the bed couple of feet from his face. "Honey, this is your Grandpa who today rose from the dead just to meet you before he goes back there again." She bent down closer to his ear. "And sooner rather than later, you son of—"

"What's going on?" a short chubby nurse interrupted. "Please, this is a resting place."

"I'm sorry," Kelly replied, face livid. "Hope, come on, say goodbye to your grandpa."

Before they turned to the next hallway, Kelly stopped and stared back at the door to his room. *I need to know.* She walked Hope to the lobby and sat her next to a magazine rack. "You wait here, I forgot to ask Grandpa something very important."

"OK, Mom, but please make it fast, I hate the smell in this place."

She walked to the desk, asked the nosy receptionist to keep an eye on her, and rushed through the hallway. The short chubby nurse was pulling the door behind her. "Excuse me, is it OK if I see my father for a couple more minutes?"

The nurse held the door ajar for her. "No problem, but please keep it low."

He was still in the same position she had left him, face up, eyes shut, and wheezing with his mouth wide open. She tip-toed to the bed and shook his shoulders, but he didn't move. He could be dead already. She shook him harder, and his eyes opened. "Why do you hate me?"

He stared up at her, motionless.

"Before you croak," she said softly, "why do you hate me so much?" Shook his powerless fragile body. "You hear me, why?"

Slowly, he leaned his head against the bed frame. "Please," he muttered, "bring that chair over."

Please? Huh. Growing up, he never acknowledged that such a word even existed. *I guess when the end is near, even beasts could turn into angels.* She grabbed the chair and brought it next to the bed few feet away from his face. "Go ahead."

"When I found out that you went back to school, I became the proudest person on earth. I just wish I had the courage and strength to come and tell you in person." He reached for a tissue and wiped his eyes again.

Her eyes bloated, and her mouth gaped. "Really? The last thing I remember, on my sixteenth birthday to be exact, you were demanding that I quit school, and now you expect me to believe that?" She sneered at him. "Look, I don't have all day. If you sent for me to clear your conscience, this is your last chance. Why have you hated me so much?"

Tears coursed down his sunken cheeks. "I never hated you. I was just an angry person that fell victim to the booze."

"So, now you're going to blame the booze?"

"No, I'm not." His hand tried to reach for hers, but he was too weak. "Please let me finish. When your mother and I fell in love, I was in the tenth grade and she was in the ninth. Throughout the rest of our high school years, we were the most envied couple around." His dripping eyes turned away from hers. "We were inseparable. We studied together and we both made the honor list every year. We had great plans. College, great jobs, get married and bring up our kids in a big ranch surrounded by acres of land, big enough to even have a stall with couple of horses in it."

"Those were pretty much my dreams too, but thanks to you, they have remained just that, at least until now."

He looked away from her and sighed. "Then I went away to college while your mother stayed to finish her senior year. Even though it was hard to only see each other once every few weeks, by talking on the phone, we were managing our distance well. Then came her cousin's wedding. After sneaking a couple of shots at the open bar, and then a couple more back at her aunt's house, we ended up in an empty bedroom on the second floor where you were conceived."

"Oh my God." She shook her head in disbelief. "And you threw me out of the house like a dog for the same thing that you and Mommy were just as guilty of?"

"Please, let me finish," he pleaded, gasping for air. "Nobody ever knew because we married right away when your mom was just one month pregnant. Trying not to have reality interfere with our long-term dreams, I committed myself to continue college at night, but it was hard to go to school with a family to feed. It was even harder to go from sitting in a classroom feeding my brain and soul to a sweat shop with greasy crumbling cement floors, dusty ceilings with more spiderwebs than lightbulbs on it, and pushing wheeled metal carts filled with wet linen from one machine to another all day long for little more than minimum wage."

Every morning, as I walk through the factory door, my mind plays the day you were conceived. The image of him seating at the kitchen table with the bottle in one hand and a shot ready in the other one saying that, rolled through her thoughts like a live picture.

"My mind couldn't cope with the sudden change, so, on my way home from work, I would stop for a drink or two at first. Then one month and a few more drinks at a time led to a semester gone. Another semester and few bottles later led to a year. Then just another bottle and just another day ultimately led me here."

Feeling both anger and pity, she stared wordlessly at him.

He dragged his body a couple inches closer to her. "You're much stronger than me, and smarter; don't let anything stand in your way."

She moved the chair back against the wall and started for the door. Stopped on the threshold, turned around, and looked straight in his eyes. "You have a nice trip, whether you're going there," her thumb pointed upward, "or there," her thumb pointed downward. "I hope they treat you better than you ever treated me." She pulled the door behind her and slowly walked down the hallway.

What do you want me to do, beat you up until you're black and blue, like my father would? Or say, I told you so. Halfway down, she leaned against the wall, looked up, and muttered. "Him, I can understand, but you? Why mom, why?"

With her dark-brown pupils barely discernable from the rest of her teary eyes, they stepped inside the car. "Honey, put your seatbelt on."

"Did Grandpa make you cry?"

"No," she said. "When I was walking through the hallway, a couple of fruit flies got inside my eyes." She wiped them with the back of her hand. "See, they're all gone now."

"Oh."

You're much stronger than me, and smarter. Don't let anything stand in your way. She tried to think back, searching for anything nice he had ever told her before today, but couldn't think of any. *Trust me, I won't. But don't go dying now worrying about me, the time you could have done that is gone.* With her mind still churning, she turned on to I95 westbound.

Hope laid her head back on the seat, placed her right elbow on the door over the open window, rested the right side of her face on the palm of her right hand, and stared at the guardrail, trees, and houses zooming by. "Why is Grandpa dying again?"

Kelly's mind now raced for an answer that would not make her sound like a liar. "See, sometime people die only in someone's heart, and other times they die for real. Grandpa is now dying for real."

"Mom, I don't understand. How do you die in someone's heart?"

"Honey, that's a long story and we have no time for that now." She turned into the diner's parking lot. "When we get in there, we are going to find you a nice table in a secluded area where you will quietly play with your drawing books, OK?"

"OK."

George was at the register giving a couple their change back. Holding Hope by her hand, they walked up to the coffee counter to wait for him to be free. Kelly approached him, explained him the situation that had unexpectedly surfaced, and asked him if it was OK for her daughter to sit in a secluded table while she worked.

"Kelly, does this place look like a kindergarten?"

His day must not have been going well because that was not his normal disposition, and she decided she better be careful. "I'm sorry, I didn't have enough time to find another sitter."

"You could have called me, and I would have replaced you."

"First, I didn't want to disappoint you, and second, you know that I need the money badly."

He stared at her for few seconds. "OK, this time I'll let it slide."

"Thank you." She walked back to Hope and led her to an empty booth next to the restrooms' hallway, settled her down, and started working.

They finished cleaning and setting the last few dirty tables for the dinner crowd. "Let's take our break before they start coming," Francis said.

Kelly looked around. There were only couple of tables occupied with customers chatting and sipping at their coffees. "Yes, let's do that."

"Do you want to go first?"

"If you don't mind, my daughter's bored look is piercing my heart."

"Sure, go ahead."

"So, let's see the drawings, young lady." Kelly caressed Hope's head and sat next to her.

"Here." Hope pushed the books to her side of the table. "I'm really bored, can we leave?"

"Just a while longer. You know, I think we both deserve an ice cream after all of this, what you think?"

Hope's face brightened right up. "An ice cream, yes."

"Kelly!" George hollered from the register with the phone receiver in his hands. "Someone wants to talk to you."

Quickly, she got up and rushed over to get the call.

"Kelly, this is Carlos. On our way to New York this morning, we got into a car accident."

"What?" Kelly's face turned ghostly white. "Oh my God, what happened?"

"We were banged up pretty bad and are in the hospital."

"What hospital are you at?"

"Bridgeport Hospital. We will be here for at least couple of days."

"I'll be right over." She turned to George, who had been eavesdropping. "My best friend has been in a pretty bad car accident, is it OK if I leave now?"

"Might as well, with that ghostly face you might scare my customers away."

***

They got the pass and directions from the front desk and rushed to the elevator. Kelly and Hope stared at Rosita and Carlos, crying.

Rosita's right leg was casted from her thigh all way down to her ankle, and her arms lying straight down to her sides, bruised, with multiple tubes hooked to it. She leaned her head to face her husband, who was stretched on a chair next to her bed, also napping.

"Mommy, can I go talk to her?" Hope whispered.

"No, not now. They need to rest, let's go downstairs for a while."

The nurse on duty motioned at Kelly to wait. "Is she awake?"

"No, we'll be back in a while." The nurse looked at the clock. "In a few minutes, it's time for her medication, there is no need for you to leave."

"Thank you." Kelly grabbed two magazines from a shelf next to the chairs they had sat in and gave one to Hope. If she had only asked Rosita earlier that she needed her to watch Hope that day, the accident might not have happened.

Sometime later, the nurse stuck her head out. "Come on in, they're both awake and eager to see you."

"My God, Rosita, what happened to you guys?" Kelly gently leaned over her and gave her a hug.

"Hope," Rosita said, "don't be afraid, come here."

Hope hesitated at first. Then rushed over and gave her a long hug.

Carlos offered them his chair and went to sit on the chair across from the bed. "Rosita, I just can't believe it."

"Kelly, me either. It must have been five to ten minutes after we got on 95 southbound. The traffic was heavy, ouch." She held her casted leg and labored her body to a straight position. "Anyway, I was on the cruising lane when this midsize car from the passing lane to my left cut in front of me and stopped at once. I yelled at it, rushed my foot to the brakes, but something snapped under my foot and the car crashed into his. When I regained consciousness, I was lying down in an ambulance with a couple of people all over me, and Carlos sitting to one side, praying and crying."

"That was scary," Carlos added. "We are lucky to be alive."

"Rosita, why would the brakes snap just like that? Didn't you have the car serviced recently?"

"Couple of months ago, but one of the cops told Carlos that when I stepped on the brakes with all my strength, the brake's fluid container cover snapped off, the fluid spilled, and the brake pressure was reduced to nothing."

"That's strange. I never heard of anything like it."

"The cop told me," Carlos added. "It's rare, but it does happen, especially with older cars."

Kelly got closer to the edge of the bed and held Rosita's hand in hers. "What's important now is that you guys are going to be fine and let the insurance worry about the rest."

"That's true, but until then, what's going to happen to my little angel here?"

"I got it under control, Rosita, just worry about getting well. And if you need me, please don't hesitate, I'll take time off from work."

"I'll never let you do that. I'm already getting ready for your graduation." She winked at Carlos. "He'll take care of me."

"Rosita, I just started school, but thanks for your confidence."

"I know what you are capable of." She looked at her husband. "What time is it?"

He looked at his watch. "It's 6:15. Why do you want to know, you're not going anywhere!"

"Oh God, we better get going." Kelly stood up. "It's already been a terrible day, I don't need to hear his mouth too."

"Yes dear, you better go. Carlos, now you see why I asked you for the time?"

On their way home, Kelly's mind churned vainly over what to do with Hope while she worked. Gilda had already spent too much time helping her with school, and Angela had just started working for her father.

***

Rocky was not even halfway through the door before he complained, "I passed by the diner around 5:30, and you weren't there!"

"So?"

"Where were you?"

She stared at him. "I'm tired, and I'm stressed, and I'm not in the mood for your bullshit!"

"But I am, where were you?"

"You really want to hear about my day?"

"Yeah, you have a problem with that?"

"Make sure you take it all in." She sneered, and step-by-step recounted her visit to hospice, her few hours at work, her visit to Rosita and Carlos. "And here we are."

He walked to the fridge to get his usual beer. "How badly is she hurt?"

"She'll be on crutches for a while."

"Well, shit happens, and this time it was their turn."

"That's all you have to say after all she has been doing for us?"

"She isn't doing a fucking thing for me."

Kelly threw her apron on one of the chairs. "You're right, shit does happen. Supper is ready there, and If you hungry, go make your own darn dish."

"Who's gon' watch Hope for you now?"

CHAPTER FOURTEEN

Upset by Rocky's cold reaction toward Rosita's and Carlos's accident, Kelly worked up the courage to follow Gilda's advice, and slept on the couch both Saturday and Sunday night.

Monday morning, Rocky pointed his index finger at her. "If I ever catch you with another man, I'll kill you both."

"I wouldn't go buy a gun anytime soon."

The weekend had passed, and Kelly still didn't have anyone to watch Hope. As Hope came out of the bathroom ready to go, Kelly held her by her shoulders. "Honey, I know this might be too much to ask of you, but you need to help me."

"Help you with what?"

"If I don't work, I must stop school and we will have no more money for us either. Which means not even to buy us an ice cream when we like."

Hope's lips curled. "That would not be fair."

"I know, and that's one of the reasons why I need to work." Kelly held her by her shoulders. "After school, you come to work with me, but this time you need to stay in the car. My boss doesn't like you to stay there while I work."

Hope's face drooped. "I have to stay in the car all alone?"

"I'll come out on my break to stay with you." Kelly caressed Hope's face. "And if Dad asks you tonight, you say you stayed at Gilda's house."

"But Mommy, you always tell me not to lie."

"Honey, that's true. But sometimes if a lie helps you and doesn't hurt anyone, it's justified."

"What's justifried?"

Kelly laughed. "No, honey, that's not the way you say. Justified. J-u-s-t-i-f-i-e-d, without the r."

Hope got her pen out and wrote each letter down. "I got it, but what does it mean?"

"It means that for the right reason, sometimes it's OK to lie."

"I get it, it will help you keep your job. Will you get me an ice cream when you come out to see me?"

"Of course. Let's go or we'll be late for school."

***

Kelly parked the car on the side of the building under a tree where she could keep an eye on it from the dining room's side windows. With her eyes welling, she looked at Hope. "Try to stay put on your side as much as you can."

"OK, but don't forget the ice cream."

"I won't." Kelly lowered all the windows an inch or so for ventilation and hugged her. "I'll be back soon." She walked toward the diner's steps, her heart sinking.

It seemed like time had come to a standstill. Kelly must have looked at the clock a hundred times, but only two hours had passed. Pondering if everything was OK, she snuck to the window to peek. No part of Hope was visible. When Kelly took her break, Hope was stretched in the back seat, sleeping. Kelly shook her gently. "Honey, wake up."

"Mom?" Hope jumped into Kelly's arms. "I'm so happy to see you."

"You sound scared, what happened?"

"A man looked in the window. Then when he tried to open the door, I screamed, and he ran away."

Was he just a concerned citizen? Kelly thought. *Or was he a creep?* "Come and sit in the front with me." Kelly drove to the grocery store, got Hope an ice cream sandwich, and drove back to park. "I have to go back now." She helped Hope to move to the back seat again. "Get some homework done, please? I'll be out soon."

"I love you, Mommy." Hope settled in the backseat and grabbed one of her books.

With a knot in her throat, and her stomach coiling, Kelly locked all the doors and slowly made her way back inside the diner.

Within a few days, their routine had become somewhat normal. She drove Hope to school first, and then drove to her school. After her classes were over, she would rush back home, prepare the main course for the evening's supper, get lunch ready, and pick Hope up from school. Then she changed in her uniform, ate a quick lunch with her, grabbed the books that Hope needed, and drove to work. At night, she got the rest of the supper ready and they all had dinner together. While Kelly would clean up, Rocky would plop on the couch with his beer and watch TV. Hope would go to her room to finish her homework or play with her toys. After cleaning, Kelly would do her homework, and when Rocky was horny, she accommodated him. That seemed to make him happy, and he hadn't stopped at the diner once.

Hope had successfully covered for her and appeared to have gotten used to the routine and the ice cream during her break, but Kelly could tell that she was forcing herself to smile. That was taking a toll on Kelly's emotions, and whenever she had a chance, she would go to the ladies' room to cry.

***

Friday afternoon, Gilda parked in the empty spot next to Kelly's white Subaru and noticed Hope stretched out in the back seat, sleeping. She knocked on the window, but Hope didn't move. She knocked harder, and Hope sprung up, rushed to the opposite corner of the seat, and screamed. Then she recognized Gilda, waved at her, and moved closer to the window.

"What're you doing all by yourself? Open the door."

"I can't. Mommy told me not to open for anybody."

"Isn't your mommy working?"

"Yes, she will come out soon, but please don't tell anybody that I'm here."

"OK." Gilda shook her head. "Does your dad know about this?"

"No, and please don't tell him."

Gilda rushed inside. Kelly was serving customers on the other end of the dining room, and George was talking to one of the cooks near the kitchen door. He looked at his watch. "What're you doing here this early?"

Gilda rushed over to him, "If you had returned my call, I wouldn't have to chase you. My paycheck is all screwed up." She took it out of her pocketbook with a sheet of paper clipped to it and handed it to him. "Attached are the correct calculations, leave the right check for me for tonight." She walked over to Kelly who was just about finished taking the orders from four customers. "Can I see you for a minute?"

"Gilda, what're you doing here this early?"

"It doesn't matter, I need to talk to you." She grabbed her arm and guided her toward the bathrooms. "What's wrong with you, leaving your eight-year-old daughter in the car all by herself?" she whispered. "Not only is it dangerous for her, but it's illegal and you could get in some serious fucking trouble."

Kelly's eyes welled. "I know, but Rosita was in an accident. I tried to find someone, but they all want almost as much money as I make."

"Have you lost my number?"

"You have your hands full already with your kids, your husband, your house, your school, and your work."

"I thought we had become close friends over the last few months?" Gilda's eyebrows lifted. "Where there is space for three, there is space for four, or even more. Monday you bring Hope to my house, and no ifs, ands, or buts."

Kelly wiped her eyes with the back of her hand. "I'm sorry." She hugged her. "It will only be couple of weeks; Rosita should be OK by then."

"Kelly, I will watch her for as long as you need me to."

"I better go put this order in before I get fired. So, Monday then?"

"You better."

After her shift was over, Kelly rushed to her car. Hope crawled into the front seat. "Mom, I'm so happy we're not doing this for two whole days."

Quickly, Kelly started the car and headed home. "Honey, guess what, starting Monday you don't have to wait in the car for me anymore, you're staying at Gilda's."

"Really?" Hope's face brightened. "Mommy, thank you." She leaned her head against her shoulder. "I get to play with Melina and Tommy, and I don't have to lie anymore."

"Yes, no more lies."

"Gee, I hope their pool is still open."

"I don't think so."

"It's OK, it's still better than staying in the car alone."

"You must do your homework there and not just play."

"Mommy, I know."

Right after they got into the house, Kelly started preparing the rest of the supper with renewed energy, and Hope headed for her bedroom to play with her toys. When Rocky walked through the door, she welcomed him with a cheerful smile. "Hi, honey."

"Hi." *What's wrong with her?* Rocky thought, walking to the fridge for his usual cold beer. "Did you win the lotto?"

"I wish."

"Then why you're smiling for?"

"I'm just happy that Rosita is getting better, that's all."

"Good for her." How the fuck was he supposed to win that war?

***

Two weeks into the fall, mother nature was clearly announcing itself with shorter days and temperatures in the low fifties. A fine rain had started that morning. Kelly had been working non-stop with a smile on from the time she had punched in. Tips were fast accumulating to an amount that she had never seen, and George had filled up the cash register drawer with an even bigger smile. He called her over, his hand on the phone receiver. "I need you to work a couple of extra hours tonight."

"I need to call Rocky and let him know first."

George told the waitress on the phone he would call her back and hung up. ""Why do you need to ask him, are you his little slave?"

"No, but I have to tell him to pick up my daughter." Kelly dialed Rocky's boss's cell phone number. She walked as far as the extension cord allowed her to.

"What the fuck you call me at work for?"

"A waitress called in sick, and I need to stay late. Can you pick Hope up at Gilda's?"

"I told you when you started working that these problems were yours."

"Supper is almost ready. We will have dinner around eight, please."

"What's in it for me?"

"I'll make you extra happy tonight, I promise."

"Everything I want, and no questions asked?"

"Yes, everything you want."

"What time do I pick her up?"

"I'm usually at Gilda's by 6:45."

"What if I go earlier?"

"I'm sure she won't mind."

"OK, this time only."

"I'll see you home, thank you." She handed the receiver back to George. "I can stay until 7:30."

"That's good enough. By then dinner time is almost over." George smirked. "So, he untied his leash for tonight?"

"No, I unleashed my own powers."

***

The house front door opened. Gilda walked to the car, shielding herself from the rain with an umbrella. "Rocky, what're you doing here?"

"Hi Gilda." He stepped out. "Kelly is working late, I'm here to pick Hope up. So, how're you doing?"

"You're just going to shake my hand, that's all?" She gave him a hug and a kiss on his cheek. "Kelly told me you had a 96 black Corvette, but I had never seen you with it."

"It's not a big deal."

"Why aren't you as excited about the Vet as you used to be about your blue Z28 Camaro?"

"Those times were different."

She stopped next to the driver door. "They were, but better I might say. Can I sit in it?"

"If you really want to, here." He opened the door and took the umbrella from her.

She rolled her sweater sleeves up to her elbows and stepped inside, hand gripping the steering wheel as she dropped her butt onto the red leather seat. With her left leg still out, her light blue skirt now stretched up to her thighs, she fully exposed her hash-brown bush and embroidered white panties. His eyes were ready to pop out of their sockets. Pretending to look away, he stood against the door panel, holding the umbrella.

She looked up at him. "Boy, that's pretty tight in here."

"Yes, it is." *Man, she is a big woman now, and that firm olive skin and that bush are getting to me*, he thought.

Noticing his bulging crotch right across from her face, Gilda opened her legs a bit more. "Hop in, I'll take you for a ride."

"No, that could be dangerous."

"The car?"

"Yes, the car."

"But you let me drive your brand new Z28 all around my neighborhood once, which was just as powerful as this, and I was only sixteen."

She is fucking horny for me, and my dick is getting harder by the second. Maybe I should get in, drive her to a secluded place, and fuck the shit out of her. But what if Kelly finds out? He shook his head. "Gilda, we'll do it some other time."

"We couldn't leave the kids alone anyway." She gave him her left hand, gripped the wheel with her right, spread her legs wide open again. "Help me out."

Rocky helped her up and out of the car.

"Rocky, do you have time for a coffee?"

"For a coffee, no, but for a beer and a shot of whiskey, yes."

"It's been a long time since you and I had couple of drinks alone. Remember those summer nights when I would sneak out, and we would drive to the park and hang around drinking and talking about your girlfriends?"

"Yes, I remember. I was twenty-four then and could have gone to jail for it too."

"True, but the memories of those times never left me. You know, I had a huge crush on you then. Kelly was only sixteen, too, but that didn't seem to bother you."

"Well, whatever happened, happened."

"Well, my husband is working late, and I need to skip school tonight, so yes, a beer and a shot it is." Gilda closed the umbrella, then the door, and hooked her right arm onto his left one. "Hope, look who's here?"

Hope and Gilda's children were in the sunken living room seating around the coffee table playing with all kinds of toys. "Hi Dad." She ran to hug him. "Where's Mommy?"

"She has to work late."

"Let me get my books and stuff."

"Not yet." Gilda looked at Rocky. "Your dad and I are going to chat for a while, you can play a little longer."

"Dad, can I?"

Rocky looked at Gilda's pleading face. "OK, just a little longer."

Gilda walked to the refrigerator, grabbed a cold beer, and snapped it open. "Follow me, the liquor is down the stairs."

"Holy fuck?" Rocky's eyes bulged. The area was almost half the size of the entire living space above, totally furnished with a wet bar with three stools and staggered glass shelves on the wall behind it full of whiskey bottles, mixers, and liquors of several types and brands.

"You like this room?"

"Fuck yeah."

Gilda got two shot glasses then pointed at the glass shelves behind her. "Your pick."

"How about a shot of that black label there?"

"Black label it is." She smiled at him and grabbed the bottle. "I like you to know that those stools are waiting for asses to warm them."

While she was pouring the shots, Rocky sat on the stool at the end of the bar.

"That's for you." She handed him a glass. "And that's for me." She moved around to the front of the bar and sat on the stool across from him. "Ready?" She put the shot to lip level. "Go!" She gulped hers almost as fast as he did his.

"Wow." Rocky shook his jaws. "That's a strong fucking shot."

"No kidding," Gilda replied.

Their bare knees touched, and her skirt hitched up to just below her thighs. Rocky snuck a peek but couldn't see more than the firm olive skin of her robust legs concealing her crotch.

"Rocky, I heard that Kelly loves going to school. Rumors are that she might make the college's top student this semester, isn't that great?"

"No, I'm not happy about her fucking school, and I'm not happy about her fucking job either."

"Why?" Gilda pretended to be surprised.

"Because I married her to be my housewife, that's why!"

"But she can still work, go to school, and be a housewife. The same thing I'm doing, and I'm not half as smart as she is."

"It's not the man's job to babysit or drive around picking his kids up because his wife is at school or at work?"

"Is that why Kelly was taking Hope to work with her when Rosita got into that accident?"

"What're you talking about, I thought you have been watching her?"

"Only after I found Hope sleeping in the car while Kelly was working."

"Fuck, they both lied to me."

"Rocky, it's not a big deal, come on." She placed her hands on his knees. "The important thing is that she is here every day now."

He gulped the rest of the beer. "Fuck, it is a big deal!" He stepped off the stool, ready to leave.

She grabbed his arms. "Don't leave yet. I'll get you another beer, and I'll join you for another shot."

He pulled away. "I'm fucking pissed off now!"

"Come on, please?" She dragged him back to the stool.

"When I asked her to marry me, I told her she was gon' be a housewife and always be ready for me for everything. In my family, women were all housewives, period. None of this fucking working and school bullshit."

She sat back on her stool and stared at him. *When he ignores me for more than a few days, my body goes into a craving mode.* As Kelly's words crossed her thoughts, her legs were slowly parting. She was so horny; she could jump him right there and then. "I'm sorry I brought it up."

"If she wasn't working, I wouldn't have to be here to pick up my daughter."

Gilda pressed her crotch against his right knee, hugged him tight, and looked straight in his eyes. "Aren't you happy that after so many years, we have a chance to drink and chat alone like this?"

"I guess so."

"Stay right here, I'll go get another beer for you."

He followed her swaying hips until she disappeared up the stairway. A big but firm ass, a huge set of tits, and a crotch as hot as a running furnace on a winter night. *She wants to get fucked, and I'm going to do her.*

"Big guy, here we go." Gilda handed him an open can of beer. "The same shot?"

As she passed, he realized she had sprayed herself with perfume. "Yes, the same shit." He set back on the stool.

She came around with both shots in her hands and stood across from him with her hot crotch pressing against his knee. Handed him one. "Ready?"

"More than ever."

She squinted and jittered. "Wow, I'm really feeling this one." She dropped her glass on the bar and rested her face on his chest.

Man, her crotch is on fire. He dropped his glass on the bar top and grabbed her ass. Parted his legs, moved his butt forward, and pulled her against him.

It's about time, she thought, gyrating her crotch against his rock-hard penis. *He should have been mine anyway.*

He snuck his hands under her skirt, squeezed her hard butt, looked straight in her blue eyes. "You got a great ass."

She pulled him off the stool and tugged him to the pantry. "Come on." Closed the door behind them, pushed him against the wall, and shed her clothing in seconds. "Take me, I can't stand it anymore." She sank her tongue in his mouth.

Faster than a lightning bolt, he dropped his shorts and underwear, bent his knees a little, and with a stealthy move, he was deep inside of her.

Oh my God, she thought as their tongues whirled and her vagina stretched. "Yes, yes…" *No wonder she takes all his bullshit.*

"Mommy?" Her little boy hollered from the top of the stairs. "Mommy, where are you?"

***

The moment Kelly walked through the door, Hope jumped off the couch, ran over, and gave her a long hug. "I missed you, Mommy."

"I missed you too." The sad thing about her working and going to school was that she didn't get to spend as much time with Hope as she used to. *Hopefully, the end will justify the means.* She looked at her husband, sitting on the couch, his eyes glued to the game. "Thanks for helping me out."

"Yep, and now I'm starving."

"It'll take me less than fifteen minutes to get the supper ready, but I'd like to shower first."

"Do that after you put my dish on the table."

"OK." She dropped her pocketbook on the kitchen table and walked to the refrigerator. Lit one of the burners and placed the pan full of chicken-nuggets with broccoli on it. Lit another one and placed the pot with hot water on it for the pasta. Surrounded by a cloud of smoke from Rocky's cigarette, Hope had kneeled by the coffee table to play with her toys. "Honey, get away from that smoke; it's not good for you."

"That's OK, it doesn't bother me."

"That's what you think. Go to your room and I'll call you when dinner is ready."

"But Mommy—"

"I said go!"

With her face drooping, Hope strolled to her bedroom.

"Why you're being such a bitch to her for?"

"I'm not. I'm concerned about her health and you should be too."

"Really?" His thin top lip was hidden below his bottom one. "Just like when you left her in your car for hours while you worked?"

She froze. "What're you talking about?"

"You know what the fuck I'm talking about. Don't play dumb with me." He walked to the fridge to get another beer.

"No, I don't."

"Oh, we've become a liar too now. Gilda saw her, and you both lied to me about it."

"And what was I supposed to do?"

"Quit your job, quit your school, and take care of me and your daughter like you used to."

"So, that we can be totally broke again?"

"Soon you will not be able to use that excuse anymore. Very soon."

She had never told Gilda not to tell him, but why would she? Kelly set the table. "Hope, dinner is ready!"

During dinner, other than the disconcerted rhythm of the utensils hitting the dishes, one could have heard the buzzing of a fly. Rocky devoured his dish, got up, took his car keys, and started for the door.

"Where're you going?"

"None of your business."

"I thought you wanted to—"

"That was then."

"I'll wait up for you."

"Don't bother." He slammed the door behind him.

"Mommy, why is Daddy so upset?"

"Honey, I'm not sure. Can you start cleaning while I take a shower?"

"Yes," Hope said, eager to please her.

Kelly relaxed in the warm water, letting the stressful thoughts wash away. Then she went to the kitchen and stood there, perplexed, and heartened. The table was spotlessly clean. The dishes and utensils were all washed and orderly, stacked in the drying plastic tray next to the sink. The sink itself and the countertop were dried and clean. And Hope, already in her pajamas, was lying on the couch watching a children's show.

"I can't believe you did everything for me."

Hope smirked. "Is it nice?"

"Honey, that is incredible." She gave her a long hug and a kiss on the cheek. "I'm so proud of you."

"You work so hard, I wanted to help you."

"Thank you." With one hand, she caressed her angel's face, and with the other, wiped the corner of her eyes.

"I don't understand why Daddy was so upset at you; he was happy when he picked me up."

"Remember those few days when you stayed in the car by yourself while I worked?"

"Yes, but Mommy, I never told him about it."

"I know you didn't, but I forgot to tell Gilda not to."

"But I told her not to tell anyone."

"You did?"

"Yes, I did." Hope held two fingers in front of her. "I told her two times."

"She must have forgotten. That's OK, Daddy will get over it."

"I begged her not to tell anyone," Hope insisted.

"Huh. Let's get you to bed now, I need to do my homework."

***

A streak of light piercing through the blind moved across her face. Her eyes burst open. *Oh God, we're going to be late for school.* She jumped out of bed and rushed to Hope's room. Shook her. "Hope. Hope, get up, we're going to be late for school."

Hope opened her eyes and stared at her for couple seconds. "Mom, it's Saturday."

"Is it?"

"Yes, Mommy, it is. Please, let me sleep a little longer."

Kelly rushed to the kitchen and looked at the clock. 9:45. Grabbed the coffee pot, stepped to the sink with her mind roiling, and got it going. It was a sunny morning with a deep blue sky, a mild breeze swirling the yellow and brown leaves from one side of the street to the other. As she relished the sight, she felt a throbbing pain in her temples. She placed her thumbs on both sides and pressed. How much wine had he pushed her to drink the night before?

On Friday, the evening after he had stormed out of the house pissed off, he came home with two bottles of wine, determined to have her make good on the promise she had made for picking Hope up the day before.

Gently, she shook Hope's shoulders again. "Come on, honey, now you got to get up."

"What's the hurry, Mommy, it's Saturday."

"We're going to visit Rosita. Please, hurry up?"

***

Standing on the threshold with a cane in her right hand, her signature smile on, and her black eyes glittering, Rosita welcomed them.

Hope gave her a hug. "I missed you, Rosita, but I do like playing with Melissa and Tommy."

"I see, you like them better than me."

"No, I like you better, but I like playing with them more."

"OK, I understand."

Kelly hugged her and handed her a box filled with Italian pastries. "I'm sorry I haven't been able to visit you more often."

"You didn't have to get me anything, and you don't have to apologize either. I know how hard it is for you with your work, school, and your two kids."

"You look great, Rosita, but how are you feeling?"

"Almost as good as new. My doctor said that I can even throw this cane away if I want to, but I figured I play with it for a little longer."

"I'm so happy for you."

Rosita led Kelly to the kitchen table. "So, how are things with you and your older kid?"

"One step forward, and at least one backwards."

"When is he gonna grow up?"

"I don't know. He still hates me for going to work and hates me for going to school. Every chance he gets, he tells me to quit both. I can't do that, and he better get over it."

"Your eyes tell me that it's not the only thing bothering you." Rosita walked toward the cabinets. "Let's make some coffee."

"Rosita, no, you sit, and I'll make the coffee."

"You know where everything is?"

"Have you forgotten that we spent over a week here this summer?"

"If you insist." Slowly, Rosita sat on one of the chairs and smiled. "How is school?"

"It's a lot of work, Rosita, but so far, it's going good."

"Kelly, I'm proud of you. I really can't wait for your graduation day."

"That's far away, Rosita. This is only my first semester, and unless I go to summer school too, I got three more to go."

"Mi amor, time flies. It seems yesterday that I used to walk to the university in my country, and that was over ten years ago."

"That's true. It seems yesterday that I got pregnant with Hope, and she can already do house chores almost as good as I can."

Rosita pulled the pastry box toward her. "Let's see what kind of goodies you got me." Her eyes bulged at the succulent pastries sprinkled with white confectionary sugar.

As they enjoyed pastries with their fresh coffee, Rosita steered the conversation back to Kelly. "Kelly, what else is bothering you?"

"It has to do with Gilda. I don't know if I should—"

"Kelly, you can tell me anything, remember?"

"I know. It's just that she has been so nice since we hooked up again. The other day, though, she did something that doesn't make any sense. On Fourth of July, you got to know her a bit. So, what you think of her?"

"Other than backstabbing her friend, she seemed nice."

"What do you mean by backstabbing her friend?"

"Remember when she introduced us to that girl that goes to school with her?"

"Yes, her name was…never mind."

"Gilda was all nice to her, but the moment she wandered away from us, Gilda trashed her."

"I do remember that. But she has done so much for me with the school and then with Hope after you got injured, I just can't believe she would do such a thing."

"What did she do?"

"While you were home recovering, I took Hope to work with me and had her wait in the car while I worked."

"That was foolish of you, what if something bad happened to her?"

"I know, but I didn't know what else to do at the time. I tried to find a babysitter, but they all wanted almost as much money as I was making."

"For how long you did that?"

"That first week, Monday to Friday. Then on Friday afternoon, Gilda came over to talk to George about her paycheck being wrong and spotted Hope sleeping in the car. After she got through with

George, she called me to the side, scolded me, and demanded to watch Hope for me, starting that following Monday."

"And what was wrong with that?"

"That was very thoughtful and caring of her. But then, this past Thursday, when Rocky went to pick Hope up for me because I was working late, she told him about it."

"And Rocky took the opportunity to start a fight."

"That too, but it's not what's bothering me the most about it. At first, I blamed myself for not asking her not to tell Rocky, but then Hope told me that she pleaded with her not to tell anyone, not once but twice."

"And Rocky loved to get one on you."

"Of course. And as usual, he told me to quit both my job and school." Kelly set her coffee down. "But why would Gilda do that? That's what I can't get my mind around."

"You should ask her straight out."

"I'm afraid that she might get offended and then—"

"And then she would stop watching Hope for you?"

"That would be bad, but I also wouldn't want to destroy the friendship we've developed over the last few months."

"As to your friendship with her, I would be wary from now on. As for watching Hope, you don't have to worry about it anymore." Rosita placed her hand over hers and looked straight in her eyes. "I feel good enough to take over the job again."

"Rosita, no, you still need to take it easy."

"Don't worry, I'm fine." She smiled. "Besides, didn't you just say that Hope can already do house chores almost as good as you?"

"Since I started working, she has grown up a lot."

"I think we'll help each other. Monday you'll bring her here."

Back home, Kelly called Gilda, determined to ask her why she had told Rocky, but after Gilda's disappointment that she would no longer watch Hope, Kelly decided to leave that question for another time.

CHAPTER FIFTEEN

By late November, Kelly had worked out her schedule to fit everything in. Rosita had happily re-embraced her surrogate grandmother role with Hope, and Rocky, taking advantage of the slow landscaping season gradually approaching, continued to expand his drug dealing business with his main goal to get Kelly to stop school and quit her job while escalating his affair with Gilda.

***

The Wednesday before Thanksgiving, Kelly and Rocky argued about his rejection of Rosita's invitation to spend Thanksgiving with them. They were barely talking, and she had been sleeping on the couch, refusing to have sex with him for the entire weekend, which pissed him off more than usual because Gilda wasn't able to get away from her family either.

The Monday after Thanksgiving was a true November day, partially cloudy and chilly with occasional gusts of wind whirling the piles of leaves that Rocky had laboriously gathered. Another pile, another gust. "Fuck this shit," he shouted, gathered his tools, and took off. Sometime later, he parked the pickup truck a hundred yards or so away from the main entrance to the school's multi-story building, the same building he had seen in a pamphlet that Kelly had brought home when she first thought about going back to school. From there, he could clearly see each student going through the door without being too conspicuous. His watch marked quarter past one. He lit a cigarette and started puffing, his eyes fixated at the building. It was fucking impossible that no one in this school had tried to go after a beautiful woman like Kelly. There she was. *Who the fuck is that guy talking to my woman so close? Goddammit, I knew it! Fuck, that son of a bitch just kissed her.* Rocky turned the key, and after a few hits and misses, the engine started. Weaved his way through the parking lot, but by the time he got to the other side, the guy was gone. Turned his eyes toward the exit and saw his wife's Subaru waiting to pull out on to the main road. He jerked the steering wheel around and rushed after her. Peered at his watch. It was almost time for Hope to get out of school. *I'll get her ass tonight.*

***

"So, how was your day?" Kelly asked Hope on their way down the stairs from Rosita's house.

"Mommy, we did a lot of things together, I even helped make dinner for Carlos," Hope replied. Then her lips pursed. "But I miss playing with Melina and Tom."

"I promise you, sometime soon we'll get together with them."

The Vet was already parked in its spot. What was Rocky doing home so early? Kelly held the door open for Hope who was struggling with her backpack and saw Rocky stretched on the couch watching TV. "Go to your room quietly, and I'll call you when dinner is ready." In her bedroom, Kelly snatched her uniform off, put her velvet light-blue jogging suit on, slipped her feet in her old brown suede slippers, and tiptoed her way back to the kitchen.

The running faucet woke him up. He looked at her for a minute or so. "Did you have a lovely day?" he asked.

Still searching for a package of spaghetti in the cupboard, she turned toward him. "I thought you were sleeping?"

"Did you have a lovely day?"

Puzzled, she squinted at him. "I guess so."

He grabbed her butt. "Are we gon' do it tonight?"

"You're hurting me, stop." She pushed him away.

"Is that a no?"

She checked the water, and it was ready to boil. Dropped a spoonful of salt in the pot, followed it with a spoonful of olive oil, and stirred them together.

He grabbed her arm and pulled her toward him until their faces were inches apart. "Goddammit, answer me! Is that a no?"

She snatched her arm away. "When you start treating me with respect again, and not like a piece of meat to be taken at will, I'll think about it."

The creases of anger on his face deepened. He grabbed her by her shoulders and shook her. "Is that how that pretty guy who was making out with you this afternoon treats you?"

"Let go of me."

"Is he your lover boy now! Answer me, goddammit, answer me!" He shook her even harder and raised his right hand, ready to strike her.

Hope ran out of her bedroom and, realizing that her dad was about to hit her mom, grabbed onto his jeans pocket and tried to pull him away with all her strength. Defeated, she fervently started punching on his back with both her fists. "Stop it, Daddy, stop it," she cried, tears streaming down her cheeks. "Stop it!"

He lifted Hope up like a baby doll and threw her on her bed. "You're gon' stay here until I call you, you hear me!"

"Don't hurt her. Please, Dad, don't?"

He shut the door behind him and walked to the fridge to grab another beer.

Kelly stood at the stove, ready to drop the spaghetti in the pot, tears streaming down her cheeks. "Are you spying on me now?"

'No, I got someone else doing it."

She stopped stirring the spaghetti. "I should take this potful of pasta and throw it on your face, so that you could look as ugly as you sound."

"If you're ready to die, go ahead."

She shut the flames under the spaghetti pot and moved it to the sink to run chilly water through it. "I never cheated on you, never." She looked at him with disdain. "And the tall pretty guy that you're talking about is gay. He kissed me on the cheek to thank me for helping him study for a test we had just taken."

"I don't fuckin' believe you. You're saying that so that I don't beat you up."

"Be there Wednesday at the same time that your spy was there today and ask him yourself."

With the menace in his voice dissipating, he asked, "Is he a faggot for real?"

"He is gay, not a faggot," she replied. "He's nice and respectful, and that's all I care about."

Well, if he's a faggot, he thought, *but I still got to get her out of those fucking brothels, and fast.*

***

At the Italian coffee shop, Angela was waiting impatiently at one of the tables next to the picture window. Kelly brushed the snowflakes from her knee length coat and rushed inside. "Hi, sorry I'm late."

"Girl, after I see your grades, maybe I'll accept your apology."

Kelly swept her hair off her shoulders. "I need a mean espresso today."

"Then let's load it with a shot of Sambuca."

"No, I have to be at work soon."

"Girl, it's five days before Christmas, you just got through your first semester of college, and winter is here."

Kelly thought about it for a second or two. "What the heck, but today it's on me."

"Sister, no." A bit later, Angela placed the tray down in the middle of their table. "What's a great coffee, if not paired with a tasty heavenly ricotta imprisoned in a crispy pastry shell shaped like a tubular flying saucer?"

"Angela, that is the most fascinating description of a Cannoli I ever heard."

"So, why were you late?"

"After I got my grades, we went to the public phone and I called you." She pulled a neatly folded paper from her purse. "Then, since it was the first time that Hope was there with me, I decided to give her a quick tour of the school. The delay got me stuck on Route 8 behind an accident, and by the time I dropped Hope off at Rosita's, I—"

"Sorry, how is Rosita doing?"

"She's totally recovered, thank God. Anyway, and here I am."

"Sister, can I see your grades now?"

"Here." Kelly handed Angela the slip of paper. "They're almost as good as in high school."

"Three As, one B plus, and one B? I'm ashamed," Angela joked. "You're right though, in high school these would have most likely been all As. But considering that you have been away from school for so many years, I forgive you."

"I could have done better if it hadn't been for…" A sad look surfaced over her face.

"If it hadn't been for what?"

"I'd rather not talk about it," Kelly said, looking through her pocketbook for a tissue.

"Since when are there things that we can't talk about?"

"You're right." She stared down at her empty coffee cup. "Couple of weeks ago, Rocky accused me of cheating on him with a classmate of mine. Someone told him that I was intimately kissing him in my school parking lot."

"No way." Angela leaned closer, held Kelly's hands in hers. "Were you?"

"Angela? Of course not. His sick mind though didn't believe me, and at one point he was ready to hit me. Then once he accepted that my gay classmate was not a threat to his manhood, he retreated."

"Kelly, it sounds like he is getting worse and worse."

"The next night, I was in bed dozing off, he flopped next to me smelling like a whiskey bottle and asked me to have sex. I slid away, a rare thing for me to do with him, and buried my face in the pillow, sobbing over what he had put us through the night before. He grabbed my left arm and forced me on my back. Locked my arms over my head and forced my legs apart. For fear of horrifying Hope again, I tried to fight him off without yelling, and the last thing I remembered afterwards was him saying, 'I told you so,' and the excruciating pain as he forced himself into me like an enraged bull."

Angela reached for her hands, shook her head. "That's terrible, what you're going to do about it?"

"What can I do?"

"I would go to the police and have him arrested."

"I thought about it for a while, but it didn't make sense. How are they going to believe me after almost nine years of marriage?"

"That son of a bitch," Angela said, enraged. "It's difficult, but not impossible."

"And if they would believe me, then what?"

"Then he'd get arrested."

Kelly rested her elbows on the table. "How could I ever explain that to Hope? She would forever remember that her mother caused her father to go to jail. And even though he is not the best father to her, she still loves him and would never forgive me."

"So, you just gon' take it?"

"If I never went back to school, things wouldn't have gotten this far." She wiped her eyes again, looked at the clock behind the counter. "It's almost two, I have to get home and get ready for work." She got up, put her coat and her beanie on, and started for the door. "Angela, thanks for listening."

"Wait. I'm worried about you, what're you going to do?"

"Maybe I'll quit everything. That for sure will put an end to this craziness."

"That will put an end to your life-long dreams too." Angela looked straight in her eyes. "Don't do it."

Kelly pursed her lips, her eyes watering, and stared at the snow falling faster and denser.

"Hey." Angela held her by her shoulders. "I'm always here for you, stay strong."

"Thanks." Kelly started walking toward her car.

Angela rushed after her. "Wait? I was not going to tell you this, but after what you just told me, I feel it is the right thing to do. A week or so ago, I was going to my office, and driving in the opposite direction on the Boston Post Road, I thought I saw Rocky in his company pickup truck with a chubby lady next to him. She had her face covered with a scarf and a set of dark sunglasses."

"He must have been driving one of those rich clients from Orange to get stuff for their yard or something. At times, he does bitch about some of them who insist on picking out landscaping stuff themselves."

"Kelly, think. A head scarf in December, OK, but sunglasses with hardly any sun out?"

"Angela, I must go now."

"Kelly, don't quit."

CHAPTER SIXTEEN

The holidays passed without any major incidents, or a reversal of Rocky's negative attitude toward her work and school. And after her fury had dispersed, being the obedient wife she had been molded to be, she again laid on her back whenever he wanted to satisfy himself, even if at times she couldn't help but to fake her orgasms.

As the school vacation days came and went, between work and chores and spending quality time with Hope, whenever her mind was not occupied with something else, her thoughts would automatically land on both her school and work dilemma. The more she churned over her choices, the clearer it became to her that quitting and falling back into the same trap she had been struggling to get out of for so long wasn't an option anymore. She decided to explore the possibility of accelerating the road to her graduation. Snuck a ride up to the school and met with her counselor to design a schedule that allowed her to graduate by the end of the next fall semester.

***

Just over a week into January, winter was beginning to make its stand. It was supposed to be Hope's first day back to school from the holiday break, but the local TV station reported that all the grade schools in New Haven County remained closed due to forecasted snow. She called Hope's school and there was no answer. The sky was a blanket of gray, cold and calm. A ghostly calm with the familiar scent that precedes a snowstorm, but there were no flakes in sight yet. Kelly checked the mailbox, and, among a couple of local store flyers, found a letter from her college dated Friday January 5th, 2001. It stated that the Spring Semester accounting class for Tuesdays and Thursdays from 10:00 to 11:30 am was canceled and had been combined with the Tuesdays and Thursdays 5:00 to 6:30 pm class.

Shit. She had been there that same day and her counselor had said nothing. Kelly dug out her upcoming spring schedule, sat at the kitchen table, and studied it for a while. If she could change her work schedule from Tuesday and Thursday to Saturday and Sunday mornings, it could work. She'd have to sell George the idea that she'll be working two extra hours on his busiest mornings of the week and beg Rocky to watch Hope Saturday and Sunday mornings.

***

At the diner, she waved at George who was halfway through the double-swing kitchen doors. He turned around and met her halfway. "What you're doing here this early?"

"I need to talk to you. In private, though, if you don't mind."

He placed his hand on her shoulder. "In private?"

She winced at his sneaky look. "Yes, in private."

George motioned Francis over. "Take care of the register, I'll be right back."

"Do I get paid extra for it?" Francis joked.

In the office, he motioned her to seat on the chair across from him. "Shoot."

"I don't think it's a big deal for you, but it is for me."

"What did I do now?"

"It's nothing about you." The chair squeaked under her. "One of my Tuesday and Thursday morning classes has been canceled and replaced with a night one on the same days. Normally it wouldn't matter, but this is one of my accounting classes that comes in sequence. If I don't take it now, it will not be offered until next spring, and I can't afford to wait until then."

He drew a sigh of relief. "Kelly, and what does that have to do with me?"

"I need you to change my schedule from my Tuesday and Thursday afternoons to Saturday and Sunday mornings."

The frown lines on his forehead became so deep they resembled tributaries. "And how do you expect me to do that?"

She was just beginning to make good money there. Her teeth nipped her bottom lip. *Shit, if he doesn't go along, I'm screwed.*

He leaned forward and folded his elbows on the desk. "Kelly, my Saturday and Sunday morning staff has been the same for years now. I can't just take any of them off?"

Her eyelids wilted over her eyes. *I guess I will have to look for another job.*

"Kelly, say something, for God's sake."

"Since you can't make the change for me, and I can't afford not to take this class now, I was thinking of where to go to look for another job that will fit my schedule." She grabbed her pocketbook from the floor and took a step toward the door.

"Wait!" He motioned her to sit back down, shook his head, and stared at her. Even though she had only been at that job for six months, she worked as if she had been a waitress for years, and customers loved her. Many would only go there when she was working, and he was aware of that too. "I thought you couldn't work weekends because your husband doesn't have time to watch your daughter."

"That was then. Now I have no choice, and if he doesn't have the time to watch her, I'll have to find someone who does."

"What's your rush anyway?"

"I have to graduate by the end of this year, and to do that, I need to take this class now."

He sank back into his swivel black leather chair. "So, if I find the way to accommodate you, and you will graduate, then you'll find a better job and good-bye George. Doesn't that sound like I will be shooting my own foot?"

"George, you're kidding me, right?"

"That's true, isn't it?"

"Getting a job in the field I'm studying for, of course, it's true. But first, I doubt if I get a job right away, and second, I can always continue to do my twenty or so hours a week here easily. Especially if you let me work on weekends."

"Sure, you say that now, but once you get that job—"

"George, one of my main goals is to buy a nice house, and that takes a lot of money. You work with me, and you're gon' have me around for a long time."

"That would be nice."

"So, are you going to work with me or not?"

He stared at her for a while. "If the girl you will replace goes nuts at me, you better come to visit me at the hospital."

"George, so that you know, I'll also be working few extra hours with that schedule."

"That's good. I like that end of the bargain. When does your new schedule start?"

"The week after next."

He grabbed a pen and a notepad and started scribbling on it. "And you will work the 7 a.m. to 1 p.m. shift, both Saturdays and Sundays?"

"Yes."

He looked at the calendar on the wall behind him and pointed his pen in one of the squares. "Let's see, that will be the week of January 21st?"

"Yes. Now I need to go up to the school. Is it OK if I take today off?"

He rubbed his large hands. "Kelly, is there any more stress you'd like to throw at me today?"

"I'm sorry, but if I don't get there before 5 p.m. today, I might be too late."

"And where am I gon' find someone to replace you in such a short notice?"

"Few weeks ago, when one of the girls called in sick, you found me only an hour before my shift ended."

"You are good." He shook his head. "You're really good."

"I have an idea. I know Francis loves breaks. I can ask her to go home now and come back around three or so, work till 6:30, and I'll take over for her now instead of two-thirty."

"In those clothes?"

She winked at him. "I'll pretend to be your assistant manager for those hours."

He dialed the number at the register. "Francis, come to the office, please?"

Kelly explained the change to her, and she went along as Kelly had predicted.

George shook his head. "Thank you, Francis, we'll be right out."

"See George, problem solved."

"You're a persistent pain in the ass, but a good one. Maybe someday you'll run this place for me."

"I'll remember that." She got up, and went to punch in. Two down, and one to go.

***

The spiraling ash-sized snowflakes were now coming down quite dense. The emergency lanes had amassed an inch or so of the white powder, but the driving lanes were still mostly black and feeling normal under the tires.

She got to school around 4 p.m., and by the time she got through the process of re-registering for a class, she stepped out of the building with the last of the school staff following her. She held her coat collar up and around her face and made a run for her car, a hundred feet or so away. Once in the car, she remembered about the mozzarella she needed to finish the lasagna prep that she had started that morning. Instead of turning onto the highway, she went downtown first.

Later, the further down Route 8 south she got, the slower the traffic was moving. And by the time she got to her exit, an hour or so had passed. How handy it would have been to have a cell phone. Through the town, the traffic was not as bad, and the snowplows were already out. Her driveway was a thick white blanket. She parked in her usual spot and rushed inside. Looked at the clock. 6:15. Picked up the phone and dialed Rosita's number.

"Kelly, are you home?"

"Yes, I got stuck on Route 8 for a long time and just got here. Rocky could be home any minute, can I pick Hope up after dinner?"

"Yes, Mommy," Hope hollered in the background. "I'm helping Rosita cooking."

"Don't worry, Hope will have dinner with us."

"Rosita, I feel so terrible to impose on you like this."

"Do what you need to do, and whenever you're ready, we'll be here."

Kelly turned the oven on, cut the mozzarella in tiny slices, took the rest of the prepping, and properly placed everything in a deep glass baking tray one layer at a time, covered it with aluminum foil, and placed it in the oven. Looked at the clock again. 6:50. Rushed to the bedroom, undressed, and jumped in the shower. Minutes later, rushed to Hope's bedroom closet, grabbed his favorite black dress and her embroidered black panties, slipped the dress over her naked body, and as she was about to step in her underwear, the front door blasted open. "What the heck!" she yelled, rushing out of the bedroom.

"Son of a bitch," he shouted, "it was only supposed to be few inches, and now it turned into a fucking storm." He hustled the door shut and started beating the snow off his clothes.

"Rocky? Darn it, you made my heart drop to the floor. Couldn't you have beeped the horn or something?"

He stared at her. "Why, you're hiding some fucking guy in here?"

She had hoped for him to make a normal entrance. Annoyed at his remark, she just walked over to the oven and checked on the lasagna.

He took his black ski mask and his black winter coat off and hung it next to her coat on the hanger. Picked up his snowplowing clients' list from the top of their TV and sat at the kitchen table.

"I hope you're hungry."

"What kind of question is that?" He flipped through the address book. "I'm fucking starving."

"Then you're up for a real treat. I made lasagna for you," she said with a smile, hoping to get him in a better mood.

He gave her a mute stare and resumed writing his clients' names and addresses on a yellow pad.

She walked back to the stove, bent down, pulled the tray halfway out, and removed the piece of aluminum foil. Instantly, a luscious aroma spread throughout the house.

His head rose at once. "It's about time that—" His jaws dropped. "What happened to your fucking panties?"

Hastily, she reached around to smooth down her dress. "Your feet were barely inside the door when you started this bullshit. What do you want to hear from me, that I'm cheating on you?" She walked closer. "I'm not, but are you?"

He smirked. "Of course, I am."

Her right eye began its impulsive twitching. She thought of asking him about the lady Angela saw him with in his company truck but considering that it would escalate the argument and cause him to dislike Angela even more than he already did, she decided to let it go. After all, her main goal for the evening was to persuade him to help her watch Hope on weekends. "You probably are."

Lips curled, he squinted at her. "Remember, I have eyes on you everywhere."

"You can have thousands of them, it doesn't matter." She turned her attention back to the stove. "I am a one-man woman."

For a while, the only audible sound was the roaring wind blasting snowflakes against the windows. He sprung up at once. "OK, then how the fuck you explain this!" Pushed his chair aside. "I called you at work, and some bitch told me that you went up to your school. Then I called you here three times, between 4:30 and 5:30, and there was no answer. I came home and found you preparing a dinner that must cost at least twenty-five dollars, and when I left the house this morning, you told me you had just enough money to put gas in your car."

"I worked for couple of hours and earned some decent tips."

"OK, I'll give you that. I stormed inside and found you with your sexy dress on, looking as shocked to see me as if you had just seen a ghost of Christmas past. You bent down to check on the lasagnas, and when I looked up, I found myself staring at your bare ass and your black hairy crotch." He pressed his fists on the table. "How the fuck you explain that?"

She placed the lasagna tray on top of the stove, looked straight in his infuriated eyes, and shook her head. "Explain what?" She picked up a butcher knife and started chopping the lasagna into serving portions.

He stepped closer to her and pointed his index finger close to her nose with his head tensed like a rooster ready for its mortal peck. "Since you're not fucking telling me what happened, then I tell you!"

"Go ahead, crystal ball, I'm all ears!"

He raised his right arm, as if ready to strike at her. "For the last time, don't fuck with me," he yelled, blending his breath with hers. "Sometime today, you brought your daughter to Rosita. Then you took off from work, came home, put your sexy dress over your bare ass, and zoomed up to school to meet someone. And after you fucked him, or he fucked you, you came home to prepare a nice dinner to cover your tracks, right?"

Her face drooped at the garbage fabricated by his sick mind. What had happened to the Rocky that she once knew?

He grabbed her shoulders and shook her. "Am I right?"

Wordlessly, she stared at her feet, her mind roaming through years' past.

"And if wasn't for this unexpected crazy storm to delay you, your plan would have worked perfectly." He shook her arms again. "Right? Answer me! Goddammit, answer me!"

With tears flowing down her cheeks, she looked up at him. "You've become a sick man. Since the first day we met, I never looked at another man that way."

"No, you're the sick one." He shook her again, but stronger this time. "Goddammit, answer me!"

"Let me go," she shouted, jerking her body back with all her strength until she managed to free herself. Snatched two overused ceramic dishes from their ancient cabinets, dumped two portions in his, one in hers, and tossed them onto the table. "Aren't you hungry anymore?"

He sat back down. "You bet your ass I am, but you don't eat until you tell me what the fuck happened today!"

The bottle of Chianti was on the counter next to the refrigerator. Hoping to cool things down, she picked it up, opened it, and sat across from him. "Here, you go first."

"Fuck the wine! Just talk!"

"OK, if you really listen, I'll tell you my day step-by-step."

He pounded his fist on the table. "Stop the bullshit and spill out the truth! The fucking truth!"

"Which truth do you want to hear? Your version would be a lie, and I can't lie. So, if I can't lie, how can I tell you your truth?"

"Goddammit, speak English!"

She poured wine in both glasses, placed one in front of him and took a sip from the other. Then rested her glass on the table and, slowly whirling it, she stared at the clear red substance. "There was a time you loved it when the only thing separating my skin from your touch was this dress." With her eyelids wilted, she peered at him. "Remember that cold December night, a little after we had moved into our first house?"

"Yeah, so what?"

"Even though we don't have a fireplace here, it's still winter and cold, and I was trying to mimic that night, hoping to open your eyes that with me going to school and getting a better job, we could have that same lifestyle again. Together we can do it," she pleaded. "I loved that house, the fireplace, and our lives then. That night you went wild when you snuck your hands under my dress and felt my bare skin. And later, our sweaty naked bodies twirled until the fire died."

He stopped chewing. "When the fuck you're gon' tell me what happened today, ah!"

"You forgot to shut the TV before you left this morning. I got up to get Hope ready for school, and while I was making some coffee, the channel you had on announced that New Haven county schools were closed due to forecasted snow precipitations. I called her school to make sure, but there was no answer. I looked outside to check the weather with my own eyes, and I noticed there was mail in our mailbox. I grabbed it, and among a couple of fliers, there was a letter from my school. It said that if I wanted to still take my accounting class, I needed to go to the registration office at once. I dropped Hope off at Rosita's, went to work for few hours, and from there, I went straight up to the school. After I re-registered, I stopped at the store to get the bottle of wine and the mozzarella for the lasagna and headed back home. I got the lasagna ready for the oven, took a quick shower, and when I was about to step in my panties, you blasted the door open."

"Wow, what a crock of shit!" he said, eyes narrowed.

"Go to hell then!" She grabbed her fork and scooped up a piece of lasagna.

"OK, what time was it when you brought your daughter to Rosita's?"

She was about to take her first bite and her forkful froze at the edges of her lips. "Really?"

"Yeah, really!" He said with stronger signs of rage surfacing all over his face. "What time did you bring her to fucking Rosita? Goddammit, answer me!"

She threw her forkful of lasagna back in her dish. "My daughter? Wow. Not Hope, or our daughter. Wasn't it you that summer night howling 'I love you' as you climaxed inside of me?"

"I want the fucking answers!"

"I have nothing else to say."

"I will be the judge of that. Why did you go to fucking school today when your classes don't start until next week?"

"I had to change my schedule."

"Why?"

"I just told you." Her eye twitching faster. "My daytime accounting class was canceled and…"

"And what?"

Her stomach was now coiling. She had only had breakfast and a muffin with a cup of coffee at work during her short shift. "I had to change it for an evening one because the same class isn't offered until next spring, and that would be too late for me. I want to get a better job as soon as possible."

He laughed. "Sure, like a decent job is just there waiting for you. You're a fucking dreamer."

"Maybe I am, but everything starts with a dream." She swallowed a mouthful of lasagna, barely igniting her taste buds. "It's a dream that I intend to make happen."

Until couple of weeks earlier, when he looked at the grades from her first semester, he was upset about

her going to school as much as he was about her working, but in the back of his mind, he had thought that

her going to school wouldn't last. As for her work, he believed that once he bought the house she wanted, she would go back to stay home, and his problems would be solved. Now though, hearing that she wanted to graduate as soon as possible, he had no choice but to take her seriously.

He devoured his last bite. "When you're planning to graduate?"

"December of this year, but to do that, I need your help."

He sneered. "You're kidding me, right?"

"No, I'm not."

"You know fucking well that I don't even want you to stay in school, and you have the balls to ask me to help you do just that?"

"Yes, and I would really appreciate it."

"And what kind of help would you need from me?"

"Once I go back to school, I need you to watch Hope on Saturday and Sunday mornings while I'll be working, and If sometimes my classes run late on Tuesday and Thursday evening, you pick her up from Rosita's at 7:30 and watch her until I get home."

His top lip disappeared below his bottom one. "What did you say?"

"I need you to watch Hope on Saturdays and Sundays while I'll be working, and if sometimes my classes run late on Tuesdays and Thursdays, you pick her up from Rosita's at 7:30 and watch her until I get home."

With rage sprouting all over his face, he just stared at her.

"Why you're looking at me like that for?"

He sprung up. "I'm not watching shit!"

The curls around her temples were now dampened. *My God, his face looks just like my father's did on my sixteenth birthday. I should have known better than to ask him.*

"I get it!" He rushed around the table. "You're fucking your accounting teacher!" Grabbed her by her arms, pulled her up, and shook her like a sieve. "What's his fucking name!"

Struggling relentlessly to free herself from his stronghold, she screamed, "You're going crazy. I'm not screwing anybody!"

"That's very clever of you! While I'll be here watching your daughter, you'll be fucking your brains out with him."

"Darn it, let me go!"

He raised his hand, ready to strike. "Am I right? Goddammit, answer me!"

With her free hand, she held him back as far as she could. "If you hit me—"

"What's his name?" he shouted, shaking her arms with his jaws nearly touching her forehead.

"Let me go!"

"You're quitting that fucking school. School no more. You're quitting!"

"You are crazy!" She pushed her body back as far as she could. "I am not a quitter!" She thrust her knee against his crouch with all her strength.

His hands jetted to his crotch, his body cringed, and his knees locked. "You're a fucking whore," he yelled, body contorting.

She ran to the door, grabbed her coat, and with one foot already out, she yelled again, "I'm not a quitter!"

Still holding his crotch with one hand, he wrestled out the door after her. "Get your ass back here, you bitch. You're not a quitter, huh? Goddammit, I'll show you!"

Struggling through the whirling winds and the amassing snow, she screamed, "I'm not a quitter! And I'm not going to be your thrall anymore either!" The visibility was bad, and as she was rushing between two parked cars to cross from the street level on to the sidewalk, her right foot hit a hidden elevation and her body fell straight down like a sawed tree trunk, her face embedded in snow, her arms stretched above her head, and her dress fluttering above her hips, leaving nothing between the snow and her naked body. Impulsively, she planted her arms to her side and sprung up in a cobra-like position. Shivering, she grabbed the freezing bumper next to her. "You bastard, why do you have to be such a thick-minded jerk?" She stretched her knee length coat around her legs and as she covered her knees, a stinging pain expelled from her left one. She caressed the area and felt the warmth of her blood. Dammit. She leaned to her right and peeked at her house a hundred feet or so away, but the fierce winds battering the snow made it difficult to discern anything. She shouted again, "I'm not going to be your thrall anymore!"

By the time she reached Rosita's front deck, she was limping badly. She sat down to catch her breath, and as she took her right slipper off to empty the snow from it, she noticed her ankle was almost double its normal size and burning hot. *Shit.* She tapped the slippers against the vinyl siding and quickly put them back on. Then struggled her way up, limped her way to the edge of the deck, and looked up. Except for the kitchen and one of the bedrooms, all the lights in Rosita's apartment were out. She put some pressure on her right ankle, and almost fell. Limped her way to the door and tried to open it but it was locked. Even if she tried to go back home, she would never make it that far. Pushed the doorbell and waited. After a few more rings and no answer, she limped her way to the back of the house, hoping to make it to the second floor through the outside deck before she froze to death.

CHAPTER SEVENTEEN

Rosita was sitting on the chair at the end of the bed with her head down, her eyes shut, and her arms wrapped around Hope's body stretched across her legs, sleeping.

Kelly's eyes had remained sealed from the time she was brought to the hospital, but now suddenly her body started jittering, her arms fluttering, and she mumbled, "I'm not a quitter, I'm not a quitter…"

Rosita's and Hope's heads sprung up like bullets. Rosita rushed to the right side of the bed and Hope to the left. "Honey, everything is gon' be fine."

"Mommy, please stop moving so crazy?"

Kelly's eyes flickered open. "Where am I?"

Tears flowed down Hope's face. "Mommy, I'm scared, please stop."

Rosita fought to keep herself from exploding into tears too. "You're in the hospital, dear."

Kelly's face was pale with scattered black and blue marks. "Why am I here, what happened?"

Rosita grabbed Kelly's hand. "Last night, I had just put Hope to bed when I heard the sound of glass shattering downstairs. I switched all the outside lights on and stepped onto the deck. I noticed the garbage pail laying on the snow with a few pieces of glass scattered around it."

With each word that came out of Rosita's mouth, her eyes narrowed, and her temples twitched.

"I realized that the shattered glass must have come from the basement door, and I worried about the cold freezing our heating pipes. I grabbed Carlos and we rushed downstairs. After he picked up the garbage pail and taped a piece of cardboard over the broken glass panels, we traced the fresh steps going up to the first-floor deck. There were wide marks next to the cleaning supplies, like somebody was dragging themselves. We approached it with caution and called out, but there was no answer or any motion in there. As we got closer to it, we saw a body covered with all kinds of rags from head to toe. Shocked, we jumped back. Then Carlos cautiously approached the hut again, carefully removed all the rags, and there you were." Rosita wiped her tears. "You were out cold. For a moment, I thought it was the worst."

"That's true, Mommy. I thought you were dead, and I started screaming like a crazy person."

"Then I screamed," Rosita continued, "and our tenants, who had just made their way into their place, stormed onto the deck. We brought you into their apartment, called 911, and here you are. Gracias a Dios we found you on time, but by God, what were you doing there?"

"I'm sorry." Kelly looked at the box of tissues on the nightstand to her right, grabbed couple of them, wiped her tears, and motioned her not to talk about it in front of Hope.

"Mom, did Daddy hit you?"

"Kelly, wake up while you're still on time, please?"

"Rosita, why you're saying that for, she is awake now?"

A nurse knocked on the door. "There is this Rocky guy at the nursing station who says is your husband. Should I let him in?"

Kelly and Rosita looked at each other, lips sealed.

"Does that mean yes?"

Kelly thought for a bit longer. "OK, let him in."

Rosita, frustrated, held her hand. "Should we stay?"

"Hope, are you hungry?"

"Hungry? Mommy, I'm starving."

Rocky pushed the door in and froze with one step still out in the hallway. "What the fuck…"

Hope rested her face on her mom's chest.

Rosita took couple of steps toward him. "You better watch yourself."

"Or what?" he muttered.

"Let's go get breakfast." Rosita grabbed Hope's hand, who was now looking at her dad with disdain, and they started for the door. "Kelly, we'll be right back."

Rocky approached the left side of her bad. "What the fuck happened?"

Wordless, she just stared at him.

"You're gon' talk to me or what?"

"What did you expect would happen to me after you chased me out of the house in that terrible storm?"

"I expected to find you home after my snowplowing rounds."

"And how did you know I was here?"

"That bitch's husband told me."

"You better watch your mouth."

He looked at her wrapped foot. "You fell and fucked up your foot."

She looked away.

"Am I right?"

Her jaw tightened. "If you hadn't been such a jerk, none of this would've happened."

"So, now it's my fucking fault that you ran away?"

She lifted herself up to a half sitting position. If looks could kill, he would have instantly crumpled into a pile of ash.

Slowly, he walked to the end of the bed and sat in Rosita's chair. "OK, maybe I did go a bit too fucking far last night. Just the thought of you being with another man drives me crazy."

There was a time when she would have taken those words as a compliment, but no more. "If you can't trust me anymore, let's put an end to us right now."

"What you're saying?"

"You heard me!" She leaned forward, her tone surly and firm. "But I'm going to repeat it for you, so that there is no misunderstanding. If you can't trust me anymore, let's put an end to us right now."

"How're you gon' afford the rent, all the expenses, and going to school too?" he said with an I-got-you kind of smirk.

"That would be my problem."

His mind wandered back to the argument they had had a few months earlier, and when the next day he went home from work, he found himself all alone. That fucking Rosita had become one of those fucking ticks that he just couldn't scrape off his skin. "I was just kidding."

"But I'm not. I'm not going to be enslaved in that dump for the rest of my life. I'm going to graduate and find a decent job so that I can have a better life for me and our daughter."

"And what happened to that staying together in sickness and health and all the other bullshit?"

"Those vows apply to you too. So, stop being a possessive jerk for no reason at all, back me up instead of working against me, and then we might talk again."

Their eyes did the talking for a while.

He hated to apologize. When you're the anvil, you take the hit, and when you're the hammer, you do the hitting, he remembered his father telling him growing up. At that moment in their relationship, he realized he was the anvil. "You're right. I have been acting like a jerk with you for no reason. I promise when you come home, things are gon' be different."

"And if I come home, you're not going to bitch about me working and going to school anymore?"

His leg shook. Then he stared at the floor, like a child caught with his hands in a cookie jar. "I guess I'll have to get used to it."

"You mean that?"

He lifted his head up. "When you're coming home?"

"I'll have to think about it, and awfully hard."

***

Rocky drove his company truck to the parking lot exit. Before he merged onto the road, he stopped. To go home from there, he should have taken left, and to go to his employer's shop, he should have gone straight. Instead, he took a sharp right and drove straight for the public phone booth a mile or so down the road. "I need to see you."

Gilda was lying on the couch, still in her red negligée, holding her cell phone to her ear. "I was just taking a nap."

"It's been almost two weeks; don't you miss me?"

"No foolin'. My husband's dick must have gone in lethargy for the winter. Not that it would make much difference. What about your wife?"

"We have been arguing a lot, and she has been a fucking bitch about it."

Gilda smiled widely. "These past two weeks, I've been getting mini climaxes just thinking about us doing it, but right now it could be dangerous. When Kevin left for work this morning, he wasn't feeling that good and could come home anytime."

"I'm sure he didn't drive almost forty miles to get to Stamford and come right back. I'm hornier than a bull in heat, come on?"

She pulled her negligee up to her hips, folded her legs up, slithered her hand through her black panties and started feeling herself. "Shit, you're getting me so fucking horny. Where are you?"

"At the pay phone in front of the Derby library."

Through the dining room French doors, she could see scattered snowflakes dancing about. "Looks like it's gon' snow though, let's do it tomorrow."

"If you don't want to get out, I'll come over, and we'll do a quick one on the floor right in front of the doors, so that we can keep an eye on the snow as I pound my exploding dick inside of you."

Her face turned redder, and her vagina got hotter and wetter. At that moment, she wanted nothing more but for him to be right there on top of her, but that would be asking for trouble. "No, I'm afraid Kevin might come home early, and the last thing we need is to get caught."

"Gilda, it's only 10 o'clock?"

"Going to work sick this morning and with those flurries dancing around, I have the feeling he could walk through that door any minute."

"Why don't I pick you up then we fuck our brains out, and before the snow starts coming down heavy, I'll take you back home."

"What if Kevin is home already, how am I going to explain you dropping me off?"

"OK, then take your car and follow me."

"Rocky, this is crazy."

"And more exciting, isn't it?"

"OK, screw it. I'll meet you in thirty minutes at that same motel we went the last time." She flew off the couch, put her winter shoes and winter coat on, and left.

An hour or so later, gasping for air, he slithered off her back and gazed at the ceiling with his arms spread wide.

Also gasping for air, she leaned against the headboard, sweating. "I swear, that was the longest orgasm I ever had."

He reached for his pack of cigarettes on the nightstand, lit one, and took a long puff. "Was my arm-twisting worth it?"

She smiled. "I wish my husband aroused me like you do. But then again, his dick is less than half the size of yours."

With a proud smirk, he looked down at his crotch for a while. "I wish my wife was more like you."

Gilda tickled his side. "And cheat on you while you're working?"

"No, not that part. I meant as horny as you and do the same things you do for me."

"I thought she loved having sex with you."

"How do you know that?"

"When we first got together for coffee, we talked about a lot of things."

He sat up, turned toward her, and leaned on his elbow. "What else did she tell you?"

"That you're a stubborn old-fashioned Italian, who got terribly spoiled by a homemaker mother and molded by a fascist-like father."

"Is that so."

"And that you're very tough to live with, and..."

"Keep going," he gestured.

"We talked about the old days back in school before she snatched you away from me."

Where was she getting the idea that his wife had snatched him away from her, when at the time he thought of her more like a younger sister than a girl to hang out with? "But you weren't my girlfriend then, how can you say that?"

"I would have been, if she hadn't come around." Her face sagged. "You have no idea how many times I regretted that moment I invited her for that Memorial Day party."

Rocky liked her firm voluptuous body, especially her ass, which was at least double the size of Kelly's. Loved her huge tits and her great blow jobs. But no way he would have ever chosen her over Kelly. "How many boyfriends did Kelly have before I started dating her?"

"She was always studying or babysitting and rarely went out with boys like my girlfriends and I did. But occasionally, she did hang around the bowling alley with Cody. You know that handsome Ansonia cop who was at my Fourth of July party."

His top lip disappeared below his bottom one. "Really?"

"Why you look upset? You were not only hanging out with a lot of girls then, but you were also fucking them all."

"Yeah, but I'm a man."

"Come on, Rocky."

"How far did he get with her?"

"I don't know, but I think Kelly was still a virgin when she started dating you."

"That I know, but did he play with her pussy?"

"She told me couple of times, but so what?"

"Goddammit, she should have told me when I asked her!" He got up, took his clothes, and walked to the bathroom.

"Where you're going?"

"To get dressed."

"Rocky, it's not even twelve yet, let's do it again?"

"No," he yelled from the bathroom, "we're going home."

Maybe that's what Kelly meant about being molded by a fascist father, because it was Rocky's way or no way. Disheartened as Gilda was at that moment, she had never been as sexually satisfied and happy since they started their escapades. She would take his fascist ways over her meek husband forever with her eyes closed. Slid off the bed and quickly started putting her clothes on. When he came out of the bathroom, she stood behind him, ready to go. He opened the door and took a quick look around to make sure there were no familiar faces or cars nearby. To their surprise, the parking lot was a blanket of white, an inch or so thick.

"Fuck, it's coming down earlier than I thought. You want me to follow you just in case your car gets stuck?"

"Yes, but I'm gon' take the side road off of Milford road, so we don't take any chance that someone from the diner sees us."

"Don't worry about it, Kelly is in the hospital."

"What happened?"

"On her way back from school, she fell and hurt her right ankle."

"That's terrible. But school doesn't start for a while, what was she doing up there?"

"She had to re-register for one of her classes that was changed from mornings to evenings. At least that's what she fucking told me."

By the time they reached Gilda's house on the hill overlooking the valley, there was at least two inches of snow on the pavements with no tire or shoe marks anywhere, which meant Gilda's husband hadn't come home from work as she thought he would. She stopped her car halfway through her circular driveway, lowered the window, and waved at him parked alongside the road.

He signaled her to wait, stepped out, and walked over to her car. "Would you like me to plow the driveway for you?"

"Mhmm," she thought for a while. After he finished plowing the driveway, if she could persuade him to sneak a shot of scotch at her bar, she could seduce him to get laid again. "That would be nice, let me drive the car straight in the garage then."

He set the truck to the beginning of the driveway and carefully started plowing. Still in her winter coat over her red negligee, she was leaning against the door frame, watching anxiously. He reached the end of the driveway, turned around, and went back to the beginning to plow the other half. While positioning the truck, he noticed Kevin's car coming up the road. Lowered the window and waved at him to follow his truck as he made his second run.

At the sight of her husband's car, Gilda's face went from looking like the bright side of the moon to its dark side, and by the time Rocky got through, Kevin had slowly driven his car in the garage. Rocky parked the truck and started walking toward him.

Meantime, Gilda had walked down the steps, and had rushed inside the garage. "Honey, are you still sick?"

"Sick as a dog," he replied, holding tissues to his red nose.

"Sorry to hear that," Rocky said.

"Thank you."

Gilda stroked his face. "You look so pale, let's go inside and I'll make some chicken soup for you."

He glowered at her. "Why did you have him plow when our guy will be here later as usual?"

Rocky realized that there were doubts brewing in Kevin's head, and quickly stepped in. "Early this morning," he said, sneaking a wink at Gilda, "I stopped for coffee at the diner and promised her that if it snowed again today, I would plow her driveway for free. You guys are always so nice to us."

"I figured our guy could be really busy and I said yes," Gilda quickly added.

Shivering, Kevin gazed at Rocky. "Don't get me wrong, I appreciate your nice gesture, but our guy never lets us down. What am I going to tell him now?"

"Kevin? Now you're gone make Rocky feel bad."

"It's OK, Gilda. Maybe that was stupid of me because I wouldn't like it either if one of my customers did that to me." He shook Kevin's hand. "Man, I hope you get better soon." Shook Gilda's hand. "And you take care of him." Then turned around and started walking toward his truck.

"Thank you, Rocky," she hollered after him. "Next coffee is on me." Then held her husband's arm. "Let's get you inside and while you rest, I'll make the soup for you."

Kevin watched Rocky drive away. He shook his head. "Our guy has been great, why would you do that to him?"

CHAPTER EIGHTEEN

Before Kelly was discharged from the hospital with minor frostbites on a few of her toes and a dislocated ankle, Gilda had called and offered to help her with all her school needs until she got better.

A week or so later, Kelly was sitting on the couch with her right foot resting on a pillow on top of the coffee table and browsing through her homework when Angela paid her a visit with a doll for Hope, and a half-dozen still-warm Cannoli for her.

Angela gave her a long hug. "Sister, how are you doing?"

"In a couple of weeks, I should be as good as new. Look, my toes are looking normal again, and the swelling on my ankle is almost gone."

"Forgive me for not coming over earlier, my father is driving me crazy."

"Hey, you don't have to apologize."

Angela whispered, "So, he blew out of control because one of your classes was changed from mornings to evenings?"

"Help me to the kitchen table?" Kelly nodded toward Hope sitting next to her.

Angela grabbed the pillow under Kelly's foot and helped Kelly. Pulled two chairs out, placed the pillow on one of them, and helped her sit on one and rest her injured foot on the other.

"Now we can talk freely." Kelly settled down and recounted her fight with Rocky up to when she woke up in the hospital, and when later she told him to either trust her or they should go their own way.

"Kelly, I am really worried about you guys."

"Angela, it was my fault too for running away in that terrible weather."

"From what you told me over the phone, it was either that, getting a beating, or calling the cops?"

"I guess I didn't have much of a choice, did I?"

Angela hugged her again. "Sister, if you need me to watch Hope on the weekends, I can always take her with me while I go around showing properties."

"If Rosita couldn't, I had you next on my list."

"Aren't you going to have one of those delicious Cannoli?"

"If you make the coffee and have one with me, I will. The coffee is inside the fridge, and our coffee pot is on the counter there."

"What're you going to do about school while you're recovering?"

"Gilda offered to get all the assignments and class notes for me, and when I go back, I'll take all the quizzes and tests I've missed."

"What about your job?"

"George has been very understanding. He told me to take care of myself, and when I am ready, my schedule will be ready for me too."

"Kelly, since the arguments seem to be getting worse and worse, what're you going to do about it?"

"So, what do you think of this rat hole?" Kelly gestured from one side of the house to the other.

"You know I'm not going to lie to you. You're right, it's not even close to the house you guys used to live in, but it's clean, organized, and cozy, and I know that it's only for a little longer."

Kelly smiled. "You really have that much confidence in me?"

"I have no reasons not to, but you still haven't answered my question."

Kelly had hoped that by changing the subject, she wouldn't have to. "Since I came home from the hospital, he's been a different person. He drops Hope off to school in the morning and picks her up later, something he had never done before. And with me guiding him from the couch there, he prepares the lunch and dinner for us. He even does laundry when needed, and together with Hope, they clean the house too. Even when he tried to have sex with me the first couple of days, I complained of pains, and he stopped without bitching. Maybe he has finally realized that he does have a problem and is trying to work it out."

"Huh," Angela muttered as she filled the two cups of coffee. "Didn't you once tell me that your grandfather used to say that a wolf changes its fur, but not its habit?"

"I did," Kelly replied with a smirk, "but he never said all the wolves."

"When I was in L.A., I had the misfortune of dating some guys like the Rocky you have been describing. And whenever they acted unusually nice, especially after a big fight, they became like a quiet storm brewing until they finally erupted into a hurricane. That fight was usually worse than the one before."

Kelly took a bite, chewed slowly. "What if he is the wolf that also loses the habit and not just the fur?"

"For your sake, I really hope you're right."

At that same instant, Rocky barged through the door and froze. "Angela?"

Angela giggled. "Yes, that's me."

"Hi, Dad." Hope jumped off the couch and ran over to hug him.

"You see what I mean?" Kelly whispered. "They were never that close before."

Angela nodded.

Rocky hung up his coat. "Were you guys mocking me?"

"No, I was telling Angela what a good father and husband you have been since I got back from the hospital."

He looked at the Cannoli box and then at Angela. "Can I have one of those?"

"Ask your wife, I brought them for her."

He placed one hand on Kelly's shoulder. "Honey, is it OK if I take one?"

"This is too much." Kelly looked up at him. "You're really spoiling me."

He grabbed one, took one bite, and more than half was gone. Brushed his free hand through her long hair. "I did it before, why not again?"

Angela had been around the block few times and easily recognized the counterfeit types like Rocky. If she stayed there any longer, she might say something that she'd later regret. She looked at her wristwatch. "It's getting late, I better get going before the roads get bad."

Rocky looked at her. "You're right. As matter of fact, tiny ice crystals are starting to fall, and I also drove over some black ice."

"Angela, why don't you stay for dinner?"

Angela gave her a long hug. "Thank you, sister," she said, "we'll do it some other time." Walked over to Hope, whose eyes were still glued to the screen, and hugged her. "Take care of your mom."

"Auntie, thank you for the doll, she's beautiful like you."

Rocky had already walked to the door and was waiting to open it for her.

She looked back at Kelly. "Sister, if you need anything, just call me."

"Don't worry, she'll be fine," Rocky said, closing the door after her. He grabbed a beer and sat on the couch next to Hope, took a long gulp. "What're all these papers and books doing here?"

"My homework from yesterday's classes. Gilda dropped it off."

"Oh." He smirked. "You want me to make dinner?"

"To tell you the truth, that Cannoli filled me up."

He turned to Hope. "Honey, how about you?"

Hope rubbed her stomach. "Daddy, I ate that whole pastry."

"I'm not gon' cook just for me then." He gulped the rest of the beer. "I was gon' meet with a new snow plowing client later, might as well go now." Got up, grabbed his coat, and headed for the door.

"Can't you just call them?"

"Kelly, my boss didn't make me a partner for nothing."

***

Rocky parked his company truck in a secluded area of the commuters' parking lot, lights off, engine running, and started puffing and grumbling, eagerly scouting the driveway five hundred feet away. "Why the fuck is she helping her with school?"

Gilda's car was making its way into the lot. He turned the lights on and flashed his high beams on and off until the car steered toward his truck. Pushed the passenger door open. "Jump in, it's fucking cold."

"No foolin'." Shivering, she hopped inside.

He put the truck in gear and drove toward the lot's exit.

"Where are we going?"

"To my shop. I'm sure my boss is still in some bar somewhere, and the place is off the main roads."

"Are you that horny to get me out of the house with my husband and my kids there?"

"And you're not?"

"What you think I'm doing here?" She moved closer to him, unbuttoned her coat, pulled her uniform up to her thighs and pointed to her dark-brown-bush.

"Fuck yes! What did you tell your husband?"

"I told him I had to get my anxiety prescription refilled, and since it would take me at least an hour at the pharmacy, I'd go straight to work from there."

"You never told me you were on anxiety pills."

She cuddled his arm. "I used to, but thanks to you, I don't have to anymore."

He pulled in the shop's parking area, parked the truck in its usual spot, switched the lights off. "It's getting too warm in here." He juggled his coat off.

"You right, help me take mine off too."

"Tell me something. Why are you fucking helping her with her homework?"

Gilda hesitated for couple of seconds. "When I called her at the hospital, she was busy with the doctors and couldn't talk. When she called me back, we chatted for a while, and then she pleaded with me to help her with the school until she got better."

"Fuck, you know I can't wait for her to quit."

"What was I supposed to do, say no?"

"Yes!"

"At that moment, I was in no position to answer her any other way."

"Fuck, you are so good at making up stories for your husband, why didn't you come up with a good one for her too?"

"Since that day that my husband found you plowing our driveway, he has been asking questions that he never used to. When Kelly called me back, he answered the phone and hovered around me during our entire conversation. I thought that if I denied her the favor after we have been so close lately, my husband would have questioned me for sure, which could have led to who knows what."

"Just find a good fucking excuse not to help her."

"Rocky, listen to me. In college, when a student isn't present at the lectures for couple of weeks or more, I don't care how smart you are, you will have a tough time catching up. Her current accounting course is a tough one, and if she fails it, she will not be able to graduate as she planned and might just give up."

His face brightened right up. "Fuck, you did have a plan then."

"You bet." *By the end of the year*, she thought, *Kelly gets her wish, and I'll get mine.*

CHAPTER NINETEEN

On Monday February 5th, Kelly had fully recovered and resumed both her school and her work schedule. As she had feared, there were several quizzes awaiting for her, while at the same time she had to keep up with the ongoing classes and more quizzes and tests resulting from them.

She was in class fifteen hours a week, at work twenty-five, and the rest of the time doing housework, house chores, and studying. After a month or so, she was so overwhelmed that at times she did entertain the thought of giving it all up. Then, when she would think of how hard it had been just to get to where she was, and for how long she had wanted it, a burst of energy would slither through her body, causing her brain's eye to see the graduation day and a brighter future ahead instead.

Rocky, on the other end, upset that she hadn't quit school, began to go back to his old self, arguing about every little thing. She wasn't spreading her legs for him as much as he wanted her to. His clothes weren't washed on time. The food didn't taste as good as it used to. Refusing to pick Hope up from Rosita's those few times she had been a half-hour or so late from her night classes. The reversal to his old self-made things more difficult and stressful for her, but after many sleepless nights, and a lot of persistence, by the third week of April she had caught up on all her school backlog and was readying to sit for the upcoming final exams with everyone else.

MY LAST CHANCE

***

"Hey, man, you got my three g's?"

"Yes, Rocky, if you give me a chance," Jay said, annoyed.

Normally, Jay would give him one gram or half-gram packages already weighted, and when he needed more, they would meet somewhere where Rocky would hand him the sales proceeds less his cut and get more product from him. That deal though was an unusual one, and Jay had collected the money in advance, so he only had to give him the responsibility to make the delivery.

"Here." Jay handed him a brown paper shopping bag. "Your money, and the stuff is all in there. I also gave you two extra packets of five grams each to cut for your own customers."

Anxiously, Rocky opened the bag and skimmed through the stack of the one-hundred-dollar bills, a few fifties, and some twenties. "What I have stashed away, plus this, I have enough to buy her the fucking house she wants," he muttered.

"Are you bitching about your wife again?"

"Who else?"

"I can't believe you still won't let that go. She wants to better herself, let her be."

Rocky looked at his watch. "It's 10:40 and it's Thursday," he said, shaking his head. "I bet you I know exactly where she is at this moment, and who she's hanging around with."

Jay sneered at him. "I don't care about your sick bets. She's in school, of course she's gon' make friends."

Rocky pounded the dashboard with his fist. "That's why a woman belongs at home!"

After numerous sneaky weaves through the car-stacked lanes on the highway, he spotted an empty space next to a light pole a few hundred feet from the building's main entrance door, close to the spot where he had parked his company truck weeks earlier. His watch marked 11:30. She was still on her break. A young couple, holding hands and tittering, was walking toward him. "Hey, you, where is the cafeteria?" Rocky asked.

The girl kept walking and chatting with her friend.

"Hey! Where is the goddamn cafeteria?"

The young man stopped his girlfriend. "We heard you, it's over there!"

"You cocky fucks, was that hard to do?"

Muttering to each other, the couple picked up their pace and never looked back.

Suddenly, like ants retreating to their nest, students from every direction of the campus grounds began to flock toward the cafeteria door. Rocky barged through them to get inside and stood next to a table already occupied by four students. There must have been hundreds of them in there, some already sitting, many in line at the food station, and many more just walking around. The hall sounded like a beehive in distress. *What the fuck is this? And what the fuck are those old women doing there with books in their hands?* He shook his head and started walking along the food station, scanning the crowd from side to side. At the sight of a female head with long curly black hair sitting at a table across from a good-looking muscular young man, Rocky stopped at once. *Goddammit, I knew it.* He rushed to their table and grabbed her shoulder. As the young woman turned to look up at him, his jaws dropped.

The young man sitting across from her stood up. "What's your problem, old man?"

Nearby students went silent, eyes fixed on the two of them.

"I thought she was someone else, that's all." Rocky forced a gentleman-like posture. "I'm sorry."

"No problem." She shrugged. "These things happen."

"Screw that!" her male friend yelled, taking a threatening posture.

Rocky gave him a reluctant stare. "Listen, I have no time for this bullshit right now." He stepped aside to walk away.

The young man blocked his path, grabbed his arm. "But I do!"

On the opposite side from where the commotion was escalating, Kelly was sitting at a table with her classmate that Rocky had accused her of fucking, and as she was talking to him, he was eyeballing the scene.

"What're you looking at?" Kelly asked, turning her eyes in that same direction. Her face became as red as a hot pepper.

"You know them?" Kelly's friend asked.

Kelly should have skipped school for the day. First, that cokehead giving her a threatening look, and now her husband ready to get into a fight in a place that he shouldn't be. She pushed the food tray to the side, gathered her books. "I need to go. I'll see you in class on Monday."

Rocky jerked the guy's hand off his arm. "You do that again, and I'll snap your fucking head right off your faggot body."

Another student approaching the food line noticed the commotion. What the heck is that Rocky guy doing here? He saw his classmate facing him in a fighting posture. Rushed over and stood between them. He grabbed his classmate's arm and pushed him back. "Are you crazy, challenging that guy?" he whispered. "He will tear you into pieces."

"Let him try."

"Let it go, man," he pleaded. Then he turned to Rocky, who stood there, still enraged. "It's all cool, man. It's all cool."

Rocky hesitated until the crowd began to disperse. Then he resumed his walk around the hall, scanning the rest of the tables, and his lips curling tighter as each new table let him down more than the one before.

***

At home, Kelly started doing her homework but was too upset to focus and decided to walk to Rosita's.

Rosita was still in her ankle length flowery robe. "What're you doing here this early?"

"I'm sorry to barge in on you."

"It's OK, I just thought you would still be in school at this time of the day."

"I should be, but…"

Rosita started filling the coffee pot with water. "What happened?"

Kelly sighed. "It's Rocky again."

"I thought he was being nice lately. What did he do now?"

"I was in the cafeteria going over some homework with a classmate when I noticed a commotion on the other side of the cafeteria. It was Rocky, ready to fight some guy! I took my books and stormed out before he had a chance to see me."

"What the heck was he doing there? That son of …"

"Maybe to embarrass me, and thinking that by doing so, I'd quit school?"

Rosita poured two cups of coffee and handed one to Kelly. "Listen to me, Kelly, people never change. They just show more of who they really are as time goes by, or as different things happen, that's all. If he gets you to quit school, he will get you to quit your job too because he wants a slave at home and not a wife. Don't do it."

"After my injury, he was being so nice, I really thought he had begun to come around."

"Kelly, the devil can be nice too when seeking to harvest a soul. But I have faith in you, you're too smart to be fooled."

Kelly gazed at her. "The road to get this far has been awfully hard. You're right, I need to stay strong."

"That's my girl." Rosita gave her a long hug. Then looked at her watch. "Let's go get Hope from school, and then we can take a ride to my favorite food discount store in Milford. What you say?"

"If I could take off from work, I could use the break." Kelly dialed the diner's number.

Rosita cleaned the table, washed the coffee cups, and put everything away. "What did George say?"

"He wasn't too happy about it, but after some begging, he said OK."

"Good, we can take Hope to Chucky Cheese too, it's only couple of minutes further down. We're gon' have enjoyable time, I promise. Just give me couple of minutes to get dressed and we'll go."

***

After Rocky had delivered his biggest cocaine deal yet, he went by the diner and didn't see Kelly's car. Went home and she wasn't there either, but her car was. Fuck it, he stepped on the gas and drove to the bar not too far from their house. Where the fuck could she be? He ordered a shot of whiskey and a glass of ale.

Staring at the smoke rising from the cigarette in his right hand, he thought. *She wasn't in the fucking school, her car is home, no one is at Rosita's, and she is not at work either. If I ever find out she is fucking someone, they're both dead.*

The new bartender noticed Rocky mumbling to himself. Pretending to be working on the cash register next to the phone, he kept a furtive eye on him.

"Hey, you," Rocky hollered, "give me another round."

"Yes sir, coming right up."

He gulped that shot too, and quickly chased it down with ale. Stared in the mirror across from him and cracked his ten knuckles one by one. *I'll fix her ass so bad, she'll never go back to school or work again.* Then he slid off the stool. "What do I owe you?"

At home, instead of finding his wife getting dinner ready and his daughter watching her usual cartoons, he found a house as quiet as a cemetery. "Where the fuck is she?" He slammed the door behind him, threw his sleeveless blazer on the couch, and headed straight for the bathroom. Locked the door, took a dollar bill from his wallet, rolled it up, and held it between his thumb and his index finger. Grabbed a small packet of cocaine from his jeans pocket and placed it in the palm of his left hand. After carefully unfolding it, with the tip of the rolled dollar bill, he separated two tiny lines from the pile and quickly snorted one of them. "That's it! It's either my fucking way, or no way!" He snorted the other tiny pile, and quickly folded the packet back together. Raised his head, looked through a clear spot in the mirror, and wiped his nose with the back of his hand. "I got the fucking money for the house now."

MY LAST CHANCE

In Hope's bedroom closet, he pushed the plywood plank covering the access into the attic to one side and pulled a plastic bag out from the other side. In it, there were a few rolls of hundred-dollar bills, a few rolls of fifties, and a few rolls of twenties, along with a few small packages of cocaine. He took the bills out, laid them on Hope's bed, counted them together with the ones that Jay had given him earlier, and stashed them in his right pocket. Grabbed a five-gram package of cocaine from the shopping bag and put it in his left pocket. Put the rest of the cocaine packages in the plastic bag, placed it back in the opening, and pulled the square wooden plank back over the hole. He stormed out the door, opened the passenger side of his wife's car, looked around, and dropped the five-gram package on the back seat next to a couple of her books. "You wanna fuck with me?" he slurred, pushing the door behind him as he rushed inside. Grabbed the quart of whiskey he had picked up on the way home, snatched a wine glass from the cabinet, and sat on the couch. He poured the glass a quarter full and gulped it at once. Then took the money from his pocket, around ten thousand dollars, and threw it on the coffee table. Grabbed an old magazine from the top of the TV and spread it over the money. Looked at his fake Rolex. "Ten of fucking seven?"

***

Rosita's car was only minutes away from their neighborhood. Kelly placed her hand on Rosita's shoulder. "Thank you for treating us to a wonderful afternoon. I really enjoyed it."

"Me too, I love Chucky Cheese." Hope held a small doll in her arms. "And I love this doll too." She gave Rosita a quick kiss on her cheek and sat back down. "Thank you."

They had looked around the food discount store for a while, and then they went to Chucky Cheese. They had a lot of fun watching Hope running from one game to another, excited. She had never been there and couldn't get enough between the games and making new friends, including a couple of boys who wouldn't let her out of their sight all afternoon, following her wherever she went.

"I had a wonderful time too," Rosita said. "Like I said many times before, you're the family I never had, and it makes me happy when I see you guys smiling and sad when you don't. If you know what I mean."

"When I was home recovering, he was so good with everything," said Kelly. "He even used to sit at the kitchen table across from me, watching me doing my homework while he quietly sipped at his beer and puffed on his cigarettes. If he could do it then, why not all the time?"

"Mi amor," Rosita said, shaking her head, "people like him are capable of wearing many faces to get what they want. I think you're just refusing to see that in him."

"Maybe you're right, but I still have faith. When I get home, I'm going to have a nice talk with him. See, deep inside, he is nothing but a big baby."

"Big baby or not, he is over thirty-two years old now and it's time for him to act his age. I could see some reasons in his actions if you were one of those irresponsible women, but you're not, and he should be working with you and not against you."

With tears sprouting in the corner of her eyes, Kelly stared at the budding trees. "You really don't believe he can change?"

"Kelly, for what I have seen up to now, and for what you have been telling me over the last few months, plus him coming to your school today, probably to spy on you, I say no. Like I said earlier, people never change, they just show more of who they are as time goes by, or as different situations arise."

"If you're right, what am I supposed to do then?"

"Keep going to school and keep working but be very watchful of him. In time, you'll figure things out."

"Mommy, I have to pee," Hope said.

"Honey, we're almost home, hold it."

"Are you sure you want to take Hope home with you?" Rosita whispered. "You haven't been around all day, and I'm sure he must be climbing the walls by now."

"You have already spent most of your day with us and—"

"It's OK, Mommy, I don't mind staying with Rosita a little longer."

Kelly shook her head. "Kids."

"Let me drop you off and when you're ready, just call me and I will bring her over."

"Rosita, no. You've already done too much for us today."

"OK, then just come over whenever you're ready."

Kelly hugged Hope. "I'll pick you up soon."

"I love you, Mommy."

"I love you more."

"I don't know what I'd do without you, Rosita."

"You'd still stumble, but you'd be fine."

As she inserted the key into the keyhole, the door opened by itself. Rocky was sitting on the couch with a glass in his right hand, and a half empty quart of whiskey in the other one. He gave her a disdainful look and gulped a shot. "Where the fuck were you all day?" he yelled before she even had a chance to cross the threshold.

Frozen, she stood in the center of the door frame, shivers of fear coursing through her body. Déjà vu. Her father on her sixteenth birthday.

He slammed the bottle on the coffee table. "I said, where the fuck were you?"

She closed the door behind her and leaned against it. "You don't have to bother the neighbors."

He stood up. "Tell me where the fuck you were, and I stop yelling!"

"Rosita took us shopping." She walked to the kitchen table, laid her pocketbook down, and stared at him. "Is that a crime?"

"And Hope is at her house, right?" He moved closer to her. "How nice, you really must think I'm a fucking fool."

"She wanted to stay with her a little longer to play with the new doll that Rosita got her."

"I thought you had school today." With his teeth gnashing, he pointed his index finger at her. "You lied to me!"

"No, I did not."

"Sure," he said with an I-got-you look on his face. "I looked all over the fucking place, and the stupid cafeteria too, and you were nowhere to be found."

She moved back to the side of the table. "I saw you."

"Bullshit!"

"I saw you when you were face-to-face with another rooster, ready to pick a fight."

Suddenly, there was complete silence except for a sporadic whistle against the windows from the wind that had just begun to blow. He stopped staring at her and walked back to the coffee table. Poured another shot, gulped that one too, picked up his pack of cigarettes, and lit one up. "Who the fuck told you I was there?"

She walked to the sink, poured herself some water, and took couple of sips. "I was on the opposite side of the cafeteria, a few tables over to the right of you. I was getting ready for the next class when I accidentally spotted the circus, and when I realized that you were at the center of it, I snuck out."

"The circus had started because of you."

"And how did that happen when I wasn't even near you?"

"This girl was sitting at a table with the back toward me, talking to her boyfriend across from her. Her hair looked just like yours. I approached her, shook her shoulder, and bent my head down to the side of her face. Her friend didn't like that and wanted to fight me."

"And you did that because your sick mind had concluded I was ready to jump in the sack with the guy, right?" She shook her head and walked to the fridge. "I can't believe you're actually spying on me. What did I ever do to deserve that?" He sat back on the couch. "I ain't fucking spying on you, I just wanted to give you the big news."

"What big news?"

He snatched the magazine off the coffee table and threw it on the floor toward her. Held a pile of hundred-dollar-bills up in his hand. "This is the big news. I have saved enough money to buy us a house."

"What?" She approached the coffee table. Never in her entire life she had seen so much money together like that. "How much is there?"

"Exactly 10,750 dollars," he replied with a proud smirk.

Hesitantly, she approached the coffee table and felt all the bills. "Did you rob a bank?"

"Yes, right before I came up to your school."

"Have you gone completely out of your mind?"

"Relax. All the sweat I poured over the past nine months paid off." He held most of the bills in his large hands. "These are all the cash jobs and my portion of the profit we shared this morning. I told you in no time I'd get us a house like we had."

She couldn't believe her eyes. Maybe she had underestimated him after all.

"So, get ready to give your notices." He picked up all the cash and started for Hope's bedroom. "Tomorrow I'll start to look for a house. Your work and school days are over now."

"What did you say?"

"You heard me." He stopped, turned around. "Our deal was that once I made enough money, you would quit everything and stay home like a housewife is supposed to."

"I can't do that anymore!" She walked to the kitchen area and held on to a chair. "That was your deal, not mine. Besides, as far as I know, you could have borrowed that money from your boss."

He jetted back and stood inches from her, his index finger pointed at her face. "In my job, the checks are just for minimum wage, the rest of my pay is in cash."

She walked away from him and picked up the phone. "Let's get your partner on, I'd like to talk to him."

He snatched the receiver from her hand. "You're calling me a fucking liar now?"

"Have you forgotten when we went to the bank for the mortgage to exercise our option? Don't you remember why they denied us?"

"That's bullshit! I have ten thousand dollars for the down payment now."

"That wasn't the only reason. They denied us because you didn't have the pay stubs to prove enough steady income, and you still don't.

Why do you think I have been wanting to go to work all along and pushing you to get a different job?"

He grabbed her arm. The alcohol on his breath was so revolting, she turned her face away. He pulled her face back with his other hand. "Look at me! I don't give fuck, I got us enough money to move out of here and you're not going back anywhere. I'm the fucking boss and you do as I say!"

She gazed deep in his furious dark green eyes and thought of what Rosita had said. *"Mi amor, people like him are capable of wearing many faces to get what they want. I think you're just refusing to see that in him."* She jerked her arm out of his grip. "Let me go!" Grabbed her pocketbook and started for the door.

He ran after her, grabbed both her arms, and pulled her within inches of his face. "Where the fuck you think you're going?"

"As far away from here as possible. Let me go, or I will start screaming at the top of my lungs." Snatched her arms from his stronghold, ran out the door, jumped in her car, and skidded out of the driveway.

He stared at the back of her car. *It's my way, or no fucking way.*

***

Racing through the street toward Rosita's house, she cried, "I can't stand this anymore." Immediately, a police cruiser flashing its lights got on her tail.

"Shit." She hit the steering wheel with her fists. "I went right through the stop sign!" Slowed her car down and pulled to a full stop. Right after the cruiser came to a stop behind her, the cop stepped out and approached her car with a flashlight pointed at her.

She lowered the window. "Officer, I'm sorry."

"Sorry? You realize that speeding through that stop sign, you could have killed someone, and yourself too."

"I'm truly sorry." She wiped her tears. "I've never done this before, honestly. I just had a big fight with my husband and ran away before he could beat me up."

"Ma'am, I feel for you, but that's not the problem of those drivers or pedestrians who could have been crossing the street at that same moment." He scanned the front seat of her car with the flashlight. "Your license, please?"

She grabbed her pocketbook from the passenger seat, pulled her wallet out, and handed him the license.

"Registration and insurance, please?"

She grabbed them from the glove compartment and handed them to him.

He went to his car, checked everything out, came back and handed everything back to her. Turned his flashlight to the passenger seat again, and then to the back seats. "Mam, what's in that small white envelope next to those books there."

"A white envelope?" She looked over her right shoulder to where he was pointing the flashlight.

"Over there, next to the books."

"I don't know. It wasn't there when I got back from school this morning." She pulled the door handle ready to step out of the car.

"Ma'am, don't move. You can't step out of the car until I tell you to do so. Can I look at that envelope please?"

"Sure." She turned around and got it for him.

"Can you open it for me?"

"OK." She ripped the top off and looked inside. "There is white powder in it."

"Can I please see it?"

She shrugged. "Here."

He put his pinky finger inside the bag, stained it, and brushed it over the tip of his tongue. Then took couple of steps back. "Ma'am, please step out of the car and put your hands behind your back. I'm placing you under arrest for possession of cocaine with intent to sell."

She hadn't quite grasped the reality of the cop's request. With creases forming in the corner of her eyes., she asked, "Officer, what'd you say?"

"Ma'am, step out of the car and place your hands behind your back." He snapped the walkie-talkie from his belt and called for backup.

Staring at the flashlight pointed at her eyes, her face turned milky white. She was sitting in the school cafeteria talking to her friend, and then in her car driving home, and then next to Rosita in Chucky Cheese smiling at Hope who was running from one game to another. Then her eyes turned at the flickering lights of the backup cruiser coming to a stop in front of her car. Why all this commotion?

"Ma'am!" the second cop called on her. "Ma'am, for the last time, step out of the car, face away from us, and put your hands behind your back!"

The louder voice of the second cop echoed through her thoughts like a slow-moving wave. "What's going on?" Tears sprouted from the corners of her eyes again.

"You must step out of the car, face away from us, and put your hands behind your back, or we'll have no choice but to force you out of there!"

In a trance, she stepped out, turned her back, and placed her hands on her back. "Can you please tell me what's happening?"

"Sure. You went through a stop sign driving at least forty miles-an-hour in a twenty mile-an-hour zone, with what it looks like five grams of cocaine in your car. Do you think that's enough for us to arrest you?"

Her mind scrambled through the time from when she had left her house up to that point, and salty tears started flowing down her face. "Officer, please, I have never touched cocaine or even seen it that close my entire life. I don't know how that packet got into my car, please?"

As the cop was hand-cuffing her, he said, "Ma'am, you have the right to remain silent. Anything you say can and will be used against you in a court of law. You have the right to speak to an attorney, and to have an attorney present during any questioning."

Shivering and crying with her hands cuffed behind her back, she turned her head at the officers. "You're really going to arrest me?"

"Mam, the car is registered in your name, the packet of cocaine was in your car, and I caught you speeding through a stop sign, probably on your way to deliver this cocaine to you customers."

"No, it's not true. I was on my way to my friend's house just a block down from here. She watches my daughter while I'm at work or in school. That stuff is not mine, why can't you believe me?"

"You'll have your chance to explain that to the judge." He walked her to the cruiser and helped her inside.

She stared at the floor, hair covering her face. "I can't believe this is happening." *My job, my school, this is going to ruin everything. Who could have done this to me?*

As the police car drove through the intersection of Rosita's street, Kelly stared through the window. *My little angel, what will she think of her mom now?* Going through the stop sign was her fault, but that packet wasn't hers. Could it be the cokehead who had harassed her again that morning? Since she had started school, he had been stubbornly asking her to party with him and might be angry because she refused to even talk to him now. What's his name? She thought for a while longer. Jordan, that's it, his name is Jordan. In the cafeteria that morning, he did give her an angry look. *Maybe he did do this to me for spite, that son of a bitch.* She looked up. *Mom, please help me.*

The two arresting officers uncuffed her, processed her fingerprints, took her mugshot, and the first officer on the scene escorted her to an interrogation room. "Ma'am, please have a seat? Normally, I would be interrogating you, but my shift is over, and the detective will be with you shortly."

The room was cold and white with a rectangular table in its center and four chairs. With her face drooped, she pulled one of the chairs and slowly sat down. This must be a terrible dream.

The door opened, and a man not taller than five-feet-six with a chubby face and carrying at least fifty pounds of extra weight walked in, an annoyed look on his face.

As he was about to sit across from her, she spoke. "Sir, that packet of cocaine is not mine."

He gave her a chilling stare. "Just a minute."

Shivering, she started massaging the red marks on her wrists where the cuffs had been.

The detective adjusted a yellow pad to his desired position, grabbed his pen, and wiggled his body.

She followed his every move. She had never had a brush with the law or had a traffic ticket.

The detective raised his head halfway with a serious face. "I know the officers have read you the Miranda Rights already, do you have any questions?"

Her right eye started its involuntary twitching. She placed her hands on her laps. "I have nothing to hide."

"Ma'am, would you like to have an attorney present here while I question you? Just say yes or no."

She leaned forward. "I heard you, and I don't need an attorney because that packet of cocaine is not mine, and I don't know how it got there."

"Who were you delivering that cocaine to?"

The twitching in her right high sped up. "Like I just said, and I also told the other officers before, I didn't even know that that crap was in my car. I am a working woman with an eight-year-old daughter and an awfully demanding husband. I go to school fulltime, and I don't do any drugs, never mind selling it."

"Many dealers don't do drugs themselves." He leaned back and took a relaxed posture. "You sped through that stop sign, why?"

"Like I told the officers, I ran out of the house after I had a big argument with my husband because I was afraid that he would beat me up." She wiped the corner of her eyes with her index finger. "I just didn't see the stop sign on time."

"You could have killed someone and yourself too." He leaned forward. "You realize that don't you?"

"I do, and I always did. I live only couple blocks from there. I go through that stop sign at least three times a day, and I always stop. I don't even have a parking ticket to my name. Please," she pleaded with her hands clasped together, "understand that it was once in a lifetime mistake for me. You must believe me; I am not that type of driver."

"You'll explain that to the judge at the appropriate time." He rested his elbows on the desk. "If you don't want to tell me who you were delivering the coke to, then tell me who is your supplier?"

"Sir, with all due respect, I told you already. I am not a user, I don't deal it, and I didn't even know that that packet was in my car."

"It must have flown in there."

"No, it didn't. I'm not that naïve."

"So, then you know who put it there?"

She looked down at her rubbing hands. "While the officers were driving me here, I did think of who could have possibly put it there, but I don't like to implicate someone just based on a theory of mine."

"Hey, anything you tell me that can help explain how it got there, can only help you."

She thought for a while. "There are these two students in my school that—"

"Where do you go to school?" He moved the notepad closer and started writing.

"Naugatuck Valley Community College."

"What are these guys' names?"

"I just know the one who bothers me from time to time. His name is Jordan. The other one I don't know, but they're close friends."

"What does Jordan do to bother you?"

"Since my first day of school, he has been asking me out repeatedly. I always tell him that I'm happily married, but he doesn't give up. He is a persistent little shit. Few times he even chased me to my car with his blabbering mouth and…"

"Go on?"

"Oh my God. Who else will know about this conversation?"

"Why you're asking?"

"If my husband gets hold of this, he will go up to school and beat that guy to death."

"Are you kidding me?"

"I'm not."

He shook his head, "OK. I'll try my best to keep it as confidential as possible. Go on."

"They're both known as cokeheads around campus, but I am not close enough to either of them to know for sure."

"Then why did you make that assertion?"

"I have heard students talking about them."

"Well—"

"You asked me to tell you whatever I can think of that could shine a light on who put that package in my car, and I am telling you who I think could have had a sick reason to do that to me."

"OK, go on."

"This morning, while I was sitting in the cafeteria going over some homework with a classmate of mine, he went by us, pointing his index finger at me with a weird kind of smirk on. Maybe he did this because I refuse to even talk to him now. Those books were there since yesterday, untouched, because they're for my Wednesday and Monday classes, and I don't need to work with them until the weekend."

He had been listening and carefully analyzing her facial expressions while scribbling things on his yellow pad.

"That's my theory. But please, it's only a theory and I wouldn't want to cause any unnecessary anguish to them, even if that persistent little shit could probably use some."

He looked at his watch. "Do you have anything else to tell me?"

"That's all I have. Anything else would be a lie, and I don't like to lie."

After focusing on every word that came out of her mouth, and every facial twitch, he couldn't think of anything he detected that indicated to him that she was lying. "I want to believe you, but if we don't get to the bottom of this, you're in some serious trouble. Do you understand?"

"What will happen to me?"

"I do believe your story, but the fact is, you were caught with five grams of cocaine, which based on the quantity reflects intent to sell. And until we get to the bottom of this, you'll be charged with possession of an illegal drug with intent to sell."

"What does it mean?"

"To start with, you get a chance for one phone call, and if you can't post bond, then you will spend the night in the holding cell. In the morning, you'll be brought to court where the judge will set your bail, and a court date for your case. And if you have someone to post bail for you, you can go home and wait for us to do our job. But if you can't make bail, you'll be detained until the court date."

As each word came out of the detective's mouth, her eyes were gushing like a rising flood. At his last word, her face dropped in her hands and burst out crying like a baby. "I can't go to jail." She needed to ask Rocky to come to court to bail her out. What if he didn't, what was she going to do then? What was going to happen to Hope without her?

If this girl is guilty of dealing drugs, the detective thought gazing at her, *I'm the worst judge of characters ever.* He got up, walked around the desk, and placed his hand on her shoulder. "Come on, let's get you to the phone." Helped her up from the chair. "I'm gon' get on your case right away. I promise you; I'll do my best to get to the bottom of this."

She stood next to the payphone. Her shivering hands labored the quarter into the slot and started dialing. After she had dialed the last of the seven numbers, she realized she had mis-dialed the last one. "Shit." Anxiously, she hung up the receiver and started all over again.

After her third number, again she misdialed the next one. "Darn it!" Started all over again and got it right. *Come on Rocky, please answer the darn phone.* After a few more rings with no answer, she hung up and decided to call Rosita instead.

"Hi Rosita, please don't tell Hope I'm on the phone."

"Did he go crazy again on you?"

"Yes, but I ran away. I jumped into my car to come to your house and didn't realize I went straight through the stop sign, the one down the street from us. A police car must have been spotting from up the street somewhere, he chased me, arrested me, towed my car away, and brought me to the police station."

"I'll come right over and pick you up."

"No, you can't," she said, scrambling for an excuse. "They won't let me go until tomorrow morning."

"That's crazy. I went through a stop sign once, and they just gave me a ticket."

"I was also speeding badly, and they charged me for that too. I have to go to court in the morning and the judge has to decide on the ticket and all."

"They're gon' keep you there for the night?"

"I think so."

"Dios mio, that's terrible."

"Don't worry, Rosita, I'll be fine."

"I told you, he'll never change."

"Please, make up some story for Hope and keep her there overnight."

"I go to work, but no worry, my husband will take care of her."

"One more thing. Please get a pen and write this number down."

"I'm ready."

"That's my friend Angela's number, please tell her where I am and what happened to me."

The detective walked over. "Kelly, you have to put it down now, your time is up."

"I got to go now, please tell Hope I love her." She hung up, and the detective handed her to the cop on duty who led her to an empty cell next to one hosting a sleazy bearded drunken man in his mid-thirties.

"Hey man," he blabbered," bring her here, I'll take loving care of her."

"If you say one more word," the escorting cop yelled, "I'll charge you with assault, and you'll go to a real jail where someone will take loving care of you instead!" With a sad look on his face the cop showed Kelly in the cell and slowly locked the door behind her. "Stay strong, we'll get to the bottom of this."

"Can you tell me when Cody is on duty?"

"I can check the schedule. Why, you know him?"

She held on to the bars. "We went to Derby High together. Can you please tell him what's happening to me?"

If she were guilty, he thought, *she wouldn't rush to publicize it*. "I'll call him right now for you."

With her back leaning against the steel-bars, she stared at the less-than-clean white walls, the open toilet, the dinky sink, and the makeshift bed in the right corner of the room. *God, please give me a hand.* She dragged her feet toward the middle of the bed, fell on it, and laid on her right side in a fetus-like position, staring at the steel bars forming the front wall.

What if they don't find the bastard that did this to me? At that thought, tears began to sprout in the corner of her eyes again.

"Hey gorgeous," the drunk from the next cell blabbered. "What you're in for?"

It was looking increasingly real that she must be cursed. She got up and started pacing around, tracing the same steps over and over. *Years from now, when you get married, remember that wives take an oath to follow and obey their husbands no matter what.* Her grandfather's words, that were often repeated to her growing up, had once again moved to the front of her lobe.

Signs of hope surfaced over her face when a man's familiar voice spoke around the corner. "Which cell is she in?"

That's got to be Cody. She rushed to the steel bars.

Cody, in jeans and sneakers, a black T-shirt and a dark-gray sweater, approached the cell with a set of keys in his hand. "It must be destiny," he said, smirking. "I didn't see you for eight or so years, and in less than a year, I get to see you two times. But never in a million years would I have ever thought that the next time I'd see you would be behind bars."

"Cody, I have been framed. That pack of cocaine is not mine. I swear over my dead mother, who aside from my daughter, I loved more than anyone else in this world."

He unlocked the door. "The detective has already briefed me. Let's go in the interrogation room and see if we can come up with anything else that might help you."

"I am going insane in here. Do you think they let me go home?"

"You can, if someone posts bond for you."

"How much would it cost?"

"I am not sure, but I can find out?"

"Never mind, I don't have any money anyway."

"Even if you did, you couldn't pay for it yourself. A bondsman would have to do that. Have Rocky call him."

She thought about it for a while. If she were to get him involved at the station, he could find out about the guy Jordan and that would cause even more problems. "No."

"What about if I'll do that for you?"

"No way, Cody, he would go even crazier. It's OK, I'll spend the night in jail and tomorrow I'll ask him to come to court to bail me out."

She sat down, clasped her hands, and rested her arms on the table. "I never even received a traffic ticket in my entire life. I'm so sorry I went through that stop sign, I was so upset and crying, I didn't realize it."

He sat across from her. "Kelly, they found five grams of cocaine on the back seat of your car. The detective believed your story, but until we can find out how it got there, these are the procedures."

She shook her head. "I can't believe this is happening."

He placed his right hand over her left one. "That's why I came right over on my day off. I want to find that bastard as soon as possible. Now try to relax, because I need you to carefully go over everything you did for the last forty-eight hours."

"OK."

He placed a yellow pad in front of him and started jotting things down. "When did you last touch those books in the back seat of your car?"

To make sure that her answer was the absolute truth, she thought for a while. "Yesterday. I got out of my last class around 1:45 p.m. I dropped them there, and I drove straight to pick Hope up from school. Then I went home, fed her lunch, dropped her off at Rosita's and went straight to work."

"I know this might sound silly," he smirked, "but was the pack of cocaine there then?"

"Of course not." She pursed her lips. "I would have seen it, picked it up, opened it and asked someone to tell me what it was, because I have never seen cocaine before."

"That's the answer I was hoping for." He ran his hand through his dirty blond hair. "Do you always lock your car when you're not driving it?"

"Of course, I do, I couldn't afford to buy the same books more than once." Then she thought for a moment. "Wait. When I'm home, if I'm in and out of the house for one reason or another, sometimes I do leave it unlocked."

"Was there any time yesterday that you didn't lock it? Think carefully."

She tilted her head to the side and ran her hand through her hair. "Yes, around two in the afternoon for a few minutes while I fed my daughter her lunch."

"Let's focus on today now. Step by step, start with when you got out of bed until this evening when you had the argument with Rocky."

She took her time and accounted for every instant of the day as Cody eagerly took notes. "And like a nightmare that I'm still trying to awaken from, I found myself here behind bars."

He reviewed his notes one by one. "The way I see it, there are only two or three occasions when someone could have planted that packet in your car. Yesterday, when you were feeding your daughter lunch. Or all this afternoon up to when your ran out of the house during your fight with Rocky. But for now, I'm going to rule out yesterday because it was a brief period, and you would have probably noticed if anyone snooped around it, right?"

"Most likely."

"What about this afternoon, did you lock it before you went for a walk over to Rosita's house?"

She frowned with her eyes squinted. "I must have not, I was too upset and didn't think of it because when I ran out tonight, I didn't have to unlock it."

"So, let's focus on this afternoon since you're not totally sure if you locked it or not. Also, does Rocky have the key to your car?"

"You're not thinking that…" She leaned forward. "Cody, please listen. Rocky might be a bully and a stubborn baby, but he would never do something like this. He loves me."

"Kelly, I'm not making any assertions about him, but we have to look at every possibility. And based on what you're telling me, possibly, he was the only one near the car most of the afternoon."

"Long time ago, he used to smoke marijuana, but he has never done cocaine," she said with a defensive posture. "And he drinks whiskey, perhaps more than he should, but no way he could be the one to have done this to me."

"I am sorry if you think I stepped out of line, but if you want us to help you, we have to look at every possible suspect."

"Cody, I'm sorry. I should be thankful to you instead."

"Not a problem. I always thought highly of you, and I just couldn't have stood on the sideline watching you suffer for some jerk. I know you have no clue how the packet got into your car, but please bear with me. You told me that Rocky showed you over ten thousand dollars in cash. Do you have any idea how long it took him to accumulate that much money?"

"September of last year, his boss made him a partner in his landscaping company. And before our argument got out of control, he had told me that this morning they split some of their profit." Puzzled, she asked him. "Why is that important?"

"Kelly, I am not rushing to any conclusions, but just so that you know, drug dealers only deal with cash, and usually a lot of it."

"But I would have noticed something before today, don't you think so?"

"I'm not saying he is one of them, but with that amount of cash on hand, and the other circumstances surrounding your case, I have an obligation to consider him as a possible suspect. As I will also consider Jordan. By the way, the detective already tracked him down and his last name is Cheswick. It's possible that Mr. Cheswick could have cleanly unlocked your car, placed the packet in there, and locked it back up while you were in one of your classes this morning. Some of these kids become neighborhood dealers themselves to support their habit."

"I understand," she nodded, "but I don't think Rocky would do this to me, even if he were one of those neighborhood dealers as you put it."

A sudden knock on the door caught their attention. The cop on duty at the front desk stepped inside. "There is this Angela lady pleading to see her," he said, looking at Cody. "What you want me to do?"

"She is my best friend," Kelly said, "can you please let her in for just couple minutes? I really need to talk to her," she pleaded. "I need her to get in touch with Rocky for the court tomorrow. He might be home now, and I have already used my phone call with Rosita who is watching my daughter."

"I thought Angela lived in L.A.?"

"You know her too?" the cop on duty asked Cody.

"Yes, we all attended Derby High together," Cody said.

"I get it, all in the family," the cop said with a smirk on.

Cody looked at him. "I think I'm going to get into a lot of trouble."

"They look like good people," the cop said to Cody. "After I'll explain that to the chief, I'm sure he'll understand."

Angela rushed through the door without even looking at Cody. "Sister, what happened?"

Kelly sprung up, hugged her, and burst out crying. "I'm in serious trouble, Angela, someone planted a packet of cocaine in my car."

"What?" Shocked, Angela held her by her arms. "Who would do such a horrible thing to you?"

"That's what I'm going to find out." Cody got up, extended his hand. "Hi, Angela. The last time I saw you, you had long dark-brown hair. I would have never recognized you on my own."

"Cody?"

"Yes, that's me. I'm sorry we had to reintroduce ourselves under these circumstances. Please, let's all sit?"

Angela placed her arm around Kelly's shoulders. "Sister, I can't believe this."

"Cody is going to get the bastard for me, right, Cody?" Kelly wiped her eyes with the back of her hand.

"Listen, I'm going to leave you two alone for few minutes. In the meantime, I'll get to work on this right away."

"Yes, Cody, thank you," Kelly said.

Cody got up, held her hand in his. "Let me get the bastard first." Then turned to Angela. "Nice seeing you again." He shook her hand and headed out of the room.

"Sister, tell me what happened."

Kelly briefly recounted her day from the time she saw Rocky in her school cafeteria to the time she got pulled over by the cop.

"Not to sound redundant, but I told you, he is sickly jealous of you."

"I'm beginning to see that much clearer now, but that's for another time. For now, I need you to get ahold of him, tell him what happened, and ask him to meet me at the Derby Court House by 9 a.m., and not to worry about Hope because she is at Rosita's for the night."

"Of course, I'll do that for you, but what kind of malicious jerk would do something like this to you?"

"My grandfather used to say that honesty doesn't guarantee you a smooth life, but it does guarantee you to always walk with your head straight. My head is straight, I'm innocent, and this too shall pass."

"I know you are, and I know Cody will do whatever he can to help you." She giggled. "You know, he almost lost his mind when he found out that you were marrying Rocky."

"How come I never heard about all of this back then?"

"Sorry, ladies, it's almost 10 o'clock and I must break you up before Cody and I get fired."

"OK." Angela got up, hugged her. "I'll go to your house right now, stay cool."

"Thank you, Angela."

After the cop locked Kelly in her cell, she took her sneakers off and climbed on the corner of the bed. Sat with her back against the wall, hugged her arms around her knees, rested her chin over them, and stared at the brown blanket. If someone would have told her that she could have ended up behind bars before the day was over, she would have stayed in bed all day whether she had believed it or not. *Does Rocky have the key to your car?* What if Rocky didn't show up to court?

CHAPTER TWENTY

Throughout the night, she had tried to get some sleep, but between the snoring and blabbering of the man in the next cell, and the negative images flashing in her thoughts every time she was about to doze off, she hardly succeeded for more than few minutes at a time.

The cop stared at her through the rear mirror. "Kelly, I understand you're Rocky Esposito's wife?"

"How do you know my husband?"

"In our younger days, we used to run into each other at various clubs and a few times we even hooked up on double dates."

"What's your name?"

"Joe, Joe Procida. I do run into him every now and then."

"I see." Never in her life she had felt so degraded and ugly, and as they approached the courthouse, she rested her face on her knees.

Joe guided her up the stairs and placed her pocketbook in her hands. "Take everything out, put it in this basket, and give it to the security guard there."

She walked through security. And while waiting for Joe on the other side of the checkpoint, she saw Rocky coming through the main door behind a few more people. She heaved a sigh of relief and waved at him. "Joe, my husband, there he is."

"How can I miss that giant?" He placed his hand on her shoulder. "I hope he hired an attorney for you."

"Why do I need one?"

He stared at her with sympathetic eyes. "You really have no idea how much trouble you could be in."

"Other than going through a stop sign, I haven't done anything else wrong."

"Until you can prove that the cocaine wasn't yours, you need an attorney to manage your case."

As Rocky approached them, she ran over and hugged him. "Some bastard framed me."

Angela's persistent knocks on the door the night before had him all shaken up. He was happy to see that it was her and not the police but pissed off when she told him to make sure to show up to court to bail Kelly out. After she had left, he laid on the couch pondering before he decided that it was in his best interest to do so. Stone faced, he removed her arms from his shoulders. "I told you that fucking school was not— "

"Man, come on," Joe said, "why add more to her ordeal?"

"From what Angela told me, you guys think someone at her school did this to her, right? So, if she weren't in school, this wouldn't have happened."

"You mean just like if it wasn't me posted at that stop sign a while back? Did you ever tell her that I gave you a warning that night, and that I also told you that the chief was serious about stationing us there indefinitely?"

Kelly didn't need to add fuel to these flames. She gazed at them, quiet.

"That's not why she's here."

"You wanna know something, you're not the Rocky I remember." Joe got closer to him and whispered, "From what I understand, if she wasn't caught going through that stop sign, or if you hadn't driven her out of the house in tears in the first place, according to Cody, the detective, and every other cop familiar with her case, this issue could have been resolved in a unique way." He turned to Kelly. "I am sure that the next time she checked her books, she would have noticed the packet and turned it in. That's how everyone feels about her."

"If this, if that, if...," Rocky replied. "The fucking attorney is here, let me go get him."

The three of them gathered in a room while Joe waited outside the door. Later, because there wasn't a thing on Kelly's record, the judge set an incredibly low bail and a court date for the 21st of July, ninety days from then.

Joe shook her hand. "You're free to go, Kelly. And don't worry, because before the ninetieth day comes, we'll catch the bastard. And when we do, I'll make sure that when we make the arrest, we use the same cuffs that were used on you."

She shook his hand, and both followed Rocky out of the courthouse.

Rocky puffed on his cigarette as they walked. "Who's this fucking Jordan guy?"

"It's just a theory of mine. All around campus he is known as a cokehead."

"I didn't ask you that!" He turned to her, enraged. "I asked you, what's he to you?"

She didn't want to infuriate him even more and decided to leave out that Jordan had asked her out repeatedly. "He is just in one of my classes, that's all."

"There has to be fucking more than that for him to do some like that," he shouted. "Maybe it dropped out of his pocket when you were making out with him. Isn't that right?"

She looked away. "You're really losing it."

"If you weren't there, this shit wouldn't have happened, and I wouldn't be out the cash to bail you out."

"I have had it. Don't worry, you might just get your wish after all."

He stopped at the gas station where her car had been towed, paid for it, and left for work without saying another word to her.

Kelly stopped on the threshold of her house for a couple of seconds. The rat hole now didn't look as bad after all. She thought about Jordan. Why would he have done something like this to her? It didn't make sense.

She plopped on the couch and stared at the ceiling, sifting through the last sixteen horrible hours before she fell into a deep sleep.

Sometime later, she awoke suddenly, panicked, until her mind settled on the loud ringing of her phone.

"Hey, I heard you didn't go to school last night, are you sick?"

If Gilda knew what had happened already, she would have said something. If she didn't, why rush it? "Who told you that?"

"Remember that girl we sat in the cafeteria with a while back? Kind of chubby like me. I think her name is Clara. What's going on?"

"I'd rather not talk about it now."

"Final exams are coming up; I hope you're up for them."

"To be honest with you, right now I really don't care."

"Kelly? That doesn't sound like you. Remember, if you fail your accounting class, you'll never graduate."

"Gilda, are you working from 6 p.m. to 6 a.m. tonight again?"

"Who else would take care of those shit-faced guys the way I do?"

She looked at the clock. 1 p.m. "OK, I'll see you then." She needed to talk to George before he heard what had happened from someone else. She rushed to the bedroom, snapped her clothes off, and got in the shower.

MY LAST CHANCE

***

"Kelly, you're early again." George winked at her as he handed a customer her change. "You miss this place that much?"

"Yes, can I talk to you in private?"

He called one of the waitresses over to work the register. "OK, let's go."

Her body squirmed and her chair screeched. "I don't know where to begin."

"Start with why your face looks as if you had just seen a ghost. Am I that scary?"

"Before…Before people start talking, I want you to hear it directly from me."

His lips curled. "What's going on?"

"Yesterday, while I was in school…" She told him exactly what had happened to her throughout the day. Her argument with her husband and everything else always up through the judge's actions earlier that morning.

His jaws dropped. "I can't believe this shit."

"So, I'm thinking that it might be better for everyone if I quit everything and be the housewife Rocky wants me to be. He is right, if I weren't in school, none of this would have happened."

"That's bullshit. A bright young lady like you should not go to waste." He folded his arms on the desk. "He is the one who should bury his stupid old-fashioned ways."

"He has been my husband for over eight years now, and—"

"I don't care, he is the one who's wrong, not you."

"I'm going to do exactly what he wants me to do, and maybe things will work out for the better."

"You're gon' give up school too?"

"There are only couple of weeks left to the end of this semester. I'll finish it, and then I quit."

"Don't forget that I have something invested in this too. Every time you needed to change your schedule to accommodate your school schedule, I went out of my way to help you do that, even if it pissed off some of your co-workers along the way."

"George, I will always be grateful to you for that and for giving me my first job, knowing that I had no experience at all."

He shook his head. "You're gon' give me at least couple of weeks to replace you."

"This is a wonderful place to work at, you'll have no problem finding someone with experience."

"You're wrong. Normally, I wouldn't say this to an employee, but you are one of the best to ever work for me."

She wiped the corners of her eyes. "OK, I'll stay on for a couple more weeks."

Kelly, I can't tell you what to do, but I think you're making the biggest mistake of your life. If you change your mind before the two weeks are over, or even after, you'll always have a job here."

"Thank you." Got up to leave, but before she stepped out, "Gilda will be the only one to know about this before the day is over. I trust her, but please don't tell anyone else, not before my shift is over."

"Don't worry. Not only would I not tell anyone, if I catch any of them just mentioning anything about it, I will…" He looked at the employees' schedule behind him. "Gilda is taking over your area tonight, I'll make sure to remind her to keep her mouth shut. As you know, she is the type that likes to bullshit a little too much."

"I am planning on telling her when she comes in."

"Anyway, think hard on what you're about to do. I am more than double your age, and if there is one thing I've learned over the years, it is that life only gives us a couple of chances."

"Thank you, I will keep that in mind."

With her shift just about over, Kelly was getting a table ready for the next guests when Gilda rushed over. "So, what happened yesterday?"

"Ask George if you can punch in few minutes late, we'll go talk outside."

"OK." Worried that Kelly might have found out about her and Rocky, Gilda's face drooped.

The two women sat in Kelly's car.

"What's so private that you couldn't tell me in there?" Gilda asked.

"I'll tell you, but you have to promise me that at least for today you're going to keep this to yourself."

"OK, I promise." Gilda was relieved that it didn't sound like it had anything to do with her and Rocky's affair.

Kelly started with the incident with Rocky in the cafeteria and went through the entire day and night, step by step, ending with her appearance in court. "I have had it. I just gave George my two weeks' notice, and after this semester is over, I'll quit school too."

"You can't do that. By December you can graduate?"

"Yes, at times I didn't even have money to buy me and my daughter clothes when we needed them, or money to have some fun, and I was stuck living in a rat hole, but at least there were hardly any arguments, and our sex life was great." She wiped her eyes. "I'll go back to be the barefoot and pregnant kind of wife that he wants me to be again so badly."

"You can't quit now. Not after what we have been through to get you where you are."

Kelly looked at her puzzled. We? What have *we* been through? OK, Gilda had helped her getting into school, and watched her daughter when Rosita was injured, and got her the class notes when she was home injured, and she appreciated that, but the rest?

"Kelly, don't do it. Look how far you got in less than a year. I'm sure that you're innocent, and Cody will work his ass off to find that jerk for you. And as for Rocky, stand up to him, and remind him that this is the 21st century."

"I'm exhausted. I love my daughter, but I was young and naïve, and now it's too late."

"No, it's not. You can divorce him."

"That's out of the question."

"I can help you go through with it."

"Thanks for the advice. I think you need to get inside before George flips out, and I need to get home and get dinner ready."

"Kelly, I'm sorry for you, I thought you were stronger than that."

"Choices have consequences, I just wish I understood that much better years ago."

Gilda stepped out of the car, looked back at her. "Is it OK if I stop over every now and then?"

"Of course, you're one of the good things that resulted from my latest choices."

***

Hope was in the living room playing with her toys. Rosita walked Kelly to one of the bedrooms and whispered, "So, what happened yesterday?"

Kelly told her what had happened step by step, like she had done with Gilda. "I'll just be the barefoot and pregnant kind of wife he wants me to be."

"That's not right of him to expect you to live his life only. What about yours?"

"I took that vow, and now I have to live with it."

"You don't have to." Anger sprouted on Rosita's face. "I took that same vow, but me and my husband share our lives, we don't live his, or mine." She held Kelly by the arms. "Listen to me, mi amor. You deserve more than what he has been giving you."

"It might sound crazy," Kelly replied, "but I still care about him, and I know that despite his crazy ways he cares about me too. If I don't do this now, though, the fights are only going to get worse and worse. Hope is getting older, and I don't want her to live in a house where there are constant fights anymore. I must resign myself to be a housewife for the rest of my life and just hope that he gets a better job someday."

"Kelly, I don't care if you get upset at me, but it's evil of him to demand that of you. Your face shone like a bright star when you showed me your first semester's grades. With your mind and your determination, you would not only succeed for yourself, but the world too would be a better place."

"Rosita, I've got to go. I have to get dinner ready for him."

As Kelly walked away, Rosita stood on the threshold, tears dripping from her eyes. "I will pray for you."

You're a child. A child, bearing a child. Her mother's words from that humid and thunderous July afternoon eight years earlier resonated within Kelly again. She had cried her heart out when she had told her mother that she was pregnant. *I hope you realize that you have just turned your life upside down. Now you must grow up fast. All your dreams about college, career, and traveling are now shattered.* She looked up. *Mom, I guess you were right.*

CHAPTER TWENTY-ONE

George was able to hire a lady with experience. Kelly started training her, and by the end of the week, the lady was ready to do the job. So, she and George decided that Kelly didn't need to stick around for her second week.

Other than keeping up with her school schedule and doing her homework, the rest of the time she was being exactly the housewife that Rocky expected her to be. To spread her legs whenever he was in the mood, whether she was up for it or not. She got up early, prepared breakfast for all, and the lunch box for him, which she had been doing all along anyway. Got dressed, drove Hope to school, exchanged a few words with some of the other mothers, and returned straight home as expected. The days she had classes, she grabbed her books and drove to school. On Fridays, she had no classes, changed into her blue leisure suit, cleaned the house, washed the few dirty clothes there were, and, if she had no more homework to do, plopped on the couch for the rest of the morning and scanned through the few channels they had for something interesting to watch. Often, while trying to make sense of why the other mothers made such a big deal about those stupid soap-operas, she dozed off and the TV ended up watching her until it was time to get up and go get Hope from school. Back home, after she would feed Hope lunch, Hope would do her homework, and Kelly would plop on the couch until it was time to prepare dinner.

Arguments with Rocky had lessened to almost none, but so had their basic communication that existed before her going to work and going to school. Their talking to each other was now limited to him telling her what he wanted for dinner, and by what time to have it ready for him. Home from work, he would devour his dinner, grab his second or third beer, and would plop on the couch to watch some weird sport or some brainless movie while she would clean up and retire to their bedroom. She would gaze at the ceiling, waiting for him to either call for another beer, or to join her and ask her to spread her legs.

***

Friday afternoon, exactly a week since she had quit her job, and not long after she had returned from picking Hope up from school, she was on the couch, her eyes dueling with the TV, when the phone rang.

"Someone told me you quit your job, is that true?"

"Cody? Well, if you guys don't find out who planted that crap in my car, I might go to jail anyway?"

"The detective and I aren't resting until we find the bastard." He hesitated for couple of seconds. "I will give it all I have to keep you out of that possibility."

"I really appreciate what you guys are doing for me."

"So that you know, the detective has been sniffing around your school about that Jordan guy. How has he been reacting toward you?"

"Since my arrest, I haven't been in the cafeteria, or the library. I just go to my classes and come home. In between classes, I have been staying in my car, or at the diner down the street from the school."

"Why?"

"I feel embarrassed. And besides, after this semester, it will all be over for me anyway."

"Maybe not. Listen to me, Kelly, we're going to get this resolved faster than you think. I asked the chief to let me work with the detective, and he agreed. So, while the detective has been focusing on Jordan, I have been doing some sniffing around here, and things look promising. Also, out of the six fingerprints, three of them are all over the packet. The other three, one is yours, one is from my colleague that handled the packet, and the third one is still unknown. We are now working on matching it with our data base. I'd like to warn you, though, be prepared for anything."

"What do you mean?"

"I shouldn't tell you this yet, but Rocky is a suspect. I figure you ought to know just in case."

"Cody, that's terrible." Her hands shivered. "He is stubborn, demanding, and even violent at times, but he would never do that to me."

"I hope you're right."

"After eight years of twenty-four-seven, don't you think I know him well enough?"

"Kelly, many times we get called to check on domestic disputes between husbands and wives who have been together for much longer than that, and one of them always ends up saying, 'All these years, I thought I knew who I was living with.'"

"Cody, I'd like you to know that I'm deeply touched by the way you're trying to help me."

"I'll be in touch soon."

She poured herself a glass of water and went back to sit on the couch. When Cody had told her that Rocky was a suspect, a dark cloud had settled above her head and a knot had formed in her heart. Why would he say so if he had little or nothing on him?

When Rocky came home from work, he went straight to the bathroom, and after he took his shower, he grabbed a beer and plopped on the couch, his eyes swaying between the TV and her as she moved around the kitchen area.

"Hope, dinner is ready, stop playing and come to eat!"

"Wait, Mommy, I'm putting my toys away."

Rocky strolled his way to the table too. He had walked in the house with a wilted face and had barely acknowledged them. Sensing a storm brewing, Kelly diverted her attention to Hope who had already finished her spaghetti and was anxiously working on her meatballs and using the bread to brush the remaining sauce from her dish. "Honey, you were that hungry?"

"Mommy, that was so good. When I grow up, I want to cook just like you."

"You're already old enough to start." Kelly gave her a gentle pinch on her cheek. "I was your age when my grandmother got me started. Tomorrow, I'll have you help me."

"Yes, I even helped Rosita once."

Rocky gazed at them wordlessly. Then he grabbed his half-full beer and went to plop on the couch again. Lit a cigarette, put the TV on, and laid-back, puffing and gulping.

"Mommy, is Dad upset at us?" Hope whispered.

"While I clean the table and wash the dishes, go show him the drawings you made in school."

Without even turning his head, Rocky said, "Bring me another beer."

Kelly stopped washing, dried her hands on her apron, and snapped it open. She placed it on the coffee table in front of him and went back to the sink.

"What the fuck does that Cody cop want from my partner?"

"What're you talking about?"

"Never mind."

Should she tell him that the police think he is a suspect? She wondered.

CHAPTER TWENTY-TWO

On Sunday morning, three weeks and two days since Kelly was released on bail, Rocky grabbed his sleeveless-blazer, and stormed out the house with an anxious look on his face.

Still in her nightgown, Kelly filled her coffee cup and sat back at the kitchen table. He rarely worked on Sundays, where was he going in such a hurry?

Kelly and Hope decided on an impromptu visit to Rosita. Down the road, two guys were tearing an old deck apart while the third guy was on his cell phone yelling at someone who apparently had not shown up to work.

"Mommy, how come we don't have a cell phone?"

Kelly sighed. "Someday, we'll get one too."

Neither Rosita nor Carlos were home. The walk was doing Kelly good. Her mind was much clearer than it had been in a while. "Let's walk a bit further, and by the time we get back she might be home."

"Yes, Mommy, let's do that."

Between walking, talking, and doing some running and chasing along the way, they had walked downtown before Kelly realized it. "Honey, are you tired?"

"No, I'm having fun."

"OK. Then let's walk to the Derby green. When I was about your age, Angela and I used to spend a lot of time there."

MY LAST CHANCE

By the time they reached the top of the hill, they had both broken a little sweat. At the traffic light, they crossed the street and sat on a wall to catch their breath. Kelly took a napkin from her back pocket and wiped Hope's forehead first and then hers. Then tickled Hope's side. "Young lady, I'm really impressed."

Hope laughed. "Mommy, that was a huge hill."

They resumed their walk, and few minutes later they sat on a bench at the center of the Derby green.

Hope hugged her mom's arm and leaned her head on her shoulder. "Mommy, I love this, we should do it again."

"You're right, we should do this more often."

Kelly gazed around, and in each of the plaza corners, she recalled memories of her past, mostly good, but some bad. Like that morning she spent in the courthouse across from the green, which also reminded her that Angela didn't show up to court to support her, and still hadn't returned her calls after multiple messages she had left at her office. Gently, she removed Hope's head from her shoulder. "Honey, ready to go?"

"Mommy, let's stay a little longer, please?"

"We have to get home before Daddy gets there."

"OK, let's run then."

"Hope, wait for me!" Kelly ran after her and caught up with her a little past St. Mary's Church. From there, walking a little and running a little, they reached Rosita's house again. Rosita saw them through one of her windows. She rushed downstairs and unlocked the front door at the same time they were about to ring the bell.

"It's so great to see you." Rosita gave Hope a hug and kiss on each of her cheeks. "I miss you so much." Then stood up and hugged Kelly. "And how you're doing?"

"OK, I guess. We just took a long walk to the Derby green and back."

"Why, is your car broken?"

"No, we just felt like walking around for a while."

"Who's in that car there looking at us?" Rosita pointed to a blue Mitsubishi that had just stopped next to her sidewalk across from them.

"That's Cody." Kelly winked at her. "You remember him, the cop that was at Gilda's party?" She whispered so Hope didn't hear. "He is the one who's trying to help me."

"Mom, who is he?"

"A friend from school. Stay here with Rosita."

Kelly approached the car to the driver side. Cody lowered the window. "This is my third time driving to your house after as many phone calls to get in touch with you."

"I'm sorry, I went for a long walk with my daughter. You have some good news?"

"We need to talk. *Alone*," he emphasized, looking at Hope who was gazing at them.

"OK." She walked back to the deck. "He needs to borrow a book from me." She winked at Rosita. "He is driving me home and will bring me right back so that I don't miss your fresh cup of coffee. Hope, you go upstairs with Rosita, and I'll see you in a bit."

"But Mommy—"

"Just do as I said, please? I'll be right back."

At the house, Kelly pushed the door inward, stepped inside, and held it open for him. "This is our palace, not much, but it does beat the cell that I spent that night in."

"It is small, but it's cozy and clean. I should hire you to clean my condo."

"Sure, that's all Rocky would need to know. Actually, we better do this quick before he shows up." She showed him to a chair at the kitchen table and sat across from him. "I'm all ears."

He leaned forward, folded his arms on the table, and smirked. "Kelly, you're off the hook."

Her chest deflated and her face brightened. "So, you got the bastard. It was Jordan, wasn't he? That little creep."

Cody stared at her, wordless, a serious look on his face.

Kelly squinted at him. "You don't look happy, why?"

"Of course, I am, but…"

She sprung off the chair, rushed over to his side, and gave him a long hug. "If I ended up in jail, I don't know what I would have done." Placed her hand on his shoulder and looked straight in his eyes. "Cody, thank you. Thank you from the very bottom of my heart." With her eyes sparkling, she gave him a brotherly kiss on his cheek.

He remained cool throughout her celebratory actions and wished that her kiss had been birthed out of a different situation, but it was a step in the right direction for him. He had never liked Rocky. He couldn't stand his rude, bullying, and vulgar nature, and always felt that Kelly deserved better. He hated him for getting her pregnant and out of school and was now thrilled that he was going to get his ass behind bars, but his heart bled because he realized that she still loved the jerk, and the news was going to hit her hard.

"Sorry, I couldn't resist." She placed her elbows on the table and leaned forward. "I hope you arrested him with the same cuffs that I was arrested with, like Joe had promised me."

While gathering his courage, he gazed at her. "Yes, we did, but the bastard who planted the coke in your car wasn't Jordan."

"Who was it then, his cokehead friend?"

His forehead sprouted sweat below his blond hairline. "No, Kelly. The bastard was your husband."

"What?" Her face sagged like a punctured balloon. "That's impossible, he wouldn't do that to me! No way, you guys are wrong!" She sprung off the chair. "I need a drink." Snatched the glass from the countertop, walked to the sink and filled it to the rim. Guzzled half of it, turned to him again. "Are you suggesting that he wanted to see me locked up?"

"Kelly, I'm not here to judge anyone, I'm here to tell you the facts as they stand now."

She stood next to the sink silently, crying as clips of her life flashed through her mind, shaking her head in disbelief. "How can you be sure?"

"Kelly, please listen carefully. Since I called you the other day, I have been talking to people in every bar that he hangs around, a few people who he regularly mows their lawns, and had a lengthy conversation with his boss, and by the way, not his partner."

"That's not true, his boss made him a partner last September."

"Kelly, he lied to you. He did that to cover up his drug dealing business."

Now she was crying a river. Was that why he had snatched the phone out of her hand when she wanted to talk to his boss? He must have been planning this from the very first day she had started school. "What do you have on him that you're so sure?"

"All the information I was gathering pointed to the fact that he must have been dealing. So, on my own time, with my own car, I got permission to surveil him. And around eleven this morning, I caught him in the middle of a transaction with one of his customers. I quickly called for backup, and the rest is history."

That's why he hurried out of the house this morning, she thought. *His partnership and working hard to accumulate that money were all lies.* She sat up straight. "But that still doesn't prove he is the one who framed me."

She's still as naïve as a teen, Cody thought, sympathetic. *Why should I be surprised though, that bastard has been controlling and manipulating her since she was sixteen years old.* Still, it was heart-breaking to watch her defend him. "I know how betrayed, discouraged, and hurt you must feel, but the reality is that he has been charged with possession of illegal drugs with intent to sell, and the clearest fingerprints recovered from the package in your car belong to him. Plus, he is the only one who had the means, the opportunity, and perhaps the motive to do this to you. I'm really sorry for you, but not for him."

"I get it," she muttered, "I get it. That was his sure way to get me out of everything, even at the cost of ruining my life, our beautiful daughter's, and his. How crazy has he become?"

Cody was silent, allowing her the space to reflect.

Slowly, she drank some more water. "What happens now?"

"Until Tuesday morning, he'll be sitting in the same cell that you were in that night. Then he will appear in court where the judge will… Well, you know the rest." He paused for a while and there was total silence. "Kelly, are you going to bail him out?"

"I don't know. But even if I wanted to, where would I get the money?"

"Assuming you could come up with the money, I still wouldn't do it. Being that heartless, who knows what else he would do now that he is about to lose total control over you? I also suggest that you get a restraining order against him just in case he makes bail somehow."

She wiped her eyes and face with a paper towel. "How am I going to tell Hope?"

"You know, the chief felt so bad for you that when I asked him to officially come to see you in my civilian clothes and my own car to avoid unnecessary neighborhood bickering, he didn't hesitate."

"Thank him for me, please?"

"I also need to tell you that the detective is on his way with a search warrant. I'm sorry, but as part of our investigation, we need to search your entire house."

"Go ahead, but please do it as quick as possible, I need to be left alone for a while."

Just as she had said that the detective rang the doorbell. He walked in and shook her hand first. "Kelly, I told you we would get him, and we did, but I'm sorry that it turned out this way."

"I'm devastated but thank you."

"We're gon' be out of here in no time." He handed her a copy of the warrant, and cautiously started searching every section and piece of furniture throughout the kitchen and living room area, while Cody started in their bedroom.

She clasped her head in her hands, and stared at the tabletop, trying to make sense of all that had happened over the previous few weeks. *I have saved enough money to buy us a house. Exactly 10,750 dollars.* What a liar.

I should have never trusted him the way I did, she thought. *I never even checked with his boss to see if he had really made him a partner when he first told me. For God's sake, how could he have done this to us?*

She remembered what Joe had said at her court hearing. *Did you ever tell her that I gave you a warning that night and I also told you that the chief was serious about stationing us there indefinitely?*

He must have been setting the fight up from that very morning, she realized. That's why he had come to the school. A painful lump was growing in her heart bigger by the second. How could he have become so heartless? Wiping her eyes, she lifted her head and caught Cody entering the bathroom and the detective walking to Hope's room.

Not long after, she heard the rumbling of a piece of wood, and seconds later, "Bingo," the detective hollered, coming out of the room holding a plastic bag up with a lot of dollar bills in it, and few small packages of cocaine. At the sight of the bag, her mouth gawked, and her eyes bulged.

Cody and the detective looked at her, and then at each other with a sympathetic look on their faces.

"We both know you are totally unaware of this but prepare yourself because Rocky is going away for quite a while," the detective said.

She buried her face in her hands. "Please, I have had enough of this roller coaster, I'd like to be left alone now."

***

"Mi amor, Hope is taking a nap. Is that jerk starting all over again?"

The shock had drained all the energy out of her, and she was not about to prolong her torment any more than she needed to. "Please, when she wakes up, say goodnight to her for me. Tomorrow I'll tell you everything."

"You be careful. Just call the police if he starts pushing you around again."

"Thank you, Rosita."

Kelly went to the fridge, took out a beer and then a clean glass from the cabinet next to it. There, hidden behind some other taller glasses, she noticed the pint of whiskey that he was drinking the night she was arrested. It still had about a quarter left in it. She stared at it for couple of seconds and snatched it. *Maybe that's what I need.* Took the phone off the hook, lowered all the window shades and blinds, shut all the lights but the one in the bedroom on her nightstand and pulled the door closed, leaving only a small crack open for some light to get through.

She sat on the couch, resting the beer can on the coffee table in front of her, poured a shot or so worth of whiskey in the glass, and, emulating both her father's and her husband's motions, she gulped it down. Then rushed her hand to the beer can, and took a long gulp, chasing the burning fluid down her gullet. *I guess that's why they drink both at the same time.*

Kelly laid across the couch and stared at the streak of light filtering through the bedroom door. *Prepare yourself because Rocky is going away for quite a while.* She sat up and poured another shot. Grabbed the beer ready for the chase and did them both. Shook her head a couple of times. *That's better.* Snatched her denim waistcoat off and threw it on the side of the coffee table. *Mommy, why isn't Daddy coming home anymore?* At that thought, her eye started twitching. *How am I going to tell her?*

She hadn't smoked a cigarette for quite a while, but now she had a sudden urge. Sure enough, there was a full pack in the cabinet. She started looking for matches. Couldn't find any, grabbed her manual sparker and turned one of the gas stove burners on. Lit her cigarette over it, and quickly turned the knob back to the off position. Went back to the couch and started puffing on the cigarette and sipping on the beer. *My mother never worked, my aunts didn't, and neither are you.* The puffing and sipping increased in speed as her mind struggled to come to terms with her new reality. *I won't let you embarrass me.*

She was all alone now. What was she going to do? Her face dripped with sweat and tears. She choked her cigarette and stormed to the bathroom. Stripped naked and jumped in the shower, where she stood still for a while as the lukewarm water splashed on her face and trickled through her hair down the rest of her slender body. *You stay home where you belong, cooking and cleaning for me. Like you have and like my mother did for her husband, and her mother before her did for hers.*

She stepped out of the shower and, drying herself, stumbled her way to the bedroom. Threw the towel on the chair at the feet of the bed, grabbed one of his T shirts from the dresser, and slowly dragged it over her head.

Stubborn jerk. *If he trusted me, we wouldn't be in this dreadful mess.* Went back to the stove, repeated the same steps, and lit another cigarette. Sat back on the couch again, poured the rest of the whiskey, gulped it at once, and followed it with another long gulp of beer. *Unplug those fucking ears of yours. I said, I don't have it!* She shook her head. It was so heartless of him to let their baby go through such a humiliation. *And they all laughed too.* And for what, a twenty-dollar bill in the twenty-first century?

Choked her cigarette, gulped the rest of the beer, waddled her way to the bedroom, and plopped on the edge of the bed. Then tried to sit up straight, but her head was too heavy. Grabbed on to the bottom sheet above her head and slowly dragged her body across and up, ending with her arms and legs spread out wide, her T-shirt ruffled up to her waist, exposing her bottom half. Extended her arm to reach the nightstand's light switch but failed. Dragged her body further up, reached for the switch and shut the light off.

She rested her head on the pillow and stared at the whirling ceiling with tears sprouting from the corners of her eyes again, trying to come to terms with what she was facing after eight years of marriage. *Hey, once the baby is a little older, there is no reason why you can't go back to school.* "Liar," she yelled. "Liar, liar, you're nothing else but a liar."

You all know the way to the fridge, but do you know how it gets there? Her body kept quivering and her hands pressing over her ears ever so tight. *Like you lived in a fucking castle when I first met you, right?*

"You crazy son of a bitch, I was only sixteen."

Kelly, I am overly impressed with you. I haven't had a student scoring a perfect hundred on that test for quite some time. Keep it up honey, and the sky will be your limit.

What was she going to do?

Longing for refuge, her fingers found her vulva, her skin prickled, her eyes shut tight, her thighs sealed tighter, her fingers rattled faster, and her body twirled like a wounded snake inches above the mattress. "Yes, yes…" she cried, leaning her head onto her shoulder as her body deflated. "Tomorrow, tomorrow, I…"

CHAPTER TWENTY-THREE

Abruptly, her eyes opened. The ceiling was no longer whirling, the T-shirt was choking her sturdy breasts, and her hands were tight between her thighs. "Shit, not again," she muttered and snatched them off. Planted them to her side to sit up, but her throbbing head dragged her right back down. Staring at the ceiling with her eyes watery, her face sank into a dismal state. *If you change your mind before the two weeks are over, or even after, you'll always have a job here.*

She made her way to the shower where she soaked, soaped, and scrubbed every inch of her body. Dressed, she got the coffee pot going. Dialed Rosita's number.

"Kelly, what's going on?"

"Is Hope near you?"

"No, she is still sleeping like an angel."

"Rocky was the one who planted the packet of cocaine in my car."

"What?"

"That's exactly how I reacted when Cody told me."

"That no good son of a bitch. Where is he now?"

"In the same jail I spent that night in, except that he'll be in one of those for a long time."

"Maybe that's what he needed all along. What about you, what you're gon' do now?"

"Other than trying to get my job back, I'm not sure. Can I pick Hope up after I get back?"

"You really need to ask me?"

"I know, I'm sorry."

"Go get your job back and don't worry about us."

***

In his white shirt and his long sleeves folded up to his elbows, George was in his office, scribbling something. She stood on the threshold and waited for him to notice her.

Surprised, but happy to see her, he smiled. "Don't just stand there, have a seat."

She closed the door behind her, sat. "I need to—"

"You know, you look great in black."

"In this cheap thing, or in your black uniform?"

"In both. And although that T shirt might look cheap on someone else, it looks great on you."

"Thank you."

His lips widened into a sneaky smile. "Hey, let's not make a habit of this, people might start talking."

"I'm sure people are going to talk about me over one thing or another anyway."

"Why you look so strained? Isn't being a housewife with no rushing to work and all relaxing?"

"OK." She placed her pocketbook on her laps. "Before the news is spread by our local newspaper, it was my husband who planted the cocaine in my car, and yesterday he was arrested for it."

"You're kidding?"

"No." She looked away. "And he might be going away for a long time."

"That son of a bitch. I tell you, if you were my daughter, I'd kill the bastard."

"George, that wouldn't make things any better now, but I appreciate your empathy."

"What you're gon' do now?"

"I'll have to figure things out, but to start with, I'd like my job back."

He stared at her. "Kelly, I don't know if I can do that. It would really piss off the girl I hired in your place."

"But I thought you said—"

"That if you changed your mind before the two weeks were over, or even after, you'll always have a job here. Yes, I did say that."

"So, did you mean it, or you just said it to comfort me?"

"Of course, I meant it but—"

"OK, I get it." She got up. "I'm all alone now, with the responsibility to put food on the table for my daughter and I and to keep a roof over our heads. So, I better get started looking somewhere else then."

"Wait!"

She turned around. "For what, to comfort me a bit more so that you can feel better about yourself?"

He shook his head. "Please, sit and let me think for a moment."

Since she had left, there hadn't been a day without a customer asking him when she was coming back to work. They loved her, and that meant cash in his register. He resumed looking at the schedule he had been working on before she had interrupted him. "And you would need the same hours you had before?"

She got up again. "Forget it. I wouldn't want you to get rid of the new girl because of me anyway."

"You got them. And don't worry about the new girl, I'll figure something out for her."

"Are you serious?"

"When can you start?"

She heaved a sigh of relief. "If you'd like me to, tomorrow."

He got up, shook her hand. "Tomorrow it is."

"George, you have no idea how much this means to me, thank you."

"Kelly, you're a strong young woman, you're smart, and you're a hard-working person, I'm sure you'll be better off without him."

"Only time can show me that."

***

"Mommy?" Hope jumped in her arms. "I missed you so much."

"Me too, very, very much." Kelly held Hope tight to her heart. "Now go back to play for a little longer, I need to talk to Rosita."

"Why can't I stay?"

"Because this is a grownup talk. Just for a little while, please?"

"But I'm almost nine now?"

"I know honey, but you're still too young for what we need to talk about, please?"

"OK…" Head wilted, Hope made her way back to the living room.

"Kelly, have a seat while I make us a fresh cup of coffee."

"I can use it, thank you."

"So, how did it go with George?"

"I'll go back to work tomorrow, and he gave me the same schedule I had before this thing started."

"That was nice of him. See, things do happen for a reason."

"What you mean?"

"Now you decide when, or if, you go to work. When, or if, you go to school, and when, or if, you want to do anything else."

Kelly gazed at her coffee. "That's true, but I feel—"

"Don't tell me you're feeling sorry for him. Kelly, don't forget that if he had succeeded, you'd be the one going to jail. Your life could've been over, and Hope would have been left with a father, who, in my opinion, doesn't care much about her either."

"I know, but for the last eight years—"

"I don't know about all your years together, but for the last couple of years, I have seen him treating you like a slave and not a wife."

"I don't know what to think anymore."

Rosita placed her hand over hers. "Less than a year ago, you had never worked, and school was only a dream. Then you fought your way to go to work, and then fought your way to go to school, reawakening that desire and strength that you always had in you, only to see them almost crushed again by his selfish actions. Maybe it was your determination that brought him to do what he did, but for sure it wasn't your fault. Now you need to make your dreams come through for you, and your little girl there."

Kelly took a sip of coffee. "Throughout my life, despite the fights and arguments with my father, and then Rocky, I never felt as alone as I do now."

"I understand, but he was never good for you. Let him go."

"Can I use the phone?"

Rosita smiled at her. "When you're gon' stop asking me if you can use my things, or my help. Mi casa es tu casa."

"I know, I'm sorry." She walked to the phone and dialed Gilda's number.

"Kelly, how come you're not in school?"

"I didn't sleep well last night."

"Was it because of the problem with the cocaine in your car?"

Hope was still playing in the living room. Kelly moved as far as the receiver cord stretched. "Yes."

"I hope they find the bastard."

"They have." Kelly hesitated for couple of seconds. "That cocaine belonged to Rocky."

"That is the craziest thing I ever heard. Rocky doesn't do drugs."

"That's what I thought too, but he was dealing it. They caught him selling it to someone."

"You got to be kidding me, that's serious shit."

"I am not, and he is going to jail now."

"So, then the problem is no longer yours."

"From that point of view, you're right."

"So, what you gon' do now?"

"To start with, tomorrow I'm coming back to work."

"Wow, that was fast."

"I have no choices; I have to be the breadwinner now."

"Hey, now you can also go back to school and graduate by December as you had planned."

"Gilda, for now I'm just focused on finishing this semester, that's all."

"If I were you, I'd take full advantage of him not being around."

"Gilda, I don't even know if I can feed us and pay all the bills, how can I be thinking about anything else?"

"Listen, if you need any money, I'll talk to my husband."

"That's nice to know, but whatever I do, I need to do it based on my own strength, but you could get me today's class notes from Clara if you don't mind."

"You got it. I'll bring them over right after school, and if you're sleeping by then, I'll put them in your mailbox."

"That's great, thank you."

Slowly, Kelly hung up the receiver and placed her hand over her forehead. How can Gilda be so sure that Rocky wasn't doing drugs when she had only seen Rocky a couple of times in the last eight years?

"What's wrong?" Rosita asked her.

"Some things Gilda said don't make sense."

"I wouldn't strain my brains over it, you know how she can be."

"I guess you're right."

"So, are you going back to school?" Rosita said with a wide grin on.

"I'd like to, but—"

"Honey, after what he did to you, he doesn't deserve any loyalty anymore."

"That's not what I meant. Now it's an all-new world for me out there."

"Listen, if you ever need help, we're here for you."

"Giving Hope a second home is more than anyone else has ever done for me, and I will forever be in debt to you for that."

"For the last time, you're my family that I could never have, and you're not in debt to us for anything."

Kelly hugged her. "After my mother died, I was lost, and then you came around."

Rosita wiped her eyes with the back of her hand and ushered her away with a smile.

On their way home, Hope gave her a detailed account of what they ate for dinner, breakfast and all the games she had played with Rosita and her husband. Then looked up at her. "Mommy, but why did I have to stay there all of that time?"

Kelly didn't want to tell what had happened and hadn't figured out how to handle it yet. "So, you had a fun time then."

"I did, Rosita said I am her princess."

"I'm happy that you like spending time with them." She pulled in the driveway and parked in her usual spot.

"Daddy must be still working."

Kelly pretended not to hear her. It was midafternoon, and after what she had been through for the last couple of days, she didn't feel like making a normal dinner for just the two of them. "Hope, while I make us something to eat, put your toys and books away." She put together two ham and cheese sandwiches, filled two glasses with orange juice, and both sat at the kitchen table to eat. In between bites, Hope asked, "Mommy, do you think Daddy will let me go swimming with Melina and Tom this summer?"

"If Gilda is OK with that, I think you'll be able to go."

"But I still have to see if Daddy says yes."

"Maybe not."

"I thought we can't do anything without Daddy's permission."

"If he was home, yes, but since he is not, we can make the decisions by ourselves."

"Mommy, we better ask him when he gets home. He is the man of the house, and I don't like it when he gets mad."

Kelly gazed at Hope's innocent face for a while and couldn't believe that her little girl was already being brainwashed. She couldn't allow Hope to fall into the same trap she herself had fallen into. "Listen to me. Men are not better than women, and women are not better than men. And married couples decide things together."

"But that's not what you and Dad do, he makes all the decisions."

"You're right, that's not what we have been doing, but yesterday when he told me that he was going to work far away for a while, we had a long talk, and he agreed that from now on, things are going to be different."

"What you mean, he went to work far away?"

Kelly looked away from her. "He found a better job in another state a few hours from here and will be back when the job is finished."

Hope started to cry. "Why didn't he say goodbye to me?"

"He had to leave in a hurry this morning, but he said to tell you that he loves you very much and will call as soon as he settles down."

"How long is a long time?"

A sudden knot took hold of Kelly's throat and a heavy weight settled on her chest. "Maybe a few months, or maybe more. Come here." She hugged her daughter. "Listen, time goes by fast, but for now, you and I are going to be fine. I need to do some homework now. Please, go to your room and play for a while?"

Kelly sat at the kitchen table. Rested her face in her hands and thought for a while. Then walked to the kitchen cabinets again, got all the paid bills, and separated them by categories. At the center top of the yellow pad, she wrote Budget for Summer and Fall semester, June 1, 2001 to January 31, 2002. To be on the safe side, she included January. Got the monthly average for each of the category and wrote them in a vertical column, name to the left, and amount to its extreme right. Her accounting courses were already profiting her. After she finished with the utility piles, she estimated her gasoline consumption, possible car repairs, essential clothes, and personal sundries. When she got to the groceries, she stripped them down to the bare minimum, and that came to a total of seventy-five dollars a week. She would dissect the chicken like her grandmother used to and get few breasts and the drums out of it for frying or baking. The stripped-down bones, she would boil them until she could pull the remaining meat from them, add it to the interior organs, the neck, the wings, and that should give her enough pulled meat and stock to make a huge pot of chicken soup to feed them at least three suppers a week. For the rest of the proteins needed, they would have to eat beans, chickpeas, and lentils, and for greens, they could eat dandelion leaves. When in season, they would pick them, clean them, freeze them in zipper bags, and then use them as needed. She was about Hope's age when her grandparents used to cook them with navy beans for a delicious soup, and at times also made them in a salad with sliced onions, olive oil, and vinegar. *Don't ever be ashamed of the means to get somewhere in life, so long as you get there with your head standing high.* She looked up. *Grandpa, please watch over us.*

She added the lines for her four hundred and fifty monthly rent, and fifty dollars a month for unforeseen expenses, added the column, and multiplied by eight. The total came to 8,875 dollars. She sighed, added them up again. To her disappointment, the total was still the same. Skipped a couple of lines and listed the tuition costs for her last thirty credits of 1,994 dollars. The books and school supplies, three hundred and fifty dollars. The grand total came to 11, 219 dollars. There was no way she could come up with that amount of money between her grants, student loans, and what she made at work.

She ripped a blank page from the yellow pad, estimated her net wages and tips for the next eight months, and came up with a total of 7254 dollars. To that, she added her five hundred dollar a semester grant and seven hundred- and fifty-dollars student loan per semester, making the total 9754 dollars. Exactly 1,469 dollars short. *I can't do it.* She pushed the yellow pad across the table and scattered the bills all over it, and to the floor. "Forget it, like Rocky would say, school no more."

With her eye twitching, she grabbed a glass of water, stood at the window, and sipped. And that did not include the health insurance that he had, which for sure would soon be canceled. It was time to come to terms that her dreams were only just dreams and leave them at that. Her destiny was to work at the diner full time and be a waitress for the rest of her life, not a shameful way of earning a living anyway. *Trust me, they will get to you after a while. Many are rude, especially at night after the bars close. And some are plain pigs, peering up our dresses every chance they get. And some, when we bent down to place the dishes in front of them, pretending to pay attention somewhere else, rub their elbows against our breasts and sometimes even our crotches.*

Gilda was totally right. Things like that had already happened to her, and she had only worked there for ten months. She picked up the bills that had fallen to the floor and placed them back the way they were before she had her second of tantrum. She shook her head. *Maybe I should get a bigger student loan, but what if they ask for Rocky to be part of the application process because it's more money? No.* She held the budget papers in her hands and kept gazing at the numbers.

In her pajamas, Hope rushed over to her. "Mommy, can I watch TV now?"

"Shut up!"

Hope jumped back, mouth agape. Kelly had never snapped at her like that before. "What did I do?" She ran to her bedroom and blasted the door behind her.

Kelly buried her face in her hands. *Oh God, what did I just do? What's happening to me?*

Hope was laying on her bed, face down, crying her heart out. She laid next to her and brushed her hand through her deep brown hair. "Honey, I'm sorry. I didn't mean it."

"You yelled at me for nothing, just like Dad does."

"It's just that you caught me by surprise." She pulled Hope up. "Come on, let's put the TV on for you."

Hope wiped her eyes with the back of her fists. "OK, if you promise not to yell at me for nothing no more."

"I promise, I won't."

Then staring at the numbers again. *I must find the way.* Re-added everything, hoping to find some errors, but there weren't any. Wait a minute. The rent was her biggest single expense. What if she talked to her landlord into taking some of her monthly rent as a loan, like she and Rocky did with their old house once? She got busy with the calculator again. If she could convince Mr. Casale to reduce her rent by two hundred dollars a month, which for eight months would come to 1600 dollars, her budget could work. She would sign a personal loan for one year and offer him fifteen percent interest, a lot more than what the banks were probably paying. After she graduated, if she couldn't get a job in accounting right away, starting with January she could work sixty hours a week at the diner, or get a second job somewhere else. That would allow her to pay the full rent again, and by June first she would be able to put together the eighteen hundred and forty dollars she would owe him with the interest.

Yes, if Mr. Casale goes along, this will work. She heaved a sigh of relief and smirked. Like her grandfather used to say though, don't count your chicks before they hatch. Nipping at the pencil rubber top, she looked at Hope's eyes opening and closing rhythmically. Walked over and helped her to bed. Now she needed to call Rosita to make sure that her schedule from June to December would be OK for her, because if it weren't, she might as well scrap everything.

"That's the best news I heard for a long time," Rosita said. "Whatever your schedule will be, don't worry because even if sometimes I need to call in sick at work, I'll do that for you."

"That's what I meant when I said after my mother died, I was lost and then you came around."

"Yes, but say no more, please?"

Sometime later, Gilda dropped by to give her the homework for the classes she had missed that morning, and Kelly told her that she was planning on staying in school.

Gilda was thrilled to hear that. "Hey, if you need help with anything, I mean anything, just let me know."

"Please, keep your voice low," Kelly whispered, "but don't just stand there, come in for a coffee."

"I can't. I got things to do at home before I go to work."

"OK, thanks for dropping off the notes."

"Like I said, whatever you need, I'll be here for you."

After Kelly watched Gilda getting in her car, she poured a cup of coffee, and while their small cheap microwave was warming it up, she put her budget papers to the side and started her homework.

An hour or so later, the phone rang. She rushed to pick it up, hoping it wouldn't wake Hope. "Hello?"

"Fuck, you are home?"

"And where would you expect me to be, in the same place where you are?"

"You think you're funny?"

"Not at all, you bastard. Why? Why did you do it?"

"To teach you a fucking lesson."

"I have no time for this crap, I have homework to do."

"I told you to quit, what the fuck you're doing?"

"It looks like you're going to be away for quite a while, and during that time, I must be the breadwinner. Tomorrow I'm going back to work, and if I can manage it, I'm not quitting school either, so that I can eventually provide our daughter with the life that I have been begging you for."

"When I get out, I'll show you who's the—"

"When you get out, you'll show me whatever, but for now the only thing I need you to do is to tell our daughter that you went to work some place far away and will be back in a few months or longer. You tell her anything different, and you will never talk to her again."

"I tell her what I want and when I want to. Get her on the phone."

"No, unless this time you think of someone else and not just yourself as usual."

"OK, this time you win. I only got two minutes left, get her on the fucking phone."

Kelly woke Hope up gently, told her that her dad wanted to say hi to her, helped her to the phone, and went back to the table with her ears wide open.

Hope was thrilled to hear from her dad. They exchanged a few words and then he had to hang up. "Mommy, he said goodnight to you too, and asked me to tell you that he loves you."

"That was nice of him."

Hope placed her arm on her mom's shoulder. "He also said he might be back in a few days for a couple of hours, and then when his job is finished, he'll be back forever."

"That's what he told me too." She looked at her. "Are you hungry?"

"A little, are you?"

"Honey, I have to finish my homework. Can you make yourself a sandwich like I made you earlier?"

"I can do that."

By the time she finished her homework, it was 10:30. She organized her books and her uniform for the next day, and while Hope was going to bed, she called Cody. "Yesterday you told me to get a restraining order against him. If he is going to be in jail, why do I need that?"

"Kelly, if he makes bail tomorrow, he is going to be out until his court date, and that could be weeks or even months, depending on how his attorney operates. If you don't have the restraining order, he would even be able to stay with you guys, and I can only imagine what he could do. Please get it?"

"Why wasn't he brought to court the day after he was arrested like I was?"

"I don't know. There must have been a mix up at the station, but he's going tomorrow morning for sure."

"What do I need to do?"

"Just come to the station first thing in the morning. We'll drive to the court to get it, and then inform his attorney of such before he's done with his court appearance."

"Cody?

"Yes?"

"What if he flips out?"

"That's even more of a reason why you need it."

CHAPTER TWENTY-FOUR

Early the next morning, she met with Cody and together drove to the court to get the Restraining Order. Then he drove her back to the station to get her car. "You go do what you need to do, and I'll take care of the rest."

"Cody, thank you. I just hope he doesn't go crazy."

"Don't worry about it, I'll be watching him. Go, go to school now."

***

Normally, in between classes she would go to the cafeteria and do as much of her previous class's homework as possible while sneaking a bite in between, but that day she needed to seek her counselor's approval for her planned summer and fall classes that would lead her to graduate by December. Of course, if she could put the money together, that is.

After she gave the counselor an intensive sales pitch that she could handle the heavy load for both the six summer classes and the four fall classes, the counselor took a second look. "I must say that I am hesitantly approving them. However, I'd also like you to know that if there is one student who I can comfortably say that could pull this off, it is you."

***

After work, she picked Hope up from Rosita and drove straight home. "Hope, I need to rest for a few minutes, please go to your room and play with your toys for a while, we'll have dinner a little later."

"It's OK, Mommy, I think I'll take a nap too."

Kelly was just about to doze off when the phone rang. "Come on, please give me a break," she whispered dragging herself up.

"You bitch, what the fuck did you do? You're kicking me out of my own house?"

"No, you are," she said in a low tone so that Hope would not hear.

"You're the one who filed the restraining order."

"And what did you expect after what you tried to do to me?" Her body stiffened. "If it weren't for Cody, you would have put me in jail. What did I do to deserve that? Tell me, what?"

"You were getting out of control."

"Out of control?" She shook her head. "What am I to you, a puppet whose strings broke? You're gon' have a lot of time to reflect on what you've become, and I hope that you do just that."

"There is nothing wrong with me. You're the one that needs to be molded again."

"I'm warning you. Follow the order and stay away from us because Cody will not be far behind you. If you don't, you might go away for even longer."

"So, Cody is your new fucking partner now?"

"That state of mind got you where you are now. Please, start judging people for who they are, and not for what your distorted mind makes them to be."

"My mind is fine. Yours is the fucked up one. Going to school and going to work, it's not what a housewife is supposed to do."

Kelly hung up at once and checked the front and back door, and then all the windows to make sure they were all locked. Went back to the phone and placed an order to have the phone number changed. At first, they gave her a tough time because the phone was in her husband's name, but after she gave them a detailed account of what had happened, they asked her to bring the restraining order with her the next day.

First thing next morning, she got her new number and gave it to the few people close to her and her boss.

***

At school, she walked out of her last final, confident that she had done well, and as she approached the elevator, she noticed her accounting professor waving at her to wait. A handsome man in his late thirties, he caught up to her, adjusted his eyeglasses, and asked her if she had time for a quick cup of coffee. She hesitated at first, then agreed. He pushed the elevator button and leaned against the door frame, facing her.

"Kelly, you must be relieved."

"Yes, it's been a long semester."

The door opened, and he motioned her to enter first. She was in her jeans, her white short-sleeve top, and her blue sneakers. He snuck a quick glance at her back and stepped behind her. Once inside, they both leaned their backs against the elevator's side walls, facing each other.

"I heard you're going to have a full schedule this summer."

"Yes, Mr. White."

"Please, call me Lenny. Being that you're still so young, can I ask you why you're working so hard?"

"It's a long story."

"Longer than the time it takes to drink our cup of coffee?"

"Yes." She nodded.

They headed straight for the cafeteria. "Kelly, how do you drink your coffee?"

"Just black."

"Is that the secret for a young mom to stay slim and fit as you?"

"Maybe?"

The cafeteria was much different from a usual school day. There were just a handful of students and staff scattered throughout the hall. He pointed to an empty table with four chairs. "Would that table there be OK?"

"Yes, that will be fine."

"I'll be right back."

After they both took their first sip. "So, now tell me why you're in such a hurry?"

She smiled. "I'll tell you an edited version." Threaded her long-curly-black-hair over her shoulders. "I work as a waitress at a diner. I make decent money, but that's not good enough for the lifestyle that I dream for my family to have. We live in a small house, and even though the expenses aren't a lot, we're always missing a penny to put together a dollar. I am tired of it, and I want to put an end to that as soon as possible."

Captivated, he was absorbing every word. "Why don't you get some financial help like many students in the same situation here do? They get everything paid for, and don't have to worry about working."

She gave him a mild sneer. "I like to earn my own way."

Puzzled by her reaction, he said, "I'm sorry if I offended you."

"That's OK." She put her books in her arms. "Thank you for the coffee, Mr. White, it was nice of you."

"Again, I'm sorry, but please wait. I'd like to talk to you about something you might be interested in."

She sensed that he was somewhat frustrated and decided to sit back down. "Just for a little longer though because I have to pick up my daughter from school."

"You're one of the best students I have had in a while." He leaned forward. "I don't know if you're aware that I am a partner in a local CPA firm. Anyway, we're always looking for smart, serious, and determined people like yourself, and…"

"And?"

"And I would like for you to join our staff. Of course, after you graduate, and after we agree on a salary, which I guarantee you it will be a good one." He smirked. "What do you say?"

She leaned back, breathless. Something like that hadn't even crossed her thoughts. "You caught me by surprise, Mr. White."

"Again, please call me Lenny."

"OK Lenny. Unless I overcome my heavy load for the next two semesters, December graduation is still only a dream for me." She paused. "What if I don't pass some of the courses?"

"What if we get a snowstorm in the month of July?" Lenny replied.

"You have that much confidence in me?"

He rested his arms on the table and leaned forward again. "Look, I have talked to every professor that had you in their classes and everyone in the administration that knows you before I made the decision to approach you. We don't want you to rush into anything, but as you go through these next seven months, keep this in mind. Around the end of the fall semester, I will invite you to our firm, introduce you to all my colleagues, and we'll take it from there. What do you say?"

She was absorbing every word gliding out of his lips as her insides sparkled like a firework display on a clear Fourth of July night. But that meant that now more than ever, she needed to resolve her financial shortfall. "I'm astonished, but I guess I can do that."

"That's great." He got up, shook her hand. "You can go get you daughter now. Come on, I'll walk you out."

"It's OK, I need to make a phone call first, but thank you."

Scanning her model-like body as she walked over to the public phone, he called, "I'll see you in my class in couple of weeks."

"See you then, Lenny."

She dialed her landlord's number and his wife answered. After a couple of friendly exchanges, Kelly asked her to tell her husband that she would like to see him that coming Sunday around 2 o'clock to talk about the next month's rent, if possible. Before they hung up, the lady promised her that she would tell her husband, and if he couldn't make it, she would have him call her.

***

Sunday before Memorial Day, the same day Kelly was to have the meeting with her landlord, Gilda invited her and Hope to spend the day at the pool. At first Kelly had said no, but after some arm twisting, she agreed with the understanding that Gilda would watch Hope while she would go back home to meet with her landlord.

"Mom, this is Osborndale Park, not Gilda's house."

"Geez, I must have lost my mind," she joked. "See those few people bending down up the hill there?"

"Yeah?"

"They're picking dandelions, and we're going up there, a little further from them, and we are going to do the same."

"Mom, why do you want to pick up weeds?"

"When I was about your age, my grandfather used to bring me here to pick them and then we used to cook them either with beans as a soup, or make a salad with them, and they were delicious. It's time that you learn about them too. He used to always say, 'If there will ever be a time when there is no more food in the stores, these will help you survive.'"

"Why would the stores have no more food?"

"Some other time I'll explain it to you."

After they had filled three grocery bags of the deep green leaves, Hope puffed, "Mommy, I'm tired, let's go."

"Go sit under that oak tree there, I'll pick two more bagful and then we'll go."

Later, while chatting with their pina coladas in their hands, they were resting under a burgundy umbrella, watching their kids jumping, laughing, and splashing water from one end of the pool to the other. When Gilda told her that if she didn't tell her whether she was going to continue school through the summer to graduate in December, she was going to give birth to her ovaries, Kelly decided not only to tell her that probably yes, but she also told her of her meeting with her accounting professor who had promised her a job right after graduation. And when Gilda followed up with what she was going to do if Rocky didn't approve of the plan, Kelly told her that she would then be open to the possibility of divorcing him.

***

"Mr. Casale, please come in." Kelly gestured.

He held her hand tight and shook it couple of times. "Kelly, how are you?"

"Good, and you?"

"Ah, the years pass, and the legs get heavier."

Kelly filled a glass with ice and water and brought it to him.

He accepted it, scanning her up and down. "Kelly, you turned out to be a beautiful woman."

"That's a nice compliment, thank you." She smiled and sat across from him.

"Tu nonnu Calogero would be very proud of you."

She shuffled the papers in front of her. "I don't know about that."

"You mean after what happened?"

Not sure whether he was referring to Rocky or not, she decided to play dumb. "What you mean?"

"If Rocky's father was alive, he would have snapped that cornuto head off with his bare hands."

Her face reddened. "How do you know?"

"Kelly, people talk." He shook his head. "But why would he want to do that to you?"

Realizing that there was no reason to hold anything back, Kelly opened to him. "I don't know if you're going to believe me or not, but these are the facts. Since Rocky lost his job a few years ago, and unable to find another one as good, we've been living just above poverty level. To help, I got a job, and then I also went back to school hoping to someday get a better and higher paying one, but he didn't want me to work and he didn't want me to go to school, so to stop me from doing that, he planted a pack of cocaine in my car. When I asked him why, he said to teach me a lesson. The rest I think you already know."

"Only a paz would do some like that to his own family." Stunned, he leaned forward. "Why he did not want you to work?"

"He always told me that none of the woman in his family ever worked a day in their lives, or gone any further than few grades in school, and I was to follow their footsteps because he had married me to be his housewife, period."

"That's his father Lorenzo talking. He was a hardworking man and respected women, but at the same time he also considered them just another piece of property. I'm sorry, I wish one of my sons had been lucky enough to marry someone like you."

"That's a breath of fresh air, thank you, Mr. Casale."

"You know, it's pretty muggy in here and yet outside is cool. This house must be like a running furnace during the summer."

"And it is."

"Kelly, I have a small used air conditioning unit that would fit right in there." He pointed to the living room window. "If you like, I'll give it to you for free."

"That would be nice, but I can't afford the cost to run it."

"Are you sure? It's a small unit; it won't cost much."

"I'm more than sure, Mr. Casale." She paused for a while. "And that brings me to the reason why I wanted to meet with you today."

He laughed. "To tell me that you can't afford an air conditioner?"

"That is funny." She laughed along with him. "Since you knew about Rocky already, you must have also wondered where your next month's rent would come from?"

"That's true, that did cross my mind. So, what about it."

She shuffled the sheets of paper in front of her couple of times and picked up her budget. "Yes, paying you the rent for the next eight months is going to be quite stressful for me, to say the least, but please hear me out. If I go to school full time this coming summer and this coming fall, by December I'll graduate with an Associate in Accounting. The way things look, soon after, I should be able to get a job in that field that will pay between twenty and twenty-four thousand dollars a year to start with, and my counselor has already approved my schedule to achieve that."

He was gazing at her with his trademark smirk on and his lips sealed.

She handed him her class schedule for the next two semesters. "But for me to achieve that, I can only work thirty or so hours a week, which means I can only earn so much money." She noticed his temples twitching and stopped cold.

"Go on." He nodded.

"Here I've listed the basic expenses that my daughter and I will incur in the next eight months, including your rent and my school. And here is the list of my estimated earnings, my student loan, and a grant that the school gives me for being in the students' honor list. The problem is that I am still around 1400 hundred dollars short. I was thinking— "

"Aspett." His chair screeched under his chubby body. "Kelly, listen to me. I think I know where you're going with this, but before you go any further, I have an easy solution for you. I have many tenants that get most of their rent, utilities, and even cable TV paid for, on top of a monthly welfare check and food stamps. And they get all of that without lifting a finger for anything even related to work or school. Why you're wracking your brains for? Just go down the welfare office, sign up, and all your problems will be solved."

Wordless, she leaned back, her right eye twitching, her lips pursing, her temples pulsating. She gazed at him as if she had just seen a ghost.

"Then you could have not one but two air conditioners, one for here and one for your bedroom."

"Sure, along with my scarred soul."

"What're you saying?"

She leaned forward and looked straight in his eyes. "If I were physically and or mentally incapable to handle a job, and I mean any job, then, and only then, I would allow myself to fall into the grips of our big brother's degrading system, and only because in those conditions, I would have no say in it."

"I am not sure about some of the words you used, but I got the message. And you sound just like your grandfather Calogero." He shook his head. "The system is there, why not take advantage of it?"

"My grandfather had many stubborn and outdated views about life, some of which I wish he hadn't instilled in us kids, but on this issue, he was totally right." She got up and went to get a glass of water for herself too.

His eyes followed her to the sink. It seemed yesterday that he had held that little girl in his arms the day she was baptized, and look at her now, a beautiful woman with an ironclad willpower and beliefs.

"Mr. Casale, you brought up the subject and I can't help it but to expand on it now. How many families who got sucked into that degrading system were able to ever get out?"

He shifted uneasily. "I got no idea."

"Anytime one of them succeeds in getting out successfully, it gets all over the national news, but they rarely, if ever, talk about the millions who have comfortably settled into a life of perpetual poverty. If that isn't slavery through dependency, then I misunderstood the basic definition of slavery, which most dictionaries define as 'submission to a dominating influence,' in this case the dominating influence being the government, and in my marriage was my husband. Mr. Casale, I have been fighting hard to free myself from one form of slavery, and I'm not about to fall into another form, which will most likely be even worse for me. Back in high school, I had a few classmates whose single parents, like myself now, were on welfare. Guess what, now *they* are the single parents depending on the system."

"Kelly, everything you said is true. I see it with my own eyes, but you are a different person, and if you graduate by December like you said, it will only be temporary for you."

"You're right, I am different, and that's why I refuse to even be contaminated by that system."

"That would never happen to you because you are strongminded and have a strong goal to work for."

"But I'm also human. I will pick dandelions, cook them with kidney beans, and have it with old bread for breakfast, lunch, and dinner if I must before I subdue myself and my daughter to those humiliating handouts."

He looked at the countertop. "Is that why you have a ton of them there?"

While she was waiting for him, she had washed the five bags of dandelions and spread them all over the countertop to dry before placing them in the freezer. "Yes."

"Kelly, but—"

"With all due respect, Mr. Casale, there is no but. I need to earn my own way and pay for everything I get, which brings me back to where we were before we got sidetracked onto this bitter subject."

"OK," he said, shocked but impressed by her convictions. "Go on."

"For the next eight months, from June first to January first, I'd like you to take two hundred dollars off my monthly rent, a total of sixteen hundred dollars, and turn that into a loan. I am willing to pay you fifteen percent interest, a lot more than what banks are paying for a twelve-month CD nowadays, at least that's what they told me. The loan will be due on or before May 31st, 2002, exactly one year from this coming Thursday. On that day, if not before then, I'll pay you 1840 dollars in total. I know I will have no problem paying you back, whether I get a job in accounting or not, because after I graduate, I can turn my classes and studying hours into working hours at the diner, or with a second job somewhere else, and will work sixty or seventy hours a week to meet my obligation. What do you say, Mr. Casale?"

Fascinated by the detailed and knowledgeable presentation she gave him, he just stared at her.

Waiting for an answer, her anxiety level was steadily rising. "So, what do you say, Mr. Casale?"

The fifteen-percent interest had caught his full attention, like she had hoped.

"Are you sure you need to finish school? I think you could teach my accountant a thing or two."

"So, is it a yes or no?"

He studied her a bit longer. "If you promise me that when you become the president of the United States, I'll be the first one to get invited to the coronation ceremony," he said with a smirk, "I'll go home and try to convince my wife to do this for you."

She labored a smirk back to him. *He is not going to talk it over with her. I'm sure in his home, like in my grandparents' home and my home with Rocky, the men make all the decisions. Who is he trying to fool?*

"My wife has your number, right?"

"Yes, I gave it to her when we spoke last week."

He shook her hand. "It's much better to talk to you than that cucuzzo of your husband. You'll hear from us soon."

"Mr. Casale, thank you for your time." She shook his hand and led him to the door" Perhaps, her last move would be to ask George for at least ten more hours a week. Her grades could suffer, but If that meant the difference between graduating or stopping school altogether, she had no choice.

CHAPTER TWENTY-FIVE

She met with George about her summer schedule and asked him if he would increase her hours to forty hours a week if she needed it. He seemed a little annoyed with the managerial roller coaster that Kelly had been putting him through since January but said yes. Her new summer schedule called for Sundays off, and to show him how much she appreciated his understanding, she made herself available to work on Sundays.

A week after she had met with her landlord, she was working a shift for one of her coworkers who had called in sick. Around 11:30, George called her to his office and handed her the phone. She looked at him with hesitation, but after he assured her that wasn't Rocky, she took it.

"Hi Kelly, this is Mr. Casale. I'd like to meet you this afternoon at your house at the same time if it's OK with you. I have a couple of more questions."

Surprised, but happy to hear from him, "OK, that will be fine," she replied, pretending to be indifferent.

"Kelly, is there a problem?" George asked her.

"No, that was my landlord. Thank you for allowing me to take the call."

The meeting with Mr. Casale felt like a rendezvous of the previous Sunday, but the fact that he wanted to talk about it gave her some sense of optimism. What a relief if she could avoid working extra hours.

MY LAST CHANCE

It had been drizzling off and on all morning with temperatures in the seventies, also hot and humid. Not an unusual New England late spring day. She put the coffee pot on. She figured that if she had it ready, this time he might accept a cup. She made herself a quick peanut butter and jelly sandwich and sat at the kitchen table. She was just about to swallow her last bite when the doorbell rang. Mr. Casale was standing at the door with his politician smirk on.

"Come in, please." She closed the door behind them, pointed to the same chair he sat on the last time.

"Thank you." He placed a manila folder down.

"Today I have the coffee ready." She smiled and filled two cups. "Do you take milk and sugar?"

"Mi cara, at my age, the doctor makes those decisions. Just black is fine."

She placed one cup in front of him, the other in her spot, and sat down. "What else would you like to know?"

"My wife told me that the last time she remembers seeing you was while having coffee at your grandmother's house, and you were around four years old then. After I described you to her, she is dying to see you." He smirked. "You know how those Italian grandmothers are."

"I don't remember her, but I'd love to meet her. Anyway, I thought you wanted to know more about the deal I proposed you."

"Oh that? Jesus, I almost forgot the reason why I came." He opened the manila envelope, took two sheets out, and handed them to her. "You notice the loan starts June first and today is June third. Starting with this month, you would pay me two hundred dollars less for the rent per month until February first, 2002, like you asked me. Read these loan papers and if you agree, sign both sheets. And then, if you agree to these other two things that are not written in there, I'll sign them too. One, not later than a couple of weeks from today, you and your daughter come to visit us. And two, you'll never tell my wife that I am charging you the fifteen percent interest."

Kelly wanted to scream with joy but restrained herself. "Mr. Casale, that's a deal." *Now for sure I want to meet with Mrs. Casale to learn a thing or two on how to deal with Sicilian men,* she thought as she was signing the loan agreement.

He borrowed her pen. "I think now you can afford the cost of running the air conditioner too."

"Not yet, but if you can, hold it for me for next summer."

"I'll do that." He handed her one of the signed sheets and headed for the door.

She opened it for him. "I really appreciate what you're doing for me, Mr. Casale, and I promise you will not regret it."

"I know. George said the same thing."

***

She had just stepped inside the house with Hope ahead of her when the phone rang. What now?

"Hello?" She had only given her number to a handful of people. "Hello?" she said again.

"Hi Kelly." It was Angela.

"Hi stranger, I left couple of messages with your dad's secretary a while back, is everything OK?"

"Yes, she gave them to me with this number. I have been busy, but it's not the reason why I didn't return your calls." She paused for few seconds. "I'm sorry, Kelly, I really am."

"Sorry about what?"

"I'm not the friend I thought I was," she said weeping. "I wasn't there for you when you needed a shoulder to lean on."

"Hey, cheer up. You did stand by me when I was arrested, and you did tell Rocky to show up to court the next day."

"Yes, but I didn't show up there to support you. And then…"

"Listen, we're fine. Come on, give me that giggle."

Angela blew her nose. "When my father heard about the reason for your arrest, he lost it, and ordered me to stay away from you, or I could just leave the house and never go back. 'Associating with drug dealers is not good for business,' he yelled at me." She started crying again. "I feel like I sold you out."

"Angela, you didn't. You believed in me because you're my best friend and know me better, but until I was proven innocent, your dad had no choice but to react the way he did. In his place, I would have probably reacted the same way too."

"But when the truth came out, believe me, I let him have it until he apologized to me. Then he also asked me to apologize to you. He knows you're better than that, he said, and shouldn't have rushed to conclusions. Can you forgive us?"

"Angela, I never doubted you. I was just wondering if everything was OK, that's all. There is nothing for me to forgive, but if it makes you feel better, of course I forgive you."

"Thank you, sister, it means a lot to me."

"Listen, sometime in the next week or so, before I start my summer semester, we should meet for a cappuccino again at our favorite coffee shop."

"I can't wait."

"I'll call you soon."

As she was putting the receiver back on the hook, she heard a car coming to a stop across the street. She looked through the blind and saw a shadow of a man inside. The moment he noticed her, he took off at once. It wasn't Rocky's Vet, or a car that she recognized. Quickly, she closed the curtain and locked all the windows and doors throughout the house.

***

Rocky had been climbing the walls at a motel room for about an hour, waiting for Gilda. "It's about time."

She sank her tongue in his mouth. Then plopped on the bed, grabbed the bottom of her black uniform, pulled it up to her hips, and spread her legs, exposing her pantyless crotch. "It's screaming your name, take me."

"We need to talk first."

"But you said you were so horny."

"And I am, but first things first." He lit a cigarette and laid next to her. "What is my bitch up to now?"

"Why you're calling her a bitch for?"

"How else you want me to call her? She threw my ass out of my own house and is stopping me from seeing my daughter when I want to."

"You're right on that, she didn't have to go that far, but stay cool and soon everything will be over."

"Bullshit, I'll be gone for at least six months."

"That's what they gave you?"

"Yeah. That fucking female judge, who was probably a slut or a lesbian when she was young, wouldn't listen to my lawyer."

"So, when are you going away?"

"Wednesday, to the Cheshire Correctional Institution, thirty minutes or so from here."

"At least it's close to home."

"What difference does it make? I'm not commuting."

"Don't be funny, I meant if someone wants to visit you."

"You told me that Kelly went back to work and is going back to school, but how she'll be paying for the bills, the rent, and all?"

"I tried to push couple of extra margaritas on her around my pool, but she wouldn't budge."

"Working part time, it's impossible for her to make enough money to go to school full time and pay all the bills. Unless that fucking Cody is footing the bill to get in her pants."

"Rocky, I don't think so, at least not yet."

"Then where will she be getting the money?"

"What difference will it make? She must have found a way and is graduating in December, whether you're still in jail or not."

"Over my dead body."

"Actually, you might not like to hear this, but she already has a job lined up with an accounting firm."

"What the fuck did you say?"

"Her accounting professor, who by the way is single, offered her a job in his firm. Sometime before the end of the fall semester, he is going to invite her to his office, introduce her to the rest of his male partners and negotiate a salary."

"Working with a bunch of three-piece suits?" He grabbed her arm in his giant hand. "Is that what she told you?"

"Word for word. She also thinks that by the time you get out you'll accept her as a partner and not just as your slave anymore. And if you don't, she said she gon' divorce you."

His face was shaped in a rectangle of rage. ""Fuck her, I'll get her ass, you'll see!"

CHAPTER TWENTY-SIX

Summer was going to be impossibly busy, between school, work, and Hope. Four days before her summer schedule was due to start, Angela called.

"I was about to get into my car when Rocky approached me from nowhere and pleaded with me to get in touch with you."

"Really, for what?"

"He would like to see you guys before he goes away. He told me he will be in at least six months and would like to say goodbye in person."

"Now that it suits him, it's OK for you to talk to me at his wish?"

"Trust me, I was going to let him have it, but I thought of Hope, and here I am."

"Besides the fact that I don't want Hope to know where he is going, the restraining order prohibits us to getting within two hundred feet of each other."

"He said that he would tell Hope he came back with his boss just for the day."

"Angela, since when has he become thoughtful of others too?"

"Sister, sometimes it takes a big screw-up to open one's eyes." She giggled.

"Not that fast, not with Rocky."

"Think of Hope for now, he's still her father after all."

"Let me talk to Cody about it first."

"He said is going away on Wednesday, five days from now."

"The same day my summer semester starts, isn't that ironic?"

"His trial was this morning. He told me the judge sentenced him to nine months, but with good behavior, he could just serve two thirds of his sentence and get out in six."

"So, he could be out by December the sixth."

"Yes."

"Unless this ordeal really made him wake up, with his temper, he'll end up doing the full term or even more."

"I honestly think he has. During our entire conversation, he never used the word 'fuck.'"

"He also looked like a different man back in January when I was home with my injured foot. Anyway, let me talk to Cody and I'll call you after work tonight."

"OK, sister, till then."

She called Cody from the diner's public phone, and after she told him about what Angela had said, he said that he didn't see a problem with it but would ask his chief about it just to make sure and would let her know that evening after eight.

There was not one customer in the dining area. Her face drooped. Not only because no customers meant less much-needed tips in her pocket, but also because she hated hanging around with little to do.

Sometime later, a familiar looking man sat a few stools down from hers. Rested his arms on the counter, a pair of thick eyeglasses covering the top of his sad face and stared behind the counter where the coffee machines and a glass shelf containing several types of pies were. After gazing at him for a couple of seconds, her mental switch turned on. This was the guy she had caught peeking under her dress. Her stomach began to coil. She should go over and tell him that pigs like him don't belong in there.

The waitress assigned to the counter was in the kitchen getting supplies. Kelly stared at him, her blood boiling. "Sir, can I get you something?" she said coldly, hoping for him to toss a spark over her fuel.

"I'm sorry, I'm sorry," he babbled, his body shivering like a frightened child, his face turning whiter than milk, and his fearful eyes staring down at the counter. "It was wrong, it was wrong."

Her anger began to cool.

"It was wrong, it was wrong," he kept babbling, his hands clasped between his knees and his body jerking back and forth.

At that moment, the other waitress stepped out of the kitchen door, looked at the guy, then at Kelly, and stopped cold.

"It was wrong, it was wrong, it was—"

"Sir, calm down, please. Sometimes we all do things that we later regret," Kelly said. She handed him a glass of ice water. "Here, this will make you feel better." She smiled and watched him sipping water

"I'm sorry, I'm sorry, it was wrong," he said. Then he dashed toward the exit, still saying, "I'm sorry, I'm sorry."

"What the heck was that?" the other waitress asked.

Kelly sighed. "That's the guy I caught looking up my dress last summer. If I knew it was going to drive him that crazy, I wouldn't have yelled at him."

"He seemed pretty normal to me the other day when he asked me about your schedule."

"He did? Then he must have wanted to apologize really bad."

"That might be true because a few days ago, one of the night waitresses told me that around 10 o'clock, she was approached by a guy looking for you, but I forgot to tell you."

"How did he know I was working this afternoon though, when this is not my usual shift, and it was only decided late this morning that I'd be working?"

"Hey, maybe it was bothering him so much that he decided to stalk you until he got it off his chest." She smiled, "Kelly, cheer up, at least you have admirers."

"Do you know what type of car he drives?"

"I have no idea."

"If you happen to serve him again, please see if you can find out."

***

"Kelly, the chief said it's fine," Cody said, "but he recommends that you have someone with you, just in case. I can go if you'd like me to."

"I don't think it's a clever idea. You arrested him, remember?"

"You tell him that the chief suggested that I be present to make sure that things will not get out of hand."

"What about Hope? She doesn't know anything about what happened, and I'd like to keep it that way."

"She knows me as a friend, not a cop, right?"

"That's true."

"We're all set then."

"How about meeting him around 1 at the boardwalk in West Haven where there will be plenty of people around?"

"That's a smart choice."

"OK, let me call Angela to arrange it."

She dialed Angela's number and reminded her that Rocky should tell Hope exactly what he had told her earlier, and although Angela didn't quite agree about lying to Hope, she did exactly what Kelly had asked her to.

***

Kelly, Hope, and Cody walked to the boardwalk across from the bathrooms, but there was no sign of Rocky.

"We're a few minutes early," Cody said, looking at his wristwatch.

A bit later, Rocky ran toward Hope with his arms open wide.

"I missed you, Dad."

He pulled her up in his giant arms and gave her a long kiss on the cheek. "I missed you too." Sneered at Kelly, and then at Cody, who were standing next to each other few feet away. "But don't worry, when that job ends, we'll all be together again." He put her back down and walked over to shake Cody's hand and hugged Kelly as it had been agreed he would do.

Then he went back to Hope, hugged her again with tears forming in the corner of his eyes. "I'm gon' miss you a lot." Held her hand, walked a few feet away from Cody and Kelly, and talked for a while. "Remember, while I'm away, your mom is the boss of you, and you listen to whatever she says."

Cody watched his every move, and Kelly stood next to him, pondering. *Angela was right, he doesn't look like the same Rocky, but I wonder what else he got up his sleeves.*

CHAPTER TWENTY-SEVEN

School was practically empty compared to the Spring and Fall semesters. Throughout the days and weeks that followed, Kelly religiously stuck to her schedule. By the third week, signs of fatigue began to show on her face. Everyone cautioned her to slow down, but she brushed them away by saying, "My grandfather used to say, 'If the end justifies the means, it's all worth it.'"

***

Just before her last final of the first summer session, Kelly came down with a severe cold and fever. Her last test was on her Tuesday evening class. Armed with a bottle of pills and a box of tissues, she dragged herself to school. Her body was shivering, her eyes streaming, and her nose dripping steadily, conditions that would keep many people in bed under a ton of blankets.

I must finish it, I must, she thought, head down, fully focused. And before the allotted hour was over, she had completed her last question. Relieved, she gathered her books and approached Mr. White, who had been gazing at her often.

He looked at his watch. "Kelly, you're sure you don't want to review it. There is still plenty of time."

"I can't."

"You finished much too fast, maybe you should."

Shivering, she blew her nose. "I can't, my head is ready to explode."

***

Since it had rained on Fourth of July, Gilda had moved her party to that Saturday. Kelly got up early and spent a couple of hours preparing a mouthwatering tray of lasagnas.

Hope, still in her pajama and rubbing her eyes, walked up to her. "Mom, why didn't you wake me up? I wanted to help you with the lasagnas."

"I'm sorry, you were sleeping like an angel. Here, let me put the water on for you. The faster you take your shower, the quicker you get to the pool."

The word pool caused Hope to move fast.

The sun was strolling its way across the deep blue sky with a few scattered clouds following it. Gilda's circular driveway was already filled with cars and Kelly parked on the street only yards from the house she used to live in.

Rosita's husband carried the paella tray, and Kelly carried the lasagna one.

Gilda and her husband were getting the grill ready. "I smelled those trays the moment you guys took your first steps onto the yard." She pointed to the table where the food warmers were. "Let's put them over there." She scanned Kelly from head to toes and hugged her. "Which modeling magazine did you pop out of?"

"Gilda, please?"

Gilda hugged Hope, greeted Rosita and Carlos, and called for everyone's attention. "For those of you who weren't at last year's party, this is Rosita and her husband Carlos, and this is my friend Kelly and her daughter Hope." Then she held Kelly's arm and whispered, "So, it must be true that when the cat is away, the mice dance."

"Not at all. I just felt like dressing different for once, that's all?"

"You don't have to answer to anyone now, go for it."

"But that's not the reason."

"If I were you today…"

"If you were me what?"

"Never mind."

Rosita and Carlos made themselves coffee and started walking around the yard, admiring the well-manicured lawn, and mingling with some of the guests they had met the year before.

With a smile on, Kelly watched Hope mingling with some of the kids she had met at last year's party and jumping in the pool. Then she noticed Cody leaning against the corner of the deck, talking to a couple of the guys.

Cody smirked at her. "You're having coffee, are you serious?"

"Yes, what's wrong with that?"

"Kelly, it's a Fourth of July party for God's sake, come on, have a beer."

"Are you going to call your colleagues in both cities and tell them not to stop me on my way home?"

"If that's what it takes."

"What the hell then, I do deserve one anyway."

He snapped the top off a beer and handed it to her. Held his can against hers. "A salute. That's how you say it in Italian, right?"

"A salute. For an Irish man, I have to say I'm pretty impressed."

"This is the first time I see you wearing something other than jeans and tops since high school. In Hollywood, you'd be second to none."

"Cody, please, you're making me blush now."

"Sorry."

She moved closer to Gilda, who was still working on the grill. "Can I help you with something?"

"You know, I just remembered your incident of few days ago."

"What incident?"

"The afternoon waitress told me that the guy you embarrassed for looking up your dress at work came back and apologized to you in a very weird way."

"Oh that? Yes, he did."

"I don't know about that guy; you better be careful."

"Why?"

"Last week, he must have come in at least three times asking about you—when you were working next, and where you lived. I don't know what the other waitresses told him, but I brushed him off."

"I know. I guess he wanted to apologize to me, and he did."

"He just looked weird to me, that's all."

"So, what can I help you with?"

"Just chill out today, you need it." She nodded toward Cody and winked at her. "Isn't he a hunk?"

"Gilda, please?"

"You're free to do whatever you want now, and if I were you, I'd take him in a heartbeat."

"That isn't true, I'm still a married woman."

"So, you're going to sexually starve yourself until Rocky gets out?"

"I'm not that type of woman."

"Do you think Rocky would do the same for you?"

"Yes, I do."

"I wouldn't be so sure about that."

"What you mean?"

"Just that most men take whatever they can, whenever they can, and from whoever they can."

"I put up with a lot of his crap over the years, but if he wants to lose me forever, that's all he needs to do."

"Like I said, men take whatever they can, wherever they can, and whenever they can. Trust me, I know; I have been with a few of them."

"Well, I hope you're wrong about Rocky."

***

The afternoon flew by. Now she stood next to the pool cuddling a cup of coffee and watching Hope and the kids in the pool still laughing, yelling, and splashing water. She could count on one hand the social events attended during her eight years of marriage and couldn't help noticing that Rocky's absence had also absented the constant edginess that she used to feel. *I hope that these next few months will open his mind to today's realities.*

Between sips, she stared at the tall evergreen trees at the edge of Gilda's property. Through the crevices between them, she could see her old back yard and part of the house. She remembered their first Christmas as a married couple. She was a little over five months pregnant when Rocky had carried her through that door in his arms for the first time, laid her on the couch in front of the ardent flames, picked up a bottle of champagne from the fridge, blew the top against the fireplace stones, and sat next to her. After they had drunk a couple of glasses of the sparkling gold liquid, he had made love to her like he had never done before. If those greedy bastards hadn't moved their company to China, maybe they would still be living there, and who knows, he did allow her to get her G.E.D. then.

Cody placed his hand on her shoulder. "Are you OK?"

She jolted. "You scared me."

"I'm sorry. Would you like me to leave?"

"No." She clutched his arm. "It's just that—"

"You were reminiscing about your times there." He pointed his beer toward her old house.

"Until last year, I hadn't seen you since high school, how do you know that I used to live there?"

"I know the owners that bought it after you guys left. Today they are at someone else's party, but I am sure they wouldn't mind if we take a walk through their yard. Would you like to do that?"

"No, that would be trespassing."

He pulled her arm. "Come on, let's take a quick walk."

"We better not get in trouble."

"I'm a cop, and that does count for something."

"Kids, get out of the pool and dry up," Gilda yelled from the deck. "Kelly, we're having some to eat again, aren't you guys going to join us?"

"We're taking a quick walk to her old home," Cody replied. "We'll be right over."

"By the time the kids get dried up, we'll be here," Kelly added.

"Take your time."

The horizon's deep orange line was surrendering to the descending dusk. They walked through the spruces and were about halfway into the neighbor's yard when her right foot stepped in what looked like a mole's track. As her hand instinctively stretched out and down, seeking to shock absorb her fall, her coffee flew out and splashed on Cody's T-shirt and shorts, but his strong hold of her arm prevented her from falling. Holding her by one arm, he threw his beer bottle away, grabbed her other arm, and pulled her straight up, within inches from his face.

Looking straight in his light blue eyes, Kelly said, "Darn it, and I only had two beers, I—" Before the next syllable left her lips, he sealed them with his. She wavered before nestling in his arms like a deflating doll, her eyes shut as their tongues twirled, their bodies stemming heat like ardent flames. His hand slithered under her dress, his fingers fondling her black panties. His hand glided under her panties, her legs parted, his fingers slithered deep in her wet vulva, her arms clutched around his neck, her legs quivered. Suddenly, she jerked her lips away. "No," she cried, hiding her face in her hands. "This is wrong, I'm a married woman."

He stepped closer to her. "I'm sorry, I got carried away."

"It was my fault too." She wiped her eyes with the back of her hand. "I should have stopped you when you kissed me."

He pulled her chin up and looked straight in her eyes. "No, I shouldn't have kissed you in the first place. Please forgive me?"

"I just hope nobody saw us." She picked up her empty coffee cup and his empty beer bottle from the ground and they walked mutely back to the party.

***

While Hope slept, Kelly sat watching the tiny rays from her neighbor outside lights disperse throughout the room, falling on her pink cassette player laying on the dresser. She gazed at it for a while. Then opened one of the drawers below and tossed the few cassettes around until she came across "November Rain." Her sixteenth birthday flashed through her thoughts. It had been a long while since the last time she had played it. Inserted it in the player, pushed the play button, and turned the volume up just enough that she could hear it as she gazed at the ceiling again.

"And it's hard to hold the candle, in the cold November rain."

As the song's lyrics carried her thoughts to that lifechanging day, tears began to flow from the corners of her eyes. She could hear Rocky's voice as if she had traveled back in time. Pulled her night gown above her hips, shut her eyes tight, stretched her legs down and apart, and rested her hands on her wet vulva. *So, you're going to sexually starve yourself until Rocky gets out?* Her imagination floated between images of Rocky and Cody, back and forth as her head swayed from one side of the pillow to the other, sweat sprouting from her pores.

"I know that you can love me when there is no one left to blame."

As the song continued, she began to breathe faster, her legs shut tight with her fingers rattling faster. *Cody, yes, don't stop*, she thought, her body twisting and turning as her fingers rattled even faster. "Yes, yes…" She cried with her arms deflating to her sides, her legs spreading wider, and tears trickling down her temple before her head jolted at the sound of screeching gravel outside the window. She jumped out of bed, stared through the blind, but nothing was there.

***

Angela sipped her cappuccino. "I thought you didn't work on Sundays."

Kelly rested her expresso on the table. "I normally don't, but George called me around ten this morning to replace a waitress who had a severe cold. I hesitated, but because I took off yesterday for the party, and because he has been giving me extra hours while I'm not in school, it's only fair to return the favor."

"That's fair."

"Angela, since you have now become the unappointed mediator, how is my husband doing?"

"Like I told you over the phone. When he called me Friday afternoon, before I even had a chance to get a word in, he said, 'Thirty days gone, and one-hundred and fifty more to go.'"

"If he behaves, that's true."

"He did ask me if he can have your new number so that he can call you directly. He said he wakes up in the middle of the night always thinking about what he did to you."

Kelly thought for a while. "No, not yet. If what he told you is true, his mind needs to keep recycling not just what he did by planting the coke in my car, but all his abuse over the years." Her eyes watered. "As crazy as it might sound, I do miss him. But I also hate him. And until I see that he's truly abandoning those crazy old ways, I'm not giving in, not anymore, no matter how much he pleads."

"And if he doesn't?"

"If he doesn't, then I'll have to seriously consider divorcing him like the three of you have been advising me to do, even though if it is against my faith."

Angela leaned forward. "He asked if you're going to visit him at some point."

"When I feel that the time is right, I'll ask you to give him my number. Then we will talk few times, and if those conversations go well, I'll consider paying him a visit. When he asks you again, please tell him everything just like I'm telling you."

"Kelly, I shouldn't be putting any good word for him, but to be honest with you, he doesn't sound as arrogant anymore, and he doesn't swear either."

"I can't afford any distractions right now. Tell him to ask for a Bible, and use his free time to read it, and to focus on the section where it says not to do onto others what you don't like to be done onto you."

Angela giggled. "Gee, that's a clever idea. I can't wait to hear his reaction when I tell him that."

"He'll probably laugh."

***

"Hey, big man." The guard opened the door to the visitor's room for him. "You have a very sexy wife."

Rocky sneered then stared at Gilda in her foxy black halter top.

"I brought you a carton of cigarettes, but they took it from me and said they will give it to you later."

"I'm so horny, I would tear you apart right here and now."

Gilda reached for his hand and whispered, "Listen, I've been masturbating every day thinking about us doing it."

"How was your fucking party?"

"A lot of food, and a lot of people."

"I wish I could have a dish of her lasagna."

Gilda looked away from him. "Maybe you'll hate her fucking lasagna when I tell you…"

"When you tell me what?"

"Maybe it's just my imagination."

"Goddammit, tell me!"

"OK but keep your voice down. I saw her and Cody disappearing behind the spruces in your old home's backyard. She had a coffee in her hand, and they stayed there for a while. I couldn't see anything, but when they got back, their faces were red, their clothes were wrinkled, and Cody's shirt and shorts had coffee stains on them."

He clenched his hands. "I know she's fucking him."

"Don't jump to conclusion, Kelly's not like that."

"What was she wearing?"

"A purple dress with a new pair of black sandals. She looked so good that when she first stepped on the deck, every guy stared at her."

"I'm sure she knew that Cody was going to be there, that's why the bitch wore a dress. That way she could just pull it up to her hips and let him give her a quick fuck."

"That Cody was gon' be there, she knew that because I told her when I called her to tell her that we had changed the party date from Wednesday to Saturday, but I don't think that was the reason for her to wear a dress."

He hit the table with his fist. "Goddammit, when I get out, I'm gon' kill them both."

"Rocky, cool down, you're talking crazy now. I told you what I saw because you asked me to report to you, but I really think nothing like that happened, and if I knew you were gon' react like this, I wouldn't have told you anything."

"I saw how they looked at each other when I was saying goodbye to my daughter. Their affair started right after fucking Cody arrested me."

"If you're right, then it wouldn't have happened had you not gotten arrested."

"OK, I fucked up, but I was doing that to buy her the house of her dreams, so that she could stop working and stop going to school."

"Well, your strategy backfired and fueled her even more. It looks like her plan to graduate by December is working, and if she accepts that offer from her accounting professor, the first week of January she'll be working in his office. Are you gon' accuse her of fucking him too?"

"She probably is."

Gilda shook her head. "That's not the Kelly I know."

"How could he offer her a job; she just started school?"

"I don't think you know your wife well at all. She was the brain of the school from first grade until you got her pregnant. When she focuses, she can move mountains. Not only that, but she has also been working over forty hours a week while not in school, and thirty hours a week while in school, besides taking care of Hope and the house."

"If wasn't for that fucking Rosita watching Hope for her, she couldn't have worked and couldn't have gone to school, and I wouldn't be in this fucking jail."

"But I watch Hope too sometimes, not just Rosita."

"Why the fuck you're doing that for, you're supposed to be helping me messing her school up?"

"If I say no now, that would for sure blow our cover."

"I guess if one wants things done right, one has to do them himself, and when I'll get out, I'll do just that."

"I think you should try to talk to her instead of getting upset for things that might not have even happened. Here," she pulled her cell phone out, "I'll give you her new number."

"It's not gon' do any good. She told Angela that I can't have it."

"I didn't know that. So, you haven't talked to Hope since you've been here?"

He got up. "No, and I do miss her."

"You're leaving already?"

He looked at the clock. "My time is up. Thanks for the cigarettes."

"Rocky?"

Halfway through the door, he turned around. "Yeah."

"Next time you call, I let you know when I am watching Hope so that you can call me then."

"You do that." As he disappeared behind the door, he thought, "I'm gon' mold that bitch again, if that's the last thing I do."

***

After class, Kelly walked to the elevator with a few of her classmates and chatted on the way to their respective cars. One of the girls was still chatting when Kelly noticed a car parked by itself few hundred feet behind the girl with what seemed like a man inside, looking their way.

While she was about to get onto the highway, she noticed that same car driving behind her. After she had merged onto Route 8, that same car was still behind her, maintaining a steady distance. Was that one of Rocky's buddies spying on her? She pressed on the gas, and the distance between them more than doubled. Exiting the highway, she looked back through the rear mirror, and the car was gone.

She hadn't been at home all day, and the house had a stuffy damp smell to it. When she opened the window in the living room, she noticed the screen was missing. Looked out the window, and saw it standing to the side. How the heck did it end up straight up like that? She walked back to the kitchen area. "Honey, are you hungry?"

Hope, eyes fixated on the TV, didn't say anything.

"Hey, look at me! I'm making me a sandwich; do you want one?"

"No, I'm still stuffed. Gilda made hamburgers and hot dogs for supper."

"That was nice of her. Did you have fun?"

"Yeah…"

"With a 'yeah' that lazy, it doesn't sound like you did." She chewed her last bite. "Honey, something is bothering you, what is it?"

Hope hesitated. Then, eyes still locked on the TV screen, she said, "I talked to Dad today."

"Really?"

"Yeah, he called Gilda's house to talk to me."

Kelly stared at her silently.

"He called there because you don't want to talk to him. Mommy, why don't you want to talk to him?"

"OK, I'll tell you." She placed her arm around her shoulders and pulled her closer to her. "The last time he called me, you were asleep. We had a big stupid fight, and because of that, I changed our number. I want him to think about that fight a lot before I'll give to him, that way he will realize how stupid our fights are, and maybe he'll stop causing them."

"But why you always fight?"

"Unfortunately, that's what some grownups do best."

"I don't understand. I fight with my friends too, but I don't stay mad at them."

"OK. Sometime soon, I'll give him our new number so we can talk to him from here, but now it's time for you to go to bed, and time for me to study."

"You promise you'll give him the number?"

"Yes, but now go get ready for bed."

"I love you, Mommy."

Kelly grabbed her books and sat back at the kitchen table. Must have been Gilda calling him when Hope got there. Whatever. As she started reading again, she heard a car coming to a full stop across the street. Got up and walked to the window above the sink. The car was parked to the right of her house. She tried to see what type of car it was, but the reflection of the kitchen light behind her made it difficult to get a good look. She shut the lights off. By the time her eyes were beginning to refocus, the car sped away. *Son of a bitch, he does have someone spying on me.* She pulled away from the window and thought of calling Cody, but before she dialed the number, she decided against it.

CHAPTER TWENTY-EIGHT

Kelly earned two As and an A-minus during summer school, thus helping her GPA that had suffered a bit the previous semester. The mysterious car had continued to periodically appear at her school and across the street from her house at night. At one of its appearances at school, she took a good look at the black four-door sedan and managed to get the plate numbers. Again, she considered calling Cody, but when she thought about what had happened at Gilda's party, she decided to put up with Rocky's stupid games.

***

Fall semester classes began with butterflies roaming her gut like her first day a year earlier, except now they gathered out of excitement and not out of fear. It was a gorgeous morning with a bright sun and comfortably warm. Fourteen more weeks.

In the elevator, she leaned her back against the wall with her books resting over her chest. A male student leaning against the wall on the opposite side smirked at her. "Hi Kelly."

He looked familiar. Perhaps he must have been in one of her previous classes. "Hi," she replied warily.

"You don't remember me, do you?"

"Which of my classes were you in?"

Before he had the chance to answer, the elevator doors opened. She stepped out.

He rushed after her with his hand extended. "That's me, Jordan."

"OK, Jordan," she said and kept walking.

"Please, wait?"

She squinted at him. "Listen, I'm in a hurry to get to my class, please?"

"You really don't recognize me. I'm Jordan, the cokehead."

She stared at him for a while. "No way. Jordan had long sandy hair, he always wore a red headband, a pair of bell-bottom jeans, and a snobbish top splashed with many colors like a painter's shirt after many years of wear."

"Kelly, it is me. My hair is still sandy but short, and I dress like a geek now instead of a hippie from the seventies, that's all."

She looked deep in his gray eyes. "OK. You're skinny and an inch or so taller than me like he was. Your eyes do look like his, and your square face could at least pass for a brother of his, but you better not be fooling me." She was going to shake his hand, but when she remembered how annoying he had become by the end of the spring semester, she quickly retrieved it.

"You must be still upset at me, but please forgive me, I'm a different person now. I really am."

Short hair, smartly dressed, and book in hands. Not only did he look like a different person, but he also didn't even sound like Jordan. She smiled. "OK, apology accepted, but what happened to the old you?"

He looked at his watch. "We must be in our classes in three minutes. Would you join me in the cafeteria for coffee during our lunch break?"

Curious to find out what had caused such a transformation in him, she agreed.

Kelly got to his table few minutes after twelve. "Hi."

He motioned her to the chair he had pulled out for her. "Please, sit."

"This place is the busiest I have ever seen it."

"Like me, maybe more people are getting serious about their lives."

"Just seeing you with books in your hands seemed weird."

He laughed. "You're not the only one telling me that, my old gang totally defriended me over it."

"Does that bother you?"

"I must admit it did for a while. When I see them now though, I see what I used to be, and that makes me want to vomit."

"Jordan, I am really proud of you."

"So, can we be friends now?"

"Yes, if you define friendship the same way I do."

"The Jordan of back then was another person."

"I can see that. What else do you do now besides school?"

"I deliver pizzas a few hours a week for a local pizza place. That gives me enough money for my car and personal things. What about you?"

"I work thirty hours a week at a diner." She put her coffee down, smirked. "And I am a mom to a gorgeous nine-year-old girl."

"You're married?"

"Is that going to interfere with our newly-made friendship?"

"No, that's not the reason why I was shocked."

"Why were you shocked then?"

"Because you work almost full time, go to school full time, and take care of a child and a husband. That's unbelievable."

"Nothing comes easy, but if one is fairly healthy and is willing to make the necessary sacrifices, anything is achievable, especially in this country of ours, my grandfather used to proudly say."

"Kelly, the only grandfather I ever met died when I was eight, and my father and I hardly ever spoke, that is, until he looked at my eighteen-credit schedule for this semester."

"I'm sorry to hear that, but stick to your new plan, work hard, and you'll get where you want to go. This summer, while most students were vacationing somewhere, I spent my days between school and work earning eighteen credits, which will allow me to graduate by December instead of next May."

"That's amazing. Maybe that's what I should do too instead of taking my extra class at night?"

"That doesn't always work out that way though. I have a night class too, and I am only taking twelve credits this semester."

"Which nights?"

"Tuesdays and Thursdays from seven to eight-thirty."

"Which class is that? Because I also have one on those nights from seven to eight-thirty?"

"My business law class."

"Shit, I was hoping it was my marketing class."

She looked at his watch. "It's 12:40 already, if you don't start telling me about your transformation, we'll run out of time because I need to go get my daughter from school."

"I had almost forgotten about that." He took a sip of coffee. "With the people I was hanging around, it was bound to happen at some point. Around the second week of April, we were walking around the cafeteria sizing girls up when this serious looking dude in a suit and tie, along with a Waterbury cop, approached us and asked which one of us was known as the cokehead. We all froze and looked at each other, speechless. Then one of my buddies pointed at me. The guy showed me a detective's badge and asked me to follow them outside. They took me into his car, and he started asking me all kinds of questions about cocaine."

Wincing, Kelly was revisiting every step of her interrogation with that same detective.

"See, a couple of years ago, I was smoking a joint with my buddies, and each of us gave the other a nickname. I ended up with cokehead. It sounded cool then, so I played along. In no time, girls began to approach me to buy cocaine. Of course, I didn't have any, but I would promise them that I would get it, and new girls kept coming around. We guessed that the girls I never got it for wouldn't say anything to anyone for fear of themselves being labeled as cokeheads. So, new girls kept coming, and our game continued until it bit my ass."

It's unbelievable the games that some guys play just to get girls' attention, Kelly thought.

"Then the detective showed me a picture of this big dude with eyes like an owl. He kept asking me over and over if I had ever known him or seen him around campus. I told him I never did, and never would want to. Later, when I was telling one of my buddies about it, he said that it sounded like a guy from the Valley who almost got into a fight in the cafeteria."

A sense of guilt invaded Kelly's heart. If she had known what she knew now, she would have never reported his name to the detective, and later insisting that Cody pursue him even harder. She was thinking of telling him the full story when he interrupted her thoughts.

"Kelly, am I boring you?"

"No, not at all, go on."

"After a while, since the detective wasn't getting what he was looking for, he let me go. I was scared shitless. I rushed home and went straight to my room, hoping that it was just a bad dream, but the news quickly got to my father, and when he came home that evening, it was hell on earth. If it hadn't been for my mother stepping in between us, we would have gotten into a serious fistfight. Then he pointed his finger at me and said, 'If that's the kind of life you want, you better get the fuck out of my house and never come back.' I went back to my room, laid in bed, and stared at the ceiling for hours."

Kelly stared at him, eyes hardly blinking. He had had to go through all that because she had pointed him out to the detective without even a crumb of evidence, or given any thought of the effects, which could have turned into a tragedy had his mother not been home when his father got there. And for what, for someone that he barely knew who was trying to save her own butt? Her right eye started twitching. *At the end of the semester, I will tell him the full story, but for now let this be my lesson to never again make choices without considering all the possible consequences.*

"At some point during that night, my subconscious must have arrived at its own conclusion as to what my conscious self-needed to do, because the next morning, I went straight to the mall for a new pair of jeans, new sneakers, and a nice matching sweater. I came home, showered, put them on and went straight to the barber shop. Then I called my buddies to meet me at the Waterbury mall. When they got there, they would have walked straight by me had I not waved for their attention. To smooth my planned separation from them, I told them that I was going to lay cool for a while because the detective had me under surveillance. When I went home later, my parents were getting dinner ready. They turned ghostly white when they saw me.

Then they smiled, and here I am now, with a positive outlook on life and proudly sitting across from a newly-made friend that I always admired."

I guess God does work in mysterious ways, Kelly thought. *Perhaps this sort of awakening could happen to Rocky too.* "Jordan, I don't think I could find enough words to express how impressed and happy I am for you."

"Kelly, to have you as a friend is just the thing I need, thank you."

Kelly got up and hugged him. "Come here. I'll be happy to chat with you anytime, but now I need to go get my daughter."

"Already?"

"Jordan, this is one of those sacrifices that my grandfather meant."

"I get it. Then, I'll see you around soon."

"You will."

CHAPTER TWENTY-NINE

The sky was a blanket of gray with a steady drizzle and a frustrating wind twirling the doomed leaves. A good reason to grab her regular jeans and her denim waist jacket and break them in for another season. By now Kelly had pinned her schedule down to the minute and was running on fourth gear. Along the way, she got to know Jordan much better and quite often they had lunch together. When their night classes happened to get out at the same time, they would chat through their elevator rides down to one of their cars, at times for longer than she could afford.

And that Tuesday, except for the miserable weather, it wasn't supposed to be much different.

At the end of her 3 to 6 p.m. shift, George called her in the office and handed her the phone. "It's your friend Angela but make it fast because I'm waiting for a couple of calls myself."

"What's going on?"

"Sister, I'm sorry I didn't call you right away, I had a client show up out of nowhere. Rocky called me about half an hour ago and told me that his phone rights were suspended because he got into a beef with a couple of inmates."

"Why am I not surprised? If he keeps that up, he'll never come home."

"I told him that. Then he said that it's been almost four months and he would love for you to visit him. Then I heard him weeping, which he later denied."

"Him weeping is great news, but did you tell him about spying on me?"

"You bet I did, but he repeatedly swore that he has nothing to do with that. He sounded worried and said that you should call either his buddy Joe or your friend Cody."

"He actually said I could call Cody?"

"Sister, I think he meant it. If I were you, I'd call Cody, he'll catch that asshole in no time."

"No, he is brown-nosing to get me to visit him." She looked at the clock across from George's desk. "Angela, I've got to go now, I have to be at school by seven."

***

"Kelly, wait for me!" Jordan shouted, holding an umbrella over his head.

"Hurry up, or we'll be late for class."

Catching their breaths, they rode the elevator up together and rushed to their respective classes. Kelly's business law professor sat down, opened his briefcase, took a bunch of papers out, among which were the previous class quizzes, and organized them on the desk before handing them out. Perusing through the results as they made their way back to their seats, some students smirked and many sneered. When her name was called, she stepped over to his desk and extended her hand, but before he released the quiz to her, he whispered, "If you ever decide to become an attorney, I'll have a place in our firm for you."

"Thank you, I'll remember that." She went back to her seat, looked through her results, and smiled.

The professor flipped through his book. "I believe the assignment for today was on Terms of Sale Contracts, but before I go any further, can anyone tell me what are the terms that a contract must contain for it to be legal?"

Kelly looked around the class. No one was raising a hand, so she decided to raise hers.

"Mrs. Esposito, go ahead."

"The parties to a contract may agree to any terms they choose as long as those terms are recognized under the rules of the General Contract Law."

All eyes were focused on her. The professor looked around the class. "Anyone else?" Waited a few seconds and turned his attention back to her. "That's a very good answer." Then looked at the entire class again. "I can see who actually takes the time to study."

At the end of the class, she and two more students were still writing down notes while the rest of them rushed out as if reacting to a fire alarm. She neatly gathered her books and note-book and rushed to the elevator but missed it by seconds. By the time it came back up again, the other two students had also come out, and they all rode the elevator down together, chatting about the class.

Outside was dark and frigid with the rain coming down stronger now. Her car, a hundred feet or so from the door, was one of only a few scattered throughout the lot. She put her books over her head and ran, but by the time she got there, her face and hair were soaked. She rushed the door open and quickly slid in her seat. Grabbed a couple of tissues from her pocketbook, moved the rear mirror to face her, a hand seized her mouth and pulled her head tight over the edge of her seat as an arm locked the top half of her body. She yelled, trying to wrestle his hand and arm, but her scream echoed no louder that a muffled mumble, and her effort to free herself was in vain. "If Rocky put you up to this, I swear to God, I—"

"Shut up and listen to me." The voice was male.

"Who are you? Let me go!"

"If you stop bitching and wrestling, I'll let you breathe."

"OK, please?"

He grabbed the gun he had laid on the seat and pressed it against her side. "I'm warning you, if you scream, I'll splatter your gorgeous abdomen all over your laps. If you agree, nod three times."

Motionless, staring at the thick rain splashing against the windshield, her mind raced to figure out what was going on. Had Rocky lied to Angela and was pulling this insane trick to scare her so that she would finally quit school, or was she being mugged? About to choke from lack of air, she nodded three times.

The captor removed his hand from her mouth, grabbed her hair, and pulled her head back until her eyes could only see the roof of the car.

She gasped for air. "Who are you? And what do you want from me?"

"If you do as I say, you'll know soon enough," he whispered, pressing the gun to the back of her neck. "If you don't, prepare your soul for a journey into the shining light." He pressed the gun against her crotch. "I hope you're wearing those embroidered black panties?"

The thoughts of Rocky playing a trick, or that she was being robbed, suddenly vanished and the realization that she was being sexually assaulted took over. It could be that bastard who's been stalking her, but how does he know about her embroidered black panties? The screen down from the window skillfully placed against the house flashed in her brain's eye, but every door and window were locked. Then her thoughts went way back to the incident with the guy looking up her uniform. That day she was wearing those panties. Instinctively, her legs shut tight. "Please, my daughter and my husband are home waiting for me," she pleaded, with tears rushing down her cheeks.

He pointed the gun to the back of her neck again. "Your husband?" he laughed. "Let's see, if he's lucky, he might get out in couple of months." He pulled on her hair even harder. "I've worked very hard to get to this point, and I don't give fuck about your husband, your daughter, or anyone else in your life."

As he was talking, she snuck a glimpse of his head, but his face was hidden in a makeshift mask made of brown pantyhose with a hole over each eye and a smaller one over his mouth. She had seen those eyes before though, and he must know Rocky because he knows where he is.

He slithered the gun's muzzle under her T shirt and dragged it all way up above her breasts.

"Please don't?" She pushed the muzzle down first, and then the T shirt.

"What did I say?" He hit her jaw with the back of the gun. "You only move when I say so, is that clear?"

"OK, but please." She wiped the corners of her eyes with the back of her hand.

The rain was denser now and the visibility had lessened. He scanned the area a hundred-and-eighty-degrees to one side, and then to the other. Pointed his gun firmly against her temple, picked up her books from the front passenger seat, threw them onto the back seat, and slowly maneuvered his body to the front next to her. "By now you must be dying to find out who I am, and I promise you, soon you will know, but for now drive to the back of that building there, and if you make one wrong turn, or scream, or act as if you're distressed, your brains will resurface the top of this dashboard."

She shivered as she maneuvered her key into the ignition slot. *I must get out of this nightmare. Think, think of something before it's too late.*

"Right over there." He pointed to a dark secluded area.

She followed his orders and parked in the spot he directed her to.

He pressed the muzzle against her temples harder. "Take your jeans off slowly and show me what I have been dreaming about for way too long."

"I can't do that. I am a married woman, please?"

"You're all the same, the prettier you are, the bitchier you become." He grabbed her hair again, held her head tight over the top of the seat, and moved the gun from her temple to her mouth. "If you like to keep wearing this pretty face and these nice lips, goddammit, do as I say. Take off your jeans!"

With tears flowing down her high cheekbones, and her body shaking, she lowered her zipper and slowly pushed the sides of her jeans down.

"Oh yeah, just like in my dreams." He forced her face toward him, put the gun in his left hand and pressed it between her lips. Then moved his right hand over her right knee and slowly started stroking her leg upward closer to her crotch when her legs impulsively locked.

"If you want to see your daughter again, spread those fucking legs."

Headlights from a pickup truck coming around the corner of the building behind them slowly shone across the car. He dropped to his knees at once. Grabbed the gun in his right hand and pressed it against her black panties. "One word, or one wrong move, I'll blow your crotch to a million pieces."

As the truck was passing behind the car. It slowed, and a morsel of hope invaded her heart. *God, please make it stop*. But before her thought had ended, the truck picked up speed and her heart sank again.

He sat back up, forced his right hand between her legs. "Spread these fuckers!"

Hesitantly, she followed his order.

"Not enough." Pushed the muzzled deeper in her mouth. "Move your ass forward and spread them wide open."

"Please, don't do this." She peeked at the books in her back seat and a spurt of adrenaline rushed through her body. If she had a chance to grab one, and hit his temple with the back of it, she could throw him off just enough time for her to jump out of the car and run.

"Goddammit, do it!"

With tears dripping down her face, she pushed her butt forward and spread her legs wide open.

"Now we're talking." He slipped his hand through the top of her panties, cupped her hairy crotch, and started fondling her. "Yes, I've been dreaming about this pussy for long time."

"Please, don't," she pleaded. "Please?"

He pulled his hand away from her crouch. "I am going to take the gun out of your mouth, but don't get me pissed."

"Please, my little girl must be very worried by now, let me go?"

"That's how that bitch my wife used to plead with me about everything, and I used to believe her. Then I found her fucking our landscaper in my own bed," he yelled with the gun pressed against her temple. "She was a beautiful woman with a gorgeous body." Gazed at her for few seconds. "Actually, you could have passed for sisters."

"I never cheated on my husband, please let me go."

He pressed the gun against her waist. "Start the car, we're getting out of here!"

"Where're you taking me?"

He pushed his seat back and crawled down to the floor space with his back against the dashboard and his head well below the windows. Put the gun against her stomach. "You'll see it when we get there. Keep your face straight, hands on the wheel, and act normal or I'll pull the trigger."

She bent down and started pulling her jeans up.

"No!" He grabbed them and pulled them back down.

"How am I supposed to drive like this?"

"Take them off then."

"But it's getting cold?"

"Put the fucking heat on!"

She put the heat on and took her jeans off.

She started the car, backed up, and slowly started driving toward the exit. About thirty feet or so to her left, she noticed Jordan under his umbrella talking to a guy. Pretending to avoid a pothole, she slowed down, hoping that he would notice her crying and do something about it, but he just waved at her. She thought of giving him an additional signal of some sort, but with her kidnapper's eyes glued on her, and his gun pressing against her stomach, she refrained. Before leaving the lot, she snuck a quick glance through the outside rear mirror and saw Jordan still waving.

"I can't believe she didn't wave back at me?" Jordan said to the guy he was talking to. "I could swear she saw me."

"You know her?"

"Yes, we're friends." He shook his head. "Damnit, I just saw her before class, and everything was OK."

"Women," the guy replied shaking his head. "They're just like the weather."

"No, not her. She's a straight shooter. Something is not right, and I'm going to find out." He rushed to his car and took off after Kelly.

Still with his gun pressing against her side, the masked man lifted himself from the floor, sat back on the seat, and snatched his mask off.

The geek? Wordlessly, she stared at the road ahead. He seemed so weak and helpless when he apologized to her, why was he doing this?

"Are you shocked?" the geek said.

"Yes, I am. I thought you were—"

"A geek?" He sneered at her. "Like everyone at the diner says behind my back?"

"No, I never thought of you like that. I thought of you as a gentleman who just happened to make a mistake."

"You full of shit. I heard you guys calling me a crazy geek and laughing about it." He pressed the gun against her side. "Do I still look like a geek now?"

"No, but what you look like right now doesn't fit you either."

"Shut up!"

"You came to the diner to apologize to me, and I believed in you."

"I said shut up!"

"I'm sorry."

He pressed the gun against her side again. "It was fun embarrassing me, wasn't it?"

"Please, I never meant it that way. You were peeking under my uniform, what was I supposed to do?"

"You could have ignored me!"

"I swear, I didn't mean for it to happen that way."

"When that fucking bitch's life was on the line, she too swore that she didn't mean to hurt me."

"Who're you talking about?"

"Stop, the light is yellow," he shouted, jerking the gun deep in her side.

Waiting for the light to turn green, she held onto the steering wheel with all her strength and cautiously lifted her body couple of inches above the seat, hoping for a cop somewhere or for one of the few pedestrians crossing the road to notice that she was driving half-nude.

"That whore of my wife."

"That was terrible that she cheated on you. I'm sorry."

"That fucking whore. Few years into our marriage, when by accident she would decide to have sex with me, she would only do it at night with the lights off. She used to say that she didn't feel comfortable with her body anymore and didn't want me to see her nude, but that all went out the window when I found her fucking a real estate agent scouting to list houses for sale. It was me that she no longer cared to see nude, or care to fuck. It took me a while, but at the end, she did get what she deserved."

"What'd you do to her?"

"You're all a bunch of fucking whores. When the light turns green, go straight."

The traffic was heavy on both sides of the road. Jordan spotted her car ahead of his, stuck his head out the window, and noticed two heads. "What the fuck?" Jordan muttered under his breath. When she went by him in the parking lot, she was all alone and couldn't have possibly stopped to pick someone because he ran after her right away and would have seen her do that. "Man, this doesn't smell good." Took his cell phone from his pocket and dialed 911. Moments later, the dispatcher came online, and he told her that his friend was in danger.

"Sir, it's not against the law for a woman to have a man in her car."

"You don't understand, she was supposed to be alone."

"We can't send an officer there simply because you have a gut feeling that something might be wrong."

"Please, listen to me? She is a friend of mine, and before class she told me that she couldn't meet me for coffee because she had to pick her daughter up right after class. Then, while I was in the parking lot talking to another student, at least half hour after her class had ended, her car came out of nowhere and went by me with only her in it, looking straight ahead and not even acknowledging me waving, which is not like her. That puzzled me, and I decided to go after her to find out what was wrong. That was less than five minutes ago. Now her car is at the red light and there is a guy next to her."

Sir, I understand, but—"

"No, you don't. I didn't see her stop anywhere to pick up that man, which means he must have been hiding in her car when she went by."

"Is your friend married?"

"Yes, she is."

"Maybe she is cheating on her husband and had the guy hid because she didn't want anyone to see him."

"No, not Kelly. She is the most loyal, honest, and honorable person I've ever met."

The light turned green and the traffic began to move again.

"Sir, I don't know what to tell you."

"Fine, I'll take care of it myself."

While moving along, Jordan searched for a way to pass the cars in front of him but had no luck. He hoped that some of them would reach their destination before she turned on to a side street.

"What happened to your wife?" Kelly asked him again.

He placed the gun in his left hand, pushed it against her waist, and reached for her crotch again.

"Please don't, we'll crash."

"Do you think I care?" He pressed the gun even harder. "Spread these fucking legs!"

God, please help me, please?

He cupped his hand around her crotch. "First, slow like this, right?" he whispered.

"Please don't."

"Answer me, isn't this the way you like it?"

"Yes, but please stop." She held her breath, resisting the unwelcome sensual waves rising through her body.

"There was enough light piercing through your blinds. You were totally nude with your hands stroking in and around your crotch. The faster your hand rattled, the faster your body contorted and the louder you moaned."

Son of a bitch, the screeching pebbles outside my window was not a cat. It was him stalking me all this time. Why didn't I think of it when Gilda warned me? Why didn't I listen to Angela and call Cody before I came to school tonight?

"Just like this, right?" he whispered with his hand rattling faster.

Her face reddened as she tried to subdue her body's natural reaction.

"Yeah, that's how you like it, just like that bitch of my wife used to before she labeled me repulsive."

"Stop. Please, stop?"

"There is no shame in moaning," he said, rattling his fingers even faster. "You're ready to come, don't deny yourself. Come on, do it, scream like she used to."

"Please don't, don't," she begged. "Stop, please stop," she then cried with the top of her body contorting as she tightly grabbed onto the steering wheel.

"You're even sexier than I could have imagined when I was watching you masturbating."

God, why have you abandoned me?

With a vengeful look on his face. "You're just as hot as my whore was. When we first got married, we used to fuck our brains out every night." Pressed the gun against her side. "You're all a bunch of fucking whores!"

"I'm sorry she treated you like that…"

"Turn there."

He's going to rape me and then kill me. Poor Hope.

"Turn right. Now!"

Still following two cars behind hers, Jordan followed. Slowed down, shut the headlights, entered the pitch-black gravel road, and followed them a few car lengths behind using her brake lights as a guide until she came to a sudden stop. Her headlights shut off and a dim light inside her car switched on, but the exhaust was still puffing smoke. Jordan grabbed his cell phone, quickly pushed the redial button, and the same dispatcher answered. "Please, listen to me carefully. I followed my friend's car onto a gravel road. I believe the fourth right from the traffic light by taking right from the college's parking lot, right after a small shopping strip. I see a man inside holding something against her head. I think something horrible is about to happen, please send the cops right away."

"OK, just stay where you are and don't do anything foolish, you hear me?"

"I won't, if they get here fast."

"Slowly, take the rest of your clothes off." The geek held his gun to her temple. "If you make me happy, maybe I'll treat you better than that whore of my wife."

"Please, let me go."

"Take off that bra!" He pressed the gun against her stomach again.

She tried to stall, hoping for someone to miraculously appear and stop her nightmare.

He got closer. "Now! You hear me?"

She unlatched it and placed it over her lap.

He grabbed it and put the gun against her temple again. "Turn around."

"Why, what're you going to do?"

"I said turn around!"

She faced the window and shut her eyes tight. *God, please watch over my little angel, and forgive me for everything I have done wrong, and for everything that I've failed to do.*

"Put your hands behind your back."

With her mind cluttered, she failed to hear him.

He pressed the gun to the back of her head. "Put your hands behind your back. Now!"

Shivering like a leaf caught in a gust of wind, she did as he asked.

He picked up her bra and tied it around her wrists. "Here we go." He turned her around. "Now you can lay back." He stared at her. "Correction, you're prettier than that fucking whore of my wife. Now we're going to have some real fun, but if you try anything stupid, you're done." He placed the gun on the mat to his side, held her by her long black curly hair, grabbed her panties, and tore them off. He bent down and started sucking on her tits.

"Please don't, please?"

He raised his head. "Why, do I disgust you like I disgusted her?"

Maybe if she pretended to cooperate, he could let his guards down. "That's not true, I think you are a nice guy."

"You're full of shit, I'm not that stupid."

What choice did she have? "I mean it. You've really got me excited. Take your clothes off, untie my hands, and we will fuck our brains out like you and your wife used to."

"You really mean that?" he said, sounding boyish.

She forced a smile. "We've gone this far, why not do it the normal way now?"

"That would be really nice."

She leaned her back against the door and spread her legs wide. "Come on."

Ferociously, he grabbed her breasts. "I love your tits."

"Oh yes," she moaned. "Untie my hands, I want to grab your dick."

He picked up the gun from the mat and pointed it to her forehead. "I'll do it, but no games."

"I promise. Come on, my pussy is on fire for you."

He put the gun back on the mat, turned her around at once, and snapped the bra off her wrists. "Let's do it." He pushed her back against the door, facing him.

The nipples on her sturdy breasts were as pointy as the tip of a spear. She pulled him tight against her chest. "Go on, keep sucking."

He cupped half of her right breast with his mouth and with his right hand felt her crotch again.

"Yes, don't stop," she moaned, while her hand felt around for the gun.

"I'm gon' fuck you so hard that…" He stood up and quickly took his shirt off. Then, just as he was lowering his khakis, four headlights lit up the inside of the car like a midday sun.

She tried to grab the gun, but he beat her to it.

"You're a fucking bitch," he yelled, placing the gun to her head. "Now you're gon' join the other whore for sure."

"No," she pleaded, her eyes shut. "Please, I don't want to die."

"This is the police. Come out with your hands behind your back," a voice from a loudspeaker yelled.

"Fuck you, I know how you guys operate." He grabbed her long black hair. "Get up, bitch, I'll show them who's in charge."

"Please, hide the gun. I'll tell them that I have been seeing you, and everything will be fine."

"You really think I am that fucking stupid."

"No," she shook her head. "You didn't rape me. The rest I'll forgive you, I really mean it."

He thought for a couple of seconds. "No fucking way. I ran away from them before, and you are my ticket now to do it again. If you follow my orders, once we're far enough up that hill there," he said, pointing through the windshield, "I'll let you go."

"Please, don't do this, my daughter needs me."

"One wrong move, and your daughter will miss you for the rest of her life." He held her hair tightly with his left hand and pressed the gun to her temple with his right one. "Now, step out of the car slowly."

"Please?" Stepping out, her sneaker bumped against the doorjamb and she lost her footing.

"Stand up, bitch," he yelled, pulling her by her hair. Then he followed her out and stood right behind her with the gun pressed against her right temple.

The heavy rain coupled with the bright light obscured her vision. Shivering non-stop, she wiped her eyes.

"Let her go." The police spoke through their loudspeakers, guns pointed at him.

"If you want her alive, you get the fuck out of here," the geek yelled

For just an instant, her hair was free of his hand and a switch went on in her thoughts. He must have wiped his eyes too. If she could catch him the next time, she could hit his stomach with her elbow hard, throw herself flat on the ground, and let the cops do the rest. As her mind roiled with her planned action, her adrenaline level began to rise and everything around her started to move in slow motion.

"Let her go. Don't make things any worse for you," said the voice through the speaker.

He dragged her back, closer to the hill he was planning on climbing, and wiped his eyes again.

Shit, I missed it. She tightened her fists, ready to strike, and focused solely on his left-hand actions.

"Again, don't make things worse for you, let her go."

She felt his hand leaving her hair again, and like a lightning strike, she plunged her right elbow below his belt line with all her strength, threw herself flat on the ground. As she rushed her arms over her head, bullets began to fly over her. Seconds later, the raindrops became louder. She lifted her head and saw three shadows running toward her.

"Don't move yet," one of them yelled while the other two ran to her side.

Shivering beyond control, she erupted, crying like a child. Jordan took his jacket off, covered as much of her body as he could, and helped her up.

"Jordan, where did you come from?" She wrapped her arms around his neck and held him tight.

"It's all over."

Still crying like a child, she sobbed, "Tell me this is just a bad dream. Please, tell me so?"

He grabbed her shoulders. "Kelly, it isn't a bad dream, but it's over now. You're safe, and that jerk is dying."

She looked at the geek that put her through the trauma of her lifetime. "No, it's not over yet." He was lying flat on the ground, moaning, and barely moving. With the back of her heel, she started kicking his face, his chest. "You bastard son of a bitch, who's in charge now, ah!" She stepped on his crotch and started jumping as if it was a trampoline. "You like it like this, right? You piece of shit." She jumped higher and harder, yelling obscenities that she didn't even know she knew, until the cops decided that it was enough. Pulled her away still kicking and yelling and dragged her back to Jordan.

"Hey, it's over," Jordan said, rewrapping his jacket around the top half of her body. "It's over."

She locked her arms around his neck again. "I'm sorry I didn't wave back at you."

"Don't be because that's why I came after you. If you had waved back at me, I don't even want to start thinking of what would have happened to you."

Still weeping and shivering, she hugged him again. "Thank you for saving my life."

"How did you get to be so brave?"

"I just didn't want to die. Not like that."

***

At the hospital, she was checked by different doctors. Other than the black and blue mark on her right cheek caused by the gun hit, and minor scratches on the front of her body from hitting the gravel stones with force, the worst thing she was experiencing was her anxiety level. The nurse treated her scratches and handed her a tiny plastic container with a small dose of valium and a glass of water. "Here, take this, it will help you relax."

"What is it?"

"Just a small dose of Valium."

"I don't need it."

"Please, take it. It will help you sleep."

"I must get home to my daughter."

"The doctors will evaluate you in the morning, and if they think you're OK, they will discharge you then."

"But I—"

"Kelly, after what you have been through, it's the hospital's responsibility to keep you under observation for at least tonight." She held her hand. "Please, take it and try to get a good night of sleep."

She thought. "Then hand me that phone please."

The nurse placed it on her lap.

"Where are you?" Rosita answered, with anxiety in her voice.

Kelly started telling her what happened, but after a few sentences, she broke out crying.

Rosita wept. "Dios mio, what kind of animal would do that to a person?"

MY LAST CHANCE

Kelly wiped her tears with a tissue the nurse had just handed her, blew her nose, and tried to compose herself. "Is Hope still up?"

"Around 10 o'clock. I didn't know what to do and I told her to get some sleep until you would show up."

"Don't wake her up, the story is all over the local news and I don't want her to know what happened to me, at least not for now."

"Don't worry, Carlos can stay with her and I'll come to get you."

"You can't, they won't let me leave the hospital until the morning."

"OK, I come to get you in the morning right after I get out of work."

"It's OK, Rosita. Jordan, my friend and savior, drove my car here to the hospital with the help of one of his friends."

"But how can you drive, all shaken up like that?"

"By the morning, I should be fine."

"Get some sleep then, and don't worry about Hope."

"If she wakes up looking for me, just tell her that I got out of school late and went straight home."

"OK, and if that loco doesn't die from the bullets he got, I will strangle him myself."

"No, we'll do it together."

"Mi amor, I can't believe this."

"It is heartening to hear your voice again, Rosita, thank you." Kelly hung up, chased the valium down with the glass of water and stared at the ceiling. *If that loco doesn't die from the bullets he got, I will strangle him myself.*

***

In the morning, she signed herself out of the hospital and went straight home. As she pulled in her driveway, Rosita jumped out of her car and rushed over. Cuddled her in her arms, like her mother used to. "I am sorry."

"Where is Hope?"

"I just dropped her off to school." Rosita took the house keys from Kelly's hand, opened the door, and followed her inside. "Let me look at that." Gently, she caressed the bruises on Kelly's face and shook her head. "Hijo de puta. Did he punch you?"

"No, he hit me with his gun." Kelly dropped her pocketbook on the kitchen table. "Don't you worry though, when he was downed by the cops' bullets, I made sure I gave him his share and plus."

"I hope those bullets will lead him straight to hell. Where do you keep your chamomile, I'll make you some?"

"Thank you, Rosita, over there." She pointed to one of the cabinets and crashed on the couch.

"Gilda and Angela are coming over too. They saw you on the news and are terrified."

"That's nice of them." She gazed at the ceiling. Every time that the pieces of her life seem to all fit together smoothly, something happened to squander them again. Darn it, when was it going to end?

Rosita had started heating water for the chamomile when the doorbell rang. She opened the door, and Cody stood outside, white-faced.

"Can I come in?"

"Sure. Kelly is lying on the couch," she whispered, "please, don't say anything that would stress her even more."

As soon as she heard Cody's voice, Kelly stood up.

Cody hugged her. "When I saw it on the news, I wished I had been one of those cops that helped you."

"I should have told you I was being stalked." She stepped back. "But I thought it was Rocky playing games with me."

"I know, a while ago, I talked to Angela."

Her eyes flooded. "I really believed that he had one of his buddies spying on me, and since I have nothing to hide, I figured that after a while, he would realize it and stop."

"Things like that should never be taken lightly, we deal with sickos like him more often than we like to."

"I know better now."

"Remember, you can always count on me."

She sat on the couch and wiped the corners of her eyes. "When he had me facing the window with the gun pointed at the back of my head, my entire life flashed before my eyes."

Cody sat next to her and held her hand. "For all that it's worth, the police are saying you're a hero. Not only for saving your own life, but to help them arrest the bastard. Where he comes from, he's a suspect in his wife's disappearance."

"He killed her! The bastard raped her and then killed her." She clasped her face in her hands. "That's what he was gon' do with me too."

"Did he say that to you?"

Rosita placed the tray on the coffee table. "Here, this chamomile will help you relax. Cody, would you like some too?"

"No, I'm fine, thank you, Rosita."

The doorbell rang again. Rosita let Gilda and Angela in.

"What did that beast do to you?" Gilda cried.

"Sister," Angela said, hugging her. "My heart shattered when I saw it on the news. Now they're saying that he might die from the bullet wounds he endured. I hope he goes straight to hell."

"When they showed the bastard's picture, a bell rang in my head," Gilda said. "He was the guy that came into the diner asking about you. Remember me telling you?"

"Yes, and two other waitresses told me the same. Instead of feeling sorry for him, I should have connected the dots when he came in to apologize, acting like a crazy person."

"What're you saying?" Angela asked.

"Feeling sorry for what?" Cody said.

"OK." She took a deep breath and went on to tell them about the earlier incident, when the kidnapper had looked up her dress, then came back to apologize.

"That son of a bitch," Cody said, anger erupting all over his face. "I'd love to run into him in a dark alley somewhere."

"The world is going loco," Rosita said.

Angela placed her arm over Kelly's shoulders. "Sister, that's over now, but I wish you had listened to me."

"I should have, and I'm terribly sorry I didn't. But as for being over, no, it's not over yet."

They looked at each other, puzzled.

Kelly rubbed her hands. "I must face the bastard once more. I scrubbed his fingerprints off my body and now I need to scrub his facial expressions out of my head. I'm going to the hospital tomorrow."

"Do you really think that's a clever idea?" Cody said.

"I need to see that face in a defeated state."

"Maybe she does have a point there," Angela added.

Rosita shook her head. "Kelly, let it go. He'll get what's coming to him, if not in this world, in the next one."

"I'm sure that the police are guarding his room," Cody said. "But if you really want to do this, I'll help you get their permission."

"What if you go with me?"

"I'd love to."

"OK," Rosita said. "I think Kelly should get some rest now."

"She should, but I don't think she should stay alone," Gilda said.

"I'll stay with her," Rosita said, "don't worry." Angela gave her a long hug. "Sister, I'll be back late this afternoon. Do you need anything from the store?"

"No, thank you." Looked up at them. "Guys, don't worry about me, I'll be fine."

"No matter what I need to do, I'll get today's assignments and notes for you," Gilda said, hugging her.

"I appreciate that, thank you."

Cody gave her a quick hug. "What time you like me to pick you up tomorrow?"

"Be at my school around 1 p.m. if you can. The hospital is only a short distance from there."

"You're going back to school already?"

"Of course, I am."

He shook his head. "You're something else."

"I am not letting anything, or anyone hold me back anymore."

"Way to go, sister, I've not seen that grit in your eyes since you beat those two girls up in fifth grade." Kelly looked at her with a lazy smirk. Kelly had always hated fighting about anything with anyone. That day though, their ridiculing her about being poor and her father a drunk, had just gotten to be too much. She needed to put a stop to it, and she did.

"Then I'll see you at your school tomorrow at 1 p.m.," Cody said, walking toward the door behind Gilda and Angela.

Before Cody stepped out, Rosita held him back. "I hope you can change her mind."

"Rosita, I will try, but I doubt it."

***

Cody arrived at the school ten minutes earlier than arranged. He parked the car in front of the building where Kelly had told him to, and lay back, sifting through the pros and cons of their hospital visit.

"You really want to do this?" he asked Kelly when she slid into the passenger seat.

"Cody, if you don't feel right about going with me, I'll understand."

"What if you go crazy and end up getting arrested?"

"I will not. I just need to stare down at his defeated eyes with me being the dominant figure."

"If that's the only thing you're planning on doing, then let's go." He pressed on the gas pedal, and in no time, they were on the highway heading toward the hospital.

"Did you call the chief of police for permission?"

"Yes, and he wasn't too happy about it, but after some arm-twisting from my chief, he agreed."

"Do they still have a cop guarding his room?"

"No, because the bastard can hardly move any of his limbs and will stay that way for a while, if he survives at all."

A mild smirk spouted on her face.

"Kelly, can you get that bag from the back seat for me?"

She placed it on her lap. "What's in it?"

"Open it."

The black and gray Panasonic case had a camera in it, a tripod for taking timed selfies, and a bunch of other attachments. "That's a nice camera, so?"

"While we're in there, if we have a chance, we're gon' do a little detective work that will help nail the bastard forever if he does survive."

Like a child who had seen a toy for the very first time, she was inspecting it all around and touching all the buttons. "I don't see any cassette inside. Isn't that what you need to make a movie?"

"No, this one has an SD memory card for that," Cody replied. He pushed a button and the card popped right out.

"Oh wow. I've never seen anything like it. You're saying that this little card is replacing cassettes."

"Yes. Not only is replacing them but can record a hell of lot more."

"Huh. That's amazing, but my law professor said that you can't record anything about anyone without their permission."

"What he probably meant was that such recording cannot be used in court, but whatever information we gather can only help the detectives on the case."

"If you think so, then do it. As for me, I just want to…"

"Let him have a piece of your mind, right?"

"Yes, something like that."

At the hospital, Kelly rushed ahead of Cody, scanning room numbers along the way, her adrenaline rising with each step forward. As they approached the nurses' station, the nurse that had helped her sign herself out the day before blocked her. "Kelly, where are you going?"

Kelly looked like a child caught with a hand in the cookie jar. Cody stood next to her. "She got permission from the chief of police to visit her kidnapper."

Struggling to remain calm, Kelly said, "I really need to do this, please?"

"My orders are not to let anyone enter that room without permission from the police. Besides, why would you want to do that when yesterday you couldn't wait to get out of here to get it all behind you as fast as possible? Didn't he hurt you enough?"

"Yes, he did. But I honestly believe that seeing his face in a defeated state will help my mind get over the ordeal faster."

"Look Kelly, the guy is really in bad shape. He can't move any of his limbs, he can't talk, and except for his eyes and his lips, his face and head, his arms, and legs, are mostly wrapped in bandages. Not that I feel sorry for him, but I have orders not to let anyone in there without permission from the police department. Do you have something in writing to show me that I can let you in?"

"Ms.," Cody said, showing her his police badge. "I talked to the chief of police himself, and he said that it was OK if I accompanied her."

"I'm sorry, unless you show me something in writing, I can't let you in."

Kelly was determined to get in that room and wasn't going to let her stand in her way. "We weren't told that we need the permission in writing. Please, call the police station and verify that what we're saying is true."

The nurse thought about it for few seconds. "OK, just step to the side while I make the call."

Cody leaned on the station's counter and gave Kelly a smirk of confidence.

She reciprocated the smirk and sat on a chair across from him, her eyes focused on the bastard's room with her adrenaline rising. She needed to see that bastard's eyes pleading for mercy.

The nurse put the phone down. "You're right. The chief said he did give you the permission, but only for a few minutes."

That was plenty of time for what Kelly needed to do. She stood at the end of the bed and stared at him. When he opened his eyes and saw hers piercing his like a spear ready to leave a warrior's grip, they flickered. He tried to raise his arms and move his legs but couldn't.

Cody was getting the camera ready when he noticed the SD card missing. "Shit. Kelly, what did you do with the card?"

"I put it in one of the pockets inside the bag."

"I can't record shit without it."

She turned away from him with a mild smirk. "Sorry, I thought you were taking the bag with you."

"I didn't want to raise any suspicions, so I just grabbed the camera and put it in my pocket."

"Then go get it, we don't have much time."

"All right, I'll be right back."

She made sure the door was fully closed. Kelly stood next to the bastard's bedside and the tubes connecting his life to a couple of machines. With a smirk, she grabbed the plastic tubes and pretended to pull them. "It looks like you have had just about enough of this lame life, right?" she asked under her breath.

He tried to see what she was doing, his mouth wheezing vague sounds of pain, and his fingers and toes lurching in an attempt of resistance.

"How does it feel to be the victim, you sick bastard?" She retrieved her oversized tweezers from her pocketbook, gripped it tightly, placed it in a stabbing position over where she figured one of his wounds was, and pressed on it with all her strength. "Isn't this where one of the bullets hit you, my dear?" She pressed even harder. "Isn't it?"

He wheezed, pleading louder and louder. "'Now we're going to have some real fun, but if you try anything, you're done.' Remember saying that to me? Or 'Don't worry, honey, you do as I say, and you'll be fine.'" She moved her tweezers to the side of his neck and pressed on a wound. "I bet you're having just as much fun as I had when you were trashing my soul with the gun deep in my mouth, aren't you, dear? Oh, I'm sorry, you can't talk. But I know the feeling, trust me."

The visible flesh around his eyes, his lips, parts of his arms and legs, had turned reddish blue. Tears bubbling from the corner of his eyes like a waning mini geyser.

"Oh, I'm sorry, did the bullets hit you there too? What about here?" She moved the tweezers over a wound in his leg and pressed even harder.

He bit his lower lip with his stained teeth.

She put her tweezers back in her pocketbook and grabbed the empty water glass from his nightstand. "Listen to me, you bastard. On my way here, I was seriously considering pulling out the tubes that are keeping you alive and letting you go straight to hell from here, but I'm not evil like you. There is something else I owe you though. Here." She hit his face with the bottom of the glass as hard as his gun had hit the same side of her face. Then sneered at him. "Now we're almost even, but I'm sure your future jail mates will do the rest for me." She placed the glass back on the nightstand and headed out the door, almost bumping against Cody's chest.

"Where are you going?"

"I told him what I needed to tell him, let's go."

"Is he crying?"

"Yes, he is. I think after listening to me, he's regretting every terrible thing that he ever did."

"I was hoping to get his reaction on camera while you told him off."

"That's OK, let the detectives do their job. I've accomplished what I came here for, so let's go."

They rushed out of the hospital and headed back to her school to get her car. "It must have worked for you because you look a lot more at ease than before we went."

Kelly gazed out the window. "I think so too. After I got through with him, I was left with the impression that if he survives, and gets out of jail someday, he'll think twice about doing to someone else what he did to me, his wife, and who knows how many more women."

"Kelly, that was very courageous of you."

"Thank you, Cody. I just hope now that whatever black cloud has been hovering over me will disappear, at least for the next couple of months, so that I can graduate in peace."

CHAPTER THIRTY

The third week after her kidnapping incident, Kelly decided to pay Rocky a visit. For a while they just stared at each other, he with a look on his face that suggested "I told you so," and she with her lips pursed and wordless.

"How the hell are you?" Rocky said.

"I'm fine. What about you?"

He looked away from her. "I was doing pretty good before…"

"Before what?"

"Before that fucking news clip that showed you standing in the rain nude with a guy holding a gun to your head."

Kelly had expected for him to bring that up, but not that early in her visit. "I've been working very hard to put it behind me, and I don't want to talk about it."

"Did you lead him on?"

She looked straight in his eyes and shook her head. The positive image of him that had been brewing in her heart over the past few weeks had just been wiped out.

"They said he used to come to the diner and one time he even looked up your bare ass. Did he rape you?"

"No, he never got that far, thank God for a student friend who led the police there and thank God for giving me the courage and strength to do what I did, but who told you about him looking up my dress?"

"I don't remember, but isn't that fucking true?"

"Yes, it's true. What also might be true though is that if I didn't embarrass him like I did when he did that, maybe he wouldn't have kidnapped me."

"If you didn't fucking go to work and didn't fucking go to school, none of this would have happened. And I wouldn't be in here either."

"Let's see, you became a drug dealer because I went to work and went to school? If anything, you should have done that before so that you could have afforded to give me money to buy new panties more often than once a year or two."

He looked away, wordless.

"I couldn't take it anymore, to have to beg even for things like that for us. And yes, I couldn't stand to be the poor, barefoot, and pregnant housewife anymore either."

He hit his fist on the table, but not hard enough for the guard to hear it. "Goddamm it, that's what I married you for!"

"You know something, it's over four months you've been here, and you still haven't come to grips with what brought you here in the first place." She pushed her chair under the table and started walking toward the exit door.

With his eyes flooding, he begged, "Please, don't go?"

Please? She stopped, turned around, and saw him staring at the table and wiping the corners of his eyes with the back of his hand. "I still care about you, but if you can't come to grips with our new reality, I'll have no choice but to part ways, and this time I really mean it."

Staring at his hands, he was listening mutely.

"It has been hard to juggle work, school, and being a single mother, but thanks to my friends, who you always fought to keep me away from, and my will, and my focus, and God's help, we have managed OK without you."

"I realized what you've been trying to do, and in time, I'll come around."

A smidgen of sorrow invaded her heart seeing him in a defeated state, but she needed to stay strong. "Rocky, how are you going to trust me if I'll be working in an office environment with mostly men?"

"I'll have to learn to live with it. You and Hope are the only thing I have left in this world. None of what's left of my family want anything to do with me anymore."

He answered her as if he already knew that she'll be working in an office with mostly men. She wondered if Gilda had told him. But why would he be talking to Gilda when he had said that he couldn't stand her much anymore?

He shook his head. "I tried so hard to find a job in my trade and…"

"That still doesn't justify you becoming a drug dealer."

"You're right, I fucked up big time."

"How do I know that you're not going to do the same when you come out? Most likely, you're not going to find a job in your trade, especially going forward. According to my economics professor, our economy is changing from a manufacturing to a service-oriented one, and most of our factory jobs will move to China, which means that those displaced workers need to retrain themselves if they intend to keep their standard of living. Doesn't that sound pretty much like what I have been saying to you?"

He nodded. "It does."

"So, what're you going to do about it?"

"Some of the guys here said that the same college you go to has all kinds of training programs. When I get out of this dump, I'll go check them out and see if I can get started with something."

Her eyes glowed. "I'm happy to hear that, if you really mean it."

"I do mean it."

Maybe Angela was right after all, but don't jump up and down just yet, she told herself.

"Then we can go back to be a family again."

"Where you going to stay when you first get out?"

"With you and Hope, where else?"

"No, not at first."

"What you mean?"

"First, I'm trying to graduate by December, and with my tight schedule, I can't afford any distractions, and second, I can't just overlook all that has happened and let you step back in our lives as if everything is normal. No, we're going to take it one step at a time."

"And where am I supposed to live until then?"

"You'll have to figure that out. I had to reorganize everything in our lives when you left, and I am sure you can do the same."

He stared at her. Was this the woman he had married?

"The restraining order will stay in place, and we will arrange when and where we can meet and talk."

"What about my daughter?"

"With our daughter, we'll do the same thing we did before you left."

"With that Cody around?"

"If you behave, that will not be necessary." She got her pen and a piece of paper from her pocketbook and wrote her new phone number down. "Here, but I'm warning you, don't use it at random. Until you get out, you can call us two times a week. Wednesday evenings, between 7:30 and 9 p.m., and Sunday mornings not later than 11 a.m. If you don't abide by this schedule, I'll change this number too. If you cooperate, after you get out, we'll talk about how many times a week you can call."

His jaw dropped. *Who's this fucking woman?*

"I hope I made myself clear." She got up. "I must go now."

With his eyes bulging, he stared at the door she had vanished behind for a long time.

***

After some extensive arm twisting, Gilda did persuade Kelly and Hope to join her and her kids on Halloween night for a trick-or-treat run. Kelly herself hadn't been on one since she could remember, and Rocky had never allowed Hope to experience it. As they watched their kids rushing from one house to another, and in between comparing their bounties and laughing, she and Gilda talked about their marriages, sex, and school, before they called off the evening.

***

"I was expecting you yesterday, what the fuck happened?"

"On Thursdays, Kelly only works from 3 to 6:30, and the rest of the day she goes back and forth from school. I didn't want to take a chance if she was looking for me."

"I'm so horny, I can't wait to fuck the shit out of you."

"I'm sure the day you get out, she'll be waiting for you, so, when is that gon' happen with me?"

"Don't worry about that, she told me to find a place to stay because we're gon' take it one step at a time, and I am sure that she and me getting laid is not one of the first steps she has in mind." He shook his head. "My wife telling me what to do, can you fucking believe that?"

"Huh. When we went trick-or-treating on Halloween night, we chatted about many things, including men and sex, and that she really missed getting laid. If so, why wouldn't she want to see you at least for that?"

"What you mean you guys went trick-or-treating?"

"Her, Hope, me, and my kids, we all went out together on Halloween night."

"That fucking bitch. She knows I never wanted Hope to do that."

"She had told me, but when I told her that they would be better off not going, she said, 'Screw him, I am in charge now.'"

"I can't believe what she's becoming."

"Don't get upset, you can always count on me."

"I better get to her before she totally loses it."

"Rocky, she has become very independent, and I don't think she has any intentions of turning back. She told me that if you ever want to go back home, it's gon' be her way or no way."

"Will see about that."

"You're supposed to get out on December 6, right?"

"Yes, and I am counting every fucking minute."

"Then, since you have no place to stay yet, I'm gon' rent you a room at our favorite motel for a week. That day you'll meet me there, we fuck our brains out, and then we talk about our next move."

"How am I gon' get there?"

"With a taxi, or a bus. In the next couple of weeks, I'll put together some money for you to carry you over until you get back on your feet."

"I know I fucked up, but I never imagined that my life would be turned upside down as it has."

"Remember, I will always be here for you."

"What if your husband finds out about all of this?"

"To be honest, I don't have any more feelings for him, and I am ready to leave on a moment's notice. I also believe that Kelly doesn't have any feelings for you anymore either."

"You wrong about that."

"Once she gets that job with all those good looking and well-dressed guys, you'll be history in no time."

He sneered at her. "That job is not going to happen."

***

Kelly headed straight for Mrs. Alston's cubicle. "I was asked to come and see you."

"Hi Kelly, please have a seat?"

With a concerned look on her face, Kelly slowly made her way to the chair. "Is something wrong with my tuition payments?"

"No, nothing like that. Your grant and your loan came through fine."

"Thank you." Relieved, Kelly placed her pocketbook and her books on the empty chair next to her.

"I wanted to see you because I have something that might interest you." Mrs. Alston smiled.

Anxious to find out, Kelly rested her elbows on the desk. "So, what is it?"

"I have a few business connections. When we have students about to graduate, we gather the names of those students who we think meet their requirements and send them the information together with a letter of recommendation."

"OK."

"Kelly, your name was on that list, and yesterday I got a phone call from two different accounting firms asking to set up an interview with you. I am so proud of you. One firm is in New Haven, and the other one in Stamford."

"That's nice, but—"

"What you mean but?"

"I have already promised Professor White that I'll consider going to work for his firm. We talked about it this summer."

That wasn't the response Mrs. Alston was expecting. Not only because she had highly recommended her to both of those firms, and that would make her look bed, but also because she would lose the perk of one week in the Caribbean for the upcoming Christmas vacation fully paid for her and her husband if Kelly didn't take either one of the jobs. She leaned back and labored not to show any sign of distress on her face. "Kelly, have you discussed salary, benefits, and all with him?"

"Not yet. Sometime in the next couple of weeks, I am supposed to get a tour of his firm, meet his partners, and discuss all of that."

"That's good, but what I suggest you do is get interviewed by all three of them before you make up your mind. I can tell you this, the other two firms also have a program that will pay for your bachelor's degree if you decide to go for it."

"Really?" Her face shone. "Of course, I am going for my bachelor's. I have been thinking to start next fall and have already been worrying how to come up with the money to pay for it."

Mrs. Alston shook her head. "It seems yesterday that you stood on that same chair making your case that you had to start school last fall."

Kelly nodded.

"And here we are, a year and a half later not only you're graduating, but already have firms competing for your service. I am so happy that

I took that chance with you. In many ways though, it's going to be sad not to have you around anymore."

"I'll never forget what you did for me, Mrs. Alston. Your decision to accept my 'I owe you' while the bank worked on my loan was my life's turning point, thank you again."

"It's enough. We're getting a bit too soft here." She got up, walked around the desk. "Here, this is the information for those two firms. They're expecting a call from you as soon as possible, and I sincerely hope that you will end up working for one of them."

Kelly took the sheets with the information. "I will call them this afternoon."

"No handshake," Mrs. Alston joked. Opened her arms wide. "Come here." They hugged. "I know you're going to make us proud for a long time to come."

"I'll make sure of that, thank you." She spun around and headed for the door with the eyes of the entire office staff beaming her out.

***

"Happy Thanksgiving. Mommy and I made it this morning." With a wide smile on, Hope showed the pie to Rosita.

"My Princess, come in." For the first time since Rosita and Carlos had moved to the valley area, they had decided not to join their relatives in New York City for the holiday weekend, and to stay home and celebrate it with Kelly and Hope instead.

Kelly hugged her. "I could smell that mouthwatering turkey from downstairs."

"Me too." Hope walked over to the kitchen table and gently placed the pie in one of the open spots.

"She woke me up at five this morning," Carlos complained, coming out of the living room, "and now my stomach is growling."

Rosita gave him a mild sneer. "Everything is almost ready. Please, hang their coats and go back to the living room."

"Mom, can I go watch my cartoons?"

"No, Carlos is watching TV, and you stay here to help us."

"That's OK. I was just flipping through the channels to waste some time. Hope, you know what to do, go ahead."

"Thank you, Carlos."

"Where are your aprons, Rosita? I'll help you with the salad."

Carlos sat at the table and watched them rushing around the kitchen like chefs in a busy restaurant. "Kelly, Rosita told me that three different companies want to hire you already?"

"Yes, that's true. I interviewed with two of them already. Both offered me a good salary and to pay for my school costs If I decide to go on to get my bachelor's degree. The other one I have an interview with next week."

"You haven't even finished school, and already have a choice of where to go to work. That is great."

"Yes, Carlos, but the best offer so far came from the firm in Stanford, which is further than I would like."

"It's too far," Rosita said. "You'll be spending too much time on the road, and too much money for gas."

"If the offer from my professor's firm is at least close to theirs, I'll probably go to work for him. His office is not too far from my school."

"That would be better for everyone."

"I think so too," Carlos added.

Rosita pulled the oven door open. "It looks ready, what you think?"

Kelly wiped her hands, grabbed a fork, dipped into the ten-pounder golden butterball, and splintered a small piece from its side. Blew on it for few seconds and placed it in her mouth. "Wow, that's not only ready, but it's also delicious."

Rosita smiled, grabbed two baker's gloves, pulled the tray out and rested it on top of the stove.

"Hope," Kelly said out loud, "go wash your hands, we are ready to eat."

"OK, Mommy." She shut the TV off at once and ran to the bathroom as the three of them got the Turkey carved and everything else in place ready to be devoured. For a while, the only sounds were those of unsynchronized utensils hitting the ceramic plates and alternate yum in between as they guzzled.

"I love this turkey, Rosita," Hope said. "We didn't have meat in a long time."

Kelly gave her a silent scolding stare, and Rosita and Carlos looked at each other, puzzled.

Hope realized that her mom wasn't happy with what she had just said, and quickly retracted her statement. "I meant turkey meat."

After they had coffee, Carlos went to take a nap, Hope went back to the living room to watch TV, and Kelly and Rosita got busy cleaning and putting everything away. Rosita washed, and Kelly dried.

"Kelly, what was that all about?"

"What you mean?"

"Hope saying that you haven't eaten meat for a long time, and you gave her an angry look."

Kelly hesitated for a while. "Money got a little too tight, and I had to cut a few things off our grocery budget."

Rosita turned to her with a disappointed look on her face. "Kelly, that upsets me. I always told you that if you needed anything, we were here for you."

Kelly's eyes flooded. "Rosita, I know. But you're already doing so much for us, and I can never thank you enough for that. The rest I need to do on my own. Yes, there hasn't been chicken or any other meat in our diet for quite a while, but I make sure that we both eat enough, and healthy. Rice, beans, and dandelion soup, pasta, and egg and cheese sandwiches with orange juice for breakfast, and sometimes for dinner too. But to be honest with you, we're both more energetic than ever before. Sure, sometimes she complains about that, or not going to the fast-food places anymore, not that I used to take her there a lot, but who needs that? Just look at some of the overweight and unhealthy kids whose mothers practically make them live in those places."

"Kelly, that is true, but it wasn't necessarily by choice on your part, and that can be sad for her."

"Perhaps, but I always think of the end justifying the means."

"What're you saying?"

"I could have avoided such a tight budget by working fulltime, going to school parttime, and taking four years or more to graduate like Gilda is doing. But as you know, with Rocky, that wouldn't have been possible. So, I had to take advantage of that window when it opened, regardless of the sacrifices required. In a few weeks, I'll start a good paying job and that will justify all the means." She smirked. "Then our lives, with, or without Rocky in it, will change for the better. However, that still doesn't mean that Hope will get to go to fast food places any more than a few times a year."

"OK, I understand, but—"

"There is no but, I'm sorry. The sacrifices I 'm asking my daughter to do along with me are minimal compared to what I had to endure at her age. Besides, I actually believe they will make her a stronger and more disciplined person all around."

"Not to get off the subject, but what's going on with Rocky?"

"With him, I am totally confused. I told you I went to visit him."

"Yes, you did. And as I remember, it didn't go as well as you had expected."

"No, it didn't, but…" She walked to the counter to Rosita's side, grabbed her pocketbook, opened it, and pulled an envelope out. "I got this letter from him." She peeked in the living room to make sure that Hope was still napping. "Would you like to hear it?"

"Yes," Rosita dried the last dish. "Go ahead."

Hi Kelly:

My comments about the ordeal you went through with that son of a bitch were wrong and I am sorry.

Right after you left, I realized that I need to do something about myself. I realized that I couldn't go on and be the jerk that I have been with you all along. So, I made an appointment with this priest that comes to the prison couple of times a week. He is kind of a psychologist. He was shocked to hear that I wanted to see him when I had refused to even shake his hand for all these months. That alone made me realize that he too must have seen something in me that needed serious help.

I had a few sessions with him already and they have been extremely helpful. He too told me that after I get out, we should take it one step at a time before we move in together as a family again. I can now see how much of a jerk I have been with you about school, work, and all. And there is no more reason to blame my parents and family for having brought me up like this. I am my own person now and must let all that crap about a wife being an object of her husband go. I promised you that I would change, and I will.

My boss too came to see me. I guess he couldn't find someone to replace me, especially for the coming winter. I apologized to him too about the embarrassment and the annoyance he had to go through with the police for my actions. He was happy to see me clean and respectful, and when I told him of our plans, he offered me a room in his house for as long as it takes for us to get back together.

I was never that good of a father either, but that will change too. We will celebrate all the holidays, including Halloween.

I miss you guys a lot. Give Hope a kiss for me and tell her that I'll see her in couple of weeks. I love you guys.

Rocky.

P.S. The day after I get out, on Friday, I like to take you guys out to eat at that restaurant on the water in New Haven. Please don't make any plans, it would be nice to surprise Hope there. The day I get out, I'll call you with the reservation time.

Rosita wiped the corners of her eyes. "I'm confused too. He really sounds like a different person."

"Doesn't he?" Kelly folded the letter and put it back in her pocketbook.

"Yes, he didn't even use the F word once through the entire letter."

"Rosita, can you see what I meant?"

"Yes, if he wrote the letter himself. Don't forget though that lying has been his main trait."

"Mommy…" Hope walked in on them rubbing her eyes. "Did you say Daddy is coming home?"

"He is coming to visit us like he did the last time." She patted her shoulders. "Now get ready, we need to go home to do our homework."

CHAPTER THIRTY-ONE

An hour or so into her shift, Kelly was taking an order when she saw Cody walking up the steps in his civilian clothes. "Hi Cody, what're you doing here?"

"Can I steal a minute of your time?"

"Have a seat on that stool near the kitchen door there, and I'll be right over."

"OK."

She sat to his left. "So, what's up?"

"I'm happy to see you smiling again."

"I've decided not to allow anything or anyone to interfere with my life anymore. Yes, that experience was horrible, and I was lucky not to get killed, but in some weird way, I think I came out of it a much stronger person."

"I am glad to hear that because now you might need that strength even more."

"What're you talking about?"

"Today is December 6."

She waited for a customer to go by them. "And my husband is being released from prison, right?"

"Yes, he's already out. He was released a couple of hours ago."

"I wasn't aware that he was out already, but before Thanksgiving, I went to visit him, and we had a long talk."

"Are you withdrawing his restraining order?"

"No, not yet. He agreed to take it one step at a time."

"That's a good decision."

"Like I said, I am not going to let anyone run my life anymore. If we both get what we want from our relationship, then I'll try to make it work again. If not, he'll go his way, and I'll go mine."

"I know you still have strong feelings for him, but don't let that bury all the terrible things he has done to you."

"Since he has been in prison, he has shown serious signs of change, and if what he seems to have become stays true, then there is hope for us."

That was not what Cody hoped to hear. "If I were you, I'd be very careful."

"The last time I heard from him, he said he wants to take us out to eat at that restaurant on the water in New Haven, and that looks like a major change already."

"People like him don't change so easily."

"Cody, only time can tell me that."

He got up. "You have my cell number. If you need anything, anything at all, just call me."

She gave him a long hug. "You're a devoted friend, thank you."

**

The night before, Rocky had called and told her that the reservation at the restaurant was for 8 p.m. Kelly rushed home from work and quickly showered and dressed up for the rare occasion.

"Mommy, what are we dressed up for?"

"I have a surprise for you."

"Mom, Halloween is already passed, and Christmas is still some weeks away?"

"It's not that kind of surprise."

"What is it then?"

Kelly pinched her cheek. "If I tell you, then it won't be a surprise anymore."

They had just passed the Yale Bowl stadium and were now in the city.

"Mom, where is my surprise?"

"Relax, we're almost there."

Kelly was slowly riding around the parking lot in search of an empty space. On Friday nights, the place was busier than usual.

"I never saw a restaurant so big," Hope said as they approached the entrance.

"Because we never took you to one."

"If this is my surprise, I like it."

"Ma'am, do you have a reservation?"

"Yes, under Esposito for 8 o'clock."

The hostess perused through the reservations. "Follow me." She led them to a table next to one of the windows overlooking the bay.

Rocky wasn't there yet. The dining area was just as crowded as the bar area. "Honey, sit here." Kelly pointed to the chair next to her across from the windows where Hope could get a better look at the tiny waves visible against the shining lights hitting them from the harbor on the opposite side of the bay.

"Wow. Mom, is that the ocean?"

"I guess you could say that. At some point far out there, yes, it is."

Just then, Kelly spotted Rocky. While making his way toward their table, Rocky gestured her to pretend not to have seen him. He was in a new pair of jeans, a dark gray fitted jacket, a black T shirt, and his long deep brown hair neatly cut. She hadn't seen him looking so sexy in a long while. Under different circumstances, she would have devoured him without delay.

He stopped behind Hope and covered both her eyes.

"Who's that?" Hope shouted.

"Guess who?" Rocky bent down, pulled his hands away, and gave her a long kiss on her forehead.

"Daddy?" Hope jumped off the chair and hugged him. "I missed you."

He lifted her up and held her angel-like face against his. "I missed you too, honey." Gave her a long kiss on her cheek and placed her back in her seat. "I think you got taller since I last saw you." Then he looked at Kelly. "Am I right?"

"I think so too." Kelly got up and gave him a quick hug. "You look nice."

"Thank you." His eyes followed her back to her seat. He had expected a warmer reception from her too, but quickly retracted his wish. Bent down, got close to her ear. "I understand, one step at a time."

Kelly smirked at him. "That's right."

"Daddy, are you coming home now?"

Kelly's face remained motionless, but with a look that said you better not screw this up.

"Honey, not yet. I got another away job. This time it's a little closer, so I will come and visit you once a week." He pinched her cheek. "Just a little longer and we will…"

As Kelly started to look angry, he realized that it was best to stop prolonging the subject and he changed the focus of the conversation. "Hey, we need to eat, let's see what we can order."

"Yes, let's do that." Kelly picked up the menu and leaned closer to Hope.

After dinner, he walked them to her car. "That was nice, wasn't it?"

"Daddy, I loved it. Are we going to come back here soon?"

He looked at Kelly. "I think so."

Kelly got into the driver's seat. "It was nice, but now kiss your dad goodbye, we need to go."

"OK." Hope grabbed him by his lapel, pulled him down, and gave him a kiss on the cheek. "Dad, will l see you next week?"

"Yes, and I'll call you guys before then."

Hope walked around the car and waved at him. "Thank you, Dad."

He moved closer to Kelly, looked straight in her eyes, and whispered. "How about a kiss?"

She had missed his lips and his hot body for so long that if she let her heart control the moment, she would jump on him. Instead, she gave him a quick hug, got her lips close to his ear. "It's too early."

"I get it," he nodded. "I get it."

"One step at a time, remember?"

He watched her car until it merged into the adjacent road. Because he had moved in with his boss right out of prison, the original plans with Gilda to fuck their brains out at one of their favorite motels the day he got out were canceled. *Goddammit, I haven't gotten laid in six months*. He thought about stopping at the diner and asking Gilda to sneak out to his truck for a quick one, but then he realized that on Fridays the diner was too busy and scrapped the idea. Stared at the restaurant's main door for a while. *Maybe I get lucky in there.*

***

Kelly sat at the kitchen table studying. Her last final exam was on Monday, a little over a week away, and to secure one of the jobs offers she had received, she was determined to get the best grades ever. She looked at the coffee pot and it had just stopped brewing. Shivering, she got up and poured herself a fresh cup. *Another hour or so, I should be done*, she was thinking when the phone rang.

"Hi, it's me." Rocky sounded cranky.

"And I am me," she whispered into the receiver. "What're you doing calling at this time of the night?"

"I can't hear you."

She raised her whisper by a few decibels. "Hope just fell asleep."

"Sorry. I got great news that I wanna share with you."

"Can it wait until tomorrow?"

"We've been waiting for a break like this for years, and I am too excited to wait until tomorrow."

"What you mean we?"

"I got hired as a full-time machinist with a good pay and good benefits too. Can you believe it?"

"I'm happy to hear that." She sounded skeptical.

"I'm starting on Monday. It's not a toolmaker position but it is close enough."

"Listen, I still have lot of studying to do, can we please talk about it tomorrow before we meet for dinner?"

"I thought you'd be just as excited."

"I am. It's just that you caught me at the wrong time."

"I can't wait to tell Hope that my job away is ended."

"Uh, uh. You're not going to do that. We have succeeded to keep all our ordeals away from her this long, and you're not going to blow it now."

"I just tell her that I am working around here now."

"And what will I tell her when she doesn't see you coming home every day?"

"I see. But why can't I come home and let things work themselves out?"

"Didn't we agree to one step at a time?" She raised her voice.

"Yes, we did, but—"

"No buts. We're not there yet."

"Goddammit, why do you have to be so stubborn?"

"Are you in a bar?"

"What am I supposed to do in my room alone?"

"Lay in bed and think about why and how you ended up there, all the crap in between, and what you need to do to make things right. Finding a better job is a step in the right direction, but it's not enough anymore."

"It's been almost a week that I have been out, and I am very lonely. I need to be with you."

"Keep doing the right things, and that day will come again."

"You're right. So, I'll see you guys tomorrow in the same restaurant at the same time?"

"Yes, we'll be there."

***

There were only a handful of women at the bar all with their guys, and the only one who was alone didn't look like she was worth the effort. He went back to the phone and called Gilda. After he persuaded her to call one of her coworkers to cover for her for an hour or so, and a story about where he had been since he got out of jail, she agreed to meet with him at the commuter parking lot where they had met once before.

Shivering, she hopped in. "You got to be crazy calling me one hour before I need to be at work."

"I'll make you extra happy tonight."

"Have you seen Kelly?"

"Yes, we had a fucking family dinner last Friday."

"You know she's graduating soon."

"Yes, I know."

"I can't believe that she has three job offers to choose from, and by early January she'll be working at one of them."

Creases of rage spawned on his face like cracks on a sheet of ice under stress.

"Rocky, I thought you were gon' stop her from graduating."

"And I thought you were supposed to help me do that while I was away?"

"I tried everything I could, but she is too smart and too determined."

He took a long puff from his dying cigarette. "I'll figure something before she goes to work."

"Did you sleep with her after your family dinner?"

"Fuck no. I didn't even get a kiss."

"I don't believe that."

"Why you think I called you this late?"

"I see." She moved away from him. "A second choice, that's all I am to you."

"Gilda, come on." He reached for her. "I didn't mean it that way."

"That's bullshit. If she had spread her legs, you wouldn't be here asking me to do it."

"You know that's not true." Reached for her shoulders again and tried to pull her closer to him.

She pushed his arm back and looked like she was about to cry. "Just drive."

"Gilda, come on, don't get soft on me." He reached out to her again and pulled her close to him. "You know how much you turn me on?"

"I thought after all this time you would care about me a bit more than just a side fuck."

"And I do, trust me, but—"

"But what, that I'm always going to be second to Kelly?"

"Come here." He pulled her close and sank his tongue in her mouth. Her body deflated like a punctured human size doll. "We have a good thing going, don't we?" He grabbed her hand and dragged it over his penis. Unbuttoned her coat, slid his hand through the top of her black uniform, and squeezed her breasts. "Don't we?"

"Yes…"

"So, let's take it one step at a time and see what happens."

"OK, no more talking, just take me to your room and fuck me."

***

The hostess showed them to the table where Rocky was already seated, waiting for them. "Hi Daddy!" Hope rushed over and hugged him.

After the waitress had done taking their orders, Rocky turned to Hope. "I have good news for you."

Sensing what he was about to say to her, Kelly's face turned livid instantly, and her right foot hit his left shin hard.

He sneered at her. "I got a new job closer to home. I was supposed to start the end of January, but now they want me to start Monday." He smiled. "Soon, we'll all be together again like old times." He looked in Kelly's prying eyes. "Unless the boss I have now wants me to finish the job I am working on first, which could take a few weeks."

Hope clapped her hands. "Dad, that's awesome. Mommy, did you hear that?"

The son of a bitch was giving her a deadline. She labored a smile at Hope. "Yes, but I am sure Daddy's boss will make him finish the job away first."

After Hope got through chewing her last bite of her meatballs, she said, "Mom, I have to go to the lady's room."

Kelly got up. "Let's go."

"No." Hope shook her head. "I am a young lady now. I can go by myself."

"OK, be careful."

They watched her until she turned into the restroom's foyer. Rocky shook his head. "I can't believe how mature and tall she got in the last six months. You're a good mother."

"So, is that a deadline?"

"If you don't recognize my new self by then, you never will. I fucked up for a long time and in many ways, but I get it. Trust me, I get it. I love my family, and I'll do anything to make it work."

"No, you still don't get it. Getting back together before we have tested our new reality, it's like gluing back together a shattered vase without finding all the pieces first."

"What the fuck are you saying?"

"You just answered your own question. Before you went away, the f word was part of your conversational vocabulary, but in the last two meetings, this is the first time you used it like then. The vase is our relationship, and you getting rid of the f word is one of the vase's pieces that also must be found before it can be put together fully.

"I get it."

"The end of next week, I'll be graduating, and I already have a job lined up. I'll be starting sometime around the middle of January. What are you going to do when I go to work all dressed up in a place where most coworkers are men?"

"Like I've already told you, I'll have to learn how to live with it."

"Are you going to show up at my job, uninvited, and embarrass me like you did in my school cafeteria? There, I had the choice to leave, and I did. At work, it will cost me the job."

Fighting to hold the anger at bay, he just stared at her wordlessly.

"You went to jail trying to stop me from doing what I will be doing for the rest of my life. I cannot be the barefoot and pregnant housewife that you expected. How're you going to accept that?"

"Like you said, one step at the time."

"That's exactly why I don't want us to rush. We should experience at least a couple of months with me working at my new job, and you getting adjusted to your new one. Then, if we can manage it through those times without any serious issues, we might be ready to try again. By then, we can also save some money and start all over in a house like we had when we first got married, which I am sure will give us a better chance of succeeding."

"OK. Let's say that we do exactly as you said, what about our desire for sex, don't you have any?"

"Of course, I do. There hasn't been one night that I don't stare at the empty pillow next to me."

He reached for her hand and whispered, "I am dying to have sex with you."

She pulled her hand away before he could touch it. "I am too, but it's the wrong time."

"Why can't we do what you said, and in the meantime get together once or twice a week somewhere to have sex? What's wrong with that picture?"

"Everything. That would muddy our thoughts and only lead our relationship back to where it was, if not worse."

Hope slid in her chair, smiling. "I'm back."

"Good, because we're ready to leave, aren't we, Rocky?"

Hope got into the passenger's seat and shut the door.

He walked closer to Kelly, who had one foot already inside the car. "You're gon' leave and not even give me a nice hug?"

"After what you pulled in there," she whispered, "you really don't deserve one, but for Hope's sake, here." She gave him a quick hug like one would to a stranger. "Good night."

"That's all?"

"One step at a time, remember?" She got in the car and slowly drove toward the parking lot exit.

He stared at the back of her car turning onto the main road. "This is fucking bullshit!"

***

On Mondays, her classes end at 1:45, Rocky thought staring at the ceiling. Then looked at his watch. 6:45. Outside, it was still dark, dense raindrops splashing against the window. No sex for over six months and she wants me to believe that she is OK with that. *Bullshit, that's not the horny Kelly I know.* He went down to the kitchen and put the coffee pot on. A couple of minutes later, his boss joined him.

"So, you're starting that new job today?"

"No, not today. Friday, they called and asked me to start after the new year." He grabbed a cup of coffee and sat at the kitchen table. "I'll be around to help you get the rest of the leaves raked up before we get hit with the snow."

"I'd appreciate that."

"Can I borrow your Buick for a while?"

"Why, what's wrong with your Vet?"

"The tires are old, and I rather not drive it on the highway in this weather. The last thing I'd need now is to get into a car accident."

"When you need it for?"

"Now, if it's OK with you."

"Go ahead." He pushed the car keys across the table. "I'll wait for you in the garage."

Rocky headed out the door. Stopped at his favorite coffee shop, and after waiting in line for a couple of minutes muttering and pacing around, he got his black-dark-roast coffee. A couple of sips later, he looked at his fake Rolex, 7:35. Walked to the public phone hung on the outside wall near the main entrance door, lit a cigarette, and dialed the number of the company where he was supposed to have started working in a few minutes. A female voice answered the phone. He introduced himself, told her a bullshit story about his current boss being upset at him leaving in such short notice, and pleaded with her to put the machine shop supervisor on. The supervisor also bought his story and told him that it was OK for him to start on Monday January 7th.

To waste some time, he took a ride to Osbornedale State Park. Under the canopy, a bunch of people of different ages stood around the fireplace having a heated conversation, holding their hands out to warm them by the fire. He parked, grabbed his coffee, and joined them.

Then he headed to Kelly's school parking lot, driving around until he spotted her car. Looked for a parking space from where he could easily keep an eye on it, but far enough for him not to be recognized, and settled in. Looked at his watch again, 1:40. A bit later, he noticed Kelly stepping out the door next to a neat-looking younger guy holding a black umbrella in his left hand, and his right arm tightly gripped around her left one, chatting and laughing as they quickly made their way to her car.

"Son of a bitch, I knew it. That's why she doesn't need sex from me." He hit the dashboard with a fist. "That's why she doesn't want to drop the restraining order." Hit the dashboard again. "And that's why she keeps pushing us getting back together further out."

Kelly opened her car door and dropped her books on the passenger seat. Turned around and gave Jordan a tight hug with her face against his. "I owe you my life," she said. "For real."

"Kelly, and I owe you who I am now. It's weird how things work out in life."

"Yes, they are." She kissed him on his cheek. "Just remember that the end will always justify the means."

"To forget that is to forget you, and that's not going to happen. It will suck though not to see you around campus when I get back in January."

"As soon as I get my new job, I'll buy a cell phone and we can text each other."

"You better." He waited for her to get in her car seat, guided the door to a close, and headed toward his car.

Rocky grabbed on to the steering wheel with his hands trembling like an engine running on fewer cylinders. "If she isn't already fucking him, it's only matter of time. I got to put a stop to this. I have paid for my mistakes, now it's time for her to get over it and get back to normal."

Back at his boss's garage, he helped set up the snowplows to two pickup trucks. Back at his favorite coffee shop for the second time that day, he looked at his watch. 6:25. Ordered his black dark roast coffee and sat back on the same stool he had sat on earlier. *If they're fucking, I swear—*

"Hey, Rocky." Richard, from the lawn-mowers repair shop, approached him with a coffee in his hand. "How's it going?"

Rocky with a sad look on, nodded. "Good."

"Hey, cheer up man. Remember that time when I delivered the lawn mower to my client who was seating on the grass working on her flower bed, before she sprung up shaking like a leaf in a gust of wind, dropping her shorts, and a baby garden gray snake landed on her foot?" Richard laughed out loud. "Remember that shit?"

"Do I remember that? Fuck yeah," Rocky said with a loud laugh of his own. "She had a nice fucking body for a forty something. I can still see her as if it were happening now, she snatched her blue panties off too. Then looked at us freaking out, jetted her hands over her black crotch and ran into the house like a frightened squirrel. Poor snake though, he was almost there."

"Hey, I am sorry about what happened to your wife a while back. Richard said. "That guy should be shot."

"Don t worry, he'll be taken care of."

"Is she OK?"

"She's good. The cops got there before anything happened. Actually, I got to go call her before I go home to see if she needs anything." At the pay phone, he dialed the number and waited for her to pick up. Five rings, but no answer. *Son of a bitch, where is she?* Slammed the receiver and started pacing, puffing, and mumbling. Dialed the number again, and on the second ring, she picked up. "Hi, I have been trying to call you for the last half hour or so. Is everything OK?"

Wow, Kelly thought, *he hasn't sound this nice since our glory days.* "Yes, we are, how about you?"

"Good, I'm having a coffee here at my favorite place and thought about you."

"How is your new job?"

"It's great. I think I am back on track."

"That's good to hear."

"Listen, in a week is Christmas. I'd like to have a nice talk with you, alone."

"I don't know. This time of the year, we're extra busy at the diner and George asked me to work sixty hours a week. I can use the money."

"But you're through with school now, aren't you?"

"Yes, but sixty hours a week this time of the year isn't going to be easy."

"Come on, let's get together Sunday afternoon the day before Christmas Eve. I'm sure the diner won't be as busy with people running around to get their last-minute presents."

She thought for a couple of seconds. Maybe she was being a little too harsh on him. "OK, but only for a little while."

"Good, we can meet right here at the coffee shop."

"OK, I'll see you there Sunday around 2:30."

MY LAST CHANCE

***

Rocky knocked at the door three times and waited. Gilda pulled him inside and quickly shut the door. "I thought you had forgotten about me."

"My fucking boss asked me to help him hook up the snowplows to two of our pickup trucks. I hated it, but I couldn't say no since I live in his house for free."

"That's not gon' change that I told my husband I'd be home around 8:30, a little over an hour from now, and I am as horny as a dog in heat."

"And you think I'm not?" He ripped her clothes off, grabbed her voluptuous ass, pulled her to him, and sank his tongue in her mouth. Then pushed her across the bed, got on top of her.

"While waiting, I got my pussy ready for you." She pushed him off her, got on top, and rode him like a jockey in a horse race until they both exploded together.

Gasping for air, he sat up against the bed frame. "Wow. You're good."

She sat up next to him. "Is Kelly as good as me?"

"She is good, but not as wild as you."

"And you still care about her more than me?"

"Come on, we talked about this already. She is my wife, and I do miss my family."

"I know, I don't cook as good as she does, and I am not as pretty and smart as she is, but I know I can make you happier. Why do you want to settle for less?"

"No." He looked in her eyes with a smirk. "We're both gon' settle for more."

"What're you saying?"

"The way I see it, we can have the best of both worlds. I get her back and turn her into the housewife she used to be. You stay with your quiet and good provider husband, and we go on with our affair as usual."

"That's not gon' be that easy anymore. I'm at the point that my husband turns me off so bad that even those two nights a week that I'm off from work, I fall asleep on the couch just to avoid him."

"Hey, I hope you don't blame me for that."

"No, I don't, but before we started our affair, it wasn't as bad. Now with the holidays coming, what am I gon' do from today until the day after New Year's with him around?"

"The same thing you did while I was in jail."

"Let's get together the afternoon before Christmas Eve for couple of hours?"

"I can't. I have an appointment that day to meet her around 2:30."

"I was right, I'll always be the second choice."

"That's not true. Fuck, why didn't you tell me that earlier?"

"I'm sorry, but you're wasting your time with her anyway."

"No, I'm not. I am gon' get her back."

"Sure," she chuckled, "after all you put her through, what're you gon' do so special that you think you'll be able to persuade her?"

"I have a job waiting for me almost like the one I had when we first got married. That will allow me to qualify for a mortgage and get her a house like we used to have. I am sure the two together will do the trick."

"That would have worked before you screwed up, which allowed her to rediscover herself and her goals. Beside the fact that her accounting professor, who she soon will be working for, is only a couple years older than you, handsome like you, but very wealthy."

"Bullshit, I am gon' make sure she never starts working for him. I molded her before, and I'm fucking doing it again."

"Listen, I knew Kelly before you met her, and I have spent a lot of time with her while you were gone. The Kelly I see now, something that you refuse to see, is the same Kelly from high school, only older and wiser. She would stop at nothing then and will stop at nothing now to be the best in everything she does. She always dreamed to become wealthy and live in a big and beautiful house, and she will not relax until she gets there. She is determined to succeed and will no longer let anything, or anyone, stand in her way. Just look at what she was able to accomplish in only a year and a half.

He grabbed the ashtray, took another puff, and choked the cigarette hard. "The first time we made love was the summer night of her sixteenth birthday at Osbornedale State Park. I'll take her back there, and I'm sure her strong feelings for me will come back."

"It's winter now, hello?"

"There is a canopy there with a huge fireplace to one side, and a bunch of picnic tables all around it. On Sunday before Christmas Eve, I'm sure there won't be anybody around. I'm going there around 1:30, an hour or so before we meet, and I am going to make a huge fire. She always loved fireplaces. Then I'll go buy a bottle of chianti, some cheese, a couple bags of chips, and give her a surprise winter picnic."

"You never did anything like that for me?"

He pulled her closer to him and gave her one of his "I got everything under control" kind of looks. "Let me get her back, and then I'll do that and more for you, I promise."

Her face sagged. She pulled away and walked straight to the bathroom.

"Gilda, come on, I mean it."

"I'll believe it when I see it," she shouted.

CHAPTER THIRTY-TWO

It seemed like the entire world had waited for that Sunday to do their holiday shopping, and what a lousy day they were dealt. Cold with a fine drizzle steadily falling from a dark gray blanketed sky, and rivers of headlights dragging along the chaotic main roads, cars beeping at each other to make way and drivers shouting obscenities when they didn't succeed. Something one would expect to experience in New York City, not on a Valley road.

"Watch, she's going to be fucking late," Rocky muttered, entering the liquor store for the bottle of Chianti. From the food store next door, he had already purchased two different kinds of cheese, a couple bags of crackers, a small package of mixed cold-cuts, and a bundle of ready firewood. He looked at his watch, enough time to get the fire going and get to the coffee shop by 2:30.

As he had hoped, there was no one around the fireplace, and other than the steady beat of the rain hitting on the huge circular wood canopy rooftop, and an occasional car driving through the adjacent road, the place was quiet and gloomy. After joggling around the few dried Oaktree twigs, he had grabbed from the side of the fireplace, the flames began to rise. Warming his hands, he stared at the flames. She used to love to have sex next to the fireplace. He hurried back to the car and maneuvered his way back to the coffee shop.

After a few minutes in line, he got his usual black dark roast coffee and sat on one of his favorite stools overlooking the parking lot. The traffic on the adjacent road was turtle paced. He glanced at his watch. 2:30 I knew it, the fucking fire is gone die. Anxiously, he lit a cigarette and started his puffing and sipping routine with his eyes fixed on the lot's entrance.

***

On the other side of town, Gilda was pretending to focus on the TV, her two kids were playing with their toys, and her husband was roving around the garage, organizing their tools. He's meeting her at 2:30. She glanced at her watch. 2:35. Sat up. *I should go there*, she thought, *but what if he gets mad and breaks up with me?* The first time Kelly had taken Rocky away from her, she was sixteen, young, and naïve. Gilda grabbed her coat and rushed to the garage.

"Where're you going?" Kevin asked.

"I got to get a couple more presents for the kids."

"Today? You're crazy." He shook his head. "The roads and the stores are all packed. Didn't you see how long it took me just to go get gas?"

"I don't care." She backed her car out. "I need to go before the stores run out of them."

***

Three cigarettes later and an empty cup in his hands, Rocky watched Kelly maneuver her car into a tight parking space. "Finally," he muttered.

"I'm sorry." She smiled and sat on the empty stool next to him. "It was a mad house at work today, and then this crazy traffic."

"No problem. What's fifteen minutes, you're here now?" He smirked, got up. "You still drink your coffee small, black, and no sugar?"

"Yes, thank you."

"He handed her the coffee, extended his right arm around her shoulders, and looked straight in her eyes. "I really miss you."

"I miss you too as my husband, but not the person you had become over the last few years."

"I understand, and I'm really trying to become the person you need next to you."

"I must admit that same feeling has been brewing in me lately. The question though is, how long is it going to last?"

"I don't want to lose you, and I don't want to lose my daughter, but how're you going to know if we don't live together?"

"I told you already. If after a month or so that I have been working at my new job, you get adjusted to my new way of life without causing any drama, then I'll be ready to try again."

"And what am I supposed to do about sex until then?"

"I don't know." She chuckled. "Perhaps do the same thing you did before your first girlfriend, or when you were in prison."

"OK…" He gazed at her. "And what about you?"

"Since you went away, I've been too busy to even think about it. But if I get the urge before then, I'll do the same thing I did before you came around, I'll masturbate."

Masturbate, my ass, he thought. *She's fucking that kid.*

"Anyway, a few weeks go by just like that." She snapped her fingers. "Just stay cool, and everything will work out."

"I guess you're right." He got up at once. "Come on, I like to show you something."

"Show me what?"

"It's something that could help us along." He helped her with her coat. "It will only take a little time."

She looked at his watch. "It's 3:10 already, I told Rosita I'll pick Hope up by 4:00."

"It's only up the street." Hugged her shoulders with his giant arm and guided her out of the place.

Maybe he wants to show me a house. The house, the job, she thought, feeling eager as he held the car door open for her, something he hadn't done in years. "Really?"

He smirked and in no time was driving up the hill leading to the park.

"Where is this house?"

"What house?"

"I thought you were going to show me our future home?"

He shook his head. "Honey, I didn't even get my first paycheck yet."

"When you said a surprise that would help us along, I thought of a future home for us. I'm sorry for jumping ahead."

As he drove through the park's entrance, he pointed to the huge stone fireplace with smoke rising from the dying flames. "Remember that place over there?"

She glazed at it in dismay.

"Remember how often we used to come here when we first got married? When we used to wrestle in the snow, and then sat at that fireplace with a glass of wine in our hands?"

"Are you kidding me? First, there is no snow on the ground, and second, what makes you think I have time to waste like this?"

"So? We can still make a nice fire and sip on our wine talking about those days, can't we?" He winked at her.

Wordless, she stared at the side of his face. *From one extreme to another, I hope he's not totally losing it.*

He parked the car in the same spot he had parked earlier. "Come on, this is going to be fun." Popped the switch to open the trunk, got out, and rushed around to open her door.

"The fricking rain is coming down stronger, couldn't you have chosen a better day?"

"You run to the canopy, and I'll get the goodies." He grabbed the bags with food and the wine, elbowed the trunk shut, and ran after her. Placed the bags on the eight-seater's wood picnic table closer to the fireplace. "Here, you organize the goodies, and I'll get the fire going again."

As she unpacked the cheese, the crackers, and all, she said, "This is no picnic weather."

"I know, but it's still romantic. I thought that bringing back some good memories instead of only talking about the bad ones would be nice for a change."

"I understand that, but it's raining and it's getting colder and darker."

"Here, look at this fire." He took her hand and pulled her closer to the flames. "Am I good or what?"

She stretched both her hands. "I must say, I do have a weakness for fireplaces."

He snapped the cork out of the bottle of Chianti, grabbed two plastic glasses from one of the bags, and poured them full. "Here, this is your favorite." He placed one of the glasses in her hand and raised his for a toast. "To a new beginning,"

"I can't drink on an empty stomach."

"Just take a sip for the toast. This reminds me when you had the first beer with me up there." He nodded to the area a few hundred feet up and away from the canopy where he had first made love to her.

"Yeah, I could have sent you to prison for enticing a minor to drink."

He clutched one end of the picnic table. "Here, let's move it a bit closer to the fire." She grabbed the opposite end and helped him.

In the meantime, Gilda drove into a lower terrace of the park out of their sight. Locked the car and walked up through the meadow leading to a cinder block building that housed the men's' and ladies' restrooms. Hidden behind the ladies' room side of the building, she had a clear view of them in front of the fire.

They sat on the tabletop with their feet resting on the seat, their goodies spread between them. Kelly sensed a sneeze developing, grabbed her pocketbook, quickly pulled a tissue out, and rushed it to her nose just in time for the burst. "It will suck if I get sick for the holidays." She rested the pocketbook on the center of the seating plank behind them, out of the way but within reach for her next sneeze, and for a while they both stared at the flames, munching on the goodies, and sipping on their wine.

"I can't believe this," Gilda muttered. "The bitch is gon' take him away from me again."

Rocky grabbed the bottle of wine and refilled his glass. Her glass was on the table to her side still half full. He reached for it, but her hand got to it first and pushed his away. "No, this is enough for me."

"OK." He nodded and put the bottle back down next to the goodies.

Gilda watched steadily, like a tiger spotting its prey. She should go over, tell Kelly about their yearlong affair, and screw everything up for them. Then for sure she would leave him, but he would hate her for it, and she would lose him too.

"All those years, we should have done this with Hope too," Kelly said, sounding remorseful.

"We should have, but we still have a lot of time." He stared at her for few seconds. Wrapped the few goodies left, put them inside a bag, and rested it on the plank to the side. Moved the bottle of wine on the plank next to her pocketbook, sled closer to her, and placed his right arm around her shoulders. Smiled at her. "How about a nice kiss?"

She slid away. "Like I told you, it's too early. Doing this now will only muddle our thoughts, or at least mine."

He shook his head. "I don't get it." Flicked the ash off his cigarette onto the flames. "I remember when you used to go crazy if I didn't have sex with you for more than a couple of days." He gulped the rest of the wine from his glass and sneered at her. "You must have someone else."

"That's it." She jumped off the bench. "Take me back to my car, please?"

He threw the glass in the fire and jumped down after her. Grabbed her arm, pulled her body tight to his, and yelled, "I saw how you hugged and kissed that fucking kid in your school parking lot."

"What are you talking about?" she yelled back. "I didn't kiss anyone."

He grabbed both her arms and pulled her face inches from his. "You hugged him tight and gave him a long kiss," he shouted. "You're fucking him, aren't you?"

Oh my God, she thought, gazing in his furious eyes. *It was only an act, and I fell for it again.*

"Aren't you?" He shook her. "That's why all this time you pretended not to care about sex while I am fucking dying for it."

What is he yelling about? Gilda squinted to get a better look. Then snuck a short run and stood behind a huge oak tree, a bit closer.

"He is the kid that saved my life!" she shouted back. "It was our last day of school, I was thanking him for it again, and gave him a goodbye kiss on his cheek."

"Bullshit, that's not what I saw. Where do you meet to fuck him, ah?" Shook her hard. "Where?"

"You're hurting me," she cried, with tears streaming down her cheeks. "Let me go! You're sicker than ever!"

He twisted her body around and pushed her against the closest edge of the table. "Here is where you're going, you cheater." He shouted and forced her to lay down on the table.

Her hasty kicks to his body were not enough to deter him. He snatched her coat off, then his coat, locked her wrists in his left hand, and held her legs flat down while laying his body firm over hers.

Good, rape the bitch, Gilda thought, *that's one sure way to finally have him for me only.*

From the adjacent road, which crossed the park's main entrance to one side and the town's high school to the other, one of a few isolated cars that had been passing by had just stopped at the stop sign. And although from there the wrestling bodies were only shadows against the fire, the couple inside the car noticed the commotion and took a second look. "Let's drive there and see what's going on," the man said, ready to turn into the park's entrance.

"No." The woman held on to the steering wheel. "What if they're a couple of drug addicts?" She grabbed her cell phone from her purse and handed it to him. "Here, call the police instead."

The guy quickly dialed 911 and reported the incident. "I think I should go over there and see if I can stop the fight."

"No sir, you stay right where you are, we'll be on our way at once."

Two faces were now flashing before Kelly's eyes, rapidly alternating between her husband and that of the geek that had kidnapped her weeks earlier. "You bastards, let me go!" she screamed. "Let me go!"

"I am your husband, and I have the right to have sex with you any time I wanna. You hear me?" he shouted in her face. "So, stop denying me," he shouted again, lifting his hips up enough for his free hand to lift her uniform up to her stomach.

Struggling to free herself from his stronghold had exerted her strength and she was now week and helpless. "Look at me. I am your wife," she pleaded. "Please, don't do this."

"Then act like my wife." He ripped her pink panties off and started fondling her. "Don't you like this anymore?" he said, breathing next to her ear.

"Yes, I do, but this is not the time or place," she pleaded. "Please stop."

"Goddammit, it's been over six months and now I'm going to have my fucking way!" He forced her legs apart with his legs and kept fondling her faster and faster. "Either you go along with me," he shouted, his lips close to hers, "or I'll force my way into you."

She stared at the canopy ceiling, motionless. "Go ahead, you can have your way. Just let go of my hands, you're hurting me."

Sensing her subduing, he said, "I will, but you try anything funny, and I swear—"

"I won't, please?"

He let her hands go, crouched over her, and lowered his clothes down below his hips.

Her wrists were bruised. She rubbed them before her arms fell to her sides, mirroring Christ on the cross before he was speared. Tilted her gloomy face to her right and stared at the sound of the steady rain hitting the edges of the cement floor, her tears mirroring the same on the tabletop. Suddenly, his forceful penetration caused her body and hands to jerk up and down as if hit by a high voltage wire, with her right-hand landing on her pocketbook. He pounded into her incessantly as his moaning accelerated. Slowly, she angled her head and started feeling her way through the inside of her pocketbook until her hand felt her tweezers. Still pounding her with his eyes tightly shut, she grabbed the tweezers and slowly maneuvered it in her hand. Waited until he was about to climax, and like a lightning strike, she plunged it into his left buttock with all the strength left in her.

"Fuck…" He screamed, the tweezer's prongs stuck deep in his bleeding flash. "You are a fucking bitch!"

She jumped off the table, grabbed her pocketbook, and ran up the high slope behind the canopy in the drenching rain like a frightened squirrel scrambling her way in the dark through shrubs and trees, ripping her uniform and scratching her legs, her arms, and her face.

"Holy shit, that bitch stabbed him," Gilda muttered in shock.

He snapped the tweezers out with a loud scream, pulled his clothes up, and limped toward the park's exit.

"Rocky, wait!" Gilda screamed, running after him. "Let her go."

Kelly heard the scream. *Gilda, what the heck is she doing here?* Without looking back, she kept rushing through the barely discernable shrubs and trees, longing for her life.

After a hundred feet or so, he realized she had run up through the high slopes and started leaping in her direction as fast as he could. "Now you did it," he shouted, holding his bleeding buttock. "I'm gon' strangle you until you breathe no more."

Kelly heard his screams coming from behind her, and instead of heading for the streetlights, she stayed alongside the ditch between the street and the woods, heading toward the top of the park where he took her on her sixteenth birthday, hoping to hide somewhere in the woods there.

The couple at the stop sign, seeing the shadow with a dress on running away from the canopy toward the woods, and the shadow with the pants on screaming and hobbling after her, parked their car on a strip of grass off the road, and anxiously waited for the loud siren on its way.

Gilda, hindered by her weight, couldn't catch up to Rocky but kept yelling, "Let her go, she's not good for you, let her go!"

"Where are you, bitch?" he yelled, closing the distance to Kelly's screeching sounds and snapping twigs ahead of him.

Kelly heard a loud siren approaching the park. *Thank God, Gilda must have called the police for me.* Rushed to the closest light on the street side, jumped over the ditch, and landed on the pavement with her knees first. Wrinkled slivers of skin hung over the bare flesh with streaks of blood slithering through her shins. "Shit," she yelled cupping her hands around both. Looked down toward the park's entrance where the sound of the loud siren was coming from and saw two headlights stop for a second or two before turning on the road toward her.

"I'm gon' cut your throat, you bitch!" Rocky kept yelling

She couldn't see him yet, but from the sound of his voice, he was only yards away. She started hobbling further up the road as the siren was getting closer and closer behind her. She stopped, stretched her arms up, and started frantically waving at the car.

Rocky saw her. "I'm coming, fucking bitch," he screamed.

The cop saw Kelly screaming and waving and sped toward her as Rocky jumped over the ditch and landed halfway onto the road. The cop slammed his foot on the brakes, but his effort was in vain. He hit him head on and threw him feet up in the air before his body landed head down on the road pavement a few feet behind his cruiser.

"No… No…" Kelly screamed, falling on her knees twenty feet or so from the cruiser's headlights with her hands cupped around her bleeding face. "No…"

The cop stormed out of the cruiser and ran to look at Rocky's body, flat on his back in a contorted position, motionless and unconscious. The next cruiser came to a sudden stop between Rocky's body and the cruiser that hit him. The rain was flushing blood from under his head and the side of his mouth.

The couple that had called the police stopped in the middle of the road, got out of their car, and ran to the scene. There, they saw one of the cops standing next to Rocky's body, frantically calling for two ambulances while the other one was crouched across from him trying to get him to show signs of life. Further up the road, Kelly was on her knees, crying with both hands cupped around her face and her dress shredded beyond recognition. The man, took his long coat off, placed it around her shoulders, helped her up, and slowly started to walk her toward the cruisers.

"Oh my God. No…" Gilda screamed, struggling to rush through the ditch and up to the road where Rocky's body lay motionless. She fell on her knees next to him. "Rocky, Rocky," she screamed, shaking his shoulder.

When Kelly saw Gilda running over to Rocky and kneeled next to him hysterically crying while totally ignoring her, her mind went blank, and her body froze as if all her blood had flowed out of her veins.

"Rocky, talk to me," Gilda screamed. "Wake up, talk to me!"

Kelly, still in shock at the sight, wiped her eyes and wordlessly stared down at Gilda sobbing over her unconscious husband's body.

The two cops looked at each other, puzzled. Then one of them bent down. "Ma'am, please let me help you up, the paramedics are coming and will do whatever they can for your husband."

Gilda stood up and stared at Kelly. "That's not my husband. If he were, this would have never happened. You're a beauty queen bitch and he would have been happier with me."

Kelly was caught off guard. "What are you saying?"

"You are very smart, but very naïve too. Two days ago, we made love." She looked down and wept. "Yes, we have been having an affair for over a year now. I'm so sorry I ever invited you to that Goddamn Memorial Day party. He was going to be mine and not yours."

Kelly opened her mouth but said nothing. *Like I said, men take whatever they can, wherever they can, and whenever they can.* Gilda's words from their last Fourth of July party resonated in her. *And what am I supposed to do about sex until then? Goddammit, it's been over six months and now I'm going to have my fucking way!*

What a perpetual liar, Kelly thought. Then her eyes lasered back to Gilda as she muttered, "Birds come together up in the sky, and human scum on earth."

One of the cops approached Kelly. "Ma'am, the ambulances are here. Come on, I'll accompany you to the hospital." As the cop was saying that, Rocky's index finger motioned at them to lean over him. "I think he wants to say something to you."

"There is nothing more I want to hear from those lying lips."

The cop kneeled and put his ear next to Rocky's wheezing lips. Then he said, "The few words I could clearly make out were, 'Kelly. I'm sorry. Rosita. Car. Brakes.' Do you know what he's trying to say?"

Kelly gave him another stare between Gilda kneeling next to him, and the paramedics working on his barely responding body and thought, *the bastard caused Rosita's accident too.*

The other cop approached Gilda. "Ma'am, you need to come with me."

"Where are you taking me?"

"To the station. We need to ask you few questions." He helped her up. "Please?"

"Wait!" She snatched her arm from his hand, looked back at the paramedics. "Is he gon' be OK?"

One of the paramedics gazed up at her. "Ma'am, he's breathing."

CHAPTER THIRTY-THREE

The usual streaks of light sneaking through the horizontal blind stretched across the ceiling. *Yes, we have been having an affair for over a year now.* Kelly pulled the comforter and sheet over herself and closed her eyes.

The siren screaming louder, Rocky tossed up in the air like a mannequin, her body jetted up like Angela Rance from the Exorcist. Shaking like a battered leaf, her hands threw the covers off. Eyes shut tight, her temples twitching, her fingers began to rattle, but then froze at once. No, not anymore. She jumped out of bed and dragged herself to the couch. Cupped her head in her hands and gazed at the streak of light crossing the coffee table. A sob and a head shake. Many more sobs and head shakes, the streak of light faded with the dawn.

She dragged herself to the kitchen sink and poured a glass of water. Sipping from it, she gazed at the dark gray sky and the steady drizzle, pondering what she could've done different. Dumped the rest of the water in the sink and dragged herself to the bathroom. Took the antibiotic cream the doctor at the hospital had given her hours earlier, got closer to the mirror's ever fading clear spot, and started applying it to the scratches on her face. Just then, the doorbell rang.

"Hey." Cody stepped inside and hugged her. "I'm so sorry."

They sat at the kitchen table.

"It's been on the news all morning."

"Cody, I need a cup of coffee; would you care to join me?"

"I had two with my breakfast already, but what the hell."

She got up and got the coffee going.

"At the diner, some were just chatting about the tragedy in general, some were feeling terrible for you, and others were condemning Gilda for having an affair with her friend's husband."

"Cody, he was like a ferocious beast."

"I am sorry I wasn't there for you."

"You couldn't have been, it happened at the park in Derby."

"I know. But if I were on duty, trust me, I would have gotten the permission to cross the city line."

Kelly recounted everything that had happened step by step from the time she had met Rocky at the coffee shop until they were both driven to the hospital.

"He raped you. That son of a bitch, he better not come out of intensive care."

"Please, don't say that, Hope would be devastated." She filled the two cups. "I have no cream, do you mind?"

"It's OK, just sugar will do."

She placed a cup in front of him and sat back on her chair. Took a sip. "Her mom with scratches from head to toe, and her dad in intensive care, what am I supposed to tell her?"

"Except for the raping part, I would tell her exactly what you just told me, step by step."

"I feel I'm just as at fault for what happened."

"Are you kidding me? Kelly, the bastard abandoned you in a snowstorm once, where you almost lost a foot. Then he planted coke in your car to get you arrested. And to top it all, he not only raped you, but had the police cruiser been a minute too late, you could be the one in intensive care now."

"That's all true, but If I hadn't been so persistent with school, maybe things—"

"Kelly, the man is not normal, and it's time for you to face that reality."

She shook her head. "When I had coffee with Mrs. Casale, right after he went to jail, she told me the same thing."

"Kelly, stop pondering about if you had done this or that, and look ahead instead."

"I hope he makes it though."

"I'm sorry, but I hope he doesn't. In my line of work, I deal with his type more often than I'd like to, and they're all the same. After each defeat, they always get worse, never better. Trust me, your life will never be peaceful or normal with him in, or even just around it."

The path that had been shining toward her reunion with Rocky was narrowing, and the flame from the candle that lit the way now barely flickered.

"Kelly, if he makes it, you should have him arrested."

"That I can't do. How would I ever explain to Hope that because of me her father is in jail?"

His chair screeched. That wasn't what he expected to hear. "Where is Hope now?

"At Rosita's house. I talked to Rosita when I got home from the hospital, and since tomorrow is Christmas, she expects us to spend tonight and tomorrow with them."

"I was going to ask you over to my parents for Christmas day. After I heard what happened, I called them, and they would be happy to have you over."

"Cody, that's very thoughtful of you, but—"

"It's OK, so long you're not home by yourselves."

"Why some people are so nice, and some so bad?"

"Which of the two sides you place me in?"

She looked straight in his eyes and smirked.

"You know, I wasn't surprised at your husband, but hearing about Gilda threw me off a cliff."

"Cody, somehow, this whole thing still feels like another nightmare that I'm about to awaken from."

"Kelly, it's all real. Rumors have it that Gilda took two weeks off from work, and her husband asked her for a divorce."

"I was so happy that she and I had turned our acquaintance into a friendship." Tears started flowing again. "She was always trying to make herself helpful and seemed so sincere about it."

"Kelly, they say keep your friends close and your enemies closer." He placed his hand over hers. "It seems like that she was doing exactly that, so that you would not get suspicious."

She looked at the small artificial Christmas tree next to her TV. "I have one present for Hope there, one for each of Gilda's kids, and one for Rocky. How could I have been so naïve?"

Cody shook his head. "You're just too kindhearted."

"I was brought up to trust people until proven otherwise. That was my mother's way. Maybe years ago, it was the right way, but as I learn more about today's world, it's not. Not anymore. From now on, I will do the opposite. Don't trust anyone until proven otherwise."

"Kelly, going from one extreme to the other is not the right thing to do either."

"If that's what it's going to take for me to survive in this new world, then let it be."

"Maybe it's wrong for me to say this, but all this might have been for the best. Your life with him would have continued to be a roller coaster. And as for who Gilda really is, you're better off to have found out now rather than later."

She took another sip of coffee. "I hope you're right."

"Listen, you're young, you're smart, and you're pretty. There are many good men out there that would love to take care of you and Hope."

"Cody, from now on, I alone will take care of me and my daughter. Never, never again will I look at a man for that, even if it's just to help me along."

"I meant you're still young with a great future ahead of you."

"True, but as far as I can see, it doesn't include a man." She took the empty cups to the sink.

He looked at his watch. "I need to go and get ready for work." Got up and started for the door, but before stepping out he turned around and held her by her arms. "Remember, you have a special place in my heart."

She gave him a long hug. "I'm very happy to have you as a friend again." Gave him a kiss on the cheek. "Merry Christmas."

***

A week into the new year, the holidays had come and gone. Not as happy as Kelly had planned for them to turn out before the tragedy struck, but nevertheless, she made the best of them with Rosita and Carlos. Hope continued to carry a grudge, and only talked to her mom when it was inevitable.

In the meantime, Kelly had accepted the junior accountant's position with the firm in Stamford and was to start on the 21st of January, two weeks away. George hadn't taken her notice with ease, not so much on her account, because from her he was expecting it somewhere along the way, but because Gilda, who was supposed to report back to work that evening, had called him minutes before Kelly got there to quit.

Kelly felt so bad to leave George stranded like that, she promised to stick around until the sixteenth of January, so that he could have more time to focus on hiring their replacements, which in turn he was able to do. And George, to show her how much he appreciated her loyalty and help, put an extra hundred-dollar bill in her last paycheck.

***

Angela knocked and waited.

Rosita opened the door and welcomed her in with her trademark smile. "I'm making some strong coffee the way Kelly likes it; would you like some?"

"Yes, please?"

Angela wiped the snowflakes off her coat, her eyes scanning the kitchen from side to side. Kelly and Rosita must have been born under the same star. Every piece of off-white appliance was properly placed and spotlessly clean, and every nick-nack above the cherry wood cabinets and the gray granite countertop was meticulously organized.

Rosita filled two cups with coffee, grabbed the cream and sugar, and sat across from her. "You know, Kelly drinks hers black with no sugar?"

"Yes, I know, but I don't know how she does it."

Rosita looked at her watch. "They should be here soon. I talked to Kelly around twelve, and they were loading her car with the few things they're taking."

"I understand her new place is also furnished."

"Yes." Tears sprouted in the corners of Rosita's eyes. "I'm gon' miss them so much."

"Me too. I was just getting used of being closer to them again."

"If that son of a bitch had been a different person…I'm sorry for swearing, Angela."

"I understand. But considering the way things are now, I think she made the right decision."

"I know, but still…" Rosita wiped her eyes with the back of her hand.

"Listen, Rosita, she couldn't have missed this opportunity. Not only the firm advanced her a chunk of money to settle down there, but they will also pay for her studies going forward. This isn't something that happens every day, at least not for someone with just a two-year degree."

A knock at the door. Rosita's face brightened. "It's got to be them."

Hope pushed the door open and ran straight to Rosita.

"My little angel." Rosita held her tight and gave her kisses on each side of her cheeks. "Where is your mom?"

"She's coming," Hope replied. "Hi, auntie."

Angela hugged her. "Who's this princess?"

In a dark purple wool coat, a white sweater over a pair of dressy black slacks, a pair of black winter shoes, a black wool sharp wrapped around her face and her shiny long deep brown curls caressing her high cheekbones, Hope could have easily passed for the daughter of a wealthy family within the general area where they were moving.

Hope's eyes sparkled. "Auntie, you like my new clothes?"

"I love them. Give me another hug."

"Hi, guys." Kelly closed the door behind her. "I am sorry for running late, I had to stop over at my landlord's house to settle the rent and give him the keys."

Rosita and Angela stared at Kelly.

Kelly's hair was still black, but the gorgeous long curls that had for so long defined her overall appearance had given way to a man's style cut, parted in the middle with the sides barely covering half of her ears, and short bangs down to just above her eyebrows and her dark sunglasses. In her unbuttoned long black coat over a knee-length purple dress, black leather gloves, a black leather purse in her right arm, and her shiny high black leather boots, she approached the table. "I hope you're not going to chastise me."

Angela was still stunned. "Of course not. Rosita, are you?"

"Me? No, I just got to get used of looking at her full gorgeous face now."

"Angela, what you think?"

"I love everything. It's just that you look so different."

Hope's face wilted. "I wanted my hair short like that too, but she wouldn't let me."

"Like I told you at the hairdresser, you're still too young for this style."

"Kelly, why now?"

"Angela, a new place of work, a new city, why not a fresh look too? And since my job will require my head to be bent over a computer screen day in and day out, I figured long hair would be more of a nuisance than anything else."

Rosita took her coat. "Dios mio, you look like a teenager."

"No, she looks like an executive already," Angela said.

"Please, guys, you're making me blush now?"

MY LAST CHANCE

Rosita poured a hot cup of coffee for Kelly and a glass of orange juice for Hope. Then picked up a box of assorted holiday cookies from one of the cabinets and placed it on the center of the table. "Come on, let's have some."

Hope dug in first.

Kelly took a sip of coffee. "You read my mind Rosita, thank you."

Rosita wiped her eyes with the back of her hand. "I can't believe we're here to say goodbye."

"If it's not me running away," Angela added, "it's you."

"Guys, please relax. I'm not going to the end of the world; Stamford is only forty-five minutes away. And remember, it's not the distance that counts, but where the heart is." She opened her pocketbook and pulled out a brand-new cell phone. "Isn't that why they make these?"

"Wow, it's about time," Angela said, "congratulations."

"Yes, mi amor, but that's not the same as talking face to face. What's the number?"

Kelly read it out loud as they entered it in their favorite contacts list.

Angela nodded her head toward Hope, who was already in the living room watching TV. "How's she taking it?"

"Not good. She has been hardly talking to me."

"My poor angel is still in shock. I tried to talk to her about it too, but she puts her hands over her ears and walks away."

"Rosita, that's another reason why we need to get away from here."

"Take your time with her, the changes have been too many and too sudden for someone her age."

"Mi amor, Angela is right. Now more than ever she needs a lot of love."

The time on Kelly cell phone marked one-ten. "Guys, we need to get going now."

"Already?"

"Rosita, we have another stop to make before we leave for Stanford. And once there, I need to stop at the firm, get a copy of my lease and drive to her new school to get her registered. Hope, come on, we need to go."

Angela hugged her. "I wish you the best of everything. And once you're all settled in, don't forget to call, I want to come and visit. And this time I don't accept any excuses."

"No, this time there is no need for. I love our new place."

Rosita hugged her tight. "I am gon' miss you so much." Then she turned to Hope, held her by her shoulders, kissed both her cheeks multiple times. "And you even more."

"Rosita, how about you and Carlos go with me to visit them?"

"Angela, we'd love to do that." She held Hope tight by her side. "What am I gon' do now without my little angel here?"

"Rosita, please give Carlos a long hug from us."

"Yes. After he got off the phone with you yesterday, his watering eyes said it all."

Hope's arms were tightly wrapped around Rosita's waist.

"Hope, we need to go now, please?"

***

As if acting on its own, the car was sliding off the narrow road straight for a tombstone. At once, her hands gripped onto the steering wheel, her foot thrust onto the brakes, her back glued to her seat, the car came to a halt within inches. In shock, she stared. "Holy shit! Honey, are you OK?"

"Yes," Hope nodded.

Since her grandfather had died, Kelly totally dreaded cemeteries, and nearly snapping a headstone from its rightful place hardly helped her cause. With no one in range of view, her adrenaline rush began to secede. She backed her car to the spot where she had originally intended to park. Still breathing heavy, she took a silent minute to herself. The last time she had dragged herself in there was at Angela's grandfather's funeral years earlier. When her mother died, her father forbade her to be anywhere around her funeral services. And when his life's journey also ended, she made sure he was repaid in kind.

"Hope, be careful, there is ice under the snow."

"I'm not going!"

"We need to do this. Please?"

"No! How many times do I need to tell you?"

"Have it your way then."

Clouds of assorted sizes and shapes rushing eastward were clearing a path for a deep blue sky and a bright sun at the start of its descending journey, flickering its bright rays through the dormant branches as the shrilling wind swirled the fading flakes up, down, and around. Two cardinals gripped their tiny feet on a branch above with their feathers fluttering and their beaks chirping as they wrestled to hang on. Soon, three more joined, chirping even faster and louder and swooping from one branch to another, back and forth as if arguing about something. Then at once, one of the original two jetted southward and the rest followed suit.

If humans could only compromise as cheerfully and quickly as they did. A slicing gust of wind whipped against her face with a sturdy scent of burning wood. On the still hazy eastern side of the cemetery, gray twirls of smoke exhaled from two adjacent chimneys. She shut her eyes and smirked at the scent coursing through her nostrils.

She was six months pregnant with Hope the night Rocky had carried her through the front door of their first home. The fireplace's ardent flames ready, an open bottle of Chianti, the sunrise had found them stripped to their birthday suits.

A sudden loud siren rushing through the adjacent road robbed her of her silent smirk. She wrapped her black and purple wool scarf around her face, pulled up the collar of her coat, and pondered for a while. The place was gloomier than ever. Headstones after headstones and chapel structures of many sizes, shapes, and forms as far as her eyes could see. Some displaying Jesus, some Mary, some Joseph, and other lesser-known saints. The Chapel-like crypts must host those who refused to accept death as the equalizer seeking to retain the status they had in life. As those thoughts crossed her mind, an old lady dressed in black from head to toe with a young girl around Hope's age to her right, and a vase of flowers in her left arms, made their way to the outer wall of a multilevel Mausoleum. The lady placed the vase down and looked up at a tomb on the third level. With a rosary in one hand, she hugged the little girl's shoulders and prayed and wept.

The young girl stared at the same tomb and cried out loud. "Mommy, why did you have to die too, wasn't Daddy enough?"

Kelly pulled her glove off and wiped the tears from the corners of her eyes. Then she turned around and cautiously started crossing the snow-covered pavement that led to the graves on the opposite side. There, the snow reached up to the top edge of her black leather boots. Twenty feet or so up the slope, one of the graves still had a plywood cross on it. Hope, her face glued to her window, was stalking each of Kelly's moves. Once at the gravesite, and confident that she wasn't stepping on the corpse section, bent over the cross, stretched her right hand, and slowly started brushing the frigid snow off a section at a time. R-o-c-c-o. With tears dripping from the corners of her eye, she whacked the rest of the snow off swiftly. Esposito, October 31, 1967, January 2, 2002. She composed herself, took few steps back, buried half of her face in her sharp and her coat lapels, stared at the cross, and thought. Groomed to live by their country of descendance's customs and believes of the early twentieth century in a society that had for long abandoned the same, was just too much for him to bear. *I wish the culprits could now see the rotting harvest of their planted seeds.*

Kelly, I haven't had a student scoring a perfect hundred on that test for quite some time. Keep it up, honey, and the sky will be your limit. With the back of her hand, she wiped her eyes again. "You stupid jerk. We could have had it all."

The End

CPSIA information can be obtained
at www.ICGtesting.com
Printed in the USA
LVHW021930190521
687904LV00014B/719